The Oar House

Books in the Thomas Night Crime Novel Series

The Oar House

A Thomas Night Crime Novel

Book III

Paul Casper Scherer

Soul Attitude Press

The Oar House

A Thomas Night Crime Novel

Published by Soul Attitude Press
Pinellas Park, Florida
www.soulattitudepress.com

ISBN 978-1-946338-50-1

Printed in the United States of America

0 3 0 6 23

Preface

The Thomas Night Crime Novel Series:

Book I - La Florida

Book II - Punta Rosa

Book III - The Oar House

Book IV - Indian Hollow Road

Book V - Chattahoochee

These novels are part of a series of works of imagination of the author introducing the public to the practice of law in the State of Florida and Central America from the 1950s through the 1980s.

The vehicle for these works is a fictitious lawyer named Thomas "Tom" Night whose law firm is located in St. Petersburg, Florida.

When Tom started his practice most of his work involved a timber and lumber/sawmill business named Commercial Carriers Corporation (CCC), a corporation located north of Ormond and Daytona Beach on the East Coast of Florida. The Barnes Family owned CCC.

St. Petersburg is located on the West Coast of Florida in Pinellas County. This is the most densely populated county in Florida. The city is on a peninsula that is surrounded by the waters of the Gulf of Mexico to the west and Tampa Bay to the east. The two major cities on Tampa Bay are St. Petersburg and Tampa. In the 1970s these cities were in flux.

In the 1970s, Tampa was an industrial city with the only major port on the West Coast of Florida. It was known as the Cigar City, but the days of rolling cigars are no more. Tampa was still trying to hang on as an industrial hub but manufacturing was on the wane in the United States.

St. Petersburg was primarily residential, a bedroom comtmunity, and it was noted for its cleanliness, natural beauty and its city-owned waterfront with parks, museums and the Pier, a tourist venue constructed in the shape of an inverted pyramid. St. Petersburg had been a tourist venue with a vibrant downtown known for its green benches, sun worshipers and the elderly who lived in garage apartments and small hostels in the downtown area.

Many residents of the Tampa Bay area were transplants and most were law abiding. But some were not. This is a novel concerning the criminal justice system of Florida in 1970s.

The Author

Table of Contents

Introduction

Trial lawyers would call this work a war story. It is a serious business – a story of occurrences that engage the participants because they are unusual and memorable, something you talk about with an appropriate audience over a stiff drink when you are old. The events show the failures of men. These matters occurred in Florida beginning on October 25, 1979 with the arrest of Thomas Night's law clerk, Alphonse Alesse.

Main Characters

Francis Aloysius Barnes

"The Senator" - retired State Senator - his family owned Plantation #7 in North Ormond, Florida. The Senator, a widower, organized a company called Commercial Carrier Corporation (CCC) that owned timberland, saw mills and semi-trucks to deliver lumber to the Northeast US used to construct housing after WWII.

Francis Aloysius Barnes II

"Frank" - the Senator's son - married to Beatrice "Bea" O'Brien. Frank headed CCC, creating the biggest privately owned timberland and saw mill operation in the Southeast USA. Frank is the natural father of Jimmy and the adoptive father of Robert, Albert and Jenny Johnson-Barnes. He and Bea lived at the Homestead which was in Holly Hill. Frank's best friend and attorney is Thomas "Tom" Night. They attended college together and they created CCC.

Beatrice "Bea" O'Brien Barnes

Married Frank when she was 15 and Frank was 17. They had a child, Jimmy, who was born breach. His spine was injured by forceps used in the delivery and he suffered severe cerebral palsy as a result of oxygen deprivation during birth. Bea devoted her life to Jimmy and her adopted children, Bob, Little Al/Albert and Jenny. Bea also operated the dairy on the Homestead and developed the dairy into a large milk and cream processing facility that shipped dairy products by rail throughout the USA.

Thomas Night, Esquire

"Tom" was orphaned as a teen. Father, Mother and brother died from pneumonia as a complication of influenza in St. Petersburg, Florida. Tom was raised by two Aunts who were professors at Stetson University in Deland, Florida. Tom met Frank at Stetson. Tom studied law and his first clients were the Barnes Family and their businesses. He began his practice in Daytona Beach and then moved back to St. Petersburg and established a law firm.

Marlene James

"Marla" grew up in St. Petersburg. She took business and secretarial courses in high school. Her first job was as Tom's legal secretary. Marla was trusted by Tom and Frank and the Senator and she helped Tom and Frank's family and the businesses. For years she was Tom's girlfriend.

The Adopted Children

Robert (Bob), Albert (Little Al) and Jenny were born to Mary and Albert Johnson Senior (Big Al). Mary was schizophrenic. Big Al was an alcoholic. Bea convinced Mary to let her take Bob into her home to help her care for Jimmy. Later, after Mary and Big Al became disabled by mental illness and the bottle and neither parent could care for the children, Frank and Bea adopted their children. The children all worked in the Barnes Family businesses.

Characters

Roger Adams – partner in Night, Adams and Street, P.A.

Thomas Night – partner in Night, Adams and Street, P.A.

Alphonse Alesse – law clerk in Night, Adams, and Street, P.A.; an accused

Lori Schaeffer – an exotic dancer, girlfriend of Clemenso Bondi, alleged victim of assault

Clemenso M. Bondi – manager of The Oar House

Sarah Rogers – dancer, girlfriend of Roger Adams

Derek Kline – manager of The Man Trap, sister club of The Oar House

Big John Curry – friend of Alphonse Alesse

Anthony Stewart – investigator for Night, Adams and Street, P.A.

Tommy Magyar – an accused; co-defendant of Alphonse Alesse

James DeMarco – Tommy Magyar's attorney

Richard Cook – detective, St. Petersburg Police Department

George Randell – detective, St. Petersburg Police Department

Regina Cameron – a/k/a the "floozy "; a/k/a "Gene"

Judge Waters – on call judge

John Hale – State Attorney in Florida

Jim Faircloth – police officer, St. Petersburg Police Department

Theresa – Tommy Magyar's girlfriend

Darlene Street – partner in Night, Adams and Street, P.A.; Tom Night's wife.

Map of the state of Florida

PART I

Many lawyers contend Justice and Truth
are only found in a Court of Law
by accident.

Chapter 1

Tom Night received the urgent call at 3 a.m. None of Tom's clients had an emergency when he was having a second cup of coffee while sitting at his desk at the office. It was always at a god awful time when he was deep in sleep.

Tom was 47 years old, married, no children and heterosexual. In the 1970's everyone was heterosexual or pretended to be same. Tom was early to bed and early to rise. He was hard working and a successful lawyer and business man. He was tall (6'), a bit over weight, but fit and athletic, and enjoyed a simple life and life's routine.

The emergency call at 3 a.m. was from Francis, the wife of his law clerk. His clerk, Alphonse Alesse, had been arrested earlier in the night. Tom was stunned by the call regarding his clerk. The police had held him incommunicado for five hours and he finally was allowed to call his wife, who called Tom. Alphonse was a nice kid. He was in his last year of law school at Stetson University. Tom was an alumnus of Stetson some 25 years ago and Tom hoped Alphonse would come on with his firm after he graduated.

Although it was late October, the weather was temperate and about 65 degrees at 4 a.m.

Tom's wife and law partner, Darlene Street, rolled over in bed, looked at the time and went back to sleep.

Tom pulled on his trousers and threw on a knit shirt (Polo) and light jacket (London Fog), stepped into his penny loafers (Weejuns) worn with no socks and kissed his wife and headed out the door to the police station. The building was about ten minutes away. He parked his 250 SL Mercedes Benz convertible and walked down the ramp to the intake office of the holding facility. There were a number of small holding cells across the back wall of the jail. Each cell had a combination toilet and water fountain. (Who thinks these things up? thought Tom. A combination toilet/water fountain? Bizarre.)

The jailer greeted Tom. He was well liked. To the police most attorneys were stuck up bastards.

"Can I speak to Mr. Alesse in a private room?" asked Tom.

"No problem," said the jailer.

"I need you to turn off the recorder," Tom emphasized. "I want privacy so I can speak confidentially with my client."

"No problem," said the jailer. "Tom, you know there is no tape recorder."

Tom ignored the denial that there was no tape recorder hidden in the interview room. "Has Alphonse Alessi been charged?"

"The detectives want to speak to John Hale the State Attorney first."

"What was the arrest for?" asked Tom.

"Aggravated Battery, I think."

"Is there a bond set?"

"$10,000," said the jailer as he led Alphonse out of the cell. He was in cuffs and the cuffs were attached by a chain to leg irons. He was shackled at his ankles. The shackles pulled him down so he appeared shorter than his six feet in height. Besides the cuffs and shackles the City of St. Petersburg had provided Alphonse with an orange jump suit and flip flops and taken his civilian clothes.

"What's this with all the iron and the orange suit?" asked Tom.

"I'm the only one here this morning," said the jailer. "I'm not having a prisoner rabbit on me."

"Okay. I don't want to argue. Let me just talk to him," said Tom to the jailer. "And would you call Billy so we can get started on posting the bond?"

"You ought to wait to talk to your law clerk before you spend money bailing him out. He may be guilty." The jailer guided Alphonse into the small interrogation room. Tom reached in his pocket and pulled out a small portable radio. He flipped it on to a hillbilly station and turned it up. The room filled up with a lot of twang.

"I told you I would turn off the tape recorder," said the jailer.

"Yes, that's what you said." Tom nodded. He didn't believe the jailer. "The music adds to the flavor of the jail." The music would also drown out Tom's conversation with Alphonse. The recording system the police used in the interrogation room would pick up the music and not record the conversation between the men.

Alphonse saw Tom and he dropped his head. Embarrassed. He told Tom he was sorry to bring him out so early. He said he had tried to get the police to let him call his wife as soon as he was brought into jail but the detectives kept trying to talk to him and ask him questions. He said he kept repeating that he wanted to talk to his lawyer. Alphonse said he did not make a statement to the police.

"What do the police think you did?" asked Tom.

"They said I assaulted an exotic dancer."

"Where did the assault allegedly occur?"

"The best I could get from them was that this dancer was assaulted in her apartment by two men. One man was tall and the other was short. I guess I am supposed to be the tall man," said Alphonse.

"What was the nature of the assault?"

"The woman was cut on her face and body, is what they said."

"Why were you arrested?"

"They said the woman identified me going in a store last night."

"Were you with anyone in the store? You know, a short man?"

"No, but the police said they had arrested another man who was supposed to be my co-defendant. That arrest was some time back, a week or two ago."

"When did they say the assault occurred?"

"The detective said it was early morning 17 days ago. I figured it out," said Alphonse. "That would have been October 8th, if I have the date right. I was home alone that night. My wife had gone to visit her mother in Jacksonville."

"Where did the detectives say you were identified?"

"The police said I was going in a Quick Mart to buy a pack of cigarettes and the woman was in the store and saw me and called the police."

"Did you see the woman in the store?" asked Tom.

"There was a woman in the Quick Mart with bandages on her face. She caught my attention because it is unusual to see a person, particularly a woman with bandages. I did look at her and she seemed to notice me."

"Did you recognize her?"

"No."

"Where did the detective say she worked?"

"At a bar called The Oar House."

"Have you ever been to The Oar House?"

"No," said Alphonse.

Tom began to read the Complaint, (A Complaint is paperwork given to the prisoner explaining why he was jailed.) "The Complaint says the victim's name is Lori Schaefer. Do you know anyone with that name?"

"No," said Alphonse.

"That's enough for now," said Tom. "I am going to have to speak to Billy the bondsman and see if he can bond you out.

Unless you have a spare $10,000 that you can put up in cash you will need to pay a bondsman a 10% fee ($1,000) and the insurance company Billy works for will post the bond."

"We have a little in savings and my wife's mother has a house that she would put up as collateral," said Alphonse. "My wife and I talked about it already, we all agreed."

"Well, talk to Billy and see if you can get out of jail and we will talk in depth once you are out of jail and back in the office. In the meantime, don't talk to anyone about the case or your arrest. In particular, don't talk to any of the prisoners. Do you understand?"

"Yes," said Alphonse.

"Can I call anyone for you?"

"No," said Alphonse and then he added, "Don't you want to know if I did it?"

"Well, did you do it?" asked Tom.

"No," said Alphonse.

Criminal clients always want to tell their lawyer they are innocent, thought Tom.

Chapter 2

Alphonse was at his desk at the office by 7 a.m. the morning of his arrest. He was working on legal research that had been assigned to him by Roger Adams, a partner and civil trial lawyer with the firm. Alphonse did not know what was going to happen to him since he had been arrested. Was he going to be fired?

It was touchy when a lawyer was arrested. The attorney was still accorded the presumption of innocence. But still, the firm had to be realistic. The law firm's clients would not appreciate it if they were left alone in a room with a lawyer who was out on bail for a heinous crime. Alphonse knew the chance he would have a job at day's end was slim.

Tom, Roger and Darlene had a meeting of the partners of the firm over coffee and donuts to determine the fate of their law clerk. The fact that a lawyer might be charged with a crime was not unusual, Tom had not only been charged but convicted of a felony charge two years earlier. His situation was different from Alphonse's in that Tom was charged with a criminal contempt. He had been convicted and sentenced to six months in jail.

Lucky for Tom, his wife, Darlene, had successfully represented him. Not only was he exonerated, but his accuser, a local judge who brought the contempt charge, had been determined to have set Tom up. The last they heard of the judge was that he was in prison and was later placed in a witness protection program after testifying against numerous criminals in a drug cartel.

A lawyer friend had heard the judge testify in Miami in a drug conspiracy trial. The judge testified in court as a State witness. To protect the judge's identity, he was seated behind a screen and his voice was disguised, but the lawyer was convinced that the person testifying was Raymond Barrow, the former circuit judge of Bushton, Summer County, Florida. Bushton was an agricultural town a two hour drive north of St. Petersburg, Florida.

Judge Barrow testified that he had provided favors for drug defendants. He would reduce bonds, rule favorably on motions that freed defendant's, such as motions to dismiss on stipulated fact (they are called C4 motions), and motions to suppress confessions and evidence. These rulings by Judge Barrow allowed the defendants to go free. In return the judge was paid handsomely. Tom was unaware Judge Barrow was a crook.

Tom's attitude toward the presumption of innocence had changed after he was incarcerated. Before his arrest he didn't see its importance-- how vital the presumption was to protect a person who was not yet convicted of a crime. Darlene had felt empathy for Tom when he was arrested. However, his partner Roger was only able to last a day before he was ready to throw Tom to the wolves. He wanted Tom to resign as a partner in the firm and retire his license to practice law. Even Tom's faith in himself was shaken. He began to question whether he should resign for the good of his clients. Even Darlene was affected emotionally by the criminal conviction. She realized that without the presumption of innocence the accused had little chance of successfully fighting a criminal charge.

Alphonse was asked to join the meeting of the partners. He was offered a donut and coffee. He declined, his stomach was in a knot and he felt ready to retch. Law school had caused Alphonse to worry himself into a small bald spot that was on the top of his head. For sure he would go totally bald from worry now with his arrest.

Tom asked Alphonse if he wanted to stay on as a clerk. Alphonse admitted that it would probably hurt the firm and might have a detrimental effect on their clients if he was employed while the charge of assault was pending. The partners agreed that he could face recriminations from their other clients, all that is, except Darlene's clients who were most likely in jail and awaiting a decision on their appeals.

The agreement they reached was that Alphonse was to continue his assignment as a clerk. The firm would write a letter to all of its present clients advising them of the arrest and that if there was any question they should call Tom and he would talk to them and try to assure them that the firm stood by Alphonse and would give him the benefit of the doubt and let the case play out in the court system. The staff at the firm had already been advised of the arrest by Darlene and none of the other clerks and secretaries were openly concerned about the arrest. To a person, no one who knew Alphonse believed he could be guilty of the charge, Aggravated Assault, but they were not aware of exactly what the facts of the charge were. They might change their minds if they knew the facts.

***

Anyone arrested for a felony charge in Florida had a right to a preliminary hearing. The purpose of the preliminary hearing was to determine if there was sufficient evidence for the arrest. Justices of the Peace handled Preliminary Hearings and decided if there was sufficient evidence to hold an accused for trial. At trial, guilt would be determined by a jury. The jury had to find guilt beyond a reasonable doubt. The prosecutor could avoid a preliminary hearing by filing a charge by Information. However, even though the prosecutor could file an Information to avoid the preliminary hearing, prosecutors had other reasons to hold the hearing. The prosecutor could test the strength of the charge by letting the Justice of the Peace hear the evidence (normally the testimony of the victim of the crime), and the JP would make a decision if the witness' testimony was strong enough to prove all of the elements of the charge. If there was enough evidence to convince the JP that there was a *prima fascia* case, the accused would be bound over for trial by jury.

If the evidence was inconclusive or unbelievable, the JP could release the defendant. The JP could also find there was only sufficient evidence for a lesser offense (For exmaple: the JP finds a theft was proven but the value of the property was less than $100, so the defendant was bound over on the offense of petty theft, which is a misdemeanor, and not grand theft, which is a felony).

The defendant could waive his right to a preliminary hearing, but that made little sense because the defense attorney got a look at the prosecutor's witness and listened to the witness and was able to cross examine the witness. The defendant never put on testimony, or at least Tom in his 25 years of practice had never heard of any defense attorney putting on a defense at a Preliminary Hearing.

Preliminary Hearings were held on Friday mornings. Alphonse's case was last on the docket two days after his arrest (swift justice). Alphonse's head was swimming.

***

There were two prosecuting attorneys representing the State of Florida this particular Friday. John Hale, the State Attorney was present, which was unusual. Hale's chief assistant was also present. Tom Night and John Hale had known each other for many years. John had personally prosecuted Tom for Contempt of Court. There was no love lost between the two of them.

Preliminary Hearings were held on the main floor of the courthouse in Courtroom A. The court room was crowded with every person who had been arrested in the circuit in the last week. The court was a cattle call. Some defense attorneys had taken a retainer and only agreed to represent a client through the preliminary hearing and they and their client were still negotiating the fee if the JP bound the defendant over for trial.

Other attorneys were trying to use the opportunity of being before the court and the State Attorney to cut a deal. If they could work out the plea to a misdemeanor offence or to probation, the defendant would be sentenced on the spot and the case would be over. That would be sweet.

There were the usual glitches. Most often the problem was the absence of a witness. Each case had a lead detective and it was his job to produce the witnesses. If the witness did not show up for court, the case had to be continued or the assistant prosecutor would cut a deal and dump the case for a plea to a misdemeanor. It really upset John Hale if he was forced by the lack of a witness to reduce or dismiss a charge. He felt the defendant was getting away without paying adequately for the crime, particularly if the reason for the plea deal was that the lead detective was too lazy to keep tabs on the witness.

John Hale was really upset today. He was not going to be able to produce Lori Schaeffer, the victim of the assault in the case against Alphonse Alesse because the lead detective, Richard Cook, could not find her.

The clerk called Alphonse's case.

John Hale stood up and he literally was red-faced.

Tom knew John. A red face meant John had witness problems.

The men approached the bench for a conference. John did not want the court reporter to record the sidebar.

"No," said the Justice of the Peace as he motioned the court reporter to come forward to record the conference. "I want a record. Mr. Hale, I assume you have a witness problem. Is that true?"

"Yes," said Hale. "We need some time."

"I am not inclined to grant extra time. I continued the case against this defendant's alleged partner in crime last Friday. You couldn't produce the victim last week and now this is the second time she is a no show," said the judge.

"We want a continuance," said Hale. "And we want to increase the amount of the bond."

"You want to increase the bond and you cannot produce the victim?" The judge was incredulous. "I am not going to do that."

"You need to look at this photograph, Judge," said Hale who was pushing an 8 by 10 inch glossy print under the judge's nose.

Tom objected. "What is the point of the photo? It has to be authenticated by the victim. The victim isn't here. The photo is therefore inadmissible. Mr. Hale is trying to prejudice the Court against my client."

"I know what he's trying to do, Tom."

"The detective can authenticate the photo," said Hale as he handed the photo to the judge.

Criminal attorneys are accustomed to seeing gruesome images. But this photo of the upper torso and face of a young woman caused the judge to grimace. Tom tried to act professionally when the judge handed the photo to him to view but Tom also averted his eyes. There were wounds carved into the woman's body, some appearing to be letters or initials, "D" and "K".

Tom began to object but the judge cut him off. "Look, fellas. I don't have time for this. I'm going to put this off for one week. Mr. Hale, you have until next Friday to be prepared for a hearing on the charges. I will hold the hearing for both of the defendants who have been arrested for this crime. Or you can file the assault charge directly by an Information, Mr. Hale. You have been the State Attorney for many years. You know the rules."

"What about the bond?" asked Hale as the judge returned his gaze to the photo. "Mr. Allesse belongs in jail."

The judge looked at Tom. "Mr. Alesse is your law clerk? Is that true?"

"Yes."

"I expect you to have Mr. Alesse here next Friday," said the judge. "He is your responsibility."

"Okay," said Tom.

"If he doesn't show up you have to answer to me."

"I agree," said Tom. "Judge, one other thing, I need a copy of the photo that Mr. Hale introduced to the court."

"I didn't introduce the photo," said Hale.

"I'm afraid you did, Mr. Hale," said the judge. "Give Tom a copy of the photograph."

On the way out of the courtroom Tom saw John Hale talking to Richard Cook, the lead detective. Tom thought he would hate to be the lead detective. There would be a ton of pressure on the detective to get a conviction in this case. Tom wondered what Hale was saying to the detective. He would like to be the fly on the wall.

After the hearing, Alphonse thanked Tom. He promised he would appear for the hearing once Tom explained what the judge required.

Chapter 3

As soon as Tom returned to the office he booked conference time with Darlene. Since their last firm meeting, the attorneys agreed to keep time records which meant they scheduled their meetings with each other and assigned the time to a particular case. The time was charged at the rate of $100 per hour to the client's account. The attorneys were skeptical this would make their practice more efficient, but they had to get with the times. The times of the attorney quoting a fee and the defendant paying the fee in cash in a brown envelope were over. The IRS wanted to know how the attorney earned his fee.

But, back to this case. Tom hoped Darlene would be able to look beyond the damning facts in Alphonse's case to an argument that would point to his innocence. Darlene saw Tom right away. She knew he was anxious. He sat in the chair outside her office waiting. Tom explained the facts that he knew to date and he described the injuries the victim suffered. He didn't want to show Darlene the photo, but she insisted.

Darlene studied the photo. "That's pretty grim."

Sitting in on the meeting was the firm's investigator, Anthony Stewart, a retired police sergeant who still knew all the men on the police force. Stewart was considered an insider and he would be able to obtain information about the State's case. The investigator was very important at this stage of the proceedings because the State Attorney had no obligation to provide Alphonse's attorney with any information as to the basis of the charge. Really though, the only evidence the prosecutor needed to prove a *prima fascia* case was the victim to testify that Alphonse cut her with a weapon such as a knife, and that she did not consent to the assault.

Tom was hopeful that Anthony could discover a defense. He needed a magician. Tom hated to be embarrassed in court playing a losing hand.

Darlene, though, had plenty of questions for Anthony to answer. Who was the other perpetrator ... the short man? What was the motive? Was it love or jealousy? Did the victim know the assailants? Was this a random act? Did a third party order it? Was there a contract ... a conspiracy? The victim was an exotic dancer. The Oar House was reputed to be tied to the Mafia. Was the Mafia disciplining their employees, making an example of the dancer?

And what about Alphonse? What is his connection to the other person charged? What was Alphonse's reaction when he saw the victim in the food mart? Did he run away or did he stay to buy his smokes? What is Alphonse's motive in this? Why? Why? Why?

"Find out Alphonse's motive, Anthony. That's what we need to know," said Darlene. "If Alphonse has a motive to commit this crime, he's guilty."

"I understand," said the investigator. "Let me see what I can find out." He left the room.

Tom and Darlene were left alone to talk.

"This is really bad," said Darlene. Her dark eyes glittered. She sat at her desk. Her hands and fingers massaged her scalp below her dark wavy hair. She was deep in thought.

"I know it's bad," said Tom, reluctantly. "You take the hand you are dealt. But if this is true and Alphonse is involved in this we cannot even consider representing him. Think of the publicity during the trial. It could destroy the firm's reputation."

"Now is the time to withdraw if that is what we intend to do. The Court is not going to be inclined to let us withdraw after the trial has been set," said Darlene. "But I think we should hang in there for a while. At least until after the hearing next Friday. You will need to talk to Francis, his wife. We will know a lot after you talk to her."

"I hoped you would talk to her. I don't know her at all."

"We are kind of friends," said Darlene. "I can't push her like she needs to be pushed. We need to know if Alphonse is in any way kinky."

"Why would she tell me that?"

"Look Tom, you just need to find out if she is afraid of her husband and I will take it from there."

"Okay, I see what you mean."

"It's self-preservation. She doesn't want this to happen to her," said Darlene. "She will be honest with you, or she is a crazy person. It's my impression from what I know of her that she is not a masochist."

***

Tom called and asked Alphonse's wife Francis to meet with him that afternoon. Darlene suggested they meet at a friend's office across from the courthouse so they would have privacy and she would not be pressured to lie for Alphonse by having her husband working just down the hall doing research. Darlene told Tom to tell Francis she could be totally honest and that her communications with her husband were protected by husband/wife confidentiality. That is, Alphonse could object to the introduction into evidence of anything Alphonse had told Francis about the crime after it occurred.

***

Tom and Francis met that afternoon as arranged. Tom talked to her about the husband/wife privilege and just let Francis speak as he took notes.

Alphonse and Francis had met in undergraduate school at the University of Florida. He worked in the student lounge and they met when she went in to check out ping pong paddles. He asked her to coffee and their relationship grew over time. Neither one of them came from wealth. Her father had died when she was a teen and she and her mother lived together until she went to the

University of Florida to become a teacher. After graduation she and Alphonse married and he went to law school. He had a scholarship and he worked as a law clerk. They had no children. He had never been in trouble with the police or academically. His personal habits were clean except he smoked cigarettes. She never worried about where he was. He had no close friends. He was in a fraternity in school but it was an academic fraternity, not a social group. His mother and father were older when he was born and they were blue collar. They were both deceased. He grew up in St. Petersburg. He lived on the same street until he went to college. He had one friend on that street from boyhood named "Big John" who he still saw on occasion when they came back to town. Francis and Alphonse lived in his parent's home but it was up for sale and heavily mortgaged.

"So, do you know the facts of the crime Alphonse is charged with?" asked Tom.

"No, not really. Alphonse said it was an assault."

"There was a woman who was cut very badly, cruelly. She even had letters carved in her chest and she was cut on her face. Probably with a razor."

"I didn't know that." Francis was visibly shaken by the facts.

"Did you ask Alphonse why he was arrested?"

"He said it was a mistake."

"Would you think he would do anything like what I described to anyone?"

"No, that is not my Alphonse."

"Was he in the armed forces?" asked Tom. "Was he trained to kill?"

"No, he was designated 4-F by Selective Service. He has problems with his intestines. Crohn's Disease. He went to the medical exam and he was turned down for the Armed Forces."

"Was he into hunting?"

"No."

"Does he have a gun or knife or any weapon?"

"No."

"Does he have any hobbies or sporting interests?"

"No, all we do is work. I took a job as a sales lady at Ivey's Department Store for the summer and I go back to teach in early September. Alphonse has a job as a clerk for a judge while he is in school. His last year of school is coming up. He starts back in mid-November. We are on the Quarter System. I have to return to teach next week. We were hoping we would have a little time to ourselves. My mother is sick and we don't think she will be with us for long. I don't know what we are going to do if he is convicted of this crime. I have learned to depend on Alphonse. He is selfless.

"I cannot see this crime as being anything he would do," she continued. "If he did it, I would leave him. I could never live with someone who could do something so cruel. I love Alphonse because he is the opposite of the criminal who did this. Alphonse is kind. He is not cruel."

Francis began to cry and then to sob. This was too much, she thought. "What will I do about my mother? How will I take care of her? How will Alphonse get a job even if he is acquitted? If anyone does an investigation they won't hire him. Poor Alphonse. He has worked so hard. This is so unfair."

Tom was rattled by Francis' agony. He felt he should hold her and hug her. She certainly didn't think Alphonse had done this. Tom was convinced of that fact.

"Let's close the interview," said Tom. "If I have other questions I will ask you to come back in."

"Okay." Francis blew her nose. Tom reached for more tissues. He waited for her to compose herself.

"Tom, we don't have any money to pay you," said Francis.

"That's alright. Don't worry about the bill. Darlene and I will work on it together. We will do it for free, pro bono."

Chapter 4

The day before Alphonse Alesse entered law school two years past, he was visited at his parent's home by his friend, Big John. Big John was four or five years older than Alphonse and at that time Alphonse was 22 years old.

But Big John looked much older than he was. He had had a rough life. He had suffered a catastrophic work injury and he was no longer able to work. He was no longer big and healthy; he was a scraggly weed of a human.

The day before Alphonse left town to begin law school his mother, who was still alive at the time, told her son that John was at the door and wanted to speak to him.

Alphonse was really confused as to why John had come by. They had few communications except they waved to each other daily as Alphonse went up the hill in his 1954 Chevrolet on his way to work or to school or both. Alphonse was off to work by 6 a.m. and home by 9 p.m. That was his schedule for the last six years, through high school, and college. He left early and came back home late.

John sat on his porch all that time. For six years, ever since his legs were crushed by a cement truck at work, "Big John" occupied the porch, sitting or lying in a variety of couches with his head propped up, and then he was in a wheel chair, and then he sat in a regular chair but walked with a walker. Finally, John had been able to balance himself to walk with canes. By the time Alphonse started law school, John could make it down the street, about 500 feet, and he sat on the bench at the bus stop for an hour or two and then he pulled himself up and worked his way back up the street using his crutches, to his porch. He lived with his mother and she would help him with the last four steps up to the stoop where his chair rested on the porch.

About a year ago, John was making real progress relearning how to walk. But he had a fall. His mother saw him fall and she tried to steady him to get him up but he was hard to handle and he had fallen again.

An investigator hired by John's employer caught the two falls on film and the film was presented in court as evidence that John had sustained a new injury. The argument was that the subsequent fall was now the cause of John's medical complaints. The employer argued they were off the hook.

Unfortunately, John had in fact suffered some new injury and the film recorded John's efforts to right himself and then the efforts of his mother and the neighbors to help. Although the film was without sound you could see from the contortions in his face that he was in great pain. The neighbors who offered assistance were called to testify. They swore under oath that John was screaming every time he was moved after the fall. The pain was exquisite and acute. The neighbors did not want to testify but they were subpoenaed.

According to the testimony of the employer's medical expert, John suffered a new subsequent injury and that new injury was the cause in whole or in substantial part of the cost of medical care since the new fall. Further, John's loss of the ability to work in the future was caused by the new injury.

John couldn't deny that he had fallen and that he was hurt. His lawyer was unable to establish that the new injury was the result of the disability he originally suffered when the cement truck drove over his knees and legs. In other words, John's attorney had to prove that, but for the original injury causing John's inability to walk, he would not have suffered the new fall, and therefore the new injury was the sequella or the consequence of the original injury and the employer remained on the hook.

The judge ruled in favor of the employer and John now received no compensation and his only medical care came at the free clinic.

Alphonse met John at the stoop in front of Alphonse's house and they sat down on a bench.

"We are all proud of you, Alphonse," said John. "You were able to finish high school and college and are now on your way to law school."

Alphonse thanked John for his good wishes. Alphonse said it was nothing. And it was. Alphonse knew he still had a long way to go.

John spent a few more minutes talking before he started to climb back up the hill to his house.

"Try to remember us," said John.

"I will," said Alphonse.

***

When Alphonse went to law school a number of his fellow students had related the same type experience where they were confronted by someone who was down and out, hurt by society. The injured party had asked the students who were now on their way to law school to have pity on the masses when they got out and began practicing law in society. The best variation of the story was one involving a cripple climbing up a hill. The story was related by a student from Georgia who, at his dad's urging, watched a man with no legs pull himself up the side of a dirt road to the top of a hill. "Life is hard. That's just the way it is. We don't provide keepers for anyone unless they give up. That man doesn't give up. He crawls up that hill every day," the dad said.

Alphonse doubted the story the Georgia student told was true. It was an embellishment. But it best told the story that the law doesn't provide men a keeper. Even if he was a lawyer, Alphonse wasn't his brother's keeper.

And now after his arrest, Alphonse knew what it meant to be Big John. He knew he could easily become the man with no legs crawling up the hill. This was America. He would have no keeper.

Chapter 5

Tom reported back to Darlene after he interviewed Francis Alesse, Alphonse's wife. Tom had also spoken to their investigator and had received Anthony Stewart's initial report so he brought her up to speed on both issues.

Tom was convinced Francis had no inkling that Alphonse could be involved in the assault. Tom was struck by the fact that Francis stated she would leave Alphonse if he had committed the crime.

"She says that he isn't leaving."

Darlene went through Tom's notes of the interview.

"So I see you have volunteered our services," said Darlene.

"What are we going to do? He definitely needs a defense and they do not have any money."

"Who is representing the other defendant? The short guy?" asked Darlene.

"I think it's someone from the Office of the Public Attorney. The short guy is a Roma, a gypsy. He is insolvent. His only possession was a truck, but it burned up in the fire at the police station." (The fire at the police department was another story.) Tom continued, "The co-defendant is an itinerant worker. He fixes leaky roofs and potholes in driveways."

"Has he had any other arrests?"

"No. None. There have been complaints that he is a shoddy workman. But no criminal activity."

"Why was he charged?"

"The police were given a description of the perpetrators. One was tall and the other was short. They rounded up about 10 short guys, 5' 5" or shorter and got the men to volunteer for a lineup. This, Roma guy was picked out by the victim."

"Why was the height 5 feet, 5 inches used?"

"The victim is 5' 5" tall and she said the man was her height or shorter than her."

"Did she know either of the assailants?"

"No."

"What is the motive for the attack?"

"None, according to the victim."

"What about the letters carved into the victim's chest? Is there any significance to the letters?"

"No one knows anything... you know... Tar Baby ain't talking."

"So we have two men picked out by the victim. One man is identified in a lineup and the other man is in a Quick Mart. No other connection. No fingerprints, no blood match. Nothing?"

"Nothing," said Tom.

"The case is very weak but we are still going to lose this case."

"I know," said Tom.

"The way it looks the State will put the victim on the stand and she will ID the two men. The men will have no defense except to say someone else did it and the jury will convict the men on the basis that anyone who might have done this needs to be off the street and in jail. The jury will not want to mistakenly release a guilty person," said Darlene.

"That's my thought," said Tom. "Besides, the jury would say, 'What is the dancer's motive for identifying the wrong men? The men have no reason why they were misidentified.'"

Darlene asked, "I guess the dancer has normal vision. She's not blind, is she?"

Tom shook his head. "No, she's not blind."

"Well you better dig up a defense or you are going to look pretty stupid standing there in court before the jury with your manhood in your hands," said Darlene.

"I know," said Tom.

"What are you going to do?" asked Darlene.

"I'm going to take Roger out for a beer."

***

After he saw Francis Alesse, Tom took the photograph of the victim he received from the State Attorney to a professional photographer who he had employed for special work over the years. Since the photo showed open wounds and a nude female torso you could not take it to a drug store to have copies made. A drug store would turn the matter over to the police and you would be arrested for trafficking in obscene material.

So what Tom wanted was to have his professional photographer reproduce the photo as is, showing the wounds, and then air brush out the wounds from the State Attorney's photo and produce two images. One would show the victim without injuries from the waist up and the other would be a head shot only. Tom ordered five copies of each.

Tom waited while the work was being done and did some reading of memos the law clerks were writing for other cases. There was a timesheet attached to each memo. As Tom read each memo he filled out a time sheet. The lowest denomination of time was one quarter of an hour (15 minutes equals $25). It took him, at most, two minutes to read a memo.

Back to the case. Why the photo work-up?

Tom would give one set of photos to Anthony, his investigator. He wanted him to try to identify the woman. To this point Tom and his firm had received no paperwork that identified the victim, only the name, Lori Schaefer. The woman was not a local. Alphonse said the detectives said that the victim worked at The

Oar House. Tom knew Roger went to The Oar House. Tom had never been there. Tom wanted to show one set of photos to Roger to see if he recognized the woman. Tom knew Roger probably never looked at any of the dancers faces so he would show him the nude torso shot. He would probably recognize her from the image showing her bare breasts.

***

Roger had been in practice with Tom for seven years since Roger was fresh out of law school. Roger and Tom were together five years when Darlene came on board. She and Tom were the same age, 47 years old. Both had practiced over 20 years. After they were partners Tom and Darlene were married. They were now expecting to expand the firm again, taking on Alphonse as an associate once he completed school and passed the Florida Bar Exam.

***

At 6 p.m. Roger and Tom got in Tom's 250 SL Mercedes Benz convertible. They put the top down and drove to a warehouse in an industrial park at the edge of the city. There was a large bill board announcing: The Oar House.

The building was surrounded by a chain link fence topped with barb wire to keep the riffraff out. The Oar House was in an old Quonset hut left over from WWII. They went inside. Roger was a member of the club. Tom had to fill out an application for membership and pay a $20 entrance fee. There was a lot of noise and tobacco smoke. Tom had a hard time reading the Disclaimer/ Release that he had to sign before he could enter due to the noise and the distraction of the naked women walking around. The paperwork he was required to sign stated that he was aware that there were artistic performances that would occur in the facility and that the performances were the artistic expressions of the individual dancers and that it was possible a customer might see the naked female form. Tom signed the paperwork and the men entered the club.

There was a large raised dance platform with chairs close to the platform. Women in various stages of undress paraded and danced about. Men were giving the women tips for particularly revealing dance moves or poses. The men close to the dance floor were into it. They cooed their love for the girls and the girls looked coy and seductive. (It was actually comical.)

There were also tables and chairs for the drinkers and there were rooms behind the tables for private parties. Roger and Tom sat at a drinker's table. Tom was drinking soda and lime (no alcohol). Roger stuck to beer. By 8 p.m. the place was full and the staff announced that there would be prize fights in the boxing ring set up in the parking lot.

Tom and Roger got up to go out to watch the fight. As they passed by one of the private rooms the door opened and a young girl, maybe 19 years old, could be seen in the room with a large man, probably a bouncer. The girls' face was bandaged. She turned her head away and spoke to the burly giant who immediately closed the door.

Tom believed that the girl in the room was Lori Schaeffer, the victim in the assault, or else this was an odd coincidence.

Tom followed Roger and the crowd out to the parking lot. The ring was lit with flood lights aimed from above. There was an announcer in a black tux and a ring girl seated on a stool. A referee was talking to an assistant outside the ring who sounded the bell for rounds. There was a real crowd, maybe 500 people, all drunk and rowdy. There was open betting with girls in bikinis touting the bets. The Oar House had listed the matches on a large classroom type chalkboard. The first fight was a super heavy weight match. "Three rounds, knock out or death," the chalk board said. Roger said they were not kidding. There had been a fight resulting in a death on one occasion.

The fighters entered the ring. They wore tennis shoes and swim trunks. Both men were fat. They warmed up a bit. One fellow appeared winded from the effort of the warm up. The announcer had the referee bring the men to the center of the ring. The ring girl held up the card for Round One and her bikini top fell off. The crowd roared.

Round One. The men charged at one another. It was more like a Sumo match than a prize fight.

The crowd loved the violence, they roared. The fighters knocked each other down from the initial impact. The ring crew had to help them up off the canvas. The crowd laughed. The men then began to dance and paw at each other. The crowd booed. One fighter turned to curse the opposing fighter's corner and he left himself open for an upper cut to the jaw (a glass jaw) and down he went with a thud. He bounced off the canvas. The other fighter had to be shown to a neutral corner. The downed fighter wasn't getting up. He was down for minutes. The Ref tried smelling salts. Finally they began to pull him off the ring and he was carried away on a stretcher. The next fight was announced. There were two fighters who were not of the same weight class. One man was short and the other was thin and tall.

Just as the men climbed into their corners, police cruisers' lights flashed and sirens blared and the spectators began to run in panic. It was a raid.

Tom and Roger moved out of the way and watched as the group ran to the back of the lot and the mob collided with the perimeter fence with such force that it bent over and they crawled out. Tom and Roger followed. The group that breached the fence was about 100 strong. Once outside the fence they entered a small one acre wooded lot. It was very dark and the group was loud and drunk. They fell down, tripping one another. When the men made it out of the woods there were 10 patrol cars waiting.

The men were all rounded up and they were all marched to the front of the facility and each man had their picture taken with a Polaroid camera. The police also took information from their driver's license. If they had no identification they went to jail, otherwise they went home.

Tom and Roger got in the Mercedes and Tom drove Roger home.

Chapter 6

Roger and his wife had separated recently. Roger had custody of the house and his wife had moved in with a girlfriend. The girlfriend had two children. The fact that Roger did not want to have children had been the latest stressor to the marriage. Other problems included Roger's alcoholism and his adultery.

It felt odd to drop Roger off to a dark house. Roger was drunk and so Tom helped him inside. It was early, about 11 p.m., Roger offered Tom a drink, forgetting that Tom had quit drinking 5 years ago. Tom declined the offer and he reminded Roger that his car was at the office. Typically Roger would call in the morning to work and ask if anyone knew the location of his car. Normally it was at the office. He would straggle in riding in a taxi. He was drinking too much. Tom knew it but didn't say anything. Roger was still producing good work. He handled all the family law and wills and estates and guardianships. He also had two very good accounts representing insurance companies. There were no complaints from his clients or other lawyers or judges. But it would just be a matter of time before his drinking would interfere with his work.

Darlene wanted to say something about Roger's behavior. Tom reminded her that Roger had seniority over her in the firm. Darlene could accept that fact but that meant that Tom should talk to him and make arrangements with their health insurance company to schedule Roger to enter a program so he could dry out. Tom hoped Roger would pull himself together and dry out on his own so he procrastinated, but knew he would have to confront Roger soon. Maybe tomorrow, Tom thought as he closed the door to Roger's house.

When Tom left Roger's house and was walking to his car, he thought he saw someone in the shadows and he looked carefully back toward the garage in the back. He saw nothing.

Tom opened the door to the car and saw the manila envelope with the retouched photographs of the victim in the Alesse case. Tom took them out of the car and went back to the front door of Roger's house and knocked. He wanted Roger to look at the girl in the photos.

Roger answered the door. He had a coffee cup in his hand filled with whiskey.

"I'd love a cup of coffee, Roger," said Tom.

"I'll have one too," said Roger. "Follow me."

Roger poured the scotch whiskey in his coffee cup into the sink in the kitchen and began to prepare the percolator for the fresh ground beans.

"I'm glad you came back in the house. I was going to start drinking all over again, but lately I can't get a good drunk going."

"Hell of a waste of good whiskey," said Tom. "So should I tell you that you are losing your battle with alcohol?"

"You don't have to tell me. I know it," said Roger. "What should I do?"

"We have insurance that will cover it if you want to have medical treatment for withdrawal from alcohol. Or you can go to AA. Or you can just quit yourself."

Roger poured the coffee. Roger stirred the brew in his cup. "So if I took a couple of weeks off, it would be alright."

"You have worked for the firm for seven years. You work seven days a week and you have never taken a vacation. I guess you have earned a couple of weeks off."

"I may not be in tomorrow, then," said Roger.

"Take the time you need. The insurance agency is aware you may need some help. I talked to them. There is a good rehab hospital in Orlando. Give the agent a call."

"I think I will," said Roger.

"Look, I wanted you to look at these photographs. This is the girl Alphonse is supposed to have assaulted. I thought in your travels that you might have seen her."

Roger pulled out the two photos.

"Nice rack," said Roger as he looked at the photo of the torso shot. When he looked at the face he said, "That's Lori. She works for The Oar House. She's private property. She's the owner's girlfriend."

"Who is the owner?"

"He's Mafia, or organized crime, I think, from Tampa or Jacksonville. Very dangerous. You need to tell Alphonse to watch his back."

"How do you know all this?"

"I have been spending some time at the bar since my separation," said Roger. "The word at the bar is that Lori tried to run away from the owner. He's a big burly guy named Clem. It's short for Clemenso."

"Do you think Clem would be violent with Lori?"

"This is another world, Tom. These people like to hurt people who get in their way. They have to show that no one can take advantage of them."

"What do you know about John Hale?"

"The State Attorney?" asked Roger.

"Does he have a clue about what is going on at The Oar House?"

"John Hale is oblivious. He doesn't know what is happening in his own back yard," said Roger. "The Oar House is not the only business the Mafia people own. They have divided up the beach. They have managers for the hotels. They run other activities, gambling and drugs and prostitution. Any State Attorney who knows his salt would know these activities are happening or he is dumb as a rock. I personally think Hale is as dumb as a rock."

"I want you to look at this photo." Tom took out the original photo of the victim before it was touched up. The photo showed Lori's injuries. "This is what happened to Lori about 17 days ago. Were you aware of this?"

"No."

"Roger, I saw this girl with bandages on her face tonight in one of the back rooms at the Oar House."

"I didn't see her," said Roger. "I don't know anything about it." Roger turned his head so Tom could not see his face.

Tom noticed that Roger's eyes were blinking rapidly. He's lying, thought Tom. Why would Roger lie to me? Tom decided not to confront his partner.

Tom took a big gulp of coffee and put the cup down. He repacked the photos in the manila envelope and made his way to the door, out to his car and directly home to the condo, still wondering what Roger was trying to hide.

***

Tom tried to sneak in the penthouse at the condo. This was Darlene's place. Very chic. They shared the home with two cats. They were six months old. The cats were new from the pound. As soon as Tom entered the foyer the cats were at his feet wanting to play. Tom went to the kitchen and poured a saucer of milk. Tom wasn't sure about the cats but knew that between him and the cats, Darlene preferred the cats.

When Tom first met Darlene, Darlene had two other cats that had recently gone to heaven. First, one old cat died and then the other died within a week. Darlene was upset. Tom went to the pound and got two more cats. They were strays, destined for euthanasia. Tom thought he was doing right. Wrong. The right thing would have been to let Darlene come around to the idea that she should replace her old friends. That was one of the reasons Darlene did not like marriage. Tom would make decisions for her and then he acted like he didn't understand why it was a problem.

The two old cats were her cats and she would decide to replace them. At first she had not interacted with the kittens. Then she noticed that they had some quirks that they shared with the old cats. She was amused. Tom noticed that she bought the kittens treats.

Tom was getting there, but he still didn't know or acknowledge what he did that was wrong in taking it on himself to replace Darlene's cats. (It's almost obvious isn't it?)

***

Darlene came into the kitchen and sat at the breakfast nook across from Tom and they watched the kittens lap up the milk.

"So where were you?" asked Darlene.

"I went to The Oar House with Roger. I guess that is his hangout or he's known there. I showed him the photo of the victim, the dancer from the bar and he knew her name. Lori is her first name. He didn't tell me her last name. I think he's dating someone at the bar. He knew information about the owner that tells me he has inside information about the place. But it was like pulling teeth.

"Oh," Tom continued. "Roger may not be in tomorrow. I gave him two weeks off and told him to go dry out."

"Do you think he will?"

"I hope so," said Tom. "I had talked to the insurance agent last week and they pre-approved him going to Beta House in Orlando."

"I hope he goes," said Darlene. "Let's go to bed. It's late."

Chapter 7

As Tom drove away from Roger's house, Roger went to the back door and turned off the light. Shortly thereafter he heard scratching on the door, like a small animal – a dog or cat.

Roger opened the door and there at the door, standing 6' 2" tall, sinewy, blonde, young and beautiful, was Sarah. He hugged her in the dark on the stoop and pulled her into his house. Sarah was wearing her costume from work – a "G" string and a sheer billowing blouse.

"Sarah," said Roger. He was 6' tall but stooped over, very thin, sickly, 145 pounds, brown hair with sideburns. The dancer towered over him.

"Your friend didn't see me?"

"No, no, don't worry about it. I don't care really." Roger had a coffee cup in his right hand. (Alas, the cup contained whiskey.) "Look, I have a few days off. Do you want to take a trip somewhere?"

"That would be nice. I was going to ask if I could stay with you for a while," said Sarah. "I haven't told anyone about you. I would be safe here."

"What is going on?"

"We had a big raid at the club tonight. I don't have anywhere to go. You have always been good to me. Could I stay?"

"Of course." Roger did not mention he had seen the police raid.

"I need a shower."

"Help yourself. The towels are in the cupboard upstairs in the bathroom."

"I don't have anything to wear except my costume. I was lucky I had that to wear. I got out the back door as the cops came in the front. We were all running. Some girls were trapped. They didn't have anything on and they had to stay inside and I suppose they were arrested. At least I had my costume and I got out."

"You must have been a sight getting here," said Roger.

"I caught a cab. They are always parked near the club to cart home the drunks. I got a lift here. You want to know what? I didn't think about payment for the cab but then I remembered a big tip – $20. I saved it in my blouse pocket and I used that money for the fare."

Roger followed Sarah up to the bath. Sarah took off her clothes and started the shower. Roger sat on the bed outside the bathroom door. He could see Sarah, nude in the full length bathroom mirror.

"What happened tonight? Why the raid?" asked Roger. "Didn't Clem pay off the police?"

"I think it has to do with Lori. I think the police were looking for her. Lori said Clem wouldn't let her go to court. He's afraid the police will ask her about his business. I guess she knows where all the skeletons are buried."

"Clem wouldn't be that stupid to tell her his business."

"You know, 'Lose lips sink ships'," said Sarah as she got in the shower and pulled the curtain.

"Hungry?" asked Roger. "I'll make some eggs."

"Great," said Sarah as she rummaged around in the drawers in the bedroom looking for clothes. She was thin and wiry. If she found a pair of long pants, she could wear them like a pair of calypso pants. She found a pullover shirt. The shirt was too short but looked like it was meant to be worn with a bare midriff. The sandals in the closet fit. She was dressed well enough to go out to a store and get new clothes. Sarah came downstairs to the table. Roger was wearing a frilly apron. Sarah covered her mouth and chuckled. Roger ignored her. He was still wearing his suit pants and didn't want to stain them.

"I think the idea of a trip is a good idea," said Sarah.

"So do I. I'm sick of this place."

"You have money?" Sarah was hoping. In Sarah's mind money was the required ingredient for a good relationship.

"I have plenty of money. I have been saving for a while. I knew my wife was going to leave and I started to put money aside."

"Do you expect to get back together?" asked Sarah.

"I don't think it will happen. Too much water over the dam or under the bridge or whatever. Listen, I need to know. Do you know a man named Alphonso Alesse?"

"Who is he?"

"He works with us at the law firm."

"I don't think so. Why would I know him?"

"They say he is one of the people who attacked Lori," said Roger. "He is supposed to be the tall guy who attacked her." Roger knew the story Lori had told the cops. Sarah had told him Lori's story to the police was a lie.

"I don't think you got this right. Lori told me that there was only one person who attacked her and he was someone she knew."

"Two men have been arrested. Have they got the wrong people?"

"I would think so. Lori let her attacker in. That tells me she knew him," said Sarah. "And there was only one attacker."

"Why did she pick out two suspects?"

"She is just nutty. Clemenso told her to throw off the cops ... confuse them."

"Do you know this? Or are you making this up?"

"I'm not making it up. Lori told me she knew the person that cut her. I assumed it was only one person."

"Listen, you need to talk to my partner, Tom, to help get this straightened out."

"I can't do that. They will kill me if I talk to Tom. You don't know who to trust. If I tell Tom he will have to give my name to the prosecutor and then the cops will know and then the cops will tell Clem and then I will be dead."

"Are you serious?"

"I am dead serious," said Sarah. "If the prosecutor gets hold of Lori he will talk to her about Clem. Clem has done bad things. Lori knows things that could hurt Clem and his friends. I think the person that cut Lori was telling her to shut up about something. She knew too much. It was a warning to all the girls in the club to shut up."

"What about Alphonse? He will go to jail."

"You don't think Lori is going to testify, do you?"

"What are you saying?" asked Roger.

"Lori has to testify against Alphonse before Alphonse can be convicted for the assault and sent to jail. Isn't that true?"

"Yes, that is true."

"She was supposed to go to court last week to testify and she didn't go. Then yesterday, she was supposed to be in court and she didn't go then. Believe me, she won't testify," said Sarah.

"They will arrest her and force her to testify," said Roger.

"Fat chance," said Sarah as she swirled the eggs on her fork. Then Sarah changed the subject. "I need to get some clothes for the trip. Can you lend me a few bucks and your car? I'll be back in a couple of hours. You can get some sleep while I'm gone."

"Sounds good." Roger gave her $200 in crisp twenty dollar bills and the keys to his old jeep wagon. "This is the only car I have here; my Chevy is at the office." He apologized. The jeep was a wreck, but it ran.

"The jeep is fine," said Sarah. She gave Roger a big kiss on the lips, pocketed the $200 and the keys and ran out the back door.

***

Roger took Sarah's suggestion and he went upstairs with his coffee cup and got out of his suit pants and got in bed. He thought Sarah would be back in a few hours. He felt very tired. Then he remembered he needed to tell Tom what he had learned from Sarah. He got up out of bed and went to the upstairs phone. Then he realized it was Saturday. It was too early on Saturday to call and he was supposed to take some time off. He had forgotten his mission – to stay sober. He forgot to stay sober because he was drunk.

Then he remembered what he needed. He went downstairs to fill his cup. He should bring the bottle of whiskey upstairs and then he wouldn't have to go up and down the stairs. It would save him some steps. He might fall on the stairs, he thought. But why am I downstairs? he asked himself. Oh, to get the bottle of "Red" (Johnnie Walker Red). What was he doing? He lay down on the couch but then needed to go to the toilet. He had to go upstairs. He took a step and miss-stepped on the first tread of the first step and he fell on his face and he almost knocked himself out.

He was bleeding from a cut on his forehead and he pissed his shorts. Now, he didn't need to think about what it was that he was supposed to do. He was sleeping and unconscious and passed out on the stairs. It was a triple play.

***

Roger woke up on the stairs of his house. He went through a checklist in his mind. Where was his wife? She left him. Why was he on the stairs? That was too difficult to answer. Then he felt his head. He was bleeding. A small pool of blood was on a stair. What time is it? It was dark when he fell. He must have fallen on the stairs. There was a broken coffee cup on the floor. There was a broken bottle of "Red". He stood in the broken glass. Luckily he didn't cut his foot. Now he remembered. He was getting a drink. He went to the kitchen and opened the cardboard flap to the case of whiskey and retrieved a new bottle. He opened it and took a swig. He was dizzy. He pulled himself up the stairs on his butt, one step at a time still holding the bottle in one hand. He used the wall to steady himself and he got in the bathroom and relieved himself and then removed his underwear.

Roger looked at his face. He had an oozing cut in his eye brow. He pinched the slit closed and rubbed in styptic from a stick he found in the medicine cabinet, then took a wad of tissue and covered his forehead and waited to see if there was more bleeding. The styptic caused him to tear up. God it burned. There was just a little more bleeding, more like seepage. He wrapped a towel around his head and then fell into bed.

"I think I am supposed to call Tom," he said aloud to no one in particular.

No one answered him.

"I will call tomorrow."

Part II

A cruel crime
sometimes traps the innocent
and makes bad law.

Chapter 8

Tommy Magyar AKA "Tommy", was a short, swarthy, ugly 24-year-old. He was Roma, born in America (a natural US citizen) to parents who migrated from Hungary. He worked with a crew of fellow Roma/Americans traveling the Eastern coast from New Jersey to Florida then out to the Southwest then back to New Jersey, repairing roofs and driveways.

His pride was his truck. There was a sign on the truck: "Magyar Roofing." The truck was new this year. He used the vehicle for work. He and his crew were moving south from town to town beginning in North Carolina where he purchased the vehicle for cash.

The crew was in St. Petersburg, Florida, when he was stopped by the police, who claimed he had a faulty taillight. Tommy was alone in the truck. The police made up a story about the faulty tail light. He was very fearful of the police and he did not assert himself to the two big officers. There could be nothing wrong with the tail light, thought Tommy. The truck was brand new.

Tommy was a little slow mentally and he relied on a lady friend named Theresa to help him if he was in a situation that was stressful. Theresa was not with him when he was pulled over by the cops. His Roma blood made him naturally fearful of authority. The governments in Eastern Europe had discriminated against his people, who they called gypsies (a pejorative in Europe). His race earned enmity, as Catholics thought the Roma were the children of Cain. During WWII, the Roma were the victims of the Nazi and the Ustasa genocide that the Roma called the "Porajmos". They were killed on sight by mobile killing units on the Eastern Front

(Einsatzgroppen), or enslaved and imprisoned and sentenced to forced labor in the concentration camps. Even after the war they were called socially degraded and their women were subject to forced sterilization to control their population.

In short, all Roma, particularly mentally slow Roma, were afraid of the authorities. The memory of their ill treatment in Europe over the centuries caused this fear.

So, when the two uniformed officers stopped Tommy in his new truck, he was afraid to step outside his vehicle. The police unholstered their weapons and approached the truck. They told Tommy to put his hands on the steering wheel. Luckily he did. One policeman realized he was simple and the officer spoke slowly and told the other officer to quit screaming.

"You are scaring the suspect, stupid."

The police were on the lookout for swarthy looking short men. From his face when he was stopped at the traffic light, Tommy had the heavy beard and lumpy, uneven, asymmetrical features the police were looking for. The police just needed to see how tall he was. So they lied and told him they stopped him because of the bad tail light. They wanted him out of the truck to verify his height. His license said he was 5'5".

When the kindly officer coaxed Tommy out of the truck they saw he was short, perfect in fact. The police were conducting a BOLO ("Be on the Look Out") for a dark, swarthy, male, 5'5" tall. Now they just had to encourage Tommy to volunteer to go to the station. Remember, this was not Eastern Europe. Tommy had done nothing wrong. His tail light was not defective. The police could get away with a traffic stop but they had no probable cause for an arrest so they had to get Tommy to volunteer to go to the station for a lineup.

"Could you please come with us to the station?"

"Sir?" asked Tommy

"We need your assistance to clear up a matter."

"Sir?"

"You want to help us don't you sir?"

"Yes."

"You can follow us in your truck and then leave once we are done."

"Yes."

Tommy got in the truck and followed the police to the station. He was said to have agreed to participate in a line up. Later, Tommy disagreed when he was told by his attorney that he agreed to accompany the police to the station for a line up.

"That's not true, " said Tommy.

At the station the detective, a big man named Richard Cook, gave Tommy a form to read but didn't ask Tommy if he could read. Tommy signed the form which said he agreed to participate in a line up. He signed with his mark (an "X"). The detective said Tommy said he understood the form. ("Do you understand that?" "Yes.")

Short story, regarding the lineup, Tommy was picked out positively by the victim as the person who cut her with a "roofer's razor". (She now said the weapon was a roofer's razor, like the one the police found and took from the floor of Tommy's truck when they conducted the search.) Tommy was said to have asked the police to move his car since he was being arrested. When they moved the truck they saw the tool in plain sight on the floor of the truck. (Tommy said he did not ask the police to move his truck. He said he did not agree to a search of his vehicle.)

Tommy was then interviewed by the police detective for many hours. When asked if he had cut the victim, he denied the allegation.

In fact Tommy Magyar never admitted he in any way hurt any woman in his life.

The police asked him to take a polygraph. Tommy agreed. He answered all the lie detector operator's questions.

The operator, a policeman who was trained to use the machine came back to the detective and reported that to the question: "Did you ever cut any person with a razor or other sharp object?" that Tommy answered "No" and the operator said there was no deception shown. In fact, the operator said Tommy did not exhibit any deception to any question asked.

"What do you mean there is no deception?" yelled Detective Cook.

"The machine says there is no deception," insisted the operator. "He is not lying."

"Can't you do any better than that? I want you to look at this picture of the victim."

The operator looked at Lori's wounds. "God that's awful," said the operator. "I could put in my report that the results are "inconclusive," but if anyone looks at the recording the test made, the raw data, they will see the correct result is that there was no deception shown. This man did not commit this crime according to the lie detector machine."

"Are you kidding me? This man is a gypsy. They are taught to lie as soon as they pop out of the womb. I'll bet this guy is part of the crew that has been gipping old people around the city out of their money for phony roof repairs."

The lieutenant heard the yelling and he told the detective, Richard Cook, to take a walk. The lieutenant then went over to the lie detector operator. "What's the problem?"

The operator explained. "According to the test I ran, this man is innocent; he did not cut this girl."

The lieutenant told the operator to write out his report and then put the report and the result together with the raw data on his desk and he would take care of it.

"Okay," said the operator. "Sorry to cause all this trouble."

"You know how it is. Crimes like what he did to this young girl make bad law for a defendant like him. He's not a sympathetic figure," said the lieutenant.

"No," said the lie detector operator. Later the operator put the evidence on the lieutenant's desk.

No one could find the evidence after that. (Tommy told his attorney about the lie detector test. The police denied a test was run.)

***

Detective Richard Cook was called out of the interview room for a phone call. It was Clemenso Bondi.

"Who is going to represent the Gypsy?" asked Clem, the manager of The Oar House. Clem was calling from the club. He and Cook spoke regularly.

"No one will represent him. His people will abandon him," said Detective Richard Cook. "His girl may help him but the rest of the crew will be gone in the morning. The only chance he has to get a street lawyer is if he can find someone who will take his truck in payment. He won't get appointed a public lawyer at the State's expense so long as he has the truck."

"He doesn't have a lawyer yet?" Clemenso asked.

"He won't be able to hire one himself," said Detective Cook. "He's simple. Mentally slow. His girlfriend is savvy. She will help him."

"Why don't we help? If he doesn't have the truck the court will appoint a brand new public lawyer who has no experience."

"Right?" said Cook.

"So burn his truck?" said Clem.

"Why do that?"

"Then he will have no assets and the court will appoint someone who has no experience. His attorney will be someone who we can deal with."

"Who will represent him?" said Cook, who was rolling a new sheet of paper into his typewriter.

"His public lawyer," said Clem.

"That could backfire," said Detective Richard Cook. Cook hung up the phone and went back to the interview room. This is too crazy, thought Cook. It's too complicated and too chancy. Clem was always willing to take a risk.

"Just do what I said. I will destroy his truck." Clem was the boss.

Chapter 9

Magyar's girlfriend, Theresa, was in her mid-30's. Theresa was more like a mother to Magyar than a girlfriend. When Magyar failed to arrive at the motel where the crew was living, Theresa immediately began to worry. Normally she rode with Magyar as he sold roofing jobs, but she had work to do washing work clothes for the crew of men on the day he was arrested. If the crew looked neat and clean potential customers had a good impression of them and they could sell a job.

Once they sold one job, Magyar went door to door in the neighborhood and informed the neighbors that they would be working in the area inspecting, repairing, and replacing roofs and they could offer discounts of as much as 30% if a neighbor needed work done to their roof. Magyar was pathetic looking and Theresa acted as his helper trying to quote the cost of the work. Sometimes he could make a sale because of his neat appearance and polite manner and sometimes the owner would take advantage of his low IQ to obtain a lower price. People pinched pennies. There was one recession after another. Times were tough in the lower middle income neighborhoods the Roma targeted. So even though they offered prices that were too good to be true, Magyar had to knock on many doors before he could make a sale.

When Tommy Magyar failed to come in from work, Theresa asked the men from the work crews as they drifted in from the different locations where they were working if they had seen Magyar. But no one had seen him since morning. Theresa borrowed a truck and went to the area where he was last seen. She went to the door of a house where part of the crew had been working. The owner said he had not seen him. But, yes, he remembered the shiny new truck.

"Come to think of it I think the truck was outside the police station," said the homeowner.

So Theresa went to the police station and there in the parking lot was Magyar's truck with the sign on the door that said: "Magyar's Roofing"

Theresa went inside the station. She was told to have a seat. Her boyfriend was with a detective and it would be awhile. When she asked, she was told that he was not under arrest. "Have a seat" she was told. The desk sergeant was friendly and smiled.

Theresa sat. She felt it would be a long wait. It was 7 p.m.

***

At 9 p.m., before the detective, Richard Cook, made his call to Clemenso "Clem" Bondi at The Oar House and then after another round of questioning Magyar, he took a break and went to the water cooler located in the lobby. He saw Theresa and guessed she knew Magyar. She was dressed the part in a peasant skirt, a blouse, and a scarf. She looked plain. He got her name from the officer at the desk and then went back to Magyar. He would use her as a pawn later. Let her stew.

Magyar had not been helpful. The lie detector test had not worked out the way it should. Normally the lie detector is used to coax a confession. The way it worked was the interrogator would listen to hours of denials and then he would offer the accused the lie detector. "You can prove you are not guilty if you pass the test." Most defendants would say they would take the test. What did they have to lose?

Most defendants were guilty and the machine would show the lie. The lie detector operator would tell the defendant he was "being deceptive" (he was lying). The defendant would then be turned back to the detective and the detective would pressure a confession by repeating that the machine said he was guilty. The interrogator never explained that the result of the lie detector test could not be used as evidence because it was not scientifically reliable. But the fact the person failed the test was enough to get at least a meager confession (An, "Okay, I did it.") out of the person.

A confession, even a weak confession, was a chink in the defendant's armor. Magyar didn't confess and he "passed" the lie detector, but he had been identified by the victim in the lineup and she had identified the roofing knife found in Magyar's truck as the weapon that cut her. The identifications were big chinks in the defense.

But this case was still weak. The police had found fingerprints in Lori's apartment that were not eliminated and probably belonged to the perpetrator. The finger print analyst said the prints in Lori's apartment were not Magyar's prints.

At the time of Magyar's arrest the crime was 10 days old and during those ten days the police had had no cooperation from the victim, Lori, or any of her friends at work. Lori had been unable to give a description that an artist could use to produce a drawing of the suspect.

The police and the State Attorney could make no sense out of Lori's statement as to how the crime occurred. She said she didn't know the perpetrator but there was no sign of forced entry. There did not appear to have been a fight in the apartment. She didn't remember a struggle. She was bigger than Magyar. How did he overpower her? The police felt there had to have been another person who held her down while she was cut. She claimed she opened the door and saw "one short, swarthy, ugly man" and she passed out. Why did she pass out? "I don't know."

The State Attorney felt Lori's statements were scripted. She was only telling the police what she had been told to say. It seemed that if she had not been told what to say she said she couldn't remember. This was exactly what Richard Cook wanted. "Confusion to the enemy," he said to Clem.

***

"Your friend is in real trouble," said Detective Cook to Theresa.

"That is hard for me to believe. Tommy is an innocent," said Theresa. "He has never done anything wrong."

"You never know. Do you want to see him?" asked the detective.

"Of course."

The detective arranged a visit. They could see each other through a glass partition and visit and speak to each other over the phone receivers. Detective Cook was not being kind. He hoped to gain evidence from Tommy and Theresa. The phones were bugged. This was allowed as a security measure so that the police could thwart escapes. If a defendant, by chance, said anything incriminating regarding the charge for which he had been arrested the statement could be used in trial.

"Why were you arrested?" Theresa asked Tommy through the phone.

"I don't know. They say I cut a girl with a knife."

"You don't have a knife."

"They said it was a roofing knife that was on the floor of the truck."

"Is that true?"

"No."

"Did you cut a girl at any time?"

"No."

"When did they say this occurred?"

"Ten days ago."

"We were in Jacksonville 10 days ago."

"I told them. They didn't believe me. They say the girl said I did it. She identified me here at the police station."

"She has to be mistaken. What is her name?"

"I don't know. They wouldn't tell me."

"I need to hire an attorney. Are they asking you any questions?"

He nodded yes.

"Don't talk to them anymore until I can get you a lawyer."

"Okay."

***

Theresa waited for the detective. Two hours later Cook met with her.

"I need the keys to Tommy's truck, please," Theresa asked the detective.

"We are holding it as evidence."

"That is the only property he has and he wants to sell it to hire a lawyer."

"Sorry, the truck has to be processed. We may decide to hold it."

"When does he go to court?"

"In the morning."

"How much is his bail?"

"There is no bail."

"Why?"

"He has not been cooperative."

"Thank you," said Teresa (trying to be cooperative) as she sat on the bench waiting for court to convene.

***

The two men from Tampa strolled into the front parking lot of the police station. It was 5:30 a.m. and dark. The shift change occurred at 8 a.m. and the police who had worked the midnight shift were sitting in their patrol cars appearing to do paperwork. Actually they were sleeping. The first thing a patrolman learned was how to look like he was awake when he was not. He was sleeping with his eyes open in the low intensity interior light of the patrol car with his chin bent down to his chest.

There were three empty patrol cars in the police parking lot. The rest of the cars were out on patrol with the officers snoozing. There was no guard in the parking lot and no activity that the two criminals could see inside through the windows of the station even though all the lights were on.

The two men were told to look for a new truck. The color was unknown. The men from Tampa were confused as there were three relatively new Ford trucks in the lot. "There must have been a sale," they commented.

The men popped the gas caps on the three trucks and slid a rag into the tank pushing the tip of the rag into the gasoline. The rags absorbed and became soaked with gas.

Once they had the rags in the neck of the gas tanks they split up and each took a truck and they lit the rag. That took care of two trucks. Now one man walked away and the other waited for a minute and walked to the third vehicle and lit the fuse and walked away.

There were three explosions. Among the trucks attacked there were two Magyar roofing trucks. Tommy Magyar owned one and the other was owned by Omar Magyar, which Theresa had borrowed to use to find Tommy.

The Lieutenant on duty was asked by the press for a comment on the cause of the fire. The fire was intentionally set, he said. "It must have been Bolsheviks or Hippies." In as much as America was in a cultural revolution you could say something like that to explain unusual circumstances and at least one half of the people in the United States would believe it.

Unfortunately that is still true.

Chapter 10

Theresa awoke when she heard the three explosions. She was curled up in her seat in the lobby of the police station. She had fallen asleep after she spoke to Tommy. She had intended to wait for the first appearance hearing. That hearing would give her a chance to talk to a judge about her friend and possibly obtain bail and the name of an attorney.

The explosions caused a stir. All the patrolmen who were on the street awoke and roared back to the station with their sirens blaring.

The fire department was next door to the police station so the firemen did not have far to go to get to the scene. The problem was dealing with the three separate fire locations. Each of the burning trucks was in a different part of the parking lot. The firemen had to call in other fire equipment units to try to keep the three scenes cool. Despite their efforts other cars in the parking lot started to explode and before it was over seven cars and trucks had been totally destroyed and almost every car in the lot suffered damage. There was a fear that the police station would go up in smoke but that was avoided by aggressive work by the fire crews. Before it was over units from three surrounding cities plus all the local units were involved in fighting the blaze.

Because of the worry of the loss of the police station in the fire, the prisoners were collected (there were only two) and taken to a gym at the high school located down the road and put in a locker room. There were other visitors (civilians who were now possible arson suspects) who were taken with the prisoners for their safety. The prisoners and the civilians were put in one locker room. There was only one door to the locker room so they only needed one armed guard outside the door of the room to secure the prisoners and the civilians. As a result, Tommy Magyar and Theresa were together and they had a chance to talk.

Theresa had been able to look out the window after the explosions first occurred and before the other vehicles caught fire. She saw that both of the Magyar Roofing trucks had been destroyed. That was the first thing she told Tommy after they had a chance to talk. Magyar began to cry. The truck was his only possession. His crown jewels.

Magyar had never been arrested before. During his lifetime, he was so afraid of the police he avoided any activity that could result in incarceration. So he was upset being in jail. Then he lost his truck and Theresa was worried. He could see it in her face. He did not like to see her worried. Most times he didn't understand why she was worried. But he could tell that now she was worried about him. And that made him worry even more.

"What are we going to do?" Magyar asked.

"We will need to get you a lawyer. A lawyer will know what to do," said Theresa.

Tommy leaned his head against Theresa's shoulder and was very quiet. They both fell asleep. Later that day they were both taken to the County Jail. The sheriff and the court made provision for Magyar to have his hearing before the judge as was required by the criminal rules. The judge had to review the charge and make sure the defendant understood what he was charged with. This was normally a simple process.

***

"You realize you are charged with assault with intent to commit first degree murder?" asked the court.

Tommy nodded.

"Do you have a lawyer?"

Tommy nodded.

The judge looked at him. The judge could see Tommy only half understood what was going on. The judge then looked in the audience and said: "Is there anyone here with Mr. Tommy Magyar?"

"Yes." Theresa stepped forward.

"Why isn't he responding to me?"

"He's afraid."

"Do you intend to hire a lawyer for him? This is a very serious charge. It is a felony. He could go to jail for a long time."

"We understand. He had a brand new truck but it was burned up in the fire at the police station. The truck was all he had. We do not have money to pay an attorney."

"He doesn't own a house, have money in the bank, any bonds or notes?"

"No, we don't have anything now."

"Well, I will appoint an attorney. Let me look out here in the courtroom and see." The judge paused as he looked around the courtroom. "Where is the Public Attorney?"

"They called and said they couldn't take any more cases right now," said the clerk.

The judge looked around the courtroom. "Ok, well I guess that leaves you sir. What is your name?"

"James DeMarco, Judge."

"Well, Mr. DeMarco, you have a client. I will give you some time to talk to Mr. Magyar. I will consider the question of bail, but I am hesitant to release him on his own recognizance on this charge unless he has substantial ties to the community. The paperwork says he cut a woman badly. But you talk to him and come back next week with a motion to set bond if you feel it is in his best interest."

"Thank you, Judge."

"Bailiff."

"Yes, your Honor," said the deputy sheriff.

The judge wrote and then signed a note to the warden of the jail stating Magyar was to be put in the medical wing and he gave the note to Attorney DeMarco.

"I want this man in the hospital ward until he can be examined," the judge said to the deputy. "I don't want him to be put in with someone who can take advantage of him. He's very small. Do you understand what I mean?"

"Yes, your Honor," said the deputy sheriff.

"Next case."

***

Theresa and Mr. DeMarco went outside and talked briefly. The lawyer gave her his card and told her to call to set an appointment the next day. Mr. DeMarco promised that he would talk to Magyar that morning after he finished his other hearings. Theresa smiled. She felt good that her friend had a lawyer. The lawyer was very young though, she thought.

***

The county jail was built in the 1920's and additions had been constructed as the county had grown. Unfortunately the jail had not increased in size in proportion with the growth of the population. This was high growth Florida. The jail was overcrowded. It was built to house 250 inmates but there was a pretty constant jail population of 600 prisoners.

The jail was four stories high. The first floor was administrative offices and prisoner intake and medical wing. The medical wing was where Magyar was supposed to be housed but it was overcrowded. There were eight beds and 17 inmates who were sick or injured. None of these prisoners could fend for themselves. That was why the judge ordered Magyar to be placed in the medical wing. He was small and vulnerable like the other 17 men.

The jail was old and awful. The interior of the jail was two-toned. The walls were a crème color and the bars were the color of Dijon mustard. It was like puke. That was the only memorable thing about the interior of the jail beside the cigarette smoke. The smell would choke a maggot.

Because of overcrowding, the jailers ignored the judge's instructions to house Magyar in a medical cell. Tommy was put on the fourth floor where there were three large cages with 20 dangerous men in each cage. The cages had steel tables and chairs welded to the floor in the center of each cell and smaller cages along the back wall with four steel cots welded to the walls in each cage. The intent was that there would be a metal door on each small cage so the men could be locked up in the small cells at night or if there was an emergency. However the doors restricted the floor space that was needed for extra cots and so the cell doors were removed. The men who did not have a steel bed used a cot on the floor at night. Therefore, the steel doors that were supposed to separate the men in the large cage were gone and each large cage contained a scrum of men.

The guards did not like the arrangement on the fourth floor. They felt it was dangerous. They could be attacked and held prisoner by the inmates. Sometimes there were more than 20 men who could wander freely in each of the three large rooms. Because the guards felt insecure entering the three large cages the two guards on duty to watch and control the 90 or so men on the floor had set up a desk outside the three rooms next to the entrance to the elevator and they did not go in the large cages. These cages were governed by the prisoners.

Tommy Magyar was in fear for his life. The guard had to push him into one of the cages with a night stick. The men were all larger than him and intimidating. He was struck by the noise on the floor. The materials used to construct the jail were "hard". There were three large rooms separated by bars with reinforced windows and concrete walls, floors, and ceilings. Every sound that was made on the floor echoed and resulted in a roar of unintelligible noise. Lawyers hated to visit clients who were assigned to the fourth floor because they had to shout their conversation at their client. Other men would crowd up next to the prisoner so they overheard the conversation. They were like biddy hens spending their time collecting information and spinning it out to the other inmates. The information was also valuable because they would trade the prisoner's statements to the prosecutor for a lighter sentence. Beware the snitch.

When James DeMarco learned that Magyar was being housed on the fourth floor he immediately went to the administrative offices and complained. The sergeant on duty said he was aware DeMarco's client was supposed to be in the medical wing where each inmate had his own room, but there were double the number of inmates in the medical wing as there were cells and there was nothing that could be done. The officer said he would make a record of the complaint and that he would advise the judge that the jail personnel failed to comply with the court's written directive because of overcrowded conditions in the jail.

DeMarco said nothing. He went to the fourth floor. As the elevator rose, the cacophony on the top floor of the jail became louder. When he arrived and checked in with the guard he asked if the guard could remove Tommy so he could speak to him. The guard smiled knowingly, thinking DeMarco was an idiot, and said, "I'm not opening the door to one of those large cells without a five man extraction team. Period."

***

James was left with nothing he could do but to retreat. He walked around the outside of the large caged rooms until he found his client. He was in a corner surrounded by three men who were poking him with their fingers, as one would test a bird in the oven to see if it was tender. It was obvious to James that Tommy was going to be in trouble if he was left on this floor.

Tommy recognized his lawyer and was able to get away from the three men who were pawing at him.

"Get me out of here," begged Magyar.

As the attorney explained that he could not get him out without a court order and that it would take at least a week to get a hearing before the court, Magyar began to cry silently.

"I can't do this," said Magyar.

DeMarco went to the elevator and back to the administrative office and walked in on the sergeant who was speaking to another guard. DeMarco interrupted, which was not his normal behavior and he said: "The fourth floor is entirely unsuitable for my client. The judge realized that and said he should be in a medical cell. That wasn't a suggestion. That was a court order. I was present when the court ruled. "The judge gave me this signed order," he said as he handed the sergeant the paper. "You have to comply."

The sergeant looked at the piece of paper. "Will you leave me be if I put him in a single cell with an old man?"

"Yes. I will keep my mouth shut," said DeMarco.

The sergeant called the fourth floor and told the guard that he was sending up two guards to move prisoner Magyar to the second floor.

DeMarco went to the waiting room and waited. Five hours later Tommy had been moved to the second floor and he and DeMarco visited and Tommy was able to give his statement to his lawyer. He explained to his lawyer that at the time of the assault he had been working in Jacksonville and that he had witnesses who were not related to him, roofing customers who would verify he could not have been in St. Petersburg at the time this crime was committed.

***

When they had finished the interview Tommy put out his hand and shook DeMarco's hand. "You saved my life," Tommy said to DeMarco. "Thank you."

"No problem," said DeMarco. The attorney was surprised he had confronted the sergeant on behalf of his client the way he had. He felt stupid that he hadn't realized at once that the piece of paper the judge signed was an order.

Chapter 11

Richard Cook was the new breed of cop. He had an Associate Degree in Science in Criminal Justice. He had obtained the degree taking classes in college during the day after working the midnight shift as a uniformed officer. It had taken him only 18 months to obtain the degree. He didn't sleep except when he was on duty and he went from work to school and didn't change his uniform to civilian wear. The detective showed two faces, though. He was one person to his boss, the Chief of Police, and another person when he was with his boyhood friend, Clemenso Bondi. To the chief, Cook was a hardworking and honest cop. To Bondi, Cook was his co-conspirator and partner in crime.

The chief was fooled, and promoted Cook to the rank of lead detective. He wore a suit and tie to work and he was assigned difficult assault cases where it took some brain power to close the case with an arrest. Most of the assault cases that remained open were unsolved because the victim did not know the assailant. The crime was a random act of violence. There might be a suspect, but there was almost never enough evidence to make an arrest unless there was a confession.

Detective Cook was also assigned follow up duty on cases where the victim of the case was difficult to handle. Once a crime is reported by an alleged victim, the police and the State Attorney have the power to prosecute the case or not. The greatest power in government is held by the cop on the beat. The cop can see a crime and let the criminal go. He can make a traffic stop and determine the driver is drunk but let a friend take the driver home.

The person in the criminal system who is the next most powerful to the cop on the beat is the prosecutor, the State

Attorney. The State Attorney can investigate and file a No Information stating that there is insufficient evidence to prosecute. Neither the victim or the arresting officer can force the State Attorney to file a charge. Conversely, the victim cannot withdraw the allegation the victim makes against a defendant and force the State Attorney to drop the charges. The only way the victim can reverse a prosecution is to state she was lying and she would be at risk of being prosecuted for perjury or making a false report of a crime. In other words, the State Attorney controls the case after the arrest, and if the State Attorney, acting on behalf of the people, is determined to bring the case he can move forward but he must have the cooperation of the victim. To retain that cooperation he needs someone to keep up with the case and follow up. That is the job of the lead detective.

Richard Cook was assigned to be lead detective in Lori Schaeffer's assault case. His ultimate job was to make sure he knew the location of the victim and to make sure she appeared in court and was available to testify. However, Cook's role in Magyar's case, so far as Clemenso was concerned, was to frustrate the police investigation and undermine the case.

There are two ways the victim can undermine a case. First the victim can fail to appear and second the victim can appear, take the stand to testify, and then claim the defendant is not the person who committed the crime, or claim she can no longer remember, or lie and state the crime did not occur. In Lori Schaeffer's case, with the injuries involved, a crime was assumed. Lori didn't cut herself, in fact it would have been impossible for Lori to cut herself the way she was cut.

Lori Schaeffer had reported the crime when she was brought into the emergency room by her friend and workmate, Sarah Rogers. Further, she had attended a line up and identified Tommy Magyar as the assailant and then she had picked out Alphonse Alesse in a convenience store as the second individual who held her down during the attack. It appeared she was cooperating but she also seemed to be sabotaging the case. At first she claimed she was assaulted by only one person then later after she was questioned extensively she remembered there was another person who held her down. So then the police were looking for a short suspect and a tall suspect.

When the police questioned her veracity, the physician who was treating her felt she could have had partial amnesia. She had gone through major physical and mental trauma and the doctor felt she may have tried to forget the incident. The doctor felt there must have been something about the taller of the two assailants that was particularly terrorizing to Ms. Schaeffer that caused her to forget that a tall assailant was also involved. The police accepted the medical explanation but a victim with amnesia would make the case difficult to prove if the prosecutor only had Lori's testimony to prove the identification of the suspect.

After the victim made the second identification the prosecution team, led by John Hale, the State Attorney, was upset. They were embarrassed by the victim. In their parlance, the witness was a "squirrel," a person who the attorney could not trust to testify consistently on the stand. One of the instructions the judge gives to the jury regarding the credibility of a witness is whether the witness was consistent in their prior statements with their testimony on the stand. If a witness can't keep the facts straight the witness' testimony can be disregarded by the jury. If Lori Schaeffer's recitation of the facts of the case was disregarded then the jury would have a duty to disregard her testimony that Tommy Magyar and Alphonse were the assailants and they would be found not guilty.

Lori Schaeffer's credibility was further in question by the fact that Magyar had a strong alibi. The alibi witnesses were non family members who established that the crew that he was part of was working in Jacksonville when the crime occurred. Fellow crew members were not the only persons to provide the alibi. Customers who had ordered roof work that was sold to the home owner by Tommy at the same time the assault was occurring provided alibi testimony. These witnesses said Magyar was with them in Jacksonville, which is a good five hours away from St.

Petersburg, when the crime occurred. Alibi witnesses can be shaken but the witnesses that had been interviewed in Jacksonville were believable witnesses. They were salt of the earth type people who were sober when they met with Magyar and they paid Magyar by check so they knew when and where the meeting took place.

Then, Lori Schaeffer identified Alphonse Alesse as the co-defendant. Identifying Alesse was not helpful. To begin with, the victim had failed to state that there was a second assailant. Worse, there was no connection that the police could find between Alesse and Magyar. They didn't work together, they had no relationship. Why would they be the ones to do this? No motive. Detective Cook was respected as a good interrogator. He spent many hours with both men and he was unable to get any statement from the men that was inculpatory. The fact that there was no confession concerned the prosecution team.

Further, nothing connected the men to the scene. No fingerprints, no blood match at the scene (the men were both AB and Lori was O positive), no bite marks. Even the location of the crime was suspect. The apartment was clean. The technicians could find no blood in the apartment that belonged to the victim except for a small amount in the bathroom. The wounds she suffered, though not deep or to a major artery or vein, would bleed profusely. The police felt the victim would have to have been assaulted on a plastic sheet to keep the apartment so free of the evidence of the assault.

The police even brought in a blood expert who sprayed Luminal solvent on the terrazzo floor and plaster walls to try to identify blood residue. Luminal was a new investigative tool that would detect the presence of blood even after the contaminated surface had been cleaned. The Luminal test was negative for all surfaces except an area of tile in the bathroom where blood had been found.

Even good news was bad. The officers working the case were buoyed when the victim identified the hook-bladed roofer's knife that was found in Magyar's truck as the weapon involved in the crime. But when they went back to their notes they saw she had described the weapon to the doctors in the ER and to the officer who took the initial report as being a razor knife of the type used to cut carpet. The blade in the carpet knife could be removed and the blade did not have a hook – it was straight. Obviously, Lori was mistaken about the description of the weapon.

Even the arrest of Alphonse Alesse was conflicting. First Alesse was an unlikely candidate to be the perpetrator of this crime. He was a law student and law clerk for Tom Night, who was highly regarded in the community. He was married. He had no criminal record. He had been a local boy made good who worked hard to obtain what he had. He wasn't a criminal type. There was absolutely no reason why he would be involved in this crime.

From his swarthy appearance, Tommy Magyar looked like a person who might be involved in this act, but there was no proof to back up the feeling a person got when looking at Magyar. Appearances could be deceiving.

And now, if there had been any other evidence in Magyar's truck, the evidence had been destroyed in the fire in the parking lot that occurred in the early morning hours after Tommy's arrest.

And now the victim was gone. The State Attorney, John Hale, had been searching for Lori Schaeffer and he could not find her. If the State Attorney could not produce her at the preliminary hearing, now only four days away, the judge would dismiss the case. John Hale was feeling embarrassed and desperate. He had to find the victim.

Part III

Ask a witness enough questions
and if the witness is lying,
the witness may be found out.
Examination of the witness
is the only form of torture allowed
in a court of law.

Chapter 12

Tom Night, his investigator, Anthony Stewart, and Jim Swan, a local court reporter, were working together out on the street interviewing witnesses, conducting an investigation of the charges against Alphonse Alesse. Alphonse had been identified in a convenience store called the Quick Mart that was located in Alphonse's neighborhood. Tom wanted to speak to the store manager and the three men drove to the store and introduced themselves.

Anthony spoke to the store manager while Tom and Jim stood back and listened. Jim was taking shorthand notes using a Parker pen. Swan was so adept at taking shorthand he could take notes behind his back.

Anthony was very direct when he introduced himself to a potential witness. "We are here on behalf of Alphonse Alesse, who is charged with an assault on a woman named Lori Schaeffer."

"Not in my store. I know Lori, but she wasn't assaulted here," said the manager, who thought Anthony was asking if Lori was assaulted in his store.

"If she wasn't assaulted here in the store, do you know where she was assaulted?"

"I think it was at her boyfriend's house."

"Is that an apartment?"

"No. He lives in a house near here. I have delivered beer and cigarettes to his house. Clem and Lori are good customers."

"Do you know Alphonse Alesse?"

"Yes. He lives in the neighborhood too. He buys cigarettes here."

"Have you ever seen Alphonse and Lori together?"

"No. He always comes in late, near closing. I think he works late doing research. He is in law school. This is an old neighborhood and everyone knows Alphonse. His mother and father are dead and he and his wife Francis live in his parents' home. He was an only child. He has worked very hard getting to where he is. His wife is very pleasant. She is from Jacksonville."

"Alphonse was arrested here at the store. Is that correct?"

"Yes," said the manager.

"Were you here the night Alphonse was arrested?"

"Yes."

"How long have you known Lori?"

"Not long. She was another in a long line of women who were involved with Clem. He runs The Oar House. He doesn't have a good reputation. Lori has been with him for a couple of months. That's the way it is. Clem's women are here today and gone tomorrow."

"When did you first know Lori was injured?"

"About two weeks ago. She came in here with bandages on her face and she wanted a couple of cases of beer for a party at Clem's house. I called Clem and he approved the purchase for his account."

"Did she say what happened to her?"

"She said she was attacked when she came into Clem's house late at night. There was someone in Clem's house. She blacked out and woke up bleeding."

"Did she know who did it?"

"She said he was a gypsy-looking person. She said the person was arrested."

"Was it just one person?" asked the investigator.

"Yes. That's what she said. That's why we were so surprised when she claimed Alphonse attacked her."

"What were the circumstances of Alphonse's arrest?"

"It was late, almost closing time at 11 p.m., and Alphonse came in for a pack of smokes. Lori was at the register and she turned and looked at Alphonse and walked out the door. I could see her through the front window. She was in Clem's car outside. I was ringing up customers. Clem got out of his car and went to the payphone outside and made a call. Later, I found out he had the number for Richard Cook, the detective. He called him and the next thing I know there is a police car outside with its lights on and when Alphonse went outside the police put him in cuffs and they left. Then Clem and Lori drove away."

"Why was Alphonse arrested?"

"Apparently Lori claimed Alphonse attacked her. But that seemed crazy because Lori said a gypsy did it. Alphonse is an all-American guy. He doesn't look like what you think of when you think of a gypsy. I think Lori got it wrong. She seems like a nice kid and whoever cut her messed her up. She is going to need surgery for her face to clean up those scars, but I think she got the wrong guy."

"Tell me again. Where was Lori attacked?" repeated Tom, who took over asking questions.

"At Clem's house. I have the address. The house is right around the corner."

"And she said only one person attacked her?"

"Yes."

"And that person was a gypsy?"

"Yes."

"Does Alphonse know Clem?"

"I don't know. I don't think so. Clem moved in after Alphonse started college. Alphonse started law school about two years ago.

We had a little party for him at his mom's house. She was still alive then. Alphonse only had one real friend in the neighborhood. A fellow named Big John. Most of the time Alphonse was working or going to school. He had an old car and when he was in high school he left early in the morning. I'd see him later at night at the store. He'd ask how I was and say something about my family and then he would be off. After he went to law school I only saw him in the summer, and he was always working. He didn't know Clem or Lori. They were lazy people. They were looking for a fast buck."

"You said this assault happened at Clem's house," said Tom. "Where is Lori's apartment?"

"She told me she lived in the new apartments called "The Gateway" when she wasn't with Clem. She lived with another girl named Sarah. They work together at The Oar House. They are very beautiful, and smart, cagey sort of."

"Why do you say that?"

"I don't know. I always had to be careful when they picked up an order for Clem. They would come in and try to add other items to the charge. Mostly it was cigarettes. Each girl asked for an extra carton of cigarettes. Clem always paid for the cigarettes but I knew when he paid the bill that he was upset they made charges that he didn't authorize. But he should have known."

"What do you mean?"

"They weren't good girls. No pedigree. You know what I mean?"

"Yes," said Tom. "Thank you for your time."

The three men went outside of the store and spoke. "Jim, did you get down everything the man said?"

"Yes, no problem." Swan, the court reporter, had taken verbatim notes of the conversation.

"Please transcribe the statement. Anthony and I are going to The Gateway to see if we can look at the apartment. Anthony, let's stop down the road at a phone. I need to call Darlene.

***

"Well, we had some success this morning at the Quick Mart," Tom told Darlene. "The manager will make a good witness."

"Glad to hear it. Does it feel good to be out on the street?"

"Yes, but it's almost too easy to crack Lori's story. We are going to keep going and see where this leads. It seems like Lori's story is a big lie, easily contradicted by other witnesses. Do we know who is representing the co-defendant, Tommy Magyar?"

"Jim DeMarco. He called this morning and he can see us this afternoon. He's a new lawyer but he seems aggressive."

***

The apartments in The Gateway were new. Most of the tenants were young professionals just starting their careers. The focal point of the apartments was a large swimming pool. The management encouraged the tenants to mingle. They called the tenants "members", like they belonged to a club. The units were expensive. Most members doubled up so there were at least two members to a unit to split the cost. The units had two bedrooms, a bath and a large room that was a combination living room, dining area and kitchen. The rooms were painted in attractive colors and new tenants could chose the color of the interior walls and their units would be repainted if they signed a three year lease. This type of apartment was new to St. Petersburg. Most other rental units looked like prisons.

Tom and Anthony went to the lobby and spoke to a woman in guest services and asked for Lori Schaeffer. The attendant then called the manager. The manager told them he could give them no information about Lori Schaeffer. They should contact Detective Richard Cook with inquires. Tom left his card and walked outside.

"Anthony, do we know where Lori lives in this complex?" asked Tom.

"Room 159, it's in the back."

"Can you park somewhere off the property and do some surveillance?"

"Yes."

"Well let's do that. Let's budget 48 hours and see what activity there is at the unit. That will bring us up to Thursday, the day before the preliminary hearing."

"I'll personally do the surveillance Tom, unless you have something else for me to do," said Anthony. "I would like to help Alphonse if I can."

***

Tom dropped Anthony off at his house so he could pick up the van. The van was outfitted for surveillance. It had dark window glass and ports on the sides where he could mount a camera inside the van to take photographs or moving pictures of activities outside the van.

After Tom left Anthony, he drove to Roger's house to check on him. He hadn't heard from him but they had agreed that Roger would take some time off, so the fact they had not heard from Roger wasn't out of the plan.

Roger's house looked like he was away on vacation. There were three days of newspapers on the front stoop. Tom went to pick them up. Tom looked through the glass on the front door; he could see that Roger was asleep sitting up on the sofa in the front room. Tom knocked on the door. No answer. Tom decided he better talk to Roger. He banged forcefully on the door and it swung open. Unlocked.

Tom went over to Roger and shook him. He was unresponsive and then Tom felt his cheek. Roger was cold as a fish on ice.

"God damn," said Tom. He looked around the room. There was a bottle of Johnnie Walker Red on the end table. Without touching the bottle he could see it was half full.

Roger did not look like he suffered any significant trauma. There was no visible wound except a red mark above his eyebrow that appeared to be dried blood. There were signs of post mortem lividity in his bare feet. He was in his pajamas. Tom lifted the pajama legs and the dark color of lividity (dark like bruising) extended from his feet up his calves.

Tom went into the kitchen and picked up the phone and dialed the police and reported the death. There was a case of scotch on the kitchen table. There were only two full bottles of scotch left. Roger had saved the empties. As he went back to the front room Tom passed the stairs and saw shards of glass and a small amount of blood that was smeared on to one of the steps. Tom continued out the front door and waited on the front stoop for the police and the medical examiner.

Chapter 13

Tom stood on the front porch. There was a large water maple tree in the front yard and the leaves were turning red and yellow and were dropping from the tree in the brisk breeze. The weather had finally turned. It was still warm in the sun, but felt cool in the shade with the low humidity. The sky was deep blue and cloudless. Perfect Florida weather.

The first car to arrive at Roger's house was a marked police vehicle with its lights on but no siren. The uniformed officer asked Tom where the body was located. Tom pointed into the living room to the corner of the couch. Roger's head was up and leaning back against the wall.

"Did you touch anything?"

"I felt his cheek and I looked at his feet and legs for postmortem lividity. I called from the phone in the kitchen and then came out to the porch to wait for you."

"Thanks," said the officer. "Stay here."

The second vehicle was an ambulance with two men. The paramedics checked the body for a pulse.

The medical examiner's car appeared and the doctor confirmed the diagnosis of the paramedics. Roger was dead.

Next appeared the dark purple Ford four-door sedan of the State Attorney. It was John Hale in person. Mr. Hale had initiated many improvements in his office. One was that he required an Assistant State Attorney (SA) to go to the scene of any death that involved trauma or the death of a younger person. If the death was unexpected the SA was to oversee the investigation and obtain verbal reports from the medical examiner as to the cause of death. If the death was suspicious the scene was processed and a uniformed officer kept outsiders out of the area to prevent contamination of the scene. The State Attorney's representative collected the names of all of the persons at the scene as potential witnesses and he spoke to persons who witnessed the death or discovered the body. This made for a professional approach to a determination of the cause of death and led to a better possibility that any suspect in a homicide would be identified and captured.

It was unusual, however, for John Hale, the State Attorney, to appear in person.

"Hello, Tom," said Mr. Hale. "Sorry for your loss."

"Thank you," said Tom.

"Do you know what happened?" asked Hale.

"I'm not sure. Roger was on vacation. It was the first one he had ever taken to my knowledge. He had left his car at the office and I didn't hear from him and thought it was odd, so I dropped by and his door was unlocked. It opened when I knocked. He didn't respond to me when I called to him and I went in and saw he was dead."

"Did you see anything unusual?"

"There was a half-bottle of scotch on the end table. I didn't touch it. I also noticed there was blood on the stairs and pieces of glass there. I saw the blood after I made the call to the police. I did not disturb the area on the stairs. I came outside and waited for the police."

"Did he have a drinking problem?"

"He drank but he was a hard worker. Alcohol never interfered with his work. He was married, but separated. His wife may be able to discuss his personal habits," said Tom.

"Wait here a minute. I want to talk to the medical examiner and the uniformed officer."

"Sure," said Tom.

Mr. Hale went inside and came out in a few minutes.

"Do you have Roger's wife's phone number?"

"They will have it at the office. Ask for Karen, my office manager. She will help you with that."

"Tom, like I said, I am sorry for your loss. I know you have that preliminary hearing in three days. I would agree to a continuance if you want it."

Tom looked at Hale. He didn't say anything at first, and then started to speak. At first he was going to agree to the offer of a continuance but then said, "No, we will be prepared on Friday morning."

Hale's face turned red. Hale had an ulterior motive for personally visiting the scene. Tom understood that Hale had personally come to the scene of Roger's death because the State Attorney's office was not prepared to go forward on Friday. This wasn't a courtesy call. Tom knew that Hale couldn't find his witness.

Tom got in his car and looked back toward Hale who was yelling at the uniformed officer.

Tom thought: They don't have their witness. Lori is gone. Hale came down here trying to take advantage of my client. He thought I would be weak because of Roger's death and would welcome a continuance. Well, thought Tom, I will prepare so hard. I won't sleep before this hearing. I will shove this down Hale's throat.

Tom went directly to the office. When he arrived he spoke to Darlene and told her about Roger. Darlene said she thought she should be with Roger's wife, Rose. When she called Rose she was told to go meet her at the ME's office. There would be an autopsy. She reminded Tom about the meeting with James DeMarco, Tommy Magyar's attorney. And she headed out to sit with Rose at the medical examiner's office.

Tom's office manager, Karen, gave him a note from Anthony. He was staked out watching the apartment in The Gateway and he was at a pay phone, he wanted Tom to call the pay phone and left a number. It was important.

Tom called. Anthony reported he had seen some activity at the apartment. A tall young woman was removing clothing and housewares from the unit. She had a U-Haul trailer attached to an old gray Jeep. The jeep was a Willis model that was badly rusted and dented. Anthony wanted to know if Tom wanted him to try to interview the woman or just stay put and wait to see if Lori made an appearance.

"By the way, doesn't Roger have an old Willis Jeep?" asked Anthony.

Tom got Anthony's exact location and while he covered the receiver with his hand he told Karen to go out and help Anthony. Tom told Anthony that Karen was on the way. Anthony was to try to get a statement from the tall woman. Tom confirmed that Roger had a gray Jeep. Tom also told Anthony that Roger was dead. He told him it appeared to have been alcohol related.

Tom told Karen she was not to take any chances and confront anyone. If she was confronted she was to just leave. Tom promised he would have someone relieve her shortly.

***

James DeMarco was very pleasant. Firm handshake, nice smile, dark curly hair. He was young. He graduated from the University of Florida (UF). They quickly discussed law school. They both laughed. They both graduated near the bottom of their classes in class rank. James had only been out of school for a few years and he primarily practiced criminal law. A number of older criminal attorneys from UF sent him cases they couldn't handle or ones where the likelihood of being paid was low. James didn't mind. He didn't want to carry someone else's briefcase around and be required to handle cases with a senior attorney watching over his shoulder. The law allowed the uninitiated attorney to learn the law by practice as a sole practitioner. You could practice with little or no practical knowledge and you learned by your mistakes while your client suffered the consequences. James had started trying cases with the Public Attorney's Office. There were a few experienced attorneys who would sit with a new attorney during trial and tell the novice when to stand and when to sit and get the attorney through trials. It was strange, but most new attorneys would win their initial cases. It was obvious to the jury members the novice didn't know what he was doing. The juries had pity on their clients most times if the crime wasn't too serious and let the criminal go. An NG (Not Guilty),

Tom and James had a brief conversation. They could speak to each other under a rule called the Joint Defense Doctrine without waiving the attorney/client privilege for their clients. It appeared they had a common defense jokingly known as the "SODDI Defense" (some other dude did it). Their clients did not know each other and had never met. Both defendants denied they committed the offense. Ergo, someone else did it.

The attorneys agreed that they would use the preliminary hearing on Friday morning for discovery purposes – to try to find out (discover) what evidence the State Attorney had against their clients. Tom told James he could question the witnesses first and Tom would mop up. Tom told James that they were just starting their investigation and they would get together on Thursday to see what they had discovered. The investigation would be work product and privileged but Tom could share the information with James without losing the privilege because they had a common defense. That would prevent James from disclosing the information. Tom wanted James and his client to sign a Joint Defense Agreement so there would be no question that the privileges would remain intact even though disclosure was made by Tom to James of their work product. The results of the investigation and the statement or comments of their clients would be confidential.

Tom had asked Karen to prepare an agreement the day before. It was signed by Alphonse and Tom and James signed while he was in the office. James said he would take the agreement to the jail so Magyar could add his signature.

The men shook hands and James left.

***

Tom asked if he had a call from Anthony or Karen. No calls from them, but Darlene called and was now at the funeral home with Rose and asked if Tom would call.

"Tom, I'm here with Rose and she is trying to make funeral arrangements. Tom, she says she doesn't have any money."

"That's hard to understand. Roger made good money," said Tom.

"Rose said he drank it up. That's why she left. She couldn't stand to watch him destroy himself."

"Roger has money in profit sharing," said Tom. "Probably way more than she needs for funeral arrangements. Tell her to decide what she wants to do for the funeral and we will give her a check to pay for it. See if she needs money now for her personal needs and we can give her his paycheck. Later we will do an accounting and we will get her a check for the balance in Roger's profit sharing account."

"She says she will go back to the house today. Will that be ok?" asked Darlene.

"I would say so. The funeral home will make arrangements to pick up the body for services from the ME."

"I'll tell her," said Darlene.

Tom hung up and was given a note. "Come at once." There was an address provided. The message was from Anthony.

Chapter 14

Tom went to the address Anthony provided. The address was in Tampa just across the old Gandy Bridge. The address was about 10 minutes from The Gateway apartments, assuming there wasn't an accident or stalled vehicle on the two-lane Gandy Bridge to block traffic.

Just over the bridge on the Tampa side, there was a winding road in an industrial area that led to a group of ramshackle homes near the water in an area called Old Port of Tampa. The house in question was painted a faded turquoise. It was two stories. There were five or six cars in the yard. Tom could see Anthony's van and Roger's jeep were parked next to each other but the trailer was unhitched and it had been pushed up to the porch and the ramp from the trailer was connected to the porch so there was a bridge between the trailer and the house. There were two tall women – one middle aged and one young – unloading boxes from the trailer. The boxes contained mostly clothes and kitchen items. There were also costumes. A lot of thin sheer cloth on hangers covered with clear plastic garment bags. There were many boxes of shoes, most with exaggerated high platform heels.

Tom and Anthony stood by and watched as the trailer was quickly unloaded. Anthony helped the young woman re-hitch the trailer and the middle aged woman drove away in the Jeep with the trailer.

The young woman wiped her brow with the back of her hand and motioned for the men to have a seat on the porch.

Anthony made the introductions. "Tom, this is Roger's friend Sarah. Sarah, Tom was Roger's law partner."

"Do you know about Roger?" asked Tom.

"Yes, he's dead. I was staying with him. He died Monday night. When I left he was sitting in the living room. I propped him up in the corner of the couch and I left and came to my Aunt's house."

"Don't you live with Lori?"

"No, Lori lives with Clem. Lori let me stay at the apartment at The Gateway when she moved in with Clem. I've been at the apartment for about two months. I stayed with Roger for a few days and I was going to move in with him and rented the trailer for the move on Sunday. But Roger got real sick. He fell and hit his head on Friday night and he fell again on Sunday. He wouldn't go to the hospital. He just stayed in his pajamas and drank whiskey. He walked from the couch to the bathroom. Then when he couldn't walk, I helped him. He made a mess of the house. I cleaned it up and propped him up in the couch after he fell on the floor the last time. His breathing got real shallow and he just died."

"Did you stay there with the body?"

"Only Monday night. On Tuesday I came to my Aunt's house here. Today I went to The Gateway apartment to pick up my stuff. That's when Anthony Stewart talked to me. I told him the two of you could talk to me but I wanted to talk over here at my Aunt's house."

"So how did you meet Roger?"

"He was at the club one night. The Oar House. He asked me out. I explained that I didn't date customers. He asked if having a cup of coffee was a date. I laughed. Coffee. I felt that was safe enough and he didn't look like he could take me in a real fight, so I said yes. After that, he would come late at work and take me home. We got more serious and we started to date. I would spend the night at his house occasionally. Last week he asked me to move in with him."

"Did you know he was married?"

"Yes. They were separated. Her stuff was still in the house. I just moved her clothes and belongings over to the side. They were having real trouble. Roger was an A #1 drinker. I put up with him. If he was on the floor, I walked over him. My Dad and Mom were drinkers. They both died from alcohol poisoning. I told Roger he was on the way to end up like them."

"Why did you stay with him?"

"He was sweet to me. He wasn't a mean drunk. He always went to work. That is until last Friday. He said he was taking a two week vacation. He wanted me to get some new clothes. I didn't though. I kept the money he gave me for clothes and got some of my old clothes from the apartment. When I got back the next day, Saturday, he was really drunk. He had fallen and hit his head. But he kept drinking."

"Why did you keep dancing after you were with Roger?"

"I didn't think it would last with him, but I decided to see. You never know. Things might have worked out. But they didn't."

Tom was surprised. There was no emotion to Sarah. It was pure fact. She was a fact machine. Ask her a question and she answered in a matter of fact way. Dead pan. She seemed truthful, but who knew. She was like Robbie the Robot.

"We have been looking for Lori. Do you know where she is?"

"I don't know but Clem will know. He controls her. He tries to control everything he touches."

"Does he control you?"

"He could if he wanted to, but he doesn't care about me. I don't interest him in a personal way."

"Where do you think Lori is? Is she still at his house?"

"If she is, she will be gone soon. Clem doesn't want her to testify on Friday at the hearing and he will get her out of here."

"Where will she go?"

"The same place all the other girls went."

"What do you mean?"

"I don't know what I mean. I just know that when Clem's girls leave him they never come back. It's permanent."

"Why do you think Lori is gone?"

"She is too much trouble. She puts Clem in danger. Clem comes first. Always. Clem comes first."

"Do you know who hurt Lori?"

"If I knew, I wouldn't tell you or anyone."

"Has what happened to Lori ever happened to another girl at the club?"

"No, not to my knowledge."

"Is there anyone I can talk to who might know where Lori is or what happened to her?"

"The only one is Clem."

Sarah's Aunt returned and the Jeep was driven back into the yard by the Aunt. The vehicle was minus the trailer.

"Is that Roger's Jeep?" asked Anthony.

"It was," said Sarah. "He gave it to me on Saturday. I have the title here in my pocket. He signed it over to me."

Tom looked at the title work for the jeep and recognized Roger's signature. Drunk or sober, Roger's signature looked the same.

***

Tom and Anthony went back to The Gateway to relieve Karen and send her back to the office. Tom and Anthony followed in their vehicles. At the office Tom spoke with Darlene and gave her an update on the day's events. Darlene said Rose was in pretty good shape, all things considered. Rose had resigned herself that Roger wasn't going to live long when she moved out of their home. Darlene and Rose went by the house and Darlene helped her straighten up. Rose was surprised the house was in relatively good shape. They threw out a load of whiskey bottles and they cleaned the upstairs bathrooms. Rose decided she couldn't live with the couch Roger died on and two of the neighbors helped carry it to the alley for pick up.

Darlene noticed there was a bra and panties on the hook behind the bedroom door that didn't belong to Rose and she wrapped them in a bag and got them in the trash before Rose noticed.

Darlene asked Rose to come and stay at the Condo but Rose said she wanted to go home. She had been living with a friend who was divorced and had two young kids (4 and 6 year olds) and she couldn't stand to stay there anymore. The kids were too noisy, but she didn't want to impose by staying in the condo. Darlene didn't say anything, but she was actually happy Rose wanted to go to her own home. Tom and Darlene would have enough to do preparing for the hearing on Friday. Darlene left Rose at her house and came back to the office alone.

When Darlene walked in the door, she was told Tom was on the phone.

"What happened to Roger's Jeep?" Darlene asked.

"I'll explain later when I get back."

***

Tom still wanted to do some work on the street. Tom told Anthony to follow him and they went out to the parking garage and got Anthony's surveillance van.

"Do you know where Clem lives?"

"Yes. The manager at the Quick Mart gave me the address. Remember he made deliveries?"

"We need to keep a lookout to see if Lori is still living at Clem's house. I'll follow you and you can set up the van to watch Clem's house. Then I want to knock on the door. Maybe Lori will answer."

***

Tom followed the van to Clem's house in his Mercedes. It was only a few blocks from the Quick Mart. Anthony parked along the street. He set up under a tree in the shade. It would be dark under the leafy canopy of the big live oak tree when the sun went down. There were no street lights and Anthony would be able to see any activity in the house as long as the shades and curtains were not drawn. There was a light on in the upstairs bedroom. Surprise. They could see a woman's figure at a set of dresser drawers. They couldn't recognize who the woman was.

Tom helped Anthony set up his cameras and then he left in his little blue convertible. After determining that the closest pay phone was in front of the Quick Mart, Tom stopped and got the number of the pay phone and came back to the van.

Then Tom walked over to the front door of Clem's house and rang the bell. An older woman came to the door. She said she was the housekeeper and she said no one else was there. Tom said he was looking for Clem and Lori. The housekeeper said they were at the club.

Tom left his card and said he would run by the business and see if they could see him. Tom inquired about Lori's health.

"She's ok," said the woman.

"Does she still live here?" asked Tom.

"I don't watch who comes and goes here." The woman was annoyed.

Chapter 15

Tom made the second visit of his life to The Oar House at 8:30 p.m. after he finished dinner with Darlene. Tom and Darlene had been married for about a year and a half. They were very mature, rational people, except when it came to their desire to competently represent their clients. They didn't always win but their clients received very thorough representation.

Tom was impressed with Darlene's legal ability. On the one occasion when he needed a lawyer, he had hired her. She had successfully represented Tom against contempt charges, the potential loss of his license to practice law and his livelihood, and his reputation. With Darlene as his lawyer, Tom won the trifecta.

So when Tom said he needed to return to The Oar House to try to locate Lori Schaeffer and Clemenso Bondi, Darlene didn't question Tom. She even asked if she could help by accompanying him to the strip club. Tom said no, if she came with him the dancers would be jealous because all the customers would be asking when she was going to perform.

Darlene blushed and told Tom to just leave but try to get home before dawn. The previous Friday when Tom was with Roger they didn't get home until late and they would have been even later had there not been a raid of the club and they were chased out and through the woods by the police.

Tom promised to try to finish his work as soon as he could. Meanwhile, Darlene still had the books from her old law library in a room in the penthouse apartment. She once used the condo as an office before she became partners with Tom and Roger. She kept the library up to date and she enjoyed using her own library to do research. The room was quiet and she could concentrate.

She wanted to work on the question of the burden of proof required for the prosecutor to prove a prima facie case of aggravated battery. Specifically, Darlene wanted to know what proof could be substituted for the testimony of the victim to prove the crime.

The testimony of the victim of an assault is not necessary to prove the defendant was the person who committed the crime if the victim was not available to testify. Another eyewitness could offer testimony, or tangible proofs such as finger prints, blood or other evidence could provide sufficient proof that the defendant committed the crime. In a murder case it is rare for a jury to hear the testimony of the victim because the victim is dead and unavailable to testify. Rarely, the victim of a murder will identify his killer by making a dying declaration identifying the killer.

The legal issue Darlene was concerned with would be one where the victim fails to appear in court and the prosecutor calls a police officer who talked to the victim and attempts to have the police officer tell the court what the victim said. This should not be allowed because the out of court (hearsay) statements or identifications by the victim cannot be used as a substitute for testimony by the victim on the stand. The reason is the defendant has a right to see (confront) his accuser. The victim has to testify in the presence of the defendant and the witness has to be subject to cross examination by the defendant's attorney.

If Lori Schaeffer failed to appear at the preliminary hearing, could her statements to the police be considered by the court as competent, admissible evidence sufficient to hold the defendants without bail pending the trial? That was the way Darlene phrased the legal question. That was the legal question she would research for the hearing on Friday while Tom was at the club.

***

On his way to The Oar House Tom parked at the Quick Mart and bought a cup of black coffee and then walked the two blocks in the dark unlit streets to Clem's house. It was very dark under the oak tree. The branches and leaves of the tree were very thick and hid the van from the light from the moon and the night sky. Tom rapped on the side of the van. Tap tap tap tap.

Anthony opened the rear door. Tom handed him the coffee and climbed in.

"Thanks for the coffee."

Tom looked through the eyepiece of a camera mounted on the inside of the van and saw what the lens of the camera could reproduce. The camera lens showed the entire side of the two story house and the side of the front porch. The house was dark.

"Has there been any activity since I left?"

"No, the only thing that happened was the housekeeper drove away. She's something. Before she left she came over to the van and walked around it. She was very suspicious, it seemed to me."

"Maybe she's with neighborhood crime watch," said Tom, joking. "Do you think she knows the van is here to surveil the house? Do you think she made the van?"

"I don't know," said Anthony. "Maybe she was just curious. Even though the house is dark now, I think I will stay here and see what happens through the night."

"Keep the doors locked. Clem doesn't like people getting into his business."

"I'll be careful."

Tom left the van quietly and walked back to his car. He bought another cup of coffee for himself and he headed out to the club.

***

The Oar House was very loud. The dance floor was dimly lit with revolving colored lights. The seats around the dance floor were filled. Tom showed the membership card he had been issued the previous Friday and paid the admission fee. He went to the drinking section at the tables set up behind the men at the bar who were interacting with the dancers offering them money – dollar bills they stuffed under their garter belts.

Tom ordered a beer. He didn't drink it. A topless barmaid in navy blue sailor pants noticed he was not drinking and advised him he could not sit at the table and not drink.

"It's my job to sell drinks. If you don't buy a drink I will get in trouble."

"Look," said Tom. "I just want to watch the dancers."

"You can't do that."

"But I paid my admission." Then Tom thought better of arguing with the waitress. "How many drinks do you have to sell me per hour?"

"Three."

"Sounds fair. Each hour, you bring me three beers," said Tom. Tom dug in his pocket and found a fifty dollar bill.

"Great," said the barmaid. For emphasis she stood up straight and her breasts stood up like a salute. How did she do that? thought Tom.

Tom sat with his three beers with his hands folded on top of the table. He noticed that there was a hierarchy of the women working in the club. There were barmaids who swarmed amongst the men at the tables and wandered around the bar. Their job was to sell drinks. They also interacted with the bouncers, big brutes who helped the women if they needed an enforcer. If someone pinched their breast the customer was out of there. If that activity was condoned by the club (touching the breast of an employee) the club could be closed by the authorities. The men could not touch the bare skin of the employees. The bouncers also encouraged the men to keep drinking three drinks an hour but the customer had to remain under the legal limit. The bouncer threw the customer out if he was drunk.

The girls at the front of the dance floor sold a close encounter for tips that were placed under the garter on the thigh of their leg. These girls were topless and, wore G-strings. The customer had to insert the dollar bill between the garters and the thigh without actually touching the dancer's skin. These girls worked about 30 minutes an hour and then got down to the floor and mingled and invited men to visit with them in one of the side rooms for a private dance (allegedly no touching was allowed). While these women worked the room, professional dancers took their place on the show floor. These performers were more like old time strippers. They danced to music and wore costumes like the outfits Tom had seen Sarah remove from the U-Haul trailer at her Aunt's house in South Tampa.

In fact, through the smoke and haze Tom saw Sarah dancing in the back. He didn't have to move to get a better view because the strip-tease dancers rotated positions so that every man in the club could remain in his seat and see each girl's routine. Tom thought Sarah was quite good. She was athletic and agile. She might make a good show girl, he thought. She had this way of looking out into the audience and it seemed that she was looking in each customer's eyes. She had a pleasant smile and she seemed to be performing her dance personally for each man in the club.

It was as he was contemplating a particularly interesting dance move. (How did Sarah do that? he thought) that Tom was tapped on the shoulder. He reached into his pocket thinking he needed to pay more money to the kitty but when he turned around he was confronted by a bouncer.

Tom knew he had done nothing wrong so he told the bouncer to leave him alone. The bouncer insisted that Tom come with him, and he grabbed his shirt at the forearm and pulled him through the crowd to the back of the club and pushed him into a room. In the room behind a desk sat a large, ugly man. He was the same large, ugly man he had seen with the girl with the bandages on her face last Friday night.

The bouncer sat Tom in a seat in front of Clem's desk and then left and closed the door.

Chapter 16

Tom and Clem were both stubborn. Both men just sat and stared at each other.

Finally Tom said, "This is ridiculous. If you force me to stay here in your office against my will it could be considered false imprisonment. I want to return to my seat and watch the show."

"You would know what false imprisonment is I guess, Mr. Night, you being a lawyer and all," said Clem, sarcastically.

Clemenso was thick and huge. He looked like he had been a pro-football player – maybe a lineman, a guard – Tom guessed. He was about 35 years old, 6'2", 260lbs, short hair. Crew cut. He was always pulling at the front of his shirt at the collar like the collar was a noose tightening around his neck.

Tom smiled. "It seems odd that your girlfriend has made a complaint to the authorities. I thought you and your group of thugs could take care of a matter like an assault on your girlfriend without involving the police."

"I could get into trouble taking the law into my own hands."

"Clemenso, what is your last name?"

"Bondi, Clemenso Bondi."

"Mr. Bondi, it seems to me that these charges against my law clerk are a case of mistaken identity."

"Why do you say that?"

"Mr. Alesse does not have any motive for attacking Lori Schaeffer. There has to be a reason this occurred. Miss Schaeffer either did something to provoke this attack or you did something to provoke the attack. My guess is that if Lori did something you would have protected her from the attack or you would have moved heaven and earth to exact revenge by your own hand on the people who did this to Lori. Scarring up a woman who relies on her beauty for her livelihood is very personal. It is not only personal to her but it is personal and an insult to the person who desires her.

"But you didn't protect her," continued Tom. "My guess is that this crime was committed to send you a message. The message is that you don't have the clout to protect your woman from the person who did this, and you are not powerful enough to seek revenge. If Mr. Alesse had cut your woman you would have killed him in the parking lot of the Quick Mart when he was identified by Lori as her attacker. You were in the car in the parking lot of the Quick Mart when Lori made the identification, weren't you?"

Clemenso stared at Tom. Then Clem lifted the phone receiver, pushed a button and the bouncer returned to the office.

"Mr. Night is leaving," said Clemenso to the bouncer. "Refund his admission."

Tom stood up and walked out the door of Clemenso's office. The bouncer took Tom's arm and led him out the exit door to his car. The bouncer waited for Tom to enter his vehicle and drive out of the parking lot.

***

Clemenso opened the side drawer of his desk and removed a .44 Caliber pistol and a heavy sheathed knife. Clem had been a pro football player. The pistol was a gift he received when he retired from The Sharks pro-team. Clem carried it with him sometimes, but he had never fired it. He went out the private entrance of the club without telling anyone. Clemenso drove down the street to a pay phone and made a call.

The phone rang on the desk of Richard Cook in the detective division of the police station. After a minute at his desk speaking on the phone, Detective Cook clocked out and left the building.

The parking lot was still being repaired. The burned out vehicles had been removed from the lot but the asphalt surface had not been repaired.

Det. Cook drove to the Bondi residence. He parked in front of the house in his unmarked car. He walked up to the door and knocked. Lori Schaeffer came to the door.

"Good evening, Richard," said Lori. "Clem isn't here."

"He will be soon."

Lori pushed the screen door open and stepped out to let the detective in the house. There were two porch lights on either side of the front door and there was a flood light that illuminated the front walk. It was as bright as daylight at the front door. After the detective went in the door, Lori looked outside and stared at the van parked next to the road on the side of the house.

***

Tom's investigator, Anthony Stewart, saw the police car drive up and park. He turned on the camera. There was enough light at the front of the house to distinguish the person at the door as Detective Cook and when the door was pushed out the film captured a woman in a white robe who had white bandages on her face. The woman looked to the side of the house and stared at the van. From a second port or hole in the side of the van, Anthony was able to focus the close up lens so that he captured the image of the face of the woman in the bandages.

The van was well suited for surveillance. It was comfortable for the investigator who would have to remain in the van for a long stretch of time and it was outfitted with the best camera equipment available. The van was Roger's idea. Many of his clients were insurance companies. They never believed anyone was hurt and they were willing to pay the expense of the van and an investigator to sneak up on a claimant. They thoroughly enjoyed catching a fraud. It made their day.

Anthony was able to view the side of the house from a third port equipped with a wide angle lens that he could swivel in the port to view from the front to the back of the house and to the garage and alley in the back.

Shortly after the detective arrived, Clemenso drove up in an old beater – a 1952 Chevrolet 4-door deluxe sedan. It was dented and rusted and invisible. It could hide in plain sight. Anthony could see the trunk to the car being opened and then closed. He could see the figure of a man in the shadows and then heard the back door slam and a light went on in the back porch. Then as the figure went through the downstairs toward the front of the house he turned on every light on the ground floor.

Anthony let the film in the two cameras roll.

***

Clemenso walked into the living room. Lori was sitting in a high wingback, upholstered chair. He raised his right arm with the .44 Cal weapon and pointed the gun at Lori. Lori opened her mouth but did not scream or say a word. She put out her hands and arms in front of her body to block the bullet just as Clemenso fired the weapon. The first slug hit Lori's right forearm and shattered the ulnar bone but the bone deflected the bullet and it burrowed into the thick cotton batting in the chair. Clemenso continued to walk forward as he emptied the gun. All the other shots missed as Lori stood and fell forward onto the Oriental rug on the floor.

Lori tried to scramble to her knees but she couldn't support her weight because of the wound to her forearm. Clemenso held her down with his foot in her back and he retrieved the knife from the rear pocket of his blue jeans. Lori screamed. Clem fell on his knees and as he came down to his knees he stabbed Lori in her spine severing her spinal column.

Lori was silent, but twitched.

Clemenso looked at Detective Cook. "Richard, I need for you to go out to that van and kill the guy in the back of the van who's taking pictures."

"Okay," said Cook.

"Make sure you get the cameras and all of the film out of the van," said Clemenso as Cook left the house through the front door.

As Clemenso was giving directions to Cook, he was attempting to remove the knife from Lori's back. It was snagged in her dorsal vertebra and he couldn't pull it out. He put his left foot on her back and pulled the knife with both hands. He was able to free the knife and she stopped quivering. Clemenso rolled Lori's body into the rug. He hefted her and the rug over his shoulder and carried her through the house and out the back door. The door slammed. He opened the trunk of the old Chevy and heard the sound of a single gunshot. The sound was from his left at the surveillance van. Clemenso returned to the house and took the wounded wing chair and slid it out the front door and dragged it through the grass in the side yard. Cook joined him and they hefted the chair up and then tied the chair to the roof of the old Chevy.

Cook went back in the house. He locked the back door. He walked through the house turning off the lights as he went. He pulled the front door closed. He didn't have a key so he didn't lock the door. Cook figured no one was going to burglarize Clem's house just like no one would report the sound of gun shots in the neighborhood.

Cook got in his car and drove around the block. When he got to the alley, Clem's car was gone. He looked down the side street, picked up a heavy police flashlight from under his seat and he shown its beam on the rear of the van. Cook hopped out of the car and went to the van. He opened the rear doors and looked in one more time. Anthony was lying on his back with a gunshot to the forehead that had entered just above the orbit of the left eye. Cook climbed in the vehicle. There was an exit wound to the top of Anthony's head. Cook shone the light on the inside of the van. There was a bullet hole in the roof of the van. The bullet would later be found lodged in a limb of the large oak tree. He saw a light blinking on the side wall of the van. It was the light on one of the cameras. He reached in and took the camera attached to the wall of the van from the view port. Then he saw the other camera. It was still filming. He removed both of the cameras together with all the film. Cook then closed and locked the rear van door and checked to make sure all the doors were locked. He took the cameras and the film and got in his car and went back to the police station. He went in the rest room. He stood before a full length mirror. He looked himself and his clothes over in the mirror.

He looked fine. He hadn't raised a sweat.

***

After his meeting with Clemenso Bondi, Tom was very up tight and he did not want to go home. He got out on the interstate and drove his 250 Mercedes very fast. The engine had a powerful growl. There were highway patrol units out on the road and they frustrated his high speed drive. Tom pulled off and drove past Roger's house. The light was on. He thought about stopping to talk to Rose but he really did not know her and didn't know what to say to her so he drove west toward Clemenso Bondi's house.

***

Tap. Tap, tap, tap.

It was 11:00 p.m. when Tom went to the van, tapping on the van's window. He intended to tell Anthony to go home and get some sleep.

Tom got no answer to his knock and he tried each of the exterior doors of the van. They were all locked. He tried to peer in the van through the windows but the window tinting was too dark. He wondered why the lens and the cameras had been removed. He could see inside through the view ports. Neither camera lens was inserted in the two camera ports. But he could see nothing inside the van because it was too dark.

Maybe Anthony's wife picked him up and he went home, Tom thought.

Tom drove to the Quick Mart. It was closed but the pay phone outside was working. He called Anthony's house. Anthony wasn't there and his wife hadn't heard from him.

Tom rifled through the yellow pages and found listings for locksmiths. He made several calls but only one locksmith was open. He would be out to Tom's location in 10 minutes. He said he was close by. Tom was told to go back and stand by the van.

The locksmith arrived and asked for $100. Tom paid the money. The locksmith got his tools and came to the back of the van. First he tried to open the lock by pushing the button as you would do if the van was unlocked.

"You'd be amazed how many times I push the button and it just opens," said the locksmith as he smiled.

That didn't happen this time. The man had to get out his tools and he popped the lock on the inside of the door panel with a thin piece of metal with a hook on the bottom end. He opened the door and he could see Anthony on the floor. The locksmith backed away. Tom stepped forward, saw Anthony and turned Anthony's foot forcefully. No verbal or visible response.

Tom told the locksmith to please go to the Quick Mart and call the police and an ambulance.

***

Clemenso drove the 1952 Chevy Deluxe from his house to a cypress swamp that abutted the interstate highway at Gandy Boulevard just outside the city limits of St. Petersburg. The road was heavily traveled. He parked on the right of way and opened the trunk and lifted the carpet including the body from the trunk and walked into the swamp. About 25 feet away from the road in the middle of the tree trunks and cypress knees he dropped his load. If any of the passing vehicles saw Clem, it did not appear they knew what he was doing or did not care. No one stopped. Like his 1952 Chevy Deluxe, he was invisible, yet he was in plain sight. He laid the rolled rug in the water and stood on the carpet as air bubbles escaped from the carpet. Once the rug was saturated it sank into the mire.

Clemenso walked out of the swamp to the side of his car. He unloosened the rope that was holding the wingback chair to the roof of his vehicle. He started the car and held on to the leg of the chair with his hand and arm out the window. He then pulled out into traffic, accelerated, let go of the chair and swerved back and forth until the chair slid off the roof and fell onto the concrete surface of the road. The chair tumbled down the road throwing off pieces of the chair as it rolled down the highway.

A semi-truck clipped the side of the chair and the arms and back flew apart from the seat and legs. Other vehicles, mostly trucks, continued to hit pieces of the chair until it was mush on the roadway. Road kill.

Clemenso returned to the club. There was a shower in his office. He showered and worked the rest of the night. He closed the business, locking the door himself.

Part IV

The root cause of most criminality
is selfishness.

Chapter 17

Roger Adams' funeral was on Saturday morning and Anthony Stewart's funeral was on Saturday afternoon. Both services were at St. Paul's Church. The medical examiner had completed the autopsy for each man and had released the bodies just in time. According to the ME, Roger died of acute ETOH (alcohol) poisoning and Anthony died of blunt trauma to the head (gunshot).

The morning service was attended by representatives of most law firms in the county. In 1970, there were only 125 attorneys in the phone book offering legal services in Pinellas County. Of that number less than fifty practiced in St. Petersburg, the largest city in the county. Tom noticed Sarah was in the back of the church. The church was full of flowers. A number of people spoke – fellow lawyers and some clients. Tom said nothing. Darlene was crying. Rose, Roger's wife, sat with them. Rose still seemed to be numb.

Also attending were Alphonse and Francis Alesse, and Tommy Magyar and his girlfriend Theresa. The preliminary hearing had been canceled on Friday because, for the third time, Lori Schaeffer did not appear in court to testify.

As Darlene had anticipated, John Hale, the State Attorney, argued he should be allowed to present the typed, sworn and signed witness statement Lori Schaeffer gave to Detective Richard Cook in lieu of requiring her testimony in court. Hale also intended to have Det. Cook testify that he was present at Magyar's lineup and at the Quick Mart when Lori identified Alphonse and Tommy as her assailants. Hale argued that the purpose of the preliminary hearing was to determine if there was sufficient evidence to hold the defendant for trial and Cook's testimony was sufficient to prove a prima facie case.

The Court ruled against the argument because the State Attorney had the power to file a charge by way of an Information and therefore the State was not prejudiced by a finding of no probable cause. If the judge found there was no probable cause, the case was not dismissed, there was simply no probable cause presented at the time of the preliminary hearing to allow the defendants to be detained. The State could file a charge by Information and proceed but the prosecutor still had to comply with the speedy trial rule and try the defendants within 180 days of their arrest or the case against the defendants could then be dismissed with prejudice, meaning it was dismissed forever.

The judge also ruled he was not going to keep Defendant Magyar in jail if Lori did not show for the hearing. The court reminded Mr. Hale this was the third time the witness had failed to appear for a hearing.

Hale threatened an appeal of the ruling. Hale became red in the face and shook his right hand and arm as he made the point.

"Fine," said the judge. "You do that. You have every right to appeal my ruling. You represent the people of this jurisdiction."

The court adjourned the hearing after the judge ordered the release of Mr. Magyar without the requirement that he post bond (on his own recognizance). The judge also ordered the requirement that Mr. Alesse post surety be waived, which released his mother-in-law's house as security for the bond. Alphonse was also released on his own recognizance.

***

James DeMarco, Tommy's attorney had spent the last year being pounded constantly by the State Attorney. He had been appointed to one bad case after another. Of course, DeMarco didn't make the facts and he didn't enact the laws. He just rode the horse he was given and most of those horses were old nags. So when the court released Tommy from jail DeMarco was thrilled. It felt good to win every once in a while. James DeMarco also attended both of the funerals with Tommy and Theresa.

Tom was impressed with Jim DeMarco. He wondered if he would be interested in working at their firm. There was a need for a lawyer in the firm since Roger's death. Tom had not been able to visit the firm's office in Belize City, Belize, in Central America, for more than a month now because of the chaos at the office in St. Petersburg. Tom had found that if it was quiet and he heard nothing from his clients and their interests in the Caribbean, there was trouble brewing. He had had problems there years back, but he was satisfied with their partner in Belize, attorney Andrew Prince, Jr., the son of the former Solicitor General of the country of Belize. Prince was a very able attorney. DeMarco could take over Roger's insurance defense work. The law firm would have to hire a new investigator. It would be hard to replace Anthony. Roger had relied heavily on his work and his good conscience. Tom knew it would take time but everything would get back to normal now.

***

Anthony's funeral was a sober affair. Before coming to work for Tom and Roger, Anthony Stewart had been with the police force for 25 years. He retired as a sergeant in charge of the traffic division.

Anthony had been with Tom for more than 10 years. He and Roger had rigged up the surveillance van and Anthony enjoyed doing investigations. He was very careful to give the claimant in the case the benefit of the doubt. He made sure that the insurance company got all the film, not just the film that showed the claimant might be healthier than he claimed. Some of the film normally showed the claimants were injured to some degree. Anthony made sure that the film proving the claimant's case, (that he was injured), did not end up on the floor of the editing room.

Anthony was well liked. He had many friends from the court system, cops and lawyers and jailers and judges. A handful of each group attended and so with family, kids, grandkids, brothers and one sister, wife and neighbors, the church was pretty full.

After Roger's service there was no grave side service, as he was to be cremated. Anthony was to be buried at Woodlawn Cemetery and his wife had a plot reserved next to him. Roger's widow left the flowers from Roger's service in the church and so the church was full of flowers for Anthony's service. Rose was unsure she wanted to be buried next to Roger. That was her reasoning for the cremation.

***

There was no suspect identified as Anthony's killer. After the graveside service there was a wake at Anthony's home. There was speculation among the guests that Clemenso had committed the crime because he and Lori had been missing since Wednesday night. He was last seen closing up The Oar House the night Anthony was murdered. He never returned to his house after that.

The police department was a bureaucracy and no one thought twice about the fact that Richard Cook, the detective in charge of the investigation of the aggravated battery of Lori Schaeffer, was placed in charge of the investigation of Anthony's death. The chief thought that since Cook was most familiar with the facts of all the cases and because Cook was an honest cop, he should handle all the cases. The chief did not consider it was possible that Cook could be a suspect in these criminal acts.

Tom felt there was something wrong with Cook's investigation of the aggravated battery charges against Magyar and Alesse; more so the charge against his clerk, Alphonse. Tom felt that there was a connection between the aggravated battery on Lori and Anthony's murder, if for no other reason than the fact that Lori was staying with Clemenso and Anthony was murdered in the van parked in the road under the oak tree at the side of Clem's house.

Tom wrote a letter to the police chief saying he thought there needed to be new blood conducting the investigation of Anthony's murder. Even John Hale was upset with Cook. He could not understand why the detective could not perform a simple task like keeping tabs on a witness. Hale had suggested that Lori be placed in protective custody. Hale had been assured by the detective that he was keeping in touch with Lori and that she would appear at the preliminary hearing. When Lori did not appear Hale felt Cook was at best incompetent, and he wasn't going to become any smarter if he was given a more difficult case like Anthony's murder, a case where there was no clear suspect.

Hale was a strong proponent of victim's rights and he was angry with the course the investigation had taken to date. Hale knew that the failure to identify a suspect quickly in a murder case would make for a difficult prosecution. Hale felt there was a suspect – Clemenso Bondi, and they should issue a warrant for his arrest. Detective Cook's theory was that Anthony was killed by a third party named John Curry, who lived in the neighborhood. The theory was based on the fact that he was a known drug addict who was seen near the van on the night of the murder.

Tom and Hale were both upset that Cook did not send an officer to The Oar House the night of the murder to locate Clemenso at the club or to get on his trail immediately. The police made no inquiry of Clemenso's whereabouts until Friday, after Lori failed to show for the preliminary hearing.

Hale was so upset he even suggested to the chief that Cook be fired.

The Police Chief refused. The Police Chief felt Richard Cook was a talented police officer. Had Cook not been named officer of the year? The Police Chief was unaware that Cook and Bondi had a history. The chief had been at the job too long. He believed what his men told him and ignored the truth when it stared him in the face. Internal Affairs had had complaints about Cook and Bondi partying with women from the club and rumors swirled that Cook did favors for Clem to keep his club free of trouble with the City Attorney. In return, Clem gave Cook tips, information that Clem heard at the bar about criminal activity that helped Cook make arrests and look good to the chief. The investigatory arm of the department tried to warn the chief, but he refused to listen.

Chapter 18

Richard Cook and Clemenso Bondi had grown up together in the same neighborhood in Daytona Beach, Florida. They were within a year of each other in school. Cook was Catholic and he attended St. Paul's Catholic School. Clemenso went to public school. Richard graduated from Father Lopez High School. Clemenso went to Mainland High School but failed to finish and later he earned a GED. Cook went on to get an associate degree in law enforcement and Clemenso played football at Appalachian State College. Clemenso did not finish college with a degree but he learned enough football to impress the pro scouts and he was drafted by Chicago. He played ball for seven years and was unceremoniously let go by Chicago. None of the major pro teams picked up his contract. He was never paid more than $11,000 per year base salary. He was on two winning teams and played in a couple of post season games and made an extra $2,500 per game.

Clem was hurt as a result of play; a herniated disc in his neck. The neck injury was diagnosed just before the end of his last season with Chicago in 1968, and that was when he was released from the team. As a result of the injury he complained that when he spear tackled an opponent he had a tingling sensation in his arms to his fingers. When he left Chicago he went to the semi-pros and to a team in Jacksonville, Florida: The Sharks. He continued to have physical problems, though he played with as much enthusiasm as when he was healthy. But it took him three days after a game to recuperate. The coach of The Sharks sent Clem to an orthopedic doctor who told him that if he hit someone with his head just the right way he could die, or worse, he could be paralyzed from the neck down.

When the coach got the doctor's report he immediately cut Clem from The Sharks and Clem was left with no job and no savings. He was a free spender. Everything that came in went out. His pockets were always empty. He spent most of his money on women and he was a regular at what he called "titty joints". While he played for The Sharks his after-hours activities were no different in Jacksonville than Chicago. He was a faithful customer of a topless bar and he got to know the manager and all the girls.

When Clem was released from The Sharks he still had credit at the bar. He told the boss his woes over drinks and he was offered a job as a bouncer, which he took in a heartbeat. Clem could watch the girls without paying admission.

Some of the topless bars in Florida were operated by organized crime. But they were legitimate businesses. First Amendment. Free Speech. The Supreme Court had made nudity a matter of free expression so a topless joint was legal. Clem came to know that the club in Jacksonville was owned by mobsters from his experiences as a regular at the club. The bar in Jacksonville was connected to the bars in Daytona Beach, Ft. Lauderdale, Miami, Tampa and St. Petersburg. Clem enjoyed working at the clubs. He made his way up to the position of assistant manager in Jacksonville. Then there was an opening as manager at the club in St. Petersburg. He was offered the position and he took it. He had an old beater of a car – a 1952 Chevy Deluxe. There were bets placed that the car would not make the trip. But all it had to carry was Clem and one suitcase. Car and baggage made the trip to St. Petersburg with no problems to his new job at The Oar House.

Part of Clem's remuneration for the job as manager was free living quarters, which was an old, two story house in an old neighborhood in the Central Plaza area. This neighborhood was built on filled land in an old swamp called the Duck Pond. The syndicate took the house in trade for a gambling debt. Clem thought the house was a bonus – like hitting the Lotto. He settled in and established a credit line at the Quick Mart.

Clem wanted the neighbors to leave him be and not interfere with his right to life, liberty and the pursuit of whatever he wanted. He held a big party inviting his buddies from the topless clubs and from the pro teams. More than 500 revelers attended. The police were called due to noise complaints but they did not take any action except to accept a case of ice cold Coors's beer for the officers at the station.

Clem mocked the neighbors by turning the music up as loud as it would go. The neighbors knew who he was. He was trouble and the neighbors left him alone.

***

Clem's bosses were happy with him. The gross at the club increased 23% immediately after Clem took over. Clem didn't do anything special. He just failed to skim the take like the previous manager. The gross receipts increased immediately. After the initial good results Clem was given a raise and the previous manager was found dead in Miami. A copy of the news story covering the account of the gruesome murder that was printed in the Miami Herald was mailed to the managers of all of the operations of the syndicate.

Enough said.

***

About a month after Clem took over he was visited by Detective Richard Cook. They were both surprised that the other ended up in St. Petersburg. They had lost touch after Clem went to Chicago. Richard had bounced around in a couple of small town police forces after he graduated, but he did not advance.

Then there were job openings on the force in St. Petersburg. Cook applied and was offered a job as patrolman. He was happy with the culture and he was appointed detective quickly. Part of his job was to visit the bars and make sure they didn't get out of hand. Gambling and prostitution were a concern of the City Fathers, but they knew they had to abide a certain amount of vice and illegality – especially among the masses; the citizens who elected them to office. It was true that there was a high stakes poker game at the Yacht and Tennis club every day except Sunday that had gone on for 40 years. Most people in town were aware of that fact, so if the City shut down betting pools on sport matches at the bars but did not close down the poker game at the Yacht Club it would be the height of hypocrisy.

Detective Cook was making the rounds of the bars trying to keep the lid on potential trouble and he ran into Clem at The Oar House. This operation had caused the city much consternation because of "B" girl activity, gambling and sex. After greeting each other like long lost friends Clem and Richard retired to Clem's office for a long talk.

Richard explained to Clem that his operation was under scrutiny. Clem said he would work with Richard to resolve their differences. That first night they established the "no touching" rule. They agreed customers could not touch the performers in the main room of the bar. What happened in the small side rooms between the dancer (generally heavy petting, hand jobs, and blow jobs) and her customer was a private matter.

Clem agreed that the bar would not take a cut of the revenue generated by the girls in the small private rooms. This was a no brainer. The girls always lied about what they were paid and if the bar was involved in the payment of money for sex, they could be charged with operating a house of prostitution. So this change in operations of the business was actually cheered by corporate counsel for the syndicate, and by the prostitutes.

Later in the year, the two men established a three drink an hour minimum for alcohol consumption, which seemed reasonable to Cook. Clem and Cook decided the bar girls couldn't be charged with a "B" Girl violation if they only encouraged customers to purchase drinks at that rate of consumption.

Gambling would be handled discreetly. There would be no more advertised betting pools. They could still hold the pools but there could be no more advertised, open gambling, except at the prize fights. No one could control that activity and no one wanted the fights to be outlawed as it allowed the customers' blood up, which was thought to be a healthy male exercise.

Over the next year Clem and Richard began to party privately at Clem's house. But they were very discrete. They were also silent partners; there was side work, making collections of gambling debts and enforcement for the syndicate. The pair made good money. Clem caught the eye of his bosses. He was smart; he made full disclosures of everything he was doing, including all of the changes that he and Detective Cook were making in the operation at the club. Clem also gave tips to Cook that he could use to make arrests to make Cook look good to his superiors.

***

Clem's immediate boss was named Derek Kline. He was the manager of the Tampa Club. He passed on the word telling his bosses what Clem was doing, especially anything that seemed negative. Derek hoped the bosses would cut Clem off at the knees but instead the regional boss who ran the Florida operation out of Jacksonville only seemed to see the positive result that was produced from the changes Clem made. The regional boss was looking for an increase in revenue and Clem produced a regular increase in the rate of return at The Oar House.

The implementation of the no touch rule made the City Attorney happy. He didn't have to prosecute as many crimes involving lewd behavior. He regularly lost those cases when they were tried before a jury in any event. The Police Chief was happy because his men were always too enthusiastic when they worked undercover in the topless bars. When they were the bait in a sting operation their actions to entice the girls into a compromising position normally constituted entrapment. Finally, the regional boss was happy because there was less business interruption caused by police raids and there was less in legal expense for the defense of the bouncers and the dancers, and therefore the profit generated by the club was greater.

Everyone was happy with the changes Clem and Cook instituted, except Derek. The fact that Clem was able to impress his bosses and the fact that the other bosses in the organization began to implement the same changes in their clubs made Derek jealous and nervous. Derek needed to knock Clem down a notch. He needed Clem to understand that Derek controlled him. He wanted to send a message, but without upsetting his boss in Orlando.

Derek's opportunity arose when Clem fell in love with Lori. Clem was smitten when he first saw Lori dance. She came to interview for a job as a strip tease artist. She was not applying for a job as a bar maid or a girl who danced for tips. Clem watched as Sarah conducted the try out. Something about the way Lori danced and moved was pleasing and sensual but not obscene. She was hired immediately. For days after she was hired, Clem spent time watching her act on the dance floor. He couldn't get enough of her. He found excuses to talk to her. Lori knew he was interested but there was a non-fraternization rule. The employees could not date one another. If that rule was not enforced, a manager would treat the employees like his harem and fire them if they did not submit to his demands. That would be bad for business. So even if true love found its way into the titty joint it was not condoned by the establishment.

Clem and Lori broke the rule. Lori secretly moved out of The Gateway and moved in with Clem. Sarah sub-leased Lori's apartment in The Gateway. Lori tried to make a normal home for the two of them while she still danced at the club that Clem managed, and they pretended to be fellow employees.

Eventually the rumor of the tryst, at first a whisper, was confirmed. The fact of the relationship spread among the dancers and then over to the club in Tampa and Derek knew about the affair. As Clem's boss, Derek had the right to discipline Clem if he did not get back in line. Derek ratted Clem out. Derek's bosses could not abide the failure of their employees following the company's rules, particularly the non-fraternization policy.

Derek ordered Clem to come to Derek's club and he told him that the relationship had to end. Clem said he would think about it. That was not what Derek or Clem's bosses wanted to hear. Derek and his bosses met and decided that the problem was not with Clem but with Lori. Lori had to be out of the picture so Clem would come around and obey the company rules.

The bosses decided that the nature and extent of the action to be taken against Lori was left to Derek's discretion. Leaving the action to Derek's discretion was a mistake. The bosses thought Derek would at first verbally threaten Lori. Instead of threatening Lori so that Clem knew she was at risk, Derek and a stooge attacked her and cut her to send a message to her and all the dancers.

After Lori was attacked she blacked out. Sarah discovered her on the floor in Clem's house. Lori told her Derek had cut her. Sarah knew Clem would want to kill Derek immediately. She called Cook for advice. Richard took control. He had Lori report the crime, but she was only to say she did not know her attacker, that he was her height and that he was swarthy looking. She was not to say the attack occurred in Clem's house but at her apartment at The Gateway. Sarah was to take her to the hospital and Lori was to report the crime there. The police would not be brought to The Gateway immediately, but only after that scene was contaminated. If other questions were asked, Lori should say she had no memory and not answer any further questions. Cook knew he would be assigned the case if he was on duty at the hospital when Sarah brought her in for treatment, and he could cover for Lori because he would be the one talking to her and writing the reports. He made up the crime as the facts developed.

The attack had actually occurred in the living room of Clem's house and the carpet was a bloody mess. Cook confronted Clem with the truth-Derek had attacked Lori. Clem exploded but Cook was able to prevail upon Clem to take no action. They would all lose if the full story of the extracurricular criminal activities at the club were discovered during an investigation by the police.

Cook was surprised that Clem accepted the advise. But Clem was a realist. He knew if Lori got to talking to the police and the victim's relief counselors he would be at risk. Clem needed to be cold and collected and protect himself.

Other than the blood there was nothing to say the crime had been committed in Clem's living room. There was no forced entry and the assailants were professional. They were in and out.

Clem cleaned the carpet as best he could and then bought an old oriental rug and covered the stain on the floor. Though Derek Kline did not talk to Clem afterward, the initials "D K" scratched into Lori's breasts sent a clear message as to the identity of the assailant.

Lori was put on medical leave at work and stayed home at Clem's. She had not been fired, but she was not working at The Oar House. So, neither Clem, Lori, nor the clubs bosses, had compromised their positions, and they were winners from that perspective. On the down side, Clem became sexually impotent after Lori was injured so cruelly, and Lori changed. She had been sweet and now she was like a shrew. She would go off, exploding for little reason.

Det. Cook was able to cover for Lori and it looked like the crime would just be another unsolved tragedy. Then the two traffic cops picked up Tommy Magyar; he was identified by Lori in the lineup, and the prosecution of the suspect had a life of its own. Lori seemed to like the attention she received being the victim, and she had something she could hold over Clem. Somehow it was his fault she was no longer perfect.

Cops want to arrest people and solve crimes and see that justice is done. That's their job. Cook was afraid that if Lori did not appear to be cooperative after the lineup that the police would turn on her. So Det. Cook told Lori to make a positive identification of someone when they conducted the lineup. By happenstance, Tommy looked like Derek Kline, so Lori identified Tommy as the perpetrator. In fact, Lori had begun to believe the story Cook had woven. She began to add to the tale and she reported there was a second assailant, a tall man who held her down. And there was in fact a tall man who held her down as Derek scratched at her head and chest with the "Exacto" blade. The tall man was one of Derek's stooges. Lori said nothing about the tall man because she had been knocked unconscious.

In her mind, Lori replayed the attack over and over each time she went to answer the front door at Clem's house. She was struck in the face and disoriented. She was held on the floor by a tall man who pinned her shoulders with his knees. The other short, swarthy man straddled her hips and ripped off her shirt. She had no bra. The short man then went to work cutting her in the face and chest. She remembered that as she was being cut the tall man covered her mouth with a wad of cloth that smelled antiseptic. She passed out. She woke up and she was bleeding. She had a headache like a hangover and she called Sarah, who called Cook. Cook said he would take care of it, just have Sarah take her to the hospital and tell the doctor she was attacked in her apartment at The Gateway, not at Clem's home. Clem did not want him or his home connected to the assault. Det. Cook would be there by coincidence and he would help Sarah and Lori get through the initial questioning by the police and the doctor.

Sarah's statement was easy: she had come home to the apartment at The Gateway and found her roommate on the terrazzo floor and she took her to the hospital. Lori was to say as little as possible. She was attacked by a short, swarthy man, maybe a gypsy.

And that's the story they told. But the lie became complicated, Lori became addled, and then Lori made the second identification of Alphonse Alesse. It was a mistaken identification. But in her mind Lori believed the man buying cigarettes in the Quick Mart was the tall man who pinned her shoulders and covered her face with the rag that smelled like alcohol. And Lori began pointing and making a scene and the police came and the arrest occurred at the Quick Mart where they were well known and Clem had credit. Clem couldn't prevent it. He was known by the manager of the Quick Mart, who saw Lori lose it when she saw Alesse. Clem had to report the identification to the police. So he called Det. Cook.

Thereafter the lawyers became involved. Det. Cook had tried to steer the court to appoint the overworked Public Attorney to represent Magyar by burning the one asset, the new truck that

Magyar could use to obtain private counsel. But that backfired. After the truck was destroyed, the court appointed a young and game but very competent attorney, James DeMarco, to represent Tommy. Even worse, Alesse was represented by his boss, Tom Night, who pushed the defense of his client and law clerk very hard. Night was making headway and Cook and Clem knew Attorney Night would discover the truth once he was able to speak to Lori. And Night was close to obtaining a statement. Tom Night had his investigator surveilling Clem's house and now Tom Night had the gumption to come to The Oar House and refuse to leave. He forced Clem to talk to him. And that went badly because instead of Clem intimidating Tom Night, Tom intimidated Clem.

The best of the bad choices for the best friends was that they had to eliminate the threat to Richard Cook and Clem Bondi, which meant Clem had to kill Lori Schaeffer and anyone who could prove he committed her murder. Unfortunately that meant Lori had to die and Anthony Stewart also had to die because he witnessed and photographed Lori's murder.

Once Clem had killed Lori and Cook had killed Anthony they were blood brothers; they had nothing to lose, and they were very dangerous.

Chapter 19

The night Clem killed Lori he worked his full shift until 2 a.m. He received two calls from his friend Detective Cook relating to the status of the police investigation of the dead man in the van. Cook had Tom Night removed from the scene. He had a detective take him to the police station to conduct an interview. After he was released at 4 a.m., Tom was driven to his car at the scene.

Since Tom was not at the scene during the police investigation he was not aware that there was no investigation of Clem's home on the night of the incident. The police believed the scene of Anthony Stewart's death was restricted to the van and did not enter or search Clem's house.

Cook knew the purpose for the van being parked on the side street was to aid Anthony and his investigation of Clem and Lori. Cook knew these things because he murdered Anthony.

Since Cook headed the investigation of Anthony's death, Cook spent the entire night while he was at the scene misdirecting the police. He was so successful that at the end of the field investigation, as the van was being towed from the scene after Anthony's body had been removed by the Medical Examiner technicians and taken to the morgue, the detectives at the scene had concluded that the preliminary working theory for the homicide was that Anthony was shot and killed by a drug addict who shot Anthony in the head and then stole the cameras to pawn for drugs.

Consequently, no police officer entered Clem's home until Friday, two days after the homicide when a patrolman was sent to find out why Lori was not in court to testify as a witness in the preliminary hearing. The patrolman knocked at the door. No one answered. He tried the door. It was unlocked and he walked through the entire house looking through drawers and the closets and under beds allegedly looking for clues as to where Lori might be.

The police officer noticed that the one thing that was out of the ordinary was that the living room carpet was gone. There was wall to wall carpet leading to the living room from the hall to the dining room and the downstairs bedroom but the carpet in the living room was missing. Det. Cook remembered that the carpet below the Oriental rug had been stained by the first attack by Derek on Lori. The stain, though barely visible after numerous cleanings, was still there, so Cook had removed the carpet. When the investigation of Clem's house was finally conducted, the crime scene had been contaminated by the patrolman who was looking for Lori and the carpet was missing from the living room floor.

***

Derek Kline, the manager of the topless joint in Tampa, received a report that Clem had failed to appear at work on Friday and Saturday. The report came to him as a rumor. No one wanted to tell Derek bad news because it made him so angry. But someone had to break the news. So one of the bartenders said he heard from a liquor salesman that when he visited The Oar House it was strange that Clem was not there. The Oar House was a big volume account and the salesman was disturbed because he had no one to talk to who had any authority to purchase new products the distributor was offering for Halloween and Thanksgiving.

Derek went berserk when he discovered that the employees at the Oar House had been operating the club for two days without a manager.

Derek personally drove over the Gandy Bridge to investigate. He hated to drive to St. Petersburg because it seemed so far and out of the way. When he arrived he was told that Sarah, the dancer, had been acting as manager. She told Derek she did not know what happened to Clem.

The clean-up crew had found Clem's keys inside the back door on the floor. Clem and Lori didn't show for opening so Sarah went to Clem's house and the door was unlocked but no one was home and the 1952 Chevy was gone. It didn't appear anything was wrong at the house except the carpet was missing from the floor in the living room. At the side of the house there was yellow police crime scene tape on the side of the road near the large live oak tree.

Sarah told Derek they didn't know who to call (which was true, the crew was told nothing about the operation of the club by Clem, except Clem was in charge). Clem ran the club like a dictator and that was the intent of the owners. The owners did not want to be actively involved in the operation of the club in case it was determined the operation was illegal.

Derek asked about receipts for the night since Clem had been gone. Sarah explained there was a drop safe in Clem's office and they had deposited the receipts in the slot of the iron safe. They did not know the combination but Sarah had counted the money and made an accounting on a paper that she gave to Derek. The tally said the amount deposited in the drop safe totaled $2,387.

Derek knew the combination to the safe and he retrieved the cash, counted the cash and was satisfied when he saw there was $2,387 in bills bound by a large rubber band.

Derek called his boss in Jacksonville and told him the situation. They decided that Clem and Lori had taken off and were on the run. There was nothing that appeared to have been stolen except for one night's receipts, for the last night Clem worked. Derek was told he would have to make that up. Clem was his responsibility. Derek was Clem's boss. Therefore, Derek owed the money that was lost.

So there was just a matter of hiring a temporary manager. Derek was to let the assistant manager from the club in Tampa run the club in Tampa and Derek would run The Oar House until a new manager was hired. Meanwhile, Derek was to get control of the operation in St. Petersburg and he was told, if he could not do that, he would be fired.

Derek was dissatisfied with the arrangement. He was concerned with spending too much time in St. Petersburg. Even though there had been two arrests for the assault on Lori. there were two lawyers out there beating the bushes trying to determine what really happened. No one really believed Tommy Magyar and Alphonse Alesse were the perpetrators, especially now that it appeared Lori and Clem had disappeared. Derek was concerned that the evidence from the crime would trail to him. He was vulnerable because Clem and Lori knew he was the assailant and to his knowledge Lori was alive and on the run with Clem. If they were arrested they could testify against him. He was also vulnerable because the tall man, his co-conspirator, was still a possible witness against him. Derek Kline would have to kill the tall man or pay to make him go away. The matter was too messy. He didn't want to be in St. Petersburg. There was too much disruption. (There was too much "there" there.)

***

Meanwhile, Clem drove to Naples and got a cheap room in a motel on the Tamiami Trail. He did not shave. He drove his car into a canal (it sank like a rock) and he bought a used 450cc Honda motorcycle. He let his hair and beard grow and got a job in construction. He laid low, but kept in contact with Detective Cook. Cook was unconcerned. He felt everything was under control.

***

It took Clem only a week to grow an inch of hair on his head and face. His hair was on steroids. Two weeks later, after his first paycheck as a laborer on a construction crew, he went to a barber who evened the new growth. He bought a leather jacket and T-shirts and jeans, high top boots and leather gloves. He looked like a new man, like a biker. He fit right in with the construction crew and he made friends quickly. If there was a fight at the local bar the members of the crew wanted Clem on their side. The men spent the work day hauling concrete blocks, setting up scaffold and pushing cement as it was poured onto the four floors of the building. They carried two by four timbers and 4x8 panels of plywood eight to twelve hours a day. You got strong and fast or were fired. The buildings had four units per story. (Total units = 16.) The market for the units was wealthy New Yorkers who would use the units for a winter retreat.

Everywhere in Naples there was anonymity. The workers constructing the condo were transplants trying to get a new start. Many were Viet Nam veterans; most were unmarried men trying to put the war behind them. The owner of the building was an insurance company from the Midwest. The owner's representative never even visited the site. Construction was left to a large development company which advertised for tradesmen in the newspaper and paid for labor from local labor pools, who cast a net for workers at flop houses, the "Y" and the Salvation Army. The condo sales force moved from town to town as similar type buildings were being completed. The salesmen were working for a percentage of the sales price and practically lived out of a model unit, attacking potential buyers who happened to stop at the showroom.

Even the unit owners were unfamiliar to their co-owners. They only lived in the building temporarily, and if they had family and roots they were "up North" where it was "better".

So everyone was unfamiliar to their neighbors and they all tended to leave each other alone and give the stranger the benefit of the doubt and, really, just not ask questions. For a criminal on the lamb it was like moving to the Dakota Badlands in the 1880's or to Mexico or Chile at any time, even today.

Clem kept to himself. He stayed in his cheap motel room with its neon signage: "Tropical Breeze Motel," with the neon palm tree with fronds that waved in the inert green gas in the inert blue gas wind. Clem had not been much of a beer drinker, but he came to like beer and to tinker with his motorcycle.

The Honda bike was very fast and there were many single lane roads tracing out from Highway 41 and Highway 301 into cattle ranches to the east of Naples and Port Charlotte. The Honda was bulky, imitating a Harley "Fat Boy". But it did not cruise like a Harley, it was built for a sprint race and it was fast, but Clem burnt out on the speed. After a week with two bad spills on the road from Bradenton to Arcadia, Clem hung up his riding boots and limped into a used car lot and bought a 1956 Chevy Bel-Air.

Meanwhile, Clem kept in touch with Det. Cook. He called religiously on Wednesday evening at 6 p.m. to Cook's direct line at the police station. Richard kept Clem informed of the lack of progress in the investigation of the Anthony Stewart homicide. Cook would tear up with laughter as he recounted to Clem how his police officers followed leads that took them farther and farther away from the truth.

"Where are they looking now?" asked Clem.

"They are looking in drug dens in Atlanta."

"Are they closing in on a suspect?"

"Yes, they have a suspect. A heroin addict. A real lowlife."

"As soon as they make an arrest I will be more free to move around," said Clem. "I have a number here at the motel. Call me as soon as we have our patsy. The number is (912) 461-1213."

"I'll call as soon as I know. I think it will be soon."

"What's happening at The Oar House?"

"They put Sarah in charge, do you believe it?"

Clem pondered the information about Sarah. "She's smart. She will do fine. She is a good choice actually. Where is Derek?" asked Clem.

"He is back in Tampa, running his old club."

"I haven't forgotten him. You call when the arrest occurs. When I get a little more freedom, he's a dead man as far as I am concerned."

"I'll do it. I'll call you."

"I also need to know if they find the Oriental rug."

"That won't be found. The maintenance crew for the interstate highway doesn't clean the swamp. That was a brilliant idea."

"It came in the moment," said Clem.

They were both smiling as they hung up.

***

When the City Manager authorized the Police Chief to purchase a new phone system for the new police station two years past, he insisted that the chief purchase a phone with a feature that allowed conversations on the dispatcher's line to be recorded so they could have a record of response times to emergencies. There were always complaint's that the police were too slow and the City Manager wanted the chief to monitor the activity for those calls.

At first the chief thought the recording and collection of the calls would be a burden, but the chief found the information gathered was helpful and they were able to improve response time. The police spokesman thought that would make a great PR story and he contacted the local paper, which normally had very little good to say about the force ("... bunch of fascists ..."), and the police had little good to say about the press ("... bunch of commies ..."). This would be great, thought the spokesman.

The editor of the local news desk assigned reporter Lucy Hale to the story. Hale was the State Attorney's daughter. She was very hungry to succeed.

Hale was very thorough and in the course of her research she discovered that the recording capability of the phone system was not just limited to the emergency calls. The system could focus on a single telephone extension and tape the calls on that phone. It could also roam from extension to extension retrieving both sides of the conversation on the call. The system could also roam to another random extension and record the call in its entirety. Actually, the entire phone system was bugged.

Lucy Hale discovered the recording/taping function was in use and there were recordings on file at the station.

The chief wanted to use this function without telling his officers what he was doing. He wanted to have the Internal Affairs unit monitor the tape of the calls without telling his officers that he could hear what they were saying. Maybe the chief had become suspicious of his men.

The City Manager was sensitive to the argument the police union would make that the officers would be hampered in their duties. The City Manager knew the union would try to protect the police from releasing how many calls from the station were personal calls.

The City Attorney was consulted. His opinion was that when the police were at work they had no expectation of privacy. So, if they were using the phone system owned and operated by the City, they had no right to object if the calls were recorded. In fact, it was the City Attorney's opinion that the police had no right to even know that the calls were being intercepted and recorded. The City Manager trusted the City Attorney's opinion and he authorized the Police Chief to have the police phones tapped using the roaming feature on the phone system.

The chief did not tell anyone besides the men in the Internal Affairs Department that the phones were tapped, and he did not tell the police spokesman, and he did not release the information to the press. That, however, did not deter Lucy Hale from discovering the various features of the phone system or asking about the roaming feature that she discovered in her research.

When Lucy Hale asked, the police spokesman denied they used the roaming feature, the police phones were not tapped, he said. Ultimately the spokesman retracted the denial. The police phones were tapped, he admitted. Lucy's editor didn't think it was that important so he left it out of the story when he edited Hale's final copy. So no one in the general public heard about the fact that there were taps of all the police calls to and from the station.

However, Detective Richard Cook came upon the information when he was talking to a dispatcher. There were no secrets in the police ranks.

When Detective Richard Cook thought about it, he was able to remember that since Anthony Stewart and Lori Schaeffer had been killed, he had spoken to Clem on three occasions. And that on those three occasions, he referred to the investigation or the fact of the cause of death, and that he and Clem were involved in the murders. The first time Clem was calling from a pay phone in St. Petersburg. The next was from a payphone in Naples and the last call was from Clem's motel.

When Cook realized the phones were tapped and his calls to/ from Clem may have been intercepted he immediately concluded that he had been caught. He left the police station. He had to get out. He could not breathe. He drove to a gas station, retrieved the key to the rest room, sat on the toilet and this news caused him to evacuate his bowels with the efficiency of an overdose of Dulcolax. He locked himself in the bathroom. He had a cold sweat and the shakes. His left arm became numb and his head hurt and he could not think. He was in total panic mode.

Only when it was dark, hours after he locked himself in the odorous room did Cook leave the toilet. He was still a wreck. He thought something was wrong with him physically and it was a permanent condition. He got back in the car. His shift was over. He drove back to the station and checked out. He merely nodded to acquaintances. No one asked him anything that required him to say anything other than to say yes or no. Then his foot began to drag, his face drooped to one side and his vision became blurry. He passed out in the hallway in front of his office.

The ER Doctor at Bayfront Hospital said he had a stroke. It was a permanent condition. He was admitted. He was on duty when the stroke occurred so worker's compensation would cover his bills and pay the main portion of his salary while he waited for his disability pension to come through.

Cook was in the cat bird's seat according to his sergeant. His sergeant visited him first. "You will be able to double dip. You will get workers comp and State disability," said the Sergeant.

"You hit the jackpot, Cook. You will make more money staying home than you would if you were working."

Cook just blinked his eyes. He could not speak. Cook never admitted he had the stroke as a result of learning his conversations with Clem might have been recorded. He never told anyone the stroke was the result of his total fear of arrest for Anthony Stewart's murder.

The Report of Injury stated the cause of injury was a "stroke at work".

Part V

The first goal of all living creatures
is self-preservation.
And to accomplish that end,
all living creatures are selfish.

Chapter 20

Clem fully intended to kill Derek Kline. He had solicited Cook in that endeavor.

When Clem and Det. Cook had last talked on the phone on Wednesday at 6 p.m., they had agreed that Cook would visit The Man Trap, the topless club that Derek managed in Tampa. Cook was to scope it out and see if Derek was there and where he spent his time in the club. On the one occasion when Clem had been required to meet with Derek in Tampa, they met in an office in a basement built below the stage. Clem had worried that if he attacked Derek in the office in the basement he would be trapped afterward. He would be an easy target as he came up the basement stairs and out on the main floor behind the dance floor. Clem remembered seeing a door to the outside about 20 feet from the basement stairs on the main floor of the club, but he would be a sitting duck for those 20 feet until he could negotiate the door and get across the parking lot and to his car on the street.

According to the plan, Det. Cook was to visit the Man Trap on Friday, late, when the bar was hopping and the business was the most frenetic. The busier the better to pull off the attack, Clem thought.

Had Cook visited The Man Trap on Friday he would have discovered that Derek had moved his office to a room on the first floor of the club. The room had a short tunnel that led directly to an exit door that opened to the outside at the rear of the building to an overflow parking lot. Derek parked his motorcycle right outside the exit door.

Clem and Cook had been scheduled to meet in Sarasota at a seafood bar and have lunch and a few beers on Saturday afternoon after Cook visited the Tampa club. They intended to discuss the best way to kill Derek in the Man Trap. But Cook did not show. That was not like him, and Clem thought there was a high probability something was wrong. Clem had a phone in his room at the Tropical Breeze Motel. Cook could have made a call if he would not make the lunch appointment.

Clem kept checking his watch. Maybe it was running slow, he thought. Clem's only jewelry was a wrist watch. He was given the watch after one of the post season play off games in which he participated. It was a Timex. It ran perfectly. Clem needed a watch because time eluded him if he tried to mark its passage on his own. He had no internal sense of time. With the exception of day versus night, he was lost in time.

Clem sat at the restaurant for two hours, waiting; checking his watch every five minutes. He drank four short beers and then left and went back to Naples. He was nervous and upset. The authorities must be on to him, he thought. He loaded his car with his belongings. He had a suitcase full of clothes and personal effects including his large heavy knife and his .44 caliber handgun. He did not check out of the motel room. He had paid for a week in advance and there was no sense telling management he had checked out. He wouldn't get a refund. Besides, if the police were after him, he wanted them to stake out his room during the five days he had left in advance rent. If the cops staked out the room he would be able to spot them. Clem didn't think he would be returning to the room, but just in case he did, he left a light on in the bathroom so he didn't trip over the bed if he came in late.

After he got back to Naples from Sarasota, Clem drove his Chevy to a dive bar down the street from the motel. His construction crew members hung out there. He felt safe and he proceeded to get drunk.

It was 4:30 p.m. on Saturday when he entered the bar. It was 2 a.m. Sunday when he exited the back door with the floozy who said she would put him up for the night. On the way to her place he passed his motel. There was no unusual activity. No one was slouched down in the front seat of their car watching his room. Maybe everything was all right, he thought. But he thought it would be better to stick to the plan and stay out of his room.

Clem and the lady friend went to her garage apartment. Although he was encouraged by the lady to have sex, he told her he could do her no good as she groped him and coaxed him to the bed. "Too drunk," he said.

She tried to pull him out of the chair and move him to bed in the back room but he was too big. He was a brute, she thought. "You'll pay for your room in the morning," she told him. And she slid off his lap and went in the back room to bed. He slept in the chair and slipped out in the early morning just before first light.

"Damn him," she said as she discovered he had escaped. She looked in her icebox. Pink Grapefruit. She had gleaned it from a local tree. She would have grapefruit for breakfast and take a walk. Clem left with his car. The floozy had no transportation.

***

Tom and Darlene Night spent Saturday night at a fundraiser for the Office of the Public Attorney. The office coordinated legal service for criminal defendants who were indigent, unable to afford an attorney to defend them.

Someone thought they were being funny. They sat Tom and Darlene at the same table as the State Attorney John Hale and Hale's third wife.

It took about five minutes before the two men were sniping at one another. Hale had prosecuted Tom for Contempt of Court. Tom was jailed and Darlene successfully defended Tom and he was released. Ultimately, Hale dropped the charges. Hale couldn't prove the charge. Tom was innocent. Tom was a patsy and Darlene proved it.

Tom thought that if a prosecutor had not just failed to prove a person guilty, but the person had been proven innocent, then the prosecutor owed the person an apology. But Hale had not apologized and he implied that Tom was guilty, but that Hale just couldn't prove the case. Since then, Tom and John Hale were not the best of friends. And this latest prosecutorial disaster involving Tommy Magyar and Alphonse Alesse made Tom all the madder.

John Hale was sensitive to the fact that his office had made a mistake bringing charges when the defendant's guilt relied on such thin evidence as the testimony of Lori Schaeffer. She was a compromised witness.

Further, Tom was upset because there was so little progress being made in the murder investigation of his friend and investigator Anthony Stewart. John Hale was left defending the police work of Richard Cook, who in Hale's opinion left much to be desired as an investigator. Although John would not admit it to Tom, Hale had privately recommended to the Police Chief that he assign someone else to investigate Anthony's death. But now the matter was complicated by the fact Cook had a stroke.

Hale had flyspecked the progress of the investigation and he felt anyone with a brain would have deduced Clem was the prime suspect. His house was being surveilled by Anthony at the time Anthony was murdered and he had run off with Lori. Then there was the missing piece of carpet in Clem's house. What's up with that? thought Hale. Something happened there in Clem's house, but Det. Cook had his men chasing down a heroin addict in Atlanta. True, the addict had been questioned by the police after the murder, and he was in the area. The addict had the opportunity to kill, but he couldn't be connected to the murder and he had been released the night he was questioned for lack of evidence. He wasn't in possession of any cameras or camera equipment or a gun. It made Hale so angry that Cook was wasting time on the addict that he could scream, and he did scream, but he screamed at Tom in public and the two men were told to leave the dinner party.

***

The few tall buildings in Downtown St. Petersburg were either Savings and Loans or condominiums.

On Sunday morning Tom and Darlene sat in the kitchen of their condo looking out the window, watching the ships in the bay cruising to the Port of Tampa and the Banana Decks, and they discussed their week. Darlene was smart enough to wait until morning to talk about the confrontation between Night and Hale the night before.

Tom had at least had the sense to back off as Hale began to rant about crooks and murders and no one understanding how hard it was to protect the victim of a crime and mete out justice. Hale had gone on and on. When the President of the Office of Public Attorney asked Tom and John to leave, Tom left quickly and quietly. Darlene was just behind him. Hale was still yelling. Tom and Darlene moved quickly to the car and went home and to bed.

Sunday morning over coffee Tom said, "I think Hale has lost his mind."

"There is definitely a problem there," Darlene agreed.

"Was his daughter there covering the dinner for the newspaper?" asked Tom.

"Yes, I think so. Hopefully they won't print a story about the blowup."

"The paper will stick to the dinner," said Tom. "By the way, who won the pro bono award?"

"James DeMarco was given the award for providing the most service to the indigent during the last year," said Darlene.

"He is just starting out and he makes very little money, but he still offers most of his time to defendants who are unrepresented. He's good for our profession, I guess." Tom wasn't sure.

Darlene changed the subject. "What are you going to do about your relationship with John Hale? It's not very professional to get in a screaming match in public."

"Agreed. I just need to avoid him unless we are in court," said Tom.

"That sounds like a good start. But you can't ignore him in the hallway at the courthouse."

"I don't know what makes him tick," said Tom.

"He's embarrassed. He lost. You embarrassed him. He can't stand to lose." She smiled. "Don't confront him unless you absolutely have to."

***

If he were not lying in bed in the hospital, Richard Cook would have begun his work shift at midnight Sunday and he would work through to 10 am on Monday.

Clem knew Cook's schedule, so at 4 a.m., Monday, Clem called the police department and asked for Detective Cook. He was routed to the Desk Sergeant, who told Clem that Det. Cook was unavailable.

"When will he be available?" asked Clem.

"Not for a while, he's out."

"Is Officer Burns on duty?"

"He's on the street. He will be back at 8 a.m. Leave me your name and number."

"I'll call back," said Clem. "I'm on a pay phone."

The Desk Sergeant rang dispatch. "I just had a call. Can you pull up the phone number?"

The dispatcher liked the new phone system, even though the dispatcher had to include the task of tracing phone numbers to his duties. It wasn't that hard. It took a minute and he called the Sergeant back.

"The call was from a Quick Mart here in the city, near the old Duck Pond. It's a pay phone."

***

At 8:30 a.m. Clem called back and the Desk Sergeant had gone home. Officer Burns was paged and he came on the line.

"So Burns, this is Clemenso. Where is Det. Cook?"

Burns recognized Clem's voice. "Where are you?"

"Around," said Clem.

Officer Burns' beat included The Oar House. That was how he knew Clem. Burns had helped Clem rousting drunks at the club and Clem gave Burns a few dollars for his trouble.

"You need to come in and talk to Homicide Division," said Burns. "They are looking for you."

Burns was so naïve, thought Clem. "No time now. Where is Cook?"

"He had a stroke. He's in Bayfront Hospital. The stroke was real bad."

"Sorry to hear that."

"Can I put you through to Homicide?" asked Officer Burns.

"Not now, I'll call back," said Clem. "Later."

Clem hung up the pay phone at the Quick Mart. He was just two blocks from his house in St. Petersburg. Clem had been a patient at Bayfront Hospital one time. He was closing the club by himself and he was blindsided by a robber who hit him in the head with an unopened beer bottle. The bottle hit him just above the nose and split his head open. He was sewed up in the ER and then kept overnight. He had a concussion. He was surprised by the fact the doctor kept him overnight. They didn't keep him in the hospital when he suffered a concussion playing football. He had concussions all the time when he played ball, but you just shook them off. The robber hit Clem with a lucky punch, Clem figured.

When Clem got out of Bayfront after being robbed he tracked down the robber. He was a habitual drunk. The man didn't take money from The Oar House the night he clobbered Clem, he took a few bottles of cheap whiskey and he hid out in the small woods near the club and drank himself into oblivion. Clem found him and hit him in the head with his fist two times. It didn't faze the man. He just laid on the ground. Clem knew he had to do the man some damage or Clem would have to fight his way out of the club every night. So Clem cut off the man's right thumb with his heavy knife. Afterward, Clem had no further trouble with robbers.

Now Clem had to figure out what to do with Richard Cook.

Chapter 21

Before Tom was asked to leave the dinner party for riling up John Hale the State Attorney, Darlene and the President of the Public Attorney's Office had spoken about a program the President was trying to initiate. Indigents were sometimes lost in the system. He wanted to try an idea where the police would call the Chief Judge in serious cases (murder, rape, robbery) after the police had made an arrest and advise the court that they had a suspect who would need an attorney and it was obvious the defendant had no money to hire counsel. The judge would then appoint an attorney from a pre-appointed list. The President wanted Darlene to work with James DeMarco and take a case to see if the idea was feasible. Darlene had agreed. Tom was opposed to this idea. You would have the police involved in the appointment of attorneys to represent indigents. "Very bad idea. Conflict."

Shortly after that conversation with the President, Darlene and Tom left the party for home. What Darlene missed besides dinner was the presentation to her of a lifetime award for continuing to offer her services without charge to the indigent.

Darlene was happy to have missed the presentation because she hated praise. Although she was a fighter, she was shy and would not have liked to have been singled out before the group.

Tom was Darlene's third husband. The first put her through law school only to lose her because they grew apart after she was a practicing lawyer. She struggled long hours to succeed in her practice. Her first husband thought she was just ignoring him.

The first husband was happy when another successful attorney in town enticed her with a partnership as his law partner. She became her second husband's partner at work and later they became husband and wife. Darlene agreed to the arrangement and she worked hard and became the highest paid lawyer in the county, rich beyond her dreams. Once she generated more wealth than her marital partner his ego was bruised and he wanted out of the marriage. He was such an egotist that he had failed to obtain a pre-nuptial agreement, and so when the marriage was dissolved Darlene was awarded half of everything owned by the couple, even what the husband owned before the marriage. The judge, like Solomon, divided the baby, and with relish, because no one in the legal community liked Darlene's second husband.

After the second divorce Darlene bought her two penthouse units in the Bay Shore Condominiums. She opened her practice in one penthouse and the other penthouse was her home. She carved out a reception area, secretarial space, library and two offices in one penthouse unit. Her residence had views of Tampa Bay and the industry at the port of Tampa. From a distance the tankers and freighters and docks were majestic. The Port of Tampa was large and alive and awake 24/7. Up close the port was grimy and dirty, but generated much legal work.

It was many years (about eight) before Darlene began to think about marriage again and by then she was mature and beautiful, slim, with athletic (bike riding) firm features. Her body vibrated in powder blue or red. She had two old cats she called her kids and she didn't think she had the patience to take care of a child, so she didn't miss children much.

What brought Tom and Darlene together was the fact that Tom needed a lawyer after being held in contempt of court. He was at risk of the loss of his liberty, livelihood and reputation. Darlene had saved him and he fell in love. Eventually Darlene fell in love with Tom and she asked him to marry her after he had unsuccessfully asked for her hand many times during a two year courtship.

Darlene moved her offices to those of Tom and Roger but her practice was unusual. She didn't just take any case that came in the door. She was very selective and tried to take cases that would make a difference in the community. This is why she said she was happy to work with James DeMarco.

James DeMarco was out of school only two years. A quick mind, athletic, too young yet for serious vices, thin, 5'8" in height, dark curly hair and quick, brown eyes.

***

The first appointment under the police appointment program, called PAP, came at 5 a.m. on Tuesday, two days after the party. James and Darlene got a call and they went to the police station to the lock-up area. They tried to speak to the client, an 18-year-old charged with beating his grandmother to death. The young man was a schizophrenic. He thought he was cured of his mental illness, and he quit taking his medication. Without the drug he became more delusional, but the grandparents could not control him. They didn't realize how dangerous he could become.

A neighbor reported to the police that he was suspicious. Something was wrong at the house because he had not seen the old couple. The neighbor heard screaming and called the police. The police found the grandmother in a living room chair, propped up in front of the TV. She had been beaten to death. The police looked but couldn't find the grandfather. They arrested the boy.

The detective called the judge because he couldn't obtain anything intelligible from the boy about what happened. The officer noted the boy was a "signal 20" (crazy). The judge appointed Darlene and James as initial temporary counsel. They visited the jail and couldn't get anything out of the boy either so they went to the scene of the crime to try to get an idea what had occurred.

The grandparent's modest house was built of concrete block. It was in a small development that was built in the early 1950's. The interstate had cut through the area and the grandparents' house and two others were isolated from the remaining homes in the development. A neighbor came up to them when they drove up.

Darlene and James explained why they were there. The neighbor had a flash light that he offered to the two attorneys.

"The lights were cut off a day ago," said the neighbor. "I think that's when it happened."

"What happened?" asked James.

"There was a lot of noise. I called the police. They found the woman dead but they couldn't find the old man."

"Let's see what we can find," said Darlene.

The house was musty and specks of dust hung in the air in the light of the flashlight. It smelled moldy. There were terrariums set on the tables in the boy's room. The animals were dead or escaped and were out in the room fending for themselves. James shone the light in the corner trying to discover the source of a sound and saw a Central American chameleon chewing on a wilted piece of lettuce.

"That was the kid's hobby, the terrariums," said the neighbor. "He had rats and all kinds of things. There's a big iguana somewhere in here."

In the boy's room the bed was shoved up against the wall.

"Is that the way the bed is supposed to be?" Darlene asked. "It doesn't look right."

James and the neighbor pulled the bed out from the wall.

"Here's the old man," said James. "He's alive."

The lights were off for non-payment of the bill but the phone worked. They called the police and an ambulance.

The paramedics said the man would probably live. He was old and thin, grizzly and tough. The man wanted to know about his wife. Darlene explained, she didn't hold back the bad news. The old man began to cry and sob. The ambulance left with Darlene and the patient. James followed in the car.

Darlene thought, Tom is right, we need to hire that young man. James will be a good asset for the firm.

***

It was 6:30 a.m. James and Darlene went to first appearance with their new client. Darlene explained to the judge that they had a question. Could they represent the boy? They were witnesses to the discovery of the grandfather. The judge left them on the case for the moment. On the question of release the court found that bail would not be granted but the court ordered a competency hearing to be held the next week and they would review the matter at that time. The judge also ordered that the defendant be put back on his medication.

James and Darlene went for coffee.

"James, why don't you come work with us?" asked Darlene.

"Let's see what happens to Tommy Magyar. I have a conflict with your office representing Alphonse and me representing Tommy. That case isn't over yet."

"You're right," said Darlene. "We'll be off this case too with the grandparents. We are going to be witnesses in this case. I feel really bad for the old man."

"I know," said James.

***

Back at the office, Tom had just arrived, making coffee and checking faxes and telexes. The fax machine was something new. It worked about half the time. It required another phone line so AT&T was happy.

Darlene told Tom about the excitement. Tom listened carefully as he tried to read the chemically infused fax paper. He loved to listen to his wife talk. She was very enthusiastic. She told him how impressed she was with James and that she had offered him a job.

"But he says he has a conflict," said Darlene. "He says as long as he is representing Tommy and we represent Alphonse on this Lori Schaeffer case he can't work for us. Tom, do you think anything is going to happen with that case?"

"It's not over. I was going through the faxes. John Hale has set an Arraignment for our mutual clients. I guess Hale thinks he can prove his case without his witness," said Tom.

"I'm starting to come around to your point of view about Hale. Something is wrong with him."

"I think I know why I am so upset with him," said Tom. "I think it's the cigarettes. I started smoking again when he threw me in jail and I haven't been able to quit. I keep chipping away at them."

"It's my fault. You keep stealing my cigarettes," said Darlene. "I need to quit. But it's only a couple of cigarettes a day."

"That's what I keep saying."

Chapter 22

Clem had no one to talk to who could help him plan Derek's murder. Det. Cook had a stroke, Lori Schaeffer was dead by his hand, and he was on the lamb, running from the law and the criminal syndicate he worked for.

The only person he could think of who could help him with logistics – the who, what, where and when of the murder conspiracy at The Man Trap – was Sarah. Originally she had worked at The Man Trap for two years and then The Oar House. Now she had taken his job as manager at The Oar House and she would have information about the sister club in Tampa that Derek managed. She would know when Derek was the most vulnerable.

Clem knew where Sarah lived in Tampa near the old abandoned port with her aunt. He didn't know her exact address, but he knew that any shopkeeper would know where her aunt lived, and everyone would probably know Sarah because she grew up in the old port area.

***

Clem had to ask only one man on the street in the old port to get the aunt's address. Clem was able to find a spot where he could park his two tone crème over brown 1956 Chevy Bel-Air and watch the house. He guessed he would not have to stay parked long because she had to be at work by 11 a.m. She had to open the club for the cleaning crew and do bookwork before the club opened at 2 p.m. It would take an hour to drive to 66th Street in St. Petersburg. So all Clem had to do was park his car in the port at about 9:30 a.m. and watch and wait.

He sat there from 9:30 a.m. to 1:30 p.m. Sarah did not show at the Aunt's house.

Maybe she had the day off or she moved. He drove to the club in St. Petersburg and parked on the street near the small one acre wooded lot and walked into the woods through the brush, past the hobo camp to the fence. He could see the manager's designated parking spot from that location. There was a blue 1970 Ford Maverick in the spot. She has poor taste in cars, thought Clem.

Clem waited in the woods until 2 a.m. when the club closed. Then he went back to the fence. He was lucky. Sarah came out the back door and went to the blue car to leave. She was alone. Clem turned from the fence and ran as fast as he could to his car. It was only 400 feet away but he had to make it through the brush and around the trees. It was like running the ball back on kick off. He jumped into his car and raced around the street to the entrance of the club. He could see her car down the street. He stayed back and followed her. The streets were straight and wide. He could see her easily. There was little traffic this early in the morning.

As he followed he realized the route was familiar. These were the roads Clem took to his home every night from work at the club. They must have moved Sarah into my old house near the Quick Mart, he thought. She'll make a left at the next light he thought and she did, but Clem didn't follow because she might see his car. Clem drove straight to the old house by a short cut. He was parked under the old live oak tree on the road on the side of his old house as Sarah parked her car in the back of the garage off the alley.

Clem could see her open the back door. They had replaced the light. The door slammed. The lights went on in the dining room and then the living room. He could see the light from her TV as it was turned on. She had a beer in her hand. He couldn't tell what brand but from the color of the bottle (brown) he could guess it was a Bud (it was a long neck with a red label). From the view he had with the naked eye Clem realized that if Anthony had good cameras the night of Lori's murder the equipment would have produced damning evidence. Clem wondered where Cook had hidden the cameras and more importantly, where was the film? He thought "Christ, I will be a dead man if they get that film."

Clem just sat in his dark car and thought. He watched Sarah. She went upstairs to the bedroom. She took her time changing. She walked around nude, picking up clothes. Finally she changed into a robe. Clem looked around his car. He was thinking somebody else must know there's a free peep show over here every night when Sarah changes her clothes. There's probably some pimply faced kid loitering around here in the bushes, he thought. Clem got out of the car and went over to a small park across the street and sat on a bench. It was a little cool. He was wearing a gray jacket and a cap. He was invisible in plain sight.

The police couldn't have the photos that Anthony took or my face would be plastered on telephone poles. "Wanted." No one is staking out the room at the Tropical Breeze Motel, he thought. "I've been wandering around, people have seen me that probably know me, but my disguise is working. They haven't recognized me. The long hair and beard and new style clothes, like a laborer, are effective. Nothing has been in the papers about the discovery of a female corpse rolled inside an oriental rug in the cypress swamp near the interstate. Maybe I'm just spooked, thought Clem.

I will just go knock on the door and tell Sarah that Lori and I are alright and play it by ear, Clem said to himself.

***

Tap ta Tap Tap.

"Who is it?" asked Sarah. She got up from the recliner and she was at the door with a .22 caliber pistol in her right hand.

"It's Clem."

"Is Lori with you?"

"No, she's in North Carolina." Clem knew Sarah would know Lori was from North Carolina. It was a secret that Lori had only told Sarah and Clem. At least Sarah thought she was the only one who knew. That being said was enough to make Sarah unlock the door.

Clem stood back from the door waiting to be let in. He saw the gun in her hand. He stood there, he was waiting for her to feel safe. Then she laughed. "Your hair and face! 'Mr. Fuzzy' is what I'll call you."

Clem put up with the joke being on him. He smiled. "Can I come in?"

"Sure, what do I care?" Sarah moved the gun around in her hand to make sure Clem saw the weapon. "Are you going to kill me?"

"No."

"You have probably been tailing me for a while and know everything I'm doing and where I work. Don't you?"

"Yes," Clem admitted.

"Beer?"

"Sure."

"So what's up?" Sarah put the gun in the pocket of her robe and shagged a beer for Clem.

"I left Lori with her mom and came back to see what kind of trouble I have here. I want to clean things up with Derek and work."

"What do you need to do?" asked Sarah. "Everyone is more afraid of you than the devil." She paused, put her finger to her cheek and asked: "But you say you are after Derek." She paused, "Really?"

"I hate that bastard. If you were going to kill him, where would you do it?" asked Clem.

"Well, not inside The Man Trap," said Sarah.

"Do you know where he lives?"

"He lives in a house down the street from The Man Trap. It's close to his work. He drives a motorcycle to work every day and when he gets home he parks it in front of the garage at the house. It's a Kawasaki."

"You know what time he gets off?" asked Clem.

"At 2:30 a.m. His hours are the same as your hours were. He will be off at 2:30 a.m. and home in 10 minutes and if you are at the garage of his house you can pop him there."

"Sounds too easy."

"It would be easy. That's the way I would do it" said Sarah. "Check it out, you'll see."

"Yeah, I'll do that." Clem finished the beer and stared at Sarah. He seemed too quiet.

"So what are you going to do with me?" asked Sarah.

"Nothing now. We'll see how things play out."

"I could shoot you now," she said as she pulled the gun from her robe pocket.

"Those .22 Cal bullets aren't big enough to kill me."

"But I have six shots."

"I won't give you that many chances," said Clem. "I didn't come here to kill you. I came here to figure out the best way to kill Derek. If you let me kill him you may get another promotion."

"I don't think they will let a woman run the Man Trap. The glass ceiling and all that."

"I don't understand. What is the 'glass ceiling'?" asked Clem.

"Never mind, I don't think I understand it either," said Sarah as she put the gun back in her pocket and went to the front door. She opened it. "Need anything more?" she said as she let her right thigh protrude through the front of the robe.

"No, nothing more," said Clem.

Sarah chuckled but it was an act. She knew Clem could explode and kill her in a second. She held tight to the pistol in the pocket of her robe ready to discharge the weapon if he attacked.

Clem walked out the door and went to his car and for an hour he watched his old house. He could see Sarah move around. She had turned off the overhead light in the living room but Clem could see her in the light from the television. Sarah was sitting in Clem's large recliner. Clem slept most nights in that chair, when he could sleep. Most nights he couldn't sleep. He would doze, no dreams, no deep restful sleep. Too many concussions.

Clem could see Sarah's head roll over to the side of the top cushion of the recliner. She was asleep.

***

Clem's old house was only a few blocks from Bayfront Hospital. Originally it was called Mound Park Hospital because it was built on an Indian burial mound. The contractors leveled the top of the mound, crushing skulls and bones and then built the first building of the hospital. Later they added on and the facility became "Bayfront Hospital". The original building became a long term care ward. It was a place where patients go who weren't going to get out soon, or who might only have a slim chance to recover to some semblance of normalcy. But most likely they would die in the ward.

The original building of the old hospital still used the original entrance, a door off of Sixth Avenue South. There was a carved stone archway. The door was imposing but it was left unguarded and unlocked. The staff could enter without being restricted by a locked door. The public could enter too, if they were so inclined; there was no guard or receptionist at the door. Clem drove up near the door and parked on Sixth Avenue and walked in the big door into a large hall.

Clem went to the first door to the left. The door opened to a large ward. There was very low lighting in the room. There were mechanical whooshing sounds from the ventilators. There were 20 beds in the ward. There was no caregiver at her station or anyone else in the ward except patients. It was 3:30 a.m. There were big windows in the room, all with heavy frosted glass. Clem looked for his friend Richard and found him on a ventilation unit. Richard was awake. Richard recognized Clem. As Clem bent over and looked into his open eyes, Cook blinked excitedly.

Cook's hands rested on a tray with a pad and pen. Clem could see notes on the pad.

Clem asked: "Where are the cameras and the film?"

Clem gave Cook the pen and set the pad on the tray, Cook wrote: "Bedroom, my place. The pocket in the ceiling."

"How are you?"

"End it," wrote Cook. "Please" He was crying.

"Okay, friend."

Clem looked below the bed for the electric cord. He pulled the plug from the wall and stood there and watched as Cook's hands turned white then blue. Cook closed his eyes and his arms turned white as did his face. Clem felt Cook's neck and there was no pulse. Clem stood over Cook until he was cool and dusky.

Clem waited ten minutes. The light was blinking on the ventilator but it made no sound since he pulled the plug. No one came into the room. Clem collected all the pages from the pad. He left the pen.

He replaced the ventilator plug back in the wall socket. The light kept blinking but there was no sound. No alarm. The ventilator did not re-start.

"So long, partner," said Clem as he walked out the door of the ward, then out of the main door with the carved stone framing.

I won't have much time, he thought.

***

The licensed practical nurse returned to her station in the long term ward. She had fallen asleep on the toilet leaning against the wall of the stall. She had slept three hours. It was 6:30 a.m. As soon as she entered the room she could see there was a light blinking on the ventilation unit attached to Det. Richard Cook.

She immediately went to the bed and saw that the patient had died. She went to the floor nurse, an RN and told her what she had discovered. A death in the long term care unit was not considered an emergency situation. The staff did not call a "code blue". There was no rushing around with carts of equipment and with staff running to the bedside. Patients in the long term unit were expected to die. In fact, it was hoped that they would die and be taken from their misery. It was God's will. Patients like Det. Cook, who were conscious and aware of their surroundings, tried to communicate the sentiment that they wished to die. Many cursed the Bishop and the priest who made them endure the Purgatory that was the long term care unit, and if they could communicate, they communicated their desire to die.

The RN called the intern who was on duty. The intern thought there must be something wrong with the ventilation unit because a buzzer was supposed to sound together with the light whenever the ventilator stopped functioning. The buzzer was a "fail safe" feature. If there was no "whoosh" there was to be the double warning of the "beep, beep, beep" sound, persistently sounding the alarm and if the caregiver was deaf there was a visual signal, the "flash, flash" of a small annoying strobe to accompany the annoying beep. The primary safeguard was the LPN who was assigned to the ward.

"Where was the LPN?" asked the intern.

"She was in the bathroom."

"What, sleeping?"

The RN defended her junior co-worker. "It's a long shift. It's very depressing in this ward. They should have two nurses in the room with that many critical care patients."

"We will have to report this. Don't use that ventilator machine until the manufacturer has someone inspect the warning buzzer on the unit. It might be the backup battery is dead."

"Could be," agreed the RN.

"While the factory rep is here, have him check all the units," said the intern as he checked Cook's chart. "Oh, this man was the police detective. Did he have family?"

"No one local. His mother is from Daytona Beach," said the RN.

"Well, call his boss at work and report his death," said the intern. "Tell them we are sorry and that we did all we could to save him."

Part VI

Hell on earth
is real.

Chapter 23

It had only been two days since Det. George Randell had taken over Det. Richard Cook's cases since Cook suffered his stroke.

Nothing about Cook's cases made sense and now Randell was at Cook's residence investigating a burglary. The entire house was a wreck. Kids probably, that's what the other cops on the scene thought. The kids must have broken in before school started. The police got the call at 6:43 am.

The house was in the Kendle section of town. The developer built houses known in Florida as "7/8th houses" because the houses were 7/8th normal size. The developer had to incorporate the project as a town separate from St. Petersburg to avoid the city's building code. The developer felt it was worth it as it reduced the builder's cost by about 12% for materials and land.

Kendle was located on the edge of the City of St. Petersburg on land governed by the County. The development regulations allowed the developer (who had also appointed himself to be the mayor) to cut the size of the houses and lots. Instead of lot sizes being 80 feet by 160 feet deep the lots were 70 feet by 140 feet deep. Where the developer could get away with it, and retain structural integrity, the buildings were smaller. The ceiling height in the homes was 7.5 feet and not a minimum of eight feet as in the houses in the City of St. Petersburg. The buyers of the houses in the Town of Kendle were given a cheaper sale price but the developer still made a lot of money.

Being 7/8th size, the residents had odd size pockets left behind the drywall used to finish the walls. These dead spaces were sometimes used as hiding places by the owner. To reach them you had to go in the crawl space area above the ceiling and below the roof. You could also reach in a vent in the ceiling and then reach the pocket between the ceiling joists and the rafters.

Detective Randell was familiar with the construction of these homes and it looked to Randell like someone was looking for some treasure in a ceiling pocket in the bedroom, but the person's arm was too heavy or too big to enter the pocket to retrieve the treasure from above the ceiling. So the burglar had pulled down the ceiling using his bare hands. The room was so poorly constructed that the ceiling came down in large chunks. The robber knew what was there and where it was located because only one pocket had been exposed in the bedroom. The culprit was a big man, thought the detective. The robber climbed over the drywall ceiling that was now on the floor to retrieve the treasure and had left a boot mark that looked to be for a size 13 or 14 shoe. The detective told the forensics unit to take a photo and take measurements of the boot mark. If they could, he wanted them to cut and save the piece of drywall that contained the boot print. They did.

Det. Randell also instructed Forensics to check the bathroom for finger or hand prints. Most of the rest of the house would yield little in prints because the surfaces were porous and not smooth and solid. After forensics finished, Randell climbed to the area where the ceiling had been pulled down. He got a ladder, placed it against the wall in the corner of the room and climbed up to see what he could see. He was a hands-on type investigator.

Randell had worked as a detective for 16 years. He was 52 years old. He was bald, overweight and out of shape. He was the first and only Negro on the force to be promoted to the rank of detective. He knew he had advanced as far as he was going. He was stuck working as a detective and if the Police Chief couldn't find a reason to terminate him first, he would retire as a detective in about four more years.

When Randell reached Inside the pocket hiding place, he found a pillow case. He pulled it out and inside the pillow case he found a lens cap from a Cannon motion picture camera. Digging deeper he found a block wrapped in paper. That's cash under the paper, he thought. And it was cash. (When it was counted, the stack of 5s, 10s, 20s, 50s and $100 dollar bills had a value of $26,025. That was two years' salary for Det. Randell or Det. Cook.)

The discovery of the cash caused Detective Randell to be immediately suspicious of Det. Cook. The other members of the team of police at the scene were grousing about the fact that someone would trash the home of a cop who was in the hospital. But Det. Randell thought it was the best time to rob Det. Cook. Cook was helpless. Randell also felt the damage done to the other rooms defacing the interior of the house was a subterfuge to throw off the cops. Randell concluded that Cook was a dirty cop and someone attempted to steal his treasure. The thief was probably Cook's partner in crime. It was genius.

Then a patrolman approached Randell and whispered to him that Richard Cook was found dead in his hospital bed. They were told death was due to a stroke – natural causes.

Randell immediately called the hospital and spoke to the nurse in charge and told her that no one was to touch anything at the scene in the ward where Cook died or touch the body until he got there.

"I don't know about that. That's not our procedure." replied the RN.

"I don't care about your procedure. Just do as I say."

Randell drove directly to the hospital. He considered it was possible that Cook had been murdered. The thief and the murderer were one and the same person. That person pulled the plug on Det. Cook then left the hospital and came to Cook's house and intended to rob the deceased cop of his ill-gotten gains that were hidden in a pocket in the ceiling of his house. The chink in the theory was why the thief left the lens cap and the cash unless the robber had been interrupted by the police. What Randell did not know was that Clem wanted the police to find the cash. Clem wanted Cook's mother to inherit the money. The cash would be part of Cook's estate and would be inherited by his mother in Daytona. Clem had missed the camera lens cap and left it in the pillow case in error. Clem was not perfect. He tended to bluff and bully his way through life.

***

Randell drove to the main entrance of Bayfront Hospital and walked in the front door. He always felt a little funny walking in the front door of Bayfront. It was not until the 1960s that Negros were admitted for treatment at the hospital. There was a Negro hospital called Mercy Hospital on 22nd Street South where the Negro community was provided medical care. Both of Randell's sons were born at Mercy Hospital. His mother died there 26 years ago. Sepsis, horrible death, slow diagnosis and diluted penicillin caused the death, but no one made a complaint or brought a lawsuit due to the fact the malpractice attorneys in the city were all white men who did not represent Negroes. Just the facts.

Randell went to the front desk and showed identification. He was escorted to the long term care ward.

The RN spoke to him and explained that it appeared the ventilator machine had malfunctioned.

"What about the duty nurse?" asked Randell, "why didn't she do anything?"

"She was in the bathroom."

"How long was she gone from the ward?"

"I don't know."

"Did someone relieve her when she went to the restroom?"

"There is only one person on duty in this ward at night."

"Let me speak to the duty nurse."

The RN called the intern who brought the duty nurse – an LPN – to Randell. The intern refused to let the LPN speak to the detective unless the attorney for the hospital was present.

"When will the attorney be available?"

"In two weeks."

Randell was able to obtain the LPN's name and address together with the names and addresses of the intern and the RN. The LPN was a young white woman. Randell smiled and thanked them. The intern stayed with the detective through the investigation. However all that was left to investigate was the empty bed and the ventilator. The staff had ignored the detectives request to keep the body in place. Randell took photographs and noted the plug for the machine was in the wall. The intern explained that there was a backup generator for the entire hospital to provide electric power if there was an outage. However there had been no report of a power outage. The intern reiterated his belief that the machine malfunctioned and the machine failed to beep when it quit working.

"Did the warning light work?" asked Randell as he pointed to the yellow light on the machine.

"I don't know", said the intern, lying to the detective. He refused to look Randell in the eye. The intern's eyes were blinking rapidly.

Randell did not believe the intern.

Randell took photos of the plug in the wall and then out of the wall. He pulled the plug out by the cord. He put the plug in a bag and taped the bag shut and initialed the tape and took another photo of the bag containing the plug.

Randell explained to the RN and intern that he was sending a print technician to dust the plug. The plug in the bag was left on the floor. The plug was not to be touched. If the plug was tampered with he would arrest the person who tampered with the plug. The charge would be destruction of evidence. He explained there may be fingerprints on the plug. He also explained that he was calling the Medical Examiner and the ME would take Cook's body into his custody. Further, the ventilator machine was evidence in a murder investigation and a subpoena would be issued by the State Attorney that day and the ventilator would be confiscated. Finally, the intern, the RN and the LPN would be subpoenaed so that John Hale, the State Attorney, could take their statements under oath, as they were considered witnesses to a suspected homicide.

Randell left them each one of his cards. He walked to his car and called the ME and the State Attorney's office.

The medical examiner's office sent an ambulance to retrieve Cook's corpse. When Randell got the State Attorney's office on the line he asked for Mr. Hale. Randell was immediately put through to him. Hale felt Randell was an excellent and talented detective and if Randell called, it was important.

Randell explained the reluctance and flippancy with which the medical workers had treated the matter of the investigation of Det. Cook's death. Nothing aggravated Hale as much as a reluctant witness and he ordered his chief assistant to drop what he was doing and issue subpoenas to the witnesses and to set the time for the statements ASAP.

***

As Clem pulled away from the curb where he had parked just down the block from Richard Cook's house, he could see the patrol cars and one unmarked police car converge on the house. It was good he parked a block down the street from Cook's house. He would have been trapped if he parked in front of Cook's house. A late arriving marked car came down the street slowly and took a look at Clem. He was sitting in his Chevy Bel-Air watching the action down the street. Clem stared back and waved to the officer. The officer turned his head to the street and Clem pulled out.

If Sarah had ratted him out, the cop would have stopped Clem because Sarah would have told the police he had a beard and two inches of hair on his head. She had called him Mr. Fuzzy. The cop would have known what Clem looked like.

So he was right to leave Sarah alone for now. She still might be some good to him later in the game. He decided not to go to Tampa to kill Derek Kline like Sarah and he discussed. To be safe he decided to head back to Naples and stay away from Tampa for a while.

***

Traffic from St. Petersburg to Naples was a nightmare. One of the two twin bridges from Pinellas County to Manatee County over the channel of the Gulf of Mexico into Tampa Bay had been destroyed when a freighter collided with the center of the west span during a storm many months back. As a result all of the traffic was re-routed to the single span and the span was a single lane in each direction. Traffic was held to 25 mph. The only alternative route was to drive northeast to Tampa to pick up one of the southbound highways, but it would add two hours to the trip and Clem was tired from his busy night.

The drive to Naples was a slog. There were a million traffic lights on US Highway 301 as he drove south. It felt like Clem caught every red light all the way back south.

***

Seven hours after Clem left Cook's house he pulled into the driveway of the floozy's garage apartment. Clem racked his brain trying to think of her name. He went up the stairs and knocked. He had a bottle. He thought she drank Jim Beam, but damn if he could remember her name. She came to the door in a light flimsy robe. A pattern of parrots was printed on the cloth that fit loosely over the floozy's breasts and flowed onto the floor. There was a smile on her face. "I remember you," she said as he lifted the bottle to within four inches of her face.

"Jim Beam. That's my drink," she said as she reached over and twisted the top button on his shirt, attempting to remove it. "You know you were a bad boy leaving me like that so early in the morning. I was uncomfortable all day."

"Yeah, sorry," said Clem. "I had to be at work early that day. We were going to pour concrete."

"It's a blow to a girl's ego, you leaving like that. But if you had to work, you know, I could understand that."

She knew he was lying. He had left on Sunday morning. They don't pour concrete on Sunday. At least she didn't think they did that on Sunday. But maybe they did. The floozy retrieved two glasses. "I forgot your name." She poured two drinks, neat.

"They call me Mr. Fuzzy," said Clem.

"You are kidding? Mr. Fuzzy, they call you that?" She did not know whether to believe him so she stared at Clem and smiled a pleasant smile with her full red lips.

"Yes, and that's what you will call me if you want to have some fun."

"Well you will have to prove your worth. We'll see what we'll call you after we have some fun."

She snuggled up close. Clem kissed her. She was a wet kisser, dripping wet. Clem pulled away and looked in her eyes. "You will have to do me a favor after we're done."

"You mean besides calling you Mr. Fuzzy?"

"Yes, something besides that."

"Does it involve murder?" she asked.

"Nothing that serious."

"Well, we'll do whatever you want if we have fun," she said.

"Agreed," said Clem.

Chapter 24

Det. George Randell returned to the police station to the security of his desk. There was a lot of noise in the squad room. The voices were normal and reassuring. When he was first promoted he had faced the stares on all the white faces of the men sitting at their desks. Hatred. That's what he saw ... hatred. He was reassured by the chief that the white detectives wouldn't kill Randell while he was in the office. There were too many wit-nesses. The noise meant people and people meant witnesses.

George Randell grew up with his mother and father in The Gas Plant. This was a 65 acre community where the majority of the St. Petersburg Negroes lived. The area was named The Gas Plant because there was a huge gas retention tank and an underground piping system that provided gas for the city. The Gas Plant had the hint of a smell like rotten eggs or sulfur.

The Negro community in the Gas Plant was serviced by separate but equal facilities. Campbell Park had a large public swimming pool for Negroes ("Coloreds Only," said the sign). The schools that serviced the area were Sixteenth Street, Campbell Park and Gibbs High School. Randell's dad said you could grow up in The Gas Plant and never meet a white person.

Randell's dad was a garbage man and he was a leader of the garbage strike. The men wanted to form a union and collectively bargain for their employment rights. Since the garbage men were employees of the city the men had no right to form a union or appoint anyone to bargain on their behalf. This rule was contained in a special act passed by the legislature of the State of Florida. It was the law. Since the city did not have anyone to bargain with, the city set the men's salaries. Period. The men got what was offered or they could walk. "Just quit if you don't like it ... God damn it," said the Mayor's negotiator.

Some years before the walkout, Randell took his Dad's advice and he joined the US Army. He was trained to be an MP (military police). Although there was supposedly no discrimination in the Army from WWII on, there were very few jobs a colored soldier could learn with transferable skills to civilian life. You could, for example, learn to cook, be a boot black/orderly for an officer, or an MP. Otherwise you would learn to kill people because you were in the infantry.

Randell's mother was a teacher at Campbell Park Elementary. She was a religious woman. She made her son promise not to kill. The best Randell could do was become an MP and then when he finished his tour he could apply to be a policeman for the city.

In the 1950's Negroes were starting to rebel collectively. They would march and protest. The City fathers felt they needed a compliment of Negro police officers to quell unrest. The Army had trained the Negro MPs to roust drunken Negro soldiers. They were also trained in putting down the Negro troops who, in the 1950's, were upset that since the Civil War they were not treated fairly. They had the lowest per capita promotion rate in the service.

Randell got good marks for calming down "uppity Negroes". He left the Army when his dad died. He returned home and was hired by the City Police.

Randell didn't have to be trained to know what his job would be for the city. Randell had done the same in the military, but there was a difference. The Negro soldiers were trained to kill and so was Randell. Quelling a riot on base was dangerous business. In St. Petersburg, the locals were untrained and at Randell's mercy. Randell knew how to handle himself physically and most of the locals did not, so he was feared. Members of Randell's race thought he would give them a break if they got in trouble with the law. Randell was in a position to help. He could let a crime slide.

But Randell was very "by the book". He didn't give anyone a break. He prosecuted every suspect to the maximum. As a result Randell was hated by the members of his race. But he did not care.

Randell was not even cowed by his fellow white officers. For example, one time when things got tense in the squad room, Randell put on a face mask of a white man (President Nixon). This broke the tension and most of the officers in the room laughed. By wearing the mask, Randell was saying he was not a threat to the white cops. He would watch their backs. He was discriminated against just the same as the white cops in the room. The general populace did not like the police because they were afraid of the police. Cops were a clique. Except in George Randell's case, the cops lived together, drank together, traded wives with each other and attended each other's funerals. So eventually Randell's fellow officers saw him as just another cop who hated his job. The only people who understood cops in general were other cops or their wives, that is, if they were able to keep a wife.

After 15+ years of service as a patrolman, Randell threatened the chief that he would quit and make a stink if he was not promoted. The chief blinked and promoted him to detective. He handled homicides on "the South side." Black on black crime. Then he was allowed to handle some big cases in other parts of the city's poor white areas, such as the neighborhood where Clem, Big John and Alphonse Alesse lived. So when Det. Cook suffered his stroke, Randell was assigned Cook's cases.

***

At his desk Randell had assembled all the case files that Det. Cook had been working for the last six months. It seemed like Cook was primarily doing liaison work between the police and the Mayor's office and the night clubs out in the industrial park. Most of the activity involved The Oar House. It was the most successful topless club in the city. It had roots and a corporate identity and it was one of a string of clubs throughout the state. It also had lawyers who fought the City Attorney on even the smallest matters. Some City Council meetings seemed to be almost totally occupied with The Oar House. There was nothing else on the council's agenda besides the Pledge of Allegiance and consideration of the topless ordinance.

So, the fact Cook was working with the clubs was a good thing. Establishing lines of communication was a good thing. The club and its topless competitors in the industrial park generated most of the crime in the City. Men were employed in crime. Women, not so much. Some criminals worked as sole proprietors and some were organized with a partner or in a group. Almost all of the criminals boozed and took drugs and they liked to carouse, and no better place to find a male criminal than a topless joint.

Cook had been able to obtain agreements with the club to clean up the "B girl" activity, where the waitresses pushed drinks on the customers. And, the "no touch rule" outside the private dance rooms had pleased City Council and the Mayor. The progress on those issues were recorded in reports to the chief. Cook also was able to gain intelligence on drug dealers and prostitutes and high stakes gambling that Cook turned over to Vice and Narcotics Division.

Cook's file began to fill up with commendations and he was nominated for policeman of the year. This was unusual because normally the recipient of the award was an officer who performed an act of bravery.

Then, three months past, Lori Shaffer was assaulted. Det. Cook was assigned Lori's case. He had asked for the assignment. The chief had approved the assignment, even though there were many reasons that opposed the appointment. The most important reason was that Cook knew Lori through Clem, the manager of The Oar House. She was Clem's girlfriend. Second, Cook was not a homicide detective and that was the training a detective would need for Lori's assault case.

Randell could not ignore the block of cash wrapped in brown paper that he discovered in the pocket in the ceiling at Cook's house. And the pillowcase with the lens cap. What's up with that, he thought. Was the lens cap evidence in a case? No telling he thought. Someone needs to start over on these cases, particularly the assault and the death of Anthony Stewart, thought Randell.

But first, Randell went to lunch.

While he was out, the Forensics' Unit delivered their report on the burglary at Det. Cook's house and the evidence from the hospital. The technicians lifted partial prints from the electric plug on the ventilator machine at the hospital and from the front door of Cook's house and his bathroom. There were enough points of similarity in the partial prints to make a match of one of the partial prints on the plug from the ventilator that serviced Cook at the hospital with two partial prints from the sink of Cook's bathroom at his house in the Kendall subdivision.

There were fibers and hair samples in the bathroom that the technicians collected but they were unable to make a match. There was a photograph of the shoe/boot print on the wallboard from the ceiling in Cook's bedroom. The heel print from the print of the shoe was identified as a Cat's Paw brand replacement heel. The report noted that the piece of drywall which contained the size 14 shoeprint was in the evidence room. There was a post-script that the technician had also submitted the three finger-prints to the sheriff's office, the state, and the FBI for an iden-tification match, to see if one could be found.

The report also contained the report of the Medical Examiner from the autopsy of Anthony Stewart. Time of death was at approximately 3:30 am. Cause of death was: "severe blunt trauma, head wound, caused by gunshot, probable homicide".

***

Randell returned from lunch. He read the forensics' report closely, memorizing it. He had also requested the forensics' report from the investigation into the death of Anthony Stewart. He inspected the photographs of the van. The door in the rear had been opened by a locksmith. There were no usable prints found. There was the photo of a body of an elderly man lying on his back inside on the floor of the van. There was a photograph of the deceased's head which showed a cruel wound caused by a single gunshot that entered at the line of the eyebrow at the bridge of the nose and exited through the top of the skull. There was a hole in the roof of the van which was believed to have been caused by the single bullet that killed Mr. Stewart. According to forensics the slug had not been found.

Photographs from the outside of the van showed that it was parked on the side of the street under a live oak tree. Otherwise there were no other photographs or maps to identify the location or particulars of the crime scene.

Randell asked for a patrolman to meet him at the crime scene with a ladder. Randell guessed the ladder would need to reach a height of 20 feet.

***

Once they reached the scene of the Anthony Stewart homicide, Randell instructed the patrolman to remove the extension ladder from the roof of the patrol car. He pointed to the spot where he wanted the ladder to be placed on the limb of the tree. The limb extended over the parking spot where Anthony's van was parked when he was murdered. Randell climbed up two steps on the ladder and the ladder began to slide on the bark of the tree limb.

The patrolman asked if he could help.

"What are you looking for?" asked the patrolman.

"A slug in the bottom of that tree limb," said Randell as he pointed to a thick lower limb of the live oak tree.

The patrolman, a 23-year-old Viet Nam War Veteran named Jim Faircloth, quickly went up the ladder. Faircloth had shoulder length hair and was always being razzed about his hair. Darlene Street had represented him when the City tried to fire him over the length of his hair. Darlene won, of course.

"Don't do anything until I have a chance to take a photo," said Randell.

"Okay." The policeman waited. Randell got his camera. He took a shot, then used the lens like a telescope to inspect the underside of the limb. He had climbed up two steps on the ladder. Faircloth steadied the ladder.

"You are going to need to move the ladder a bit."

Randell got down. The patrolman moved the ladder and looked under the limb as he climbed up. He could see a piece of bark was missing and he looked carefully and saw the back end of the bullet slug. Randell made him stop and then he handed the camera up the ladder and had his assistant take photographs at his direction. The piece of bark had been recently dislodged. Finally he had the patrolman take his pocket knife and cut the bark and wood from around the slug until the slug fell out and to the ground.

Randell and the patrolman inspected the slug. It was deformed from its flight through brain and bone and the thin metal roof of the van into the bark of the tree limb.

"Looks like a .38 caliber. Those are issued to us for our service revolvers," said the Patrolman. "What do you think, Detective Randell?"

"I think you're right. Put it in a plastic sleeve and take it to forensics with this film for developing." They had used all 24 frames of film on the roll.

Randell helped the patrolman with the ladder and he went over to the house closest to where the van would have been parked.

Randell noted it was 1:15 p.m. on his watch. He knocked on the door.

Sarah Rogers answered. Randell introduced himself. He asked her name and she was pleasant and provided the information he asked. She was a renter. She said that she did not live at the house on the night of the murder, which was a Thursday, 27 days ago. She said she was late for work. He gave her a business card and she promised to call him in the morning. She went back inside, closed the door, and went out through the back. The door slammed and she got in her blue Maverick and drove away.

Randell watched her leave. Randell didn't remember if any statements had been taken of the neighbors to see what they knew or heard that was unusual the night of the homicide. That needed to be done. The only person interviewed by the police the night of the murder was a young man, 27 years old, a heroin addict who ultimately became the prime suspect. He was questioned and released the night of the crime. (Lack of prima facia evidence.) Then later, Cook felt the addict was the culprit and there was a desperate search for him. He was found in Atlanta. He had been picked up and he was on his way back to St. Petersburg accompanied by two police officers, compliments of the city. It looked like all manner of investigation had ceased once Det. Cook decided the addict was the killer. Randell couldn't see how the suspect was the killer from the evidence in the file. Randell would have a chance to see how culpable the young man was. He was scheduled to interview him at midnight that night at the police station.

Randell called in to the office and said he was going to the forensics' unit and it would take an hour to review the evidence from the Stewart case with the technicians. He could be reached in forensics. He wanted to find out what the technician could tell him about the slug they found in the tree. Also, was the size of the hole in the roof of the van consistent with the size of the bullet? It could be the slug was not connected to the case at all, thought Randell. Could be, it was just a random shot by a person celebrating a holiday who squeezed off a round in the moment? When he spoke to the weapons expert in forensics, the expert said the damage to the bark looked fresh, though it would be a question for the jury. It would be interesting if the slug is from a .38 caliber police special, he thought. The slug was a .38 Caliber according to the expert and it was consistent with the ammunition issued to the officers by the department.

***

Randell placed a call to Anthony Stewart's employer, attorney Thomas Night. He had a few questions. Attorney Night returned the call promptly. Tom had been upset with the investigation of his friend's death by Det. Cook.

Randell introduced himself as the new investigator; that he had taken over since Cook had had his stroke. Randell also told Tom that Cook had died that morning.

"Sorry about that," said Tom.

"I needed to know, was Anthony working the night he was shot?"

"Yes."

"Who was he working for?"

"Me. He was on assignment to surveil a house on the street where he was killed."

"Who was he looking for?"

"Lori Schaeffer. She is the victim and a witness in an assault case. I represent the defendant involved in that case,"

"According to County Records, the house is owned by The Oar House," said Randell. "Who actually lived in the house the night Anthony was killed?"

"To the best of my knowledge, Lori and her boyfriend, Clemenso Bondi, lived in the house."

"Is Clemenso Bondi also known as Clem?" asked Randell.

"Yes."

"Does he manage The Oar House?"

"He did. He and Lori have not been seen since Lori was due in court for a preliminary hearing. She was a no show."

"That's all I need," said Randell. "Thank you for now."

"Have you found out anything about Anthony's death?" asked Tom.

"I'm getting there."

Randell hung up and set a meeting with State Attorney Hale for the next morning at 8 am. Randell hoped he would be through with the interrogation of the drug addict and he could give Mr. Hale an update. Hale had ordered a quick, but thorough, review of the case in light of Det. Cook's demise.

***

Randell had dinner in his car. He was at a Steak Burger restaurant. He liked the ambiance. The waitresses had short skirts and tight blouses and they delivered orders on roller skates. Randell enjoyed the reaction he got from whites when he ogled white chicks.

Randell ordered a burger and fries and a large sugary drink. While he waited, he flipped through his note pad and added to the notes, and changed or emphasized certain facts.

This is one screwed up investigation, he thought. It looked to Randell like Cook was the dumbest cop on the beat, or he was intentionally trying to throw everyone off track. "It's concerting," he said out loud to himself. "Or is it the word concerning?" he asked.

The burger was good though. He was going to have to let out his trousers if he kept eating at the Steak Burger. But he got no sleep, worked 12 hour days, and needed fuel. Animal fat was fuel.

***

Randell drove to the waterfront and aired out his brain from the sugar rush and the rise in his blood pressure. It was a beautiful evening, late autumn. We finally broke the back of summer, he thought.

Randell took a walk. His wife was on him about his weight and his kids got after him, too. He walked out to the pier and back to the car. He knew if he sat there for a few minutes he would fall asleep, so he drove to the police station.

The two patrolmen who went to Atlanta were back with their prisoner. Randell reviewed the paperwork. The prisoner's name was John Curry a/k/a "Big John". He was 27 years old and lived with his mother in a house in the neighborhood where the murder occurred. He had scars on his body from numerous surgeries. He was disabled and did not work. He had become addicted to drugs as a result of the surgeries to treat his injuries from a work related accident. A garbage truck ran over his legs. He was hooked on Vicodin, and when he couldn't get the pills he used heroin. He had been unsuccessfully treated for addiction. He had been on methadone to get off the heroin. Randell was surprised the suspect had no prior criminal record ... no arrests or convictions.

The paperwork also said Big John admitted the murder of Anthony Stewart to the team of police who drove him back from Atlanta.

That was news to Randell.

Randell searched for the men who transported John Curry back from Atlanta. He found them in the cafeteria. They were surrounded by other cops and they were all laughing. When Randell came to the table the cops dispersed and Randell sat down.

"Did you get a confession from Mr. Curry?" Randell asked.

"Yes, on the way back he confessed. He said he shot an old man in a van."

"Did he say why?"

"Said he was hurting for drugs and he shot the man to get drugs."

"Did he take anything from the man?"

"He said he took some cameras."

"Did he say what type weapon he used?"

"He said it was a small caliber weapon – a .22 caliber. He said the gun is at his house in his room. We asked the State Attorney to get a warrant so we can search for it."

"Good work," said Randell. He scratched his head. Maybe Richard Cook wasn't so dumb after all. But Randall knew the ME contradicted the addict. Cook was shot with a .38 caliber weapon, not a .22.

***

Randell walked upstairs to the interrogation room. He would have to wait for his interview. The room was still in use. The room contained a heavy metal table and three matching heavy chairs.

The furniture was bolted to the floor. There was a one way mirror built into the wall of the room. There was an officer watching the show from behind the mirror. The officer could hear the conversation in the room as he watched the interrogation. It was better than TV.

Randell joined and watched through the one way glass and listened as the officers in the room finished up sweating a confession out of a burglar. The prisoner hated lawyers and broke into his attorneys' offices and stole their stamps and small change. Lawyers never kept large sums of cash in their office. To show his dislike for the profession the suspect urinated on the floor before he left. The cops thought it was funny. They felt a kinship with the burglar. Many cops wanted to pee on a lawyer's rug at some point in their career.

The officer who was witnessing the interrogation of the burglar was red faced from laughter. After the burglar finished spilling his guts, the officer left to get Mr. Curry from his cell. When he returned he held the forearm of a skinny man who walked with a distinct limp. This is "Big John?" thought Randell.

"He has braces for his legs and forearm crutches," said the officer. "I didn't think you would need him to have them for the interview. Does he need his braces and crutches?"

"No."

***

Randell got Curry situated and as comfortable as he could be in the hard chair.

"I'm good," said Curry. "The nurse gave me my meds."

"What are you taking?"

"Vicodin."

Randell was meticulous in taking a statement. He used a form with a checklist (a fill in the blanks form), that he completed with every statement he took of a suspect. Randell had suggested to the chief that they record the statements on tape so there was no question that the suspect who made an incriminating statement was not coerced. The Police Chief refused to allow the practice.

Enough said about cops coercing confessions.

"Mr. Curry, this is a process," said Randell. "I am going to ask you a series of factual questions. Your name, et cetera, and then we will get to the charges. Do you understand you are charged with murder in the first degree?"

"Yes."

"So let us begin," said Randell and he went through all the fact questions and he filled in the blanks with the responses given by the suspect. The first set of questions included a review of Curry's Miranda warnings.

Then they got to the crime. This would be a narrative that would be hand printed by Randell then read by Curry and corrected if there were mistakes, and then signed and acknowledged by the prisoner.

The long and the short of the written statement was that Big John denied he killed Anthony Stewart.

"I was out walking. I can't sleep at night because of the pain. I was in my braces and using my crutches. I had a Vicodin an hour before I went out. I wasn't high, but the pain was tolerable. I walked to the Quick Mart for smokes. It was closed. I was heading home and an officer in a car stopped me. I told him what I told you today. I did not kill anyone. The officer searched me. He asked if I had a gun. I told him I had a .22 caliber pistol at home in my room for protection. I did not have the gun with me. The officer took my name and address and let me go."

"When did you go to Atlanta?"

"The day after I was stopped by the officer."

"Why did you go to Atlanta?"

"I always wanted to see the city."

"When did you last take a trip out of town?"

"Back before the accident when I was hurt. Quite a few years ago."

"Who do you know in Atlanta?"

"No one, really."

"Where were you going to stay?"

"I had a few bucks. I stayed at the YMCA."

"Mr. Curry, did you tell the officers who drove you back to St. Petersburg that you killed an old man who was in a van by shooting him in the head with your gun?"

"Yes, I said that."

"But you now say that is not true?"

"That is correct. It is not true."

"Why did you tell them that?"

"I told them I was hurting and they said they would get me pain meds when we got to the police station if I talked to them about the crime."

"How did you know what to tell them?"

"They told me what happened to the old man. I also read about it in the newspaper. I realized that was why the police officer stopped me the night of the shooting. That's really why I went to Atlanta. I was afraid."

"Did the officers talk to the nurse about giving you your medication?"

"Yes, they talked to the nurse and she gave me the Vicodin."

"One more question," said Randell. "What is your shoe size?"

"My shoe size is 10-D."

"You ever wear a size 14?"

"No, I'd swim in a shoe that big."

Randell and Curry read what was written and then he was asked to initial each page and to sign the statement if it was correct.

"Big John" signed the statement.

Chapter 25

Mr. Fuzzy and the Floozy were finished. Mr. Fuzzy had successfully completed a sexual cycle. He was aroused. He made penetration of his penis in the Floozy's vagina and he reached a climax and ejaculated. Before this night, Mr. Fuzzy had not accomplished sexual fulfillment in years. He had put on a good show with Lori on his arm and he talked a good game. He was able to accomplish an erection but not sustain the erection until he had "shot his wad" as he liked to say. Acquaintances were convinced that he had to be a sexually satisfied man. But looks were deceiving. Until this night, he could not reach a climax and ejaculate.

The Floozy was regularly bedded but she too was unfulfilled. She was only satisfied in her sleep. The man of her dreams was like a gladiator. He was a man of the same constitution as Mr. Fuzzy. He didn't say much. He took quick action when it was needed and he was strong like a big hairy animal. She desired to be ravaged like a beauty by a beast.

Mr. Fuzzy made the Floozy's heart flutter. She was confused after the first round of the passionate encounter as to whether she wanted him inside her or if she just wanted him to touch her. She was like the hungry donkey placed between two bales of hay who starved because she couldn't make up her mind which of the bales she should eat from.

Mr. Fuzzy, though, did not let her make a choice. He had been so frustrated for years, and particularly since Lori was cut, that when he was able to complete one act and reach a climax with the Floozy he could not stop. He attacked, drowning sexually.

The Floozy had found her Gladiator. They slept and woke and repeated the exercise a number of times and then slept all night without eating all day. They fed on each other.

The Floozy was asleep again.

Mr. Fuzzy took a moment to look at the woman in his arms. Rather than a floozy, Mr. Fuzzy could see the woman was beautiful. Her hair was clean and shiny and long and red. She had very light freckles on her cheeks and nose and wonderfully shaped ears. High cheeks. Her neck and body were slender. She had ample hips and breasts. Her fingers and toes were long and slender and her nails well-manicured. He guessed she was 25 years old.

The only defect he could find from his careful inspection was that she had a bad tooth, black to the root that he saw in the side of her mouth as she smiled when he stroked her soft belly with his rough hands as she slept.

***

"I need your help." Mr. Fuzzy had promised to ask a favor.

"Anything," she said as she rubbed her eyes.

"I need you to go in a bar up in Tampa and apply for a job."

"I may do that for you, but I need to know your real name."

"You tell me your name first," insisted Mr. Fuzzy.

"Regina Cameron, my nick-name is 'Gene'," she said. "And what is your name?"

"Clemenso M. Bondi."

"That's not so bad. Do you have a middle name?" she asked.

"Me."

"Do you have a middle name?" she repeated,

"Yes. It's Me." he said.

"What is 'Me'?"

"My middle name."

"Who gave you the name 'Me'?"

"I did."

"Is it a legal name?"

"Yes, the court gave me a name change, Clem insisted. "There was a court order and everything. I had to hire a lawyer, even."

"Why did you do that?"

"I had a girlfriend who complained that I just thought of myself, that I was selfish. I told her I would make it official and change my middle name to 'Me'."

"I don't get it," said Regina.

"You know 'Me. Me. Me. Me. Me,' " he paused, "I only think of myself."

Regina Cameron looked at Clemenso Me Bondi and she laughed and laughed.

"What?" said Clem. "What, what?"

***

The pair finally succeeded in arising from bed to shower and dress, and then went down the street to an all-night diner. They ordered ham and eggs, hash brown potatoes, toast and guava jam in little packets manufactured by Plantation #7.

"Do you have any money?" asked Gene.

"I have a couple thousand," Clem bragged. "They also owe me money at work. We will need to go by and pick up my check on the way out of town."

"Why do we have to leave? Are you in trouble?"

"I don't know yet. But I have to do something that could get me in trouble unless I do it the right way."

"If you need some help, I will help you."

"What if it involves murder?" asked Clem as he chewed his bacon.

"That's ok as long as we are working together." She was kidding about participating in a murder, of course.

"Working together. You mean, like a marriage?" asked Clem.

"Conspiracy is probably as close as I will get to marriage."

"Me too," said Clem.

"Would you call me Gene?"

"Yes I will, if you will call me Clem."

***

Clem and Gene walked back along the water from the diner toward her garage apartment. There was a bench tucked back in the bushes along the trail and they sat and watched a fingernail moon that rose in the sky as the sea fog moved in to hover above the Intracoastal Waterway. Clem and Gene sat on the bench, side by side, hand in hand. It was cool. Gene had goosebumps when Clem touched her skin. The fog covered them like cotton batting. They were invisible.

Clem lifted Gene's right leg and laid it on top of his left leg. Gene shuddered as Clem rubbed Gene's bare inner thigh and then, as he moved his right hand over her mons venires and began to rub the soft mound, Gene began to pant and her underwear became moist. Gene rolled her leg back, stood in front of Clem and unzipped and lowered Clem's pants.

Gene dropped her panties onto the ground, climbed on the bench and straddled his thighs with her feet on the seat of the bench. Clem kissed her sweet dewy stomach. Gene squatted and tucked her knees under Clem's arms and her face hung over his right shoulder with her arms around his neck. Clem assisted her as she mounted him. She rode him slowly until they were both flush and satisfied.

Afterward, they sat on the bench for an hour in the fog, murmuring, intoxicated, nude from the waist down. Finally, Clem stood and buckled his trousers and he pulled Gene to her feet. She dressed and they found their way back to her garage apartment.

Gene packed her trousseau in a suitcase and a small night case and two cardboard boxes. They were together now, united, and would leave Naples, Florida, together.

***

Gene was renting month to month and her rent was due so there was nothing lost by leaving her garage apartment. Before they could get everything moved to the car a big man, fat, lumbered up the stairs. There was a skinny man with him. "You owe me, Gene" the fat man yelled up the stairs.

Gene cowered. She didn't like confrontation. She returned to the apartment to Clem.

"What's the problem?" asked Clem.

"I borrowed some money from the man," said Gene. "He's my boss. The skinny guy is the cook at the diner where I work."

"Is he an idiot?"

"Yes, pretty much. He'll raise hell until he gets his money."

"You coming out?" said the man.

"Just a minute," she yelled and then turned to Clem, "I owe him fifty bucks. Lend it to me, please?" she asked.

"Here," Clem gave her the money. "Pay him."

Gene went outside and went down the steps and handed the fifty dollar bill to the fat man.

"You missed work yesterday. I should charge you for that."

Gene said nothing. The fat man and the skinny man went away. Gene went back in the room. She started crying.

"Thank you for giving me the money," said Gene. "I will pay you back."

"You were right to pay him. It was better than me beating him up. He brought the skinny guy along to run to a phone and call the police. I would have beaten him to a pulp if the skinny guy wasn't with him."

"You did right," said Gene. "You are a smart man."

***

They finished packing the car and drove to Riverview, Florida. It was off Highway 301 and about 25 miles from Tampa, which was to the west on US 92. The Man Trap Night Club was off Dale Mabry Highway in an industrial area near the "Sombrero", the nickname for Tampa Stadium, the home of the Tampa Bay Bucs, a football franchise. The nickname of the Bucs was the "Yucks". Clem had tried out for the team after he was let go by Chicago. He remembered thinking that he wasn't bad enough for them to hire him. The Buccaneers had lost 26 games straight when he tried out. He did get the job with the Sharks but then he was let go by the team because of the injury to his neck. Then he worked in Jacksonville and then was moved to St. Pete to manage The Oar House. He never was rooted in any community in his life.

Clem liked Riverview. It wasn't really a town; it had one traffic light – a blinking yellow light. The Alafia River ran through the town. The river was pleasant so long as the phosphate processor's slag heap did not spill slurry into the river. When there was a spill, the phosphate neutralized the natural acidity of the river and killed the fish. Then the fish stank and it was unpleasant. But no one was allowed to complain or the phosphate industry would be upset and threaten to maybe leave town and take all the minimum wage jobs with them. Basic economics.

Anyway, Clem and Gene were not concerned about the local environment or the quality of the river, so long as it didn't stink. At this time the river didn't stink, so they pulled into a fish camp and got a cabin that had a river view.

Clem lied and told the owner of the camp he had lost his fishing equipment. The owner said he was lucky, an old man had died and he had his equipment for sale cheap. They negotiated a bit and Clem got a tangle of rods and reels and line and pliers, et cetera, and a bucket for bait, altogether for $20.

Gene was happy. She kissed Clem on the cheek through his beard and insisted that they go fishing.

Clem smiled and thought, that will be ok. We can fish now and wait to start working on the problem that is Derek Kline in a couple days.

***

Clem and Gene spent the next day together. They tried to get to know each other but they each had so much baggage from their past that the conversations were short. Gene urged Clem to tell her about football. They talked about games he played and the people he played with who were accepted as heroes in the USA. Clem avoided the pain he suffered and the way the players were treated in the 1960s by the owners. The men were depreciable assets. If they became hurt and unable to play they were just another business write off. Though Clem had hurt his neck, he was lucky because he could still walk. He couldn't run or lift heavy weights like he could before his injury. But he probably was lucky he got out of the game when he did. He didn't have problems with knees like most players had after they quit. They had to booze or wipe out the pain with drugs to make it day to day. He also had not ended up with mush for brains, sitting on the front porch repeating conversations with an imaginary friend.

The pair had nothing else to do so they went fishing. Clem rented a boat and rowed to Beer Can Island, located in the middle of the Alafia River. They sat in the sand and waited for a nibble on the worm on the line (really, they were having no luck with the fish). They were getting a good suntan (really for her, with her sensitive skin, it was a burn).

Gene became impatient.

The island was a bit of sand beach on the shore and then woods, large oak trees and pines and Sabal palms. When she could stand the heat no longer, Gene retreated into the shade. It was late October and if you were out of the direct sun the air was cool, 70-like. Gene had brought a blanket and food, beer and sandwiches. If they weren't fishing the pair had nothing to do but talk, and after football they had little they wanted to discuss that they were proud of.

"So, what is this job you want me to apply for?" asked Gene.

"It's in a topless bar in Tampa called The Man Trap."

"I've never worked topless. I think I would be too embarrassed," she said.

"Can you dance?"

"Yes."

"If you have talent and can dance you can apply for a job as a teaser. You don't have to take off all of your clothes if you are a strip tease dancer. I think you would be hired for that job. You have a beautiful body. Your hair is so red; it's your 'hook'. It's what you can sell. You will need an act. We can work on that together and I can buy you some costumes. Peek-a-boo type stuff. We can find it at Goodwill. You need a lot of layers of sheer material. You let the man's imagination tell him what he sees. He sees sex and beauty but it's just material. You just have to move your body, just dance seductively. You did that as a teen in front of the mirror, didn't you?"

"Yes."

"Well, what I want you to do is apply for a job as a dancer. I don't want you to show your goods. I want you to dance, a strip tease without dancing nude. I want you to tell them you want to be a 'teaser'. They will know what you mean. We will practice a routine."

"Why am I doing this?"

"I want you to get a good look at the layout of the inside of the club. I intend to kill the manager, a man named Derek."

Gene looked at Clem. "Can I ask why?"

"He killed a girl. Her name was Lori."

"Who was she to you?"

"I loved her."

Gene just looked at Clem and she smiled. This man is crazy, thought Gene. She drank a swallow of beer. Her bad tooth ached. She pushed against her cheek putting pressure on the black bud of the tooth. "Could we go to the dentist? I need to get this tooth pulled. It's killing me."

"Sure," said Clem. He thought he saw something in her gaze, but it didn't really connect.

"I need to go back to shore," she said. Gene had enough sense to be in deathly fear of Clem.

After rowing back, they went to the dentist. He examined her mouth. The doctor offered to pull the tooth. There was no way to save it. After the procedure, she needed a stitch and she had to gargle with salt water. He told her to come back in three days to remove the stitch. She said she would, but lied. The thread would dissolve in time. He gave her some pain meds. They went home to bed. That night she took the drugs and she slept with strange erotic dreams that embarrassed her.

Next afternoon, Clem took Gene to a used clothing store. It was the Halloween season and they told the clerk they were going to a party. Clem wanted to dress up to be a bum and Gene wanted to be Salome and dance the dance of the seven veils. The attendant got into the fantasy and took time to help.

That evening, Clem bought some fish, spotted trout locally caught and fresh. They bought vegetables at a roadside stand. There was a gas stove in the cabin and they had pan fried fish and a salad and baked potato.

They got to bed early. Gene's face still hurt and Clem could see it was swollen. Gene was out of pain medicine. Clem said goodnight and rolled into his side of the bed. Gene lay awake next to him and tried to figure out the best way to escape from the mad man. The pain from the tooth extraction kept her awake most of the night.

Chapter 26

Detective George Randell had spent the night reviewing the investigation notes and records for the homicide of Anthony Stewart and the aggravated battery of Lori Schaeffer. He had previously read all of Detective Cook's files involving the negotiations regarding operations of The Oar House. He had also had the fingerprints of Det. Cook, Tommy Magyar, Alphonse Alesse and Big John Curry compared with the latent prints found at Cook's house and the electric plug from the ventilator used to keep Cook alive at the hospital. The prints found did not match the known prints. Forensics had prints for everyone but Clemenso Bondi, but none existed for him, according to Forensics.

Randell seemed to be the only officer who understood that the Anthony Stewart homicide was connected to the aggravated battery of Lori Schaeffer. The homicide was connected to Clemenso Bondi's home, and Lori Schaeffer lived there with Bondi. Randell believed the motive for the murder of Anthony Stewart was the fact that the investigator saw or photographed something that incriminated someone in the Bondi house.

Further, Detective Cook appeared to have been taking bribes. That was the only logical explanation for the fact that he had $26,025 in the pocket behind the drywall in the ceiling of his house. The other thing they found in Cook's home was a lens cap. Randell believed that cap was for a camera that was in Anthony's van. That meant that Cook had possession of the cameras and film that were taken from the van the night of the murder. If Cook had possession of the cameras and film that was strong evidence he was complicit in the murder of Anthony Stewart. In addition the .38 caliber slug removed from the tree limb was consistent with the slug that passed through Anthony Stewart's skull and the roof of the van. The .38 caliber slug was a match with the slug in the ammunition that was in Det. Cook's revolver, a Smith and Wesson "Police Special". Last, the latent fingerprints lifted by the police technicians from the bathroom at Cook's house had enough similarities with the latent print found on the plug to the ventilator to conclude the person who unplugged the ventilator causing the death of Richard Cook had also been the person who had burglarized Cook's home and taken the cameras and film.

The assumption that Randell made from this evidence was that Cook was a dirty cop. Cook was being paid off by The Oar House. Lori Schaeffer, an employee of The Oar House and the girlfriend of Clemenso Bondi, the manager of The Oar House, was assaulted because of her employment and/or her relationship with Clemenso, and they disappeared together the night of Anthony's murder because they were complicit in the murder of Anthony Stewart or they themselves were murdered.

Randell felt that if he could identify the owner of the latent prints discovered at Cook's home and on the plug of the ventilator he would identify Anthony Stewart's murderer. None of the fingerprints of Tommy Magyar, Alphonse Alesse or Big John Curry matched the prints from the bathroom or the electric plug. The men did not wear a size 14 shoe. This evidence showed these men were not involved in Anthony's death or Cook's death. In fact, there was so little tangible evidence connecting the three men to any of the crimes that Randell would have suggested the State Attorney not file any charge against these men, including the aggravated battery charge that was filed against Tommy and Alphonse or the murder charge for which Big John had been arrested.

Randell's best guess was that Lori Schaeffer was dead.

***

State Attorney John Hale walked into Det. Randell's office just as the detective completed typing his report. Hale said he was short of time and asked if he could read the report to save some time.

"Sure," said Randell. The detective sat watching Hale read the report.

Then Hale read the report again. Hale's face turned red. "So, you wouldn't charge any of these men?"

"No."

"But Lori Schaeffer identified Magyar and Alesse."

"When she gave her initial statement to the police, Lori Schaeffer said she was only attacked by one person," Randell argued. "Weeks later she identified a second person. The second person she identified is a law clerk who has no connection with the first person she identified, or any motive to commit the crime. Magyar has two independent witnesses who place him in Jacksonville giving a roofing estimate at the time of the assault. There is documentation to back up the alibi witness' testimony. The initials scratched into the young lady's breasts, the "D" and the "K" do not relate to either of the defendants. This was a very personal crime, one where the victim knows the assailant or knows why the crime was committed. Yet, other than making the identifications, which the evidence contradicts, the victim states she cannot remember what happened or the motive for the attack. Both of the men deny committing the crime."

"What about this 'Big John' Curry? Didn't he confess to killing Anthony Stewart?"

"Here is my report regarding the confession," said Randell, and he passed Hale the report of the statement Big John made to the transport officers and the report Randell made of the statement Big John gave to Randell.

Hale read through them. "These statements just contradict one another. Defendants recant their confessions all the time."

"I concede that point, however, the reason Big John gave for making his confession is plausible. The transport officers withheld his pain medication. The nurse confirmed that. The jury will be instructed to ignore a confession that is coerced. There is ample evidence this confession was coerced.

"You also need to understand why Big John was on medication. His legs were crushed in an industrial accident. He cannot function without the pain meds. He can barely walk. He uses forearm crutches and braces to help him walk. He did not have the strength in his legs to climb into the back of the van and remove the cameras and film. There is no evidence he ever had the cameras and film. The only piece of the equipment we found was a lens cap and that was found behind the drywall in Cook's house. Cook also had $26,025 in cash in his house. All of these cases are connected to the operations at The Oar House. They are not separate crimes. Big John is not connected to The Oar House. Neither are Magyar and Alesse."

"Who do you think is the key witness who would solve this case?"

"If he is alive and he will talk, the person I think will know all the answers is Clemenso Bondi."

"Then that is your assignment. Find Clemenso. And make your best effort to find Lori Schaeffer, dead or alive."

***

George Randell asked for an officer who would assist him in the search for Clemenso Bondi and Lori Schaeffer. He specifically asked for Officer Jim Faircloth. He was the officer who helped Randell retrieve the bullet from the oak tree. Faircloth was 23 years old. He was married and had two children. The other cops called him a hippy or a faggot because of his long hair. He was apolitical and did not belong to the police union. Randell did not belong to the union either, but that was because he was not invited. No one ever said he was not asked to join because he was a Negro. But no one said he wasn't invited to any organization, or that he could not live peacefully in certain parts of town, because he was a Negro. It was just understood.

Randell thought Faircloth saw him as a colleague. He did not see him as a member of a particular race. Randell felt that if Faircloth could put race behind him, the two could make good partners.

The first thing Randell wanted to do was a follow up interview with Sarah Rogers. Sarah had taken Randell's business card, but she had not called after he saw her at Clem's house. She had promised she would call and she seemed sincere, but there was no call.

Randell wanted Faircloth to follow him to Clem's house in an unmarked vehicle and park under the live oak tree on the side of the house and wait and follow Sarah and see where she went after Randell spoke to her. Faircloth was excited. This was his first undercover assignment. He wore blue jeans and a red checkered shirt and boots. Randell thought he was dressed too casually but that's the way they dressed, very casual. Not like Randell, who dressed in a white dress shirt with wool blend trousers, dress shoes and a jacket.

Randell explained to Faircloth the elements of the tail. "Stay back and if you lose her, you lose her. I don't want Sarah to think we are tailing her. She is the only connection we have to Clem and Lori. I don't want to spook her. If you lose her we can find her again here at the house and start over tomorrow."

Faircloth left the station 15 minutes before Randell. He was driving an undercover narcotic's vehicle, a non-descript dirty Ford Galaxy, some shade of dull blue. He parked under the tree and slouched down in his seat. It was 11:30 a.m. He looked like a worker taking a nap at lunch time. The weather was warm, in the 70s, and it seemed reasonable that there was a man parked in his car under the tree taking a snooze.

Randell gave Faircloth a little extra time. He started out a little later than he said. He drove down the alley behind Clem's house. There was a blue Maverick parked behind the garage. Randell had run Sarah's name with the DMV and they had reported that she owned a blue Ford Maverick. Randell pulled into the street, looked to his right and saw Faircloth's Galaxy parked under the tree. He made a right hand turn and passed the Galaxy and saw the top of Faircloth's head. Randell made another right turn and he was in front of Clem's house. He parked, then walked to the door and knocked. Then knocked again. Then knocked again.

Randell backed away from the door and walked to the left side of the house, passing the large living room window in the front of the house. If Sarah was in the living room he wanted to make sure she got a good look at him. Randell figured that if she saw him, panicked, and left, she might tell them more by driving to another location than if she talked to him. They would have the name of more potential witnesses once she got to her destination. He doubted she would be honest with him if he was able to find her and talk to her again. As Randell turned around and headed back toward the front door and passed the large living room window, he could see a tall woman in the living room through the sheer drapes. That's her he thought. Randell went to the door and left his card with his private number and he drove away. Randell knew the best chance they had to follow her was for him to go back to the station and wait for her to leave home and Faircloth could establish a tail.

***

Faircloth was able to communicate that about 15 minutes after Randell left his card on the door Sarah had left out the back door and got in her Ford Maverick and she appeared to be on her way to the Gateway area. Randell started the Galaxy and headed north on Fourth Street toward the Gateway area. The station was only eight blocks from Fourth Street, so Randell was able to drive to Fourth and head north and he could stay within two miles of Faircloth and they could communicate.

"It looks like she is headed north for Tampa. She is going the wrong direction if she was headed to work at The Oar House. That's west of Clem's house." A little later Faircloth reported he could see the blue Maverick turning onto Gandy Boulevard. "She's heading for the Gandy bridge."

"The sister topless club, the Man Trap, is in Tampa just off Dale Mabry near Tampa Stadium. If she's heading north after she crosses the bridge, that is probably where she is going. She will probably head north on West Shore Boulevard and then east on

Boy Scout." Again Randell warned Faircloth to stay back so she wouldn't know she was being followed. Randell tried to stay within range and he was pretty much successful. The closer the Maverick and the Galaxy got to the Man Trap the more confident Randell became that that was Sarah's destination.

Within the next half hour the three cars had proceeded across the bridge (East) then north on West Shore. Then east on Boy Scout to Dale Mabry and then south on North Street. At that point Randell lost the two vehicles.

Randell began to drive up and down the streets that ran parallel to Dale Mabry until he saw the blue Maverick. It was parked in front of a home at 1324 Arrow Street. There was a motorcycle in front of the house in the driveway. Randell was unable to see the tag number of the bike from the street. There was a cul-de-sac at the end of Arrow Street, two blocks from the house. Faircloth was parked on the curb in the turn around. There were trees and shrubs in the center of the cul-de-sac and there behind the bushes was Faircloth's Ford Galaxy. Randell pulled up next to the driver's window and said, "Were you able to get the tag number on the motorcycle?"

"Not yet. But I will get it."

"Do you think she made you?"

"I don't know. I stayed back like you said. She seemed to come here to this house on Arrow Street by the most direct route, so my guess is she didn't see me."

"Let's leave it like that. I need you to leave your car parked here and walk down the street to that house and get the license number of the motorcycle. Then we will head back to St. Petersburg."

It only took Faircloth a couple of minutes to walk down the street and get a good angle on the tag so he could read it, memorize it and walk back to his car.

***

Derek Kline was looking out the window. "Who is this idiot out there looking at my motorcycle?" he said to Sarah as he got up and went to the door. "Can I help you?" Derek said in his most sarcastic voice.

"Is this bike for sale?" said the man.

"Do you see a 'for sale' sign?"

"No."

"Then it's not for sale. Move along," said Derek to the man, who took another look and then walked down the street.

Derek made sure the man had left. He pulled up his underwear. He was 5'6" tall. He was fat, bald, smelly and obscene.

Sarah looked out the window. She was hoping the person looking at the bike was the man in the Ford Galaxy who had followed her from her house to Derek Kline's house. One hundred to one, the guy in the red checkered shirt driving the Galaxy is a cop, she thought. He's got to be Randell's partner, she thought. This was the best way to give Randell a clue without actually talking to the police. I've brought the police to the home of the man who cut Lori, thought Sarah. They should be able to figure it out from here.

Derek turned to Sarah after he shooed the man away from the bike and settled into the couch in the sunken living room. "So what do you think of the new couch?" asked Derek. "It's pretty sexy, don't you think?"

"I may have to try it out sometime," said Sarah. He could tell she was joking.

"You're just a tease," said Derek. "So, why are you here anyway? What's the emergency?"

"I had a visit from Clemenso the other night," said Sarah. "He intends to kill you, or so he said."

"He'll have to get in line," said Derek. "Half of Florida and all of Tampa wants me dead."

"Well," Sarah pointed her finger at Derek. "Write down somewhere that I warned you about Clem so your friends don't come after me when they find you rotting in an orange grove."

"Why would they suspect you, sweet, sweet Sarah?"

"Because, they know I hate you for cutting Lori. She was a good friend to me. If you wanted to send a message to Clem you should have confronted him man to man, not by hurting Lori." Sarah was pushing back hard.

"I didn't touch Lori," Derek spat back. "And it wasn't my decision that she be cut. You know the drill. You work for the same people I do."

"Pants on fire, you liar." Sarah talked like a kid in a school yard. "If it wasn't you it was one of your stooges."

"Says you. If that's all you have to say, it's time for you to go." Derek was laughing. Sarah had a cutting tool for a tongue, he thought. She's vicious, but I don't think she would actually hurt a fly.

"We need to get to work," said Sarah.

"You sure you don't want to take a roll on the couch before you go?'

Sarah rolled her eyes again and walked out the door. She looked up the street to the cul-de-sac. The Galaxy was gone. Doesn't look like I'll have any company on the trip back to St. Pete, she thought.

***

As soon as Faircloth and Randell returned to their desks at the station they called the Property Appraiser and DMV and asked for ownership records for the house on Arrow Street and the motorcycle. The owner of the house and the vehicle was The Man Trap, Inc.

Chapter 27

In the early 1970s the criminal procedures were relatively simple following an arrest in the State of Florida. There was a First Appearance Hearing where the Judge advised the defendant of the charge against him and inquired if he had a lawyer and reviewed the amount of the bond. This hearing occurred within 24 hours of the arrest. If the defendant was unable to post the bond set, his attorney could make a motion to reduce the bond later. If no charge had been filed by the State Attorney or the Grand Jury (respectively, an information or an indictment), the defendant had a right to a preliminary hearing to have a judge hear whether the State Attorney had enough evidence to hold the defendant.

The next proceeding, assuming an information has been filed or an indictment returned, was the Arraignment. At or before the Arraignment, the defendant who wanted to challenge the legality of the charge had to file a motion to dismiss the charge, attacking the sufficiency of the information or the indictment. (The question was: Did the charging document state sufficient, ultimate facts to state the charge filed?) Few motions to dismiss were filed and few of the motions filed were granted.

The next issue at the Arraignment was the plea. The defendant could plead Guilty, Not Guilty or No Contest (Nolo Contendere). If the defendant pleaded guilty or no contest there could be a negotiation with the State Attorney for the plea. The State and the defendant could have an agreement to the sentence to be imposed, or to a reduction of the charge to a lesser crime, such as a misdemeanor, and the defendant would be sentenced at the Arraignment and the case was resolved.

If the defendant pleaded Not Guilty the case was set for trial. When the Defendant pleaded Not Guilty he could file a written demand that the State Attorney provide discovery to the defendant. The "discovery" was contained in a document that listed all the witnesses the State Attorney knew through his investigation who could have any testimony relevant to the guilt or innocence of the defendant. The State Attorney also had to provide a list of tangible evidence that was relevant to the guilt or innocence of the defendant. Items of tangible evidence were things like fingerprints, documents, or photographs. The State Attorney also had to provide the substance of any inculpatory statement or confession the defendant made to the crime charged, and identify the person to whom the statement was made.

If the defendant made a demand for discovery, the defendant was also required to provide reciprocal discovery to the State Attorney which consisted of a list of the defendant's witnesses and any evidence the defendant had to prove any defense. If the defendant did not make a demand to the State, he did not have to reveal the names of his witnesses or evidence. Whether the defendant requested discovery or not was a tactical decision.

If a defendant was going to plead guilty or agree not to contest the charges he had to be present in the Courtroom so the Court could ask him questions to make sure he was competent and knew what he was doing. He was asked if he discussed the case with his attorney and if he was satisfied with the representation he received. Last, he was told what his sentence was going to be in return for his plea of guilty or no contest, and he was asked if he had been promised anything else. The judge then accepted the plea. If there was no problem with the plea, the sentence was imposed.

If the defendant intended to plead not guilty, he could enter his plea in writing and make a demand for discovery at the same time in writing, and then he did not have to appear in Court at the Arraignment.

Tom Night and James DeMarco wanted to have their clients present in court to enter their pleas verbally. They wanted their clients to say the words "Not Guilty" on the record.

Tommy Magyar and Alphonse Alesse were called before the Court last at the arraignment hearing. They had been charged together in the information that had been filed by the State Attorney. Tom and James did not want to waive their client's right to a separate trial and they requested the court defer the time for a motion for a separate trial to be filed until after discovery was completed. The Court granted the request.

"Do your clients intend to make a demand for discovery?" asked the Court.

"Yes," they replied.

"Mr. Hale, since the defendants have made a demand for discovery, you will have to produce the complaining witness who is listed in the Information as Lori Schaeffer. The preliminary hearings in this case were set before me on three occasions and the alleged victim did not show for any of the hearings. Isn't that correct?"

"Yes, your Honor."

"And I understand the lead detective is deceased. Detective Cook had a stroke and died."

"That's correct."

"Mr. Hale, I hope you will be prepared when this case is called for trial."

"Yes, your Honor."

"You will also comply with the criminal rules as they relate to discovery. I don't want to be back here with the defendants complaining that you failed to make the alleged victim available for deposition. And also for an examination by an expert, if that is necessary."

"Yes, your Honor."

"Mr. Night and Mr. DeMarco, do your clients waive the reading of the information?"

"For the convenience of the court, Mr. Alesse dispenses with the requirement that the information be read in open court."

"Mr. DeMarco, does your client also waive the requirement?"

"Yes, your Honor."

The Judge then had both of the defendants stand and the judge asked each of the men how they pleaded to the crime of Aggravated Battery as charged in the information.

"Not guilty," said Alphonse Alesse.

"Not guilty," said Tommy Magyar.

***

Both Tommy Magyar and Alphonse Alesse appeared to state the words "not guilty" with conviction, without yelling, but both were feeling the effect of the stress of being charged with a violent felony. Neither man had been exposed to this pressure of standing on their feet in court and speaking before an audience in the past. The only time either man had been before a judge to enter a plea was when they had received a traffic citation.

Tommy was still traumatized by the few hours he spent in the zoo in the jail. Being in a common cage where men were treated like animals had made him aware of the frailty of life, and the fact that if they wished, men could force another person to do what they wished. Tommy Magyar was convinced that he would have been raped if he had been in the cage much longer. The fact that his attorney, James DeMarco, insisted he be housed in the jail hospital or in a two man cell with an older inmate had saved his life.

It took time for Theresa, his girlfriend, to reassure Tommy that he had a good attorney and he would not have to return to prison. He would be found not guilty. To help him gain confidence and earn a living, they got a job together as janitors at night in a savings and loan in one of the office towers downtown. That way they spent all their waking hours together.

Tommy was trying to recover the value of the loss of his truck. His insurance company denied his claim, stating the loss was caused by a criminal act and they did not cover a loss by intentional act, only a negligent act. Tommy also made a claim against the city. He had been told to park the truck in the city lot while he was questioned and participated in the lineup. He had also been asked for the keys to his car. He surrendered the keys and the car was in police custody and control. The truck had just been searched when it exploded.

The city took the position that the truck malfunctioned in some way and burst into flames and destroyed city property (four police cars), and damaged the parking lot. Therefore the city was making a claim against Tommy and his insurance company for the city's alleged loss. James had been asked if he would represent Tommy for the loss of his truck and he agreed.

Long story short, Tommy and Theresa purchased an old Ford Pinto. Basic transportation. If anything, the experiences they suffered since visiting St. Petersburg had made their relationship stronger and sustained Tommy.

Alphonse Alesse was less secure since he was charged. The female staff at work went into revolt after they saw the picture of Lori and her wounds. They told Darlene that they would quit if they had to work with Alphonse. They were convinced he was guilty because he had been identified and arrested, and they were afraid of him. He was a freak. They didn't want to be his next victim. Panic set in. Alphonse may have been presumed innocent under the law but that didn't mean he was not, in fact, guilty, at least so far as the staff was concerned.

Tom's solution was that Alphonse be lent to the Office of the Public Attorney to provide legal service to indigent defendants during the period between their arrest and the appointment or engagement of an attorney. Some defendants suffer from mental illness or learning defects and they become lost in the jail. This was a not infrequent occurrence. Alphonse could act as an investigator and as a paralegal for the Public Attorney until his own charges were resolved. He would receive his regular salary from the law firm as though he was still clerking in the firm's office. Alfonse knew the staff was fearful. He felt the same way when he dealt with defendants at the office of the Public Attorney who had been recently arrested for a violent crime. The suspects were sometimes emotionally spent and sometimes angry with him, and dangerous. They smelled of crime. Blood and anxiety were mixed in their sweat. Yet Alphonse was willing to do this work.

He understood he was a pariah and he had to work his way back into the good graces of society. Worse though, he had problems at home. Francis, his wife, made him sleep on the couch. She wasn't totally sure with him. She had pressure at work. Some co-workers could not understand why she stayed with Alphonse. His crime reflected on her and if she would not leave him she was somehow complicit, even if it was just that she offered him her support by remaining by his side. Another group of women felt that she "should get on with her life" and get divorced. She was happy that she would leave next week to return to teach in Deland.

Alphonse's reputation as a hardworking man with a future was not helped by the newspaper, that dwelled on the crime from the victims' standpoint and described Lori's injury graphically in the paper. Lucy Hale, the reporter, followed each event in court (First Appearance, Arraignment, etc.). With each event in the process taken in the case as it proceeded through the system, she wrote a story re-telling the crime in graphic detail.

Alphonse was affected physically by the stress. He was skinny before and lost more weight. His black hair began to thin and gray almost overnight, and his eyes became deep set and with dark rings. He looked like he could not sleep. He was happy he had the couch. He hoped he would be found "not guilty". This was a nightmare. It just could not be happening to him.

***

James DeMarco, Tommy's attorney, had a different perspective on the proceedings. He saw the statement of his client that he was "not guilty" to be a statement of innocence.

Tommy Magyar stated he was "not guilty" because he was innocent. It is rare that a criminal attorney is given the chance to represent a person who is truly innocent. Actually, guilt or innocence is irrelevant. An attorney has to use the same effort for a client whether he is guilty or innocent. At times an attorney has to put in more effort on behalf of the guilty client. And some attorneys don't even want their client to tell them if they are guilty or innocent. Having an innocent client puts too much pressure on the attorney. And most clients lie to their attorney in any event.

But to James DeMarco it was different. Representing an innocent man was a privilege and he was pleased the first innocent man came to his practice so early in his career. He was also relieved that he was joint counsel with Thomas Night, an experienced and confident attorney who could offer him the benefit of his experience.

***

Thomas Night had practiced law for 27 years. At best, at this point in his career, he was tired and he merely abided the practice of criminal law. That was as far as he would go with his poor opinion of the practice. He abided an imperfect system that regularly allowed the innocent to be imprisoned on mistaken identification testimony of a victim who was staring at the gun pointed at them during the robbery and not at the robbers face. Bad facts make bad law. The more heinous the crime, the easier it is to convict. Voodoo science, hair and fiber matches and luminol and modern science, when it is the only evidence offered and is not coupled with other solid evidence like fingerprints, did not establish guilt beyond a reasonable doubt in Tom's opinion. But juries love "science" and the jury will regularly convict a defendant based on circumstantial evidence.

Tom felt that plea bargains were the true salvation of the innocent. A good plea bargain erases most of the inequity in the criminal system. It lets everyone in the system save face.

Only in a violent crime where the need for justice screams out does the roll of the dice become a necessity. Unfortunately,

Alphonse Alesse's alleged crime was one of those cases. Tom promised God in his prayers that he would do the best he could for Alphonse. Otherwise, if he did not do his best, Tom Night would not be able to sleep at night.

Chapter 28

Gene realized the third night she slept with Clem that he either did not sleep, or his sleep was so shallow that if she moved in bed he was awake and then sitting on the side of the bed. Based on that fact Gene realized that she would not be able to sneak away from him in the middle of the night. She had hoped it would be easy; she could take the keys to the car and slip out at night. But, she realized that Clem was such a light sleeper that she gave up an escape attempt and decided to play out the cards she was dealt and try to find someone who would save her. Meanwhile, she was stuck with his plan. She was to obtain information for Clem so he could kill Derek and then the two of them would escape together.

Clem's plan required Gene to try out as a stripper at The Man Trap. She needed a dance routine. The pair settled on a routine based on an Alabama theme. They had abandoned the idea of the dance of the seven veils. Tampa was full of rednecks. The residents were even proud to describe themselves as rednecks. Jacksonville was the same, so Clem had experience with the species. He felt he knew what they would like. Clem liked the tale of the swashbuckler, only in this case the pirate was a woman. Gene wore a flamboyant black felt hat with a big fluffy red feather that accentuated Gene's red hair. The rest of the costume consisted of a bra covered with a vest and black "hot pants" and thigh high, high heel boots.

The dance routine was composed by Gene. There were movements involving the use of a buccaneer's sword that sliced through the air and led Gene's body through twists, turns and slithers. She would remove her vest and wear only her blood red bra and unbutton the row of buttons on the side of her pants to reveal the flesh on the side of her hip but never reveal her breasts or buttocks.

Clem pushed the bed sideways up against the wall of the cabin and that provided enough space for Gene to practice. He sat in a dining room chair watching the show, offering tips on how she should segue from one move to another. She would only have a limited area in which to perform on stage at the club. He helped her, suggesting moves that were the most economic, yet sensuous.

She would need music. The Alabama Crimson Tide Football Team's fight song was the ticket. It would blend the red neck theme with the football theme. Perfect, thought Clem. Gene liked it too.

***

Randell and Faircloth were only discouraged for a short time after finding that the owner of the house on Arrow Street would not lead them directly and unequivocally to Anthony's killer, but the information did connect some dots. Sarah was connected to the Oar House and The Oar House was connected to The Man Trap. Both were operated by the same corporation, named Booty Call, Inc., a Florida corporation. Its sole officer and director was a man named Harry Heade. That name had to be a joke, thought Randell.

Randell thought putting a little pressure on The Man Trap would be good. He contacted the number for the club in Tampa and spoke to an unidentified male. He told him that he would like to set an appointment with the manager to discuss the whereabouts of Clemenso Bondi. There was a long pause on the other end of the line. Then, "Our corporate attorney is in Jacksonville, we will have to call them and we will get back to you," said the man. "Please give me your number and we will call you back."

Randell gave the number for his private line.

The call from the police really made Derek sweat. He had personally accepted the call. Randell had spoken in his most officious voice, saying the matter was important and involved a homicide. Derek called HQ in Jacksonville. As usual he was told to handle it himself at his own expense.

"How do I handle it?" asked Derek.

"Just handle it," they said.

Derek decided to handle it by ignoring the call.

Meanwhile, Randell sent Faircloth to Jacksonville to visit Corporate Headquarters of Booty Call, Inc. He was told to ask for the following information from whoever would speak to him:

Where is Clemenso Me Bondi? Where is Lori Schaeffer? Is there a connection between the death of Anthony Stewart, an investigator who was killed while tailing Clem and Lori, and the fact that the two former employees of The Oar House are missing? Is there a connection between The Man Trap in Tampa and The Oar House in St. Petersburg?

Randell told Faircloth to let his imagination run with this idea. The point was that they were going to put heat on the organization of Booty Call, Inc. Faircloth was told to be insistent and not at all pleasant.

"The idea is that we are under pressure to solve these cases," Randell explained. "Anthony Stewart was one of us. He was a retired police officer and a respected member of the community. You can even tell them the Mayor was his fishing buddy. Really, what we want to do is to cause HQ to pressure the local management so they will give up whatever information they have. While you are in Jacksonville I will sit on Sarah's doorstep and wait for her to come home and I will speak to her. If I have to, I will get the State Attorney to apply for a search warrant for Sarah's house."

"It's a good plan," said Faircloth.

***

John Hale and Det. George Randell met late the day of the trip to Arrow Street in Tampa at the office of Judge John R. Waters. He was assigned as the On Call Judge to handle emergency matters.

Judge Waters had also presided over the three prior preliminary hearings and the Arraignment of Tommy Magyar and Alphonse Alesse. Judge John R. Waters seemed like he was the only judge ever available in the six story court house. The matter scheduled before Judge Waters by Mr. Hale was the State's petition for the issuance of a search warrant to search the home of Clemenso Bondi, which was presently occupied by Sarah Rogers.

Judge Waters was normally a stickler who asked many questions about the necessity of the warrant. That was why Hale brought Randell to give testimony. Randell was the most knowledgeable officer available to explain why there was probable cause for the warrant.

The first question Judge Waters asked Randell was how the house was connected to the death of Anthony Stewart.

Randell explained that the murder investigation had revealed that Anthony Stewart was conducting an investigation of the people in the house at the time he was killed. "There is an alternative theory to the motive that Det. Cook proposed that the murder was a crime of convenience by a drug addict. The motive proposed by Cook was that Stewart was robbed. Alternatively, the investigator could have been murdered because Anthony Stewart witnessed a crime committed in the house and he filmed the crime. He was silenced because he was a witness to a crime committed in the house. We need to enter the house to investigate that probability."

"Is it only a possibility?" asked the Judge. "Or is it a probability?"

"I think it's a probability."

"Why?"

"Because Clemenso and Lori are no longer in the area. They were not seen after the murder. It is also probable that Det. Cook was the victim of a homicide because he suffocated. The ventilator was inspected and was not found to be defective. His house was burglarized. Prints from his home contained the same latent prints as a print found on the plug of Cook's ventilator. There was a lens cap found in Cook's home that is consistent with the lens cap for one of the cameras that was taken from Anthony Stewart's van after he was murdered. Last, we found $26,025 in cash in Cook's house."

"Thank you, Detective." Judge Waters signed the warrant and gave Det. Randell the Return and Inventory for the warrant that had to be filed with the Clerk of Court after the search occurred. The Inventory stated what, if anything, the police had taken as evidence from the house.

***

The next morning Faircloth was back from Jacksonville. He had not been able to see anyone at Booty Call, Inc. offices who would answer any questions about the house on Arrow Street or the Kawasaki motorcycle that were both titled in the name of their subsidiary company, The Man Trap. They shuffled him from one office to another. He asked for Harry Heade. He pronounced the name "Heade" as "head". The employees of the Booty Call were not amused.

"Well?" Randell asked. "Were you at least able to make a pest of yourself?"

"Yes, I did that. What are we up to now?"

"We are going to serve a search warrant on Clem's house this morning. I am hoping Sarah will be home when we knock on the door. We are rounding up a crew to help with the search and to secure the house. I don't want to wait too long or someone will spill the beans."

"Can we ride together?" asked Faircloth. "I need to talk to you about what I was able to find out in Jacksonville."

As they drove Faircloth explained that he tried to speak to one of the officers of the parent company, Booty Call, Inc., but "no one was available".

"I did get to sit in the waiting room and I paged through some trade journals. Booty Call, Inc. is a mover and a shaker in the night club industry. They are noted for being able to operate with the least interference from law enforcement and yet provide a 'quality product' and a superior revenue stream, mostly cash."

"One thing that was interesting is their hierarchy," continued Faircloth. "The managers of each of their locations are a member of their board of directors. The pamphlets also named each of the managers and assistant managers of the club. One officer was named Harry Heade. That has to be an a/k/a." Both men laughed.

As they turned the corner and they pulled up in front of Clem's old house, Randell said "Go secure the back of the house, I will serve the warrant."

Randell went to the front door and rapped hard. "Police! Open the door! Police."

The door opened and Sarah was in her flimsy robe. "What can I do you for, Detective?"

Det. Randell believed she was intoxicated. "I need you to have a seat in the living room where you will be comfortable. There will be a female officer here shortly. She will help you get dressed. In the meantime I have to read the search warrant," and Randell read the warrant out loud, word for word.

The female officer took Sarah upstairs to dress. The crew began the search of the rooms at the front and looked at and into everything. There was a .22 caliber pistol in the chair Sarah had been lounging in. "That could have been bad if she decided she didn't want to cooperate with the search," said Randell to the officer who found the gun.

Randell wandered around as the search continued. He told a technician who was taking pictures to take a sample of the wall to wall carpet. There was a black stain in a portion of the carpet. (Might be blood, he thought) The tech also took a sample of the wood flooring in that area. In the center of the room it was evident that a large piece of carpet had been removed. Two of the techs measured the area of carpet that was missing. It was an area

9' by 12'. There was a case of bourbon on the dining room table. There was a glass with ice and mint leaves. Probably a Mint Julep, thought Randell. If I tasted it, it would have sugar as an ingredient and a little water. They took a sample in a sterilized glass bottle with a cap.

In the living room there was scoring in the floor like drag marks from a heavy chair and they discovered there was a bullet hole in the wall.

The tech removed the slug. It had passed through wallboard and plaster and was intact. It appeared to be a slug from a .44 caliber weapon. Maybe a Magnum shell, everyone was guessing. Randell told the men to put the slug in a plastic sleeve and list it on the Return and Inventory. The crew was not concentrating, thought Randell. He went back over the walls in the living room and found entrance holes for four other slugs.

Randell pointed out the slugs that were overlooked. The crew quieted down and retraced their steps to make sure they had not missed anything. It was noted that all of the holes were in a pattern in the wall that began about two feet off the floor and continued to rise by about six inches for each of the five shots until the last hole was four and one half feet above the floor as though the shooter was losing control of the pistol with each shot due to the recoil after each blast. Someone in the neighborhood had to have heard these shots, thought Randell. These were like the sound of shots from the gun in the "Dirty Harry" movie. Very loud.

When the crew got upstairs, next to the bed they found Valium pills in a bottle in the drawer. The bottle contained seven pills. There was no label on the bottle. There was also a baggie of what appeared to be marijuana.

Randell had the female officer bring Sarah into the room and he read her the Miranda warnings and asked her about the pills and weed. Sarah said she had nothing to say. Randell asked her if anyone else lived in the house. Sarah said she was there only temporarily and "mostly I stay downstairs. This house is a perk for being the manager of The Oar House, you know, free rent."

"I thought Clem was the manager," said Randell.

"No. He and Lori left and they put me in charge, at least temporarily."

"When did you last see Clem?"

"A couple of days ago."

"Where is he living now?"

"He didn't say."

"Was Lori with him?"

"I didn't see her."

"Did he say where she was?"

"He said she was in Carolina where she grew up."

"Did he say anything else?"

"What do you mean?"

"What specifically did he have to say?"

"Idle threats, is all. His bark is worse than his bite."

"How did he look?"

"Tired. Oh. I remember now. He had a beard and he let his hair grow."

"Do you know where he is right now, today?"

"No."

"Who lives at 1324 Arrow Street, Tampa, Florida?"

"The manager of The Man Trap. A fellow named Derek."

"Last name?"

"I'm not sure. I know him as Derek."

"Do you anticipate seeing Clem again?"

"Not really," then Sarah paused and said, "I don't understand these questions. I'm trying to help. Were you going to ask me about the weed and the pills?"

"Yes, yes I was. Are those items yours?"

"I don't think I should answer that question until I speak to an attorney."

"Okay," said Det. Randell.

"Am I under arrest?"

"No, unless something comes up. We should be done in a few hours. Oh, downstairs there are bullet holes in the wall of the living room."

"Is that what those are?" asked Sarah coyly.

"I don't guess you know anything about those holes. Do you?"

"No," said Sarah.

"What about the carpet? The carpet seems to be missing in the living room. Do you know anything about the carpet?"

"No."

"Well, stay with the officer until we finish. We will give you a copy of the Return and Inventory. It will tell you everything that we took as evidence."

"Okay," said Sarah. "Thank you."

Part VII

God may forgive the worst criminals.
Society never does.

Chapter 29

Gene and Clem had visited the thrift shop now a number of times, searching for a dance costume. They went first for the Hobo and Salome get-ups. Then they returned in their search for a pirate costume with the red bra and hot pants and the sword. They became familiar to the manager. He would drop what he was doing when he saw them come in the door. He would ask what they wanted and he would help with the search. One request that he thought was not in his inventory was a phonograph record (45 revolutions per minute, RPM, hopefully) of the University of Alabama Fight Song.

When Clem played football for Appalachian State College, they played a game against the University of Alabama (UA). UA scheduled the game as a warm up for their annual game against Georgia and so Clem heard their fight song time and time again as Alabama piled on, running up the score against his team. Appalachian State was beaten 84 to 21. Each time Alabama scored their band would play the song and the 60,000 UA fans in the stands would blast out the tune and spew a mist of bourbon out into the field. Clem and his teammates became intoxicated breathing in the alcohol mist as they played ball.

They searched and searched for a recording of the tune in the boxes of black discs in a backroom in the store. Finally, Clem found a record, a 78 RPM recording of college football fight songs that included "Alabama, Yea Alabama".

"This is just what we need," said Clem.

Gene had a small Victrola and it was old enough to have a setting for the speed of a 78 RPM record. Clem made her practice until she had blisters on her toes. Because of the blisters Gene made Clem rub her feet and paint her toe nails red. They never got through the foot massage without having sex. She was a good dancer but lazy and she whined that she knew the routine and she just wanted to read a magazine. But she also loved sex and that pleased Clem, now that he had regained his confidence. When it was time to try out at the club they went to use the phone at the fishing camp office and Clem placed the call to The Man Trap. He had Gene speak to the assistant manager.

"The tryouts are every afternoon at 1:00 p.m. You have to bring your costume and music. Nothing will be provided by the club," said the assistant manager. His name was Peter.

Gene then started with the rumbling in her stomach and went in the bathroom at the cabin and threw up. She was so nervous. To save her life, she couldn't stand pressure of any kind.

Clem settled Gene down by talking to her quietly. He explained what she had forgotten or did not hear from Clem's previous explanation of what she had to do at the try out. There was no total nudity.

She wasn't nervous about dancing at the club now that she knew she wouldn't have to dance topless or in a "G" string. After their talk, she was nervous because this tryout would be the best chance she would have to escape from Clem. Clem could not enter the club. The chances were high that he would be recognized even with his long hair and beard. Someone would tag him by his build, gestures or speech. The closest he figured he could safely come to the club without being identified would be to drop Gene off in the parking lot and wait there. No one knew his 1956 Chevy Bel-Air, so he would take the chance of parking and waiting. If security approached the car he would stay in the car and introduce himself as Gene's brother and hope he wasn't recognized.

Gene's job was to try to remember the layout of the club. Clem instructed her to try to get downstairs to the dressing room and look for exit doors leading to the outside. She should also look for Derek's office and see if there was an outside exit from there.

Clem thought there would be an escape route in case of a police raid. The exit would lead to the outside. Clem thought there was such an exit but he wasn't sure. When Clem was there last, Derek's office was in the basement.

Gene tried to get Clem to let her take the car and go by herself.

"Do you have a license to drive?" asked Clem.

"No," admitted Gene.

"Then you can't take my car. Maybe if they offer you a job I will teach you to drive and you can get a car."

"I thought this was a one-time thing. I don't want to work there."

This woman is a pain in the ass, thought Clem. "You know we may have to change the plan, Honey."

"I guess." Gene felt she was getting in over her head. Clem would say one thing and then, because he said it, it became a fact, something that was now true. The previous evening they had talked about the try out and what to say if Gene was offered a job.

"You should accept the job and agree to work the afternoon and evening shift the day you are hired. You will get off at 7:00 p.m. and I will pick you up then," said Clem.

When Clem dropped Gene off for the tryout at 1:00 p.m. he told her he would see her at 7:00 p.m. Gene had to remind him that she didn't have the job yet.

"Oh yeah, I forgot. You are sure to get the job though. If you aren't back out here in an hour I will know you got the job and you are working 'til 7:00 and I'll be out here then."

Clem stated a mixture of fact and fiction.

***

Derek tried to run The Man Trap like a regular business, like a barbershop or a grocery store. He expected the workers to arrive on time and there were schedules for each day of the week except

Sunday, which was, (how should one say this?), the Lord's Day. Actually, Derek was a Jew. He didn't believe in Jesus as God, but a prophet. But if you were an outsider, unfamiliar with the nature of the operation of The Man Trap, and you conducted a business audit, you would think that it was a normal, everyday, small town enterprise.

Derek Kline had a secretary named Peter. He doubled as a security guard, and he answered the phone, handled the inventory and deliveries, and controlled Derek's calendar. Derek conducted auditions. He hired all employees. When Gene called for a try out, Peter scheduled the appointment and listed it on Derek's calendar. The early crew punched in at noon. Derek was in at 11:30 am. He looked at his calendar first thing and saw the entry in his book and he began to curse. He did not want to do the audition.

"What do I know about dancers? I can interview barmaids and nude women all day but the dancers, I can't pick a winner."

"We need some fresh meat," said Peter. "Some of the regular dancers are a bit long in the tooth. We need some new acts. I'm hearing complaints from the customers."

Derek didn't say anything to his secretary. He couldn't run the place without Peter. And as a plus, Peter was homosexual and didn't bother the girls. He was actually good with them. They were kindred spirits. Together, they claimed that they were handled roughly and unfairly by men.

***

Derek went in his office at 12:45 p.m. and closed the door. Gene arrived at 1:00 p.m. on the dot. Peter helped her set up. She had her Victrola and was looking for a wall plug. Peter showed her where the Club's sound system was located. They had a man who spun records, a disc jockey. Peter said he would put her record on one of the turn tables. Gene had a more traditional 'bump and grind' record to play first and then she told Peter when she wanted to segue into the football fight song. Peter said he understood and the music began. It was something from Gypsy Rose Lee that Clem had heard a million times and thought appropriate. Derek was in his room at his desk and listened to the first song and thought, I don't even have to go out there. That is terrible noise. I won't hire her.

Then the "Alabama, Yea Alabama" song began to play and Derek began to sing along and he opened the door to his office and was now singing in a full roar as the song went into the chorus and then it repeated and he belted out the lyrics like he did back at school. He watched Gene dance and remove her vest and begin to unbutton the side of her hot pants:

Yea, Alabama! Drown' em Tide!

Every "Bama man's behind you:

Hit your stride!

Go teach the Bulldogs to behave,

Send the Yellow Jackets to a watery grave!

And if a man starts to weaken,

That's a shame!

For "Bama's pluck and grit

Have writ her name in crimson flame!

Fight on, fight on, fight on, men!

Remember the Rose Bowl! We'll win then!

Go, roll to victory,

Hit your stride,

You're Dixie's football pride, Crimson Tide!*

*Written by Ethelred Lundy (Epp) Syke; courtesy of University of Alabama Million Dollar Band.

The dance and song ended simultaneously. Derek and Peter and the crew applauded and cheered. "Sign her up," everyone yelled. Gene was embarrassed and blushed; her cheeks were as red as her bra. She was still clothed in all the important places. She had her bra and her pants.

Her vest was absent as were her thigh high boots and her hat with the large red feather.

Derek asked her to turn around slowly. "I want to look at the merchandise."

Gene turned to Derek. "What do you mean?"

"That's nice but I want to see it all."

Gene hesitated. Then she took off her bra and pants and struck a pose like she was a young girl standing before a mirror pretending to be Marilyn or Betty or Kim or Rosie. She stood with her hands on her hips and with her feet shoulder width apart.

They can all see me, but they can't hurt me. She stood there nude and beautiful and proud. I have nothing to be ashamed of. I am what I am. Everyone likes who I am, she thought.

Peter told her to dress. "You were fantastic."

***

Derek took Gene into his office and sat her down at his desk and placed a pile of papers in front of her. Gene studied the room carefully and saw a second door behind Derek's desk but she couldn't tell if it was an outside door.

"I want to hire you, if you want the job."

"How will I be paid?"

"You will dance five times a night. You will work 7:00 p.m. to midnight, six days a week. You're off on Sunday."

"How much will I be paid?"

"One hundred dollars a night. You are expected to circulate among the customers for some of the time when you are not performing. The more you circulate, the more likely you will get tips. You can give private dances in the side rooms and you get to keep what you receive from the customer, but you will be expected to be totally nude if you go in a side room and the further you go with a customer the more you will be paid."

"I don't want to do that," said Gene.

"Fine. No pressure. I am hiring you because you are a good dancer and a beautiful woman. You will brighten up the place," said Derek. "You know, I went to Alabama. I loved the school and I loved Tuscaloosa. It was like the Old South, a totally different environment. Quite a few men moved to Tampa from Alabama and whether they went to UA or not, if they are from Alabama they see the school as their school. I think you will do real well with your act and I intend to spend some money promoting you. I may even put an ad in the Tribune for the Friday morning edition. Would you like that?"

"Yes I would. I would be proud if you did that."

"I will give you a $100 bonus to start. You have to sign these papers to get that money."

"What do the papers say?"

"Essentially it says that if you leave the club you can't take a job with any other topless club in Jacksonville, Orlando, Ft. Lauderdale, Tampa or St. Petersburg. We have clubs in those cities. We don't want to invest money building your reputation and have you compete against us."

"That sounds fair," said Gene as she began to sign the papers.

"Go with Peter, he will show you around. I also want you to work with the disc jockey and work out your routine, and your music. We need to eliminate the 'bump and grind' stuff. Keep the 'Alabama Fight Song'. That should be your trademark. When someone hears the song they should think of you. But we want to change the other music."

"Okay."

"What is your real legal name Gene?"

"Regina Cameron."

"Perfect, I love that name. We will use your real name 'Regina' in the ad campaign. It sounds classy."

Gene quickly signed the papers. Derek counted out the $100 bonus in a pile on the desk.

***

Peter stayed with Gene, showing her around, introducing her to co-workers and the staff, bartenders, janitors, security men, and the dancers.

She worked with the disc jockey and he wove some new popular music in with the fight song. Then he taped the routine so it could be played whenever she was to do her routine. She practiced two times and it really worked well. She was complimented by everyone. To be complimented was new to Gene. When she was in Naples, working in the diner, people laughed at her. She had trouble keeping her orders straight and men would bother her for dates. She went to the bar to relax often after work and there she was called 'The Floozy'. The men thought they could use her. She became their patsy. She didn't care what they did to her as long as she was close to oblivious.

Gene didn't forget the reason Clem sent her to the club. Peter was showing her around. She told him she was afraid of being caught in the club if there was a fire. Peter said he understood. He gave her a floor plan of the building and took her to each exit, and each fire door so she could see they were unlocked and that if there was a fire there were easy escape routes that went directly outside the club.

Gene asked if she could keep the floor plan and study it at home. She lied.

"Once I was in a bar that had a fire in its kitchen. There was grease smoke and I had to get down on the floor and crawl to get out of the smoke. Other customers were clawing each other and climbing over each other to get out. There was panic. At one fire exit the door was locked. When the fire was extinguished a pile of corpses were discovered at the door. I never was so scared," she said. Gene had quite the imagination.

Peter said he understood. She could take the floor plan home. He also told her she did not have to worry about the men in the club. "I am here at night as a bouncer. I am here every night we are open. If you need any help, if you feel frightened, come and talk to me. If I tell a man to leave you alone, he will. If I have to roust someone out of here I will do it. I know I act like a fairy, but I can be a brute. I will protect you."

"I understand," Gene lowered her eyes, "looks can be deceiving. I am starting to learn that you can't help who you are or what you have done."

"Water over the dam," said Peter. They hugged.

***

Clem left the club at 2 p.m. and went to the cabin and he cleaned his car. When he came back at 7 pm. to wait for Gene to come out, Clem parked out of the light in a corner of the parking lot. His Chevy Bel-Air two tone crème over tan was spotless. Clem had nothing to do at the cabin and so while he had waited he had meticulously cleaned the car inside and out. On his way back to The Man Trap he stopped at a liquor store and purchased a quart of Jim Beam. Clem figured that since Gene didn't come out at 2 p.m. she had been hired and it would be late before she got out. Clem stayed in the car slouched down in the seat in the shadows and he sipped at the whiskey, listening to the radio.

When Gene came out she was in a pair of cotton slacks and a long sleeve flannel shirt. Her boots were gone. She was wearing sneakers and athletic socks.

"Where's your costume?"

"I left it in my locker."

"Where did you get these clothes?"

"They were in the locker. They fit me pretty good. We have to leave our costume at the club in the dressing room. They clean and repair our show clothes."

Clem pushed the passenger door open.

"I guess they hired you?"

"They did. They said I was very good. They watched and applauded and cheered. It was great. I feel really good."

"Yeah?" Clem sounded intoxicated. "They treated you good, huh. Better than I treat you?"

"No one's better than you," said Gene. "They gave me some money to start. I want to give you this money." Gene handed over a wad of bills.

"What's this for?"

"I owe you that. It's $175. Fifty to pay you back for the money I owed my old boss and $125 that I owe you for the dentist."

"Is that all you got?"

"No, I made another $100 dollars for dancing and I got a bonus of $100."

"Let me see."

She held the cash out in front of her and he grabbed the bills.

"Hey, that's mine." Gene tried to pull the cash back to her chest.

Clem slapped her in the face. It stung and tears welled up in her eyes.

"You don't have anything that I don't give you. You want some money? Here's a fiver." Clem threw a five dollar bill on the floor in front of her. "You don't need more than a five spot a day. You're probably still holding back on me."

"No, I swear, I don't have any more money." Gene wiped her lip on her sleeve. He had drawn first blood. "You drinking?" she asked.

"I bought you a bottle of Jim Beam so we could celebrate your new job. Here, have a sip. I was thinking we could do it till the cows come home."

Clem gave her the bottle. She took a deep drink and wiped her face and sucked the blood from the cut in her lip. The whiskey stung her mouth. Must be cut inside too, she thought.

"We won't be making whoopee for a few days. I got my period."

"How could you do that today?" complained Clem.

"Look, I am sorry about that. I didn't do it on purpose. That's probably why I'm making you so grumpy. It's all my fault."

"Yeah, it's your fault alright," said Clem.

"I got you a present." She handed him the floor plan of the club.

"I can't look at it while I'm driving. Put it in the glove box." Clem had driven out west on US 92 and he turned on US 301 and headed south to the cabin.

"You should not have hit me. That hurt."

"I do not care. What I want to know is what you had to do to get all that cash. Were you working a side room? I don't want to end up with some social disease."

"No, I was hired as a dancer. I don't do lap dances. I got $100 for the night to dance on the dance floor, not in the side rooms. And I made some tips walking around the room talking to the customers. Derek also gave me a bonus for signing a contract."

"You dumb broad. You signed a contract. Did you read the contract?"

"No. Derek told me what it said."

"You can't believe anything that Heebe says. You probably sold your soul to the company store. You're probably no better than a share cropper now. They own you."

"I don't believe that. They were good to me. They didn't treat me like a floozy."

"For sure, Derek took advantage of you. I'm the only one who treats you right," said Clem.

As Gene started to respond, Clem looked at her and without saying a word, he hit her in the left side of her head full force with his fist. The blow threw Gene across the front bench seat of the Chevy and she hit the right side of her head on the glass. Gene was still conscious and managed to open the door and fall out of the car onto the pavement of US 301. She rolled into the dark street. There was a railroad siding that was on the east side of the road. She got up, crossed the road and ran south along the tracks knowing that if Clem caught her she was dead.

The Chevy had a three speed standard transmission with a shift lever on the column. Clem had downshifted to first gear just before he slugged Gene in the left side of her head. The car shook as the transmission tried to operate at 30 mph in low gear.

Clem turned the vehicle to the left. Clem stopped the car with the foot brake. The car stalled in the street. Then he grabbed his gun from beneath his seat and jumped out and began running after Gene, down the access road next to the railroad tracks. There was no traffic.

While he ran, Clem squeezed off two shots. The gunpowder charge in the large .44 caliber bullet caused an explosion of flame around the cylinder and out the barrel and muzzle of the weapon. The retort was almost drowned out by a train moving south on the tracks that was loading lumber fencing on a flatbed on the siding. The gun was more powerful than Clem. As Clem ran and fired, holding the gun in one hand, the recoil caused the weapon to fire high and he missed Gene, who continued to run at all deliberate speed up the tracks to the lights of a business to her left.

She was running to safety, she hoped.

Clem stopped and held the weapon with both hands. He fired once, twice and saw the puff of the slug impacting the gravel in the roadbed at Gene's feet. Too low. Gene turned left heading to the lights in the parking lot of the Showtime Bar. She ran into and through the front door, and was lucky the door opened in. As the door flew open another shot was fired from the parking lot 20 feet from the door. The patrons could see the flash from the cylinder and the muzzle. Some customers later swore the slug was so big they could see it coming and then hear the projectile slice through the heavy air. There was another roar from the weapon and the slug crashed through the barroom and through the back wall. The occupants swore they could feel wind as the bullet passed through the room.

Clem ran in the door and he was immediately tackled by a fat woman and a bunch of dwarfs and midgets. A skinny man, who when he performed on the carny circuit put a 6 inch spike up his nose grossing out sightseers, hit Clem in the face with his cane.

Some women grabbed Gene and took her to a back room and locked the door and then they went back out to the front to help the men in the melee. There was cursing and biting and clawing. Literally, there was clawing, one of the participants had claw like hands and he used them to scratch at Clem's eyes. Clem cried aloud. "Help me, Lord." and he pushed with all his might and unseated the fat lady and he got to his knees and crawled out the door dragging two midgets, one on each foot.

Clem got up on his feet, shook off the little people and ran down the road, holding his eye in the socket for fear that it had been clawed out by the man with the deformed hands whose stage name was "Crab Boy". Clem found his gun halfway down his pants. He felt it slip down his right leg as he ran. He stopped and shook his leg and the pistol fired (hair trigger) burning his pants and leg. He wasn't hit. Clem pulled his pants down and retrieved the gun. He ran to his car. It was still stalled in the intersection. There was still no traffic and no police. The headlights from his car were shining at a sign that said, "Gypsumton".

"Damn," said Clem. "I will never come here again."

***

Clem drove to the cabin at the fish camp and moved all his belongings in his suitcase to his car. He was limping more and more as he moved his stuff. His groin hurt like he had a hernia. He threw Gene's things in a pile in the front yard and set the clothes and her "stuff" on fire, then drove out of the parking lot and north on US 301.

***

Inside the Showtime Bar there was excitement. "Drinks all around," said the men and each pointed to the other as the barkeep tried to collect the cost of the free round. "That was a good one." They all said to each other.

"He was big, mean and strong. But he doesn't know how bad he'll feel in the morning," said the fat lady. "I about pulled his balls out of his intestines." They all laughed and continued to exaggerate their pugilistic prowess.

The women went to the back room and unlocked the door and helped Gene up off the floor and into the rest room. There was a couch and tissue and soap and water. The woman helped Gene get cleaned up. Except for her lip, you couldn't see that much damage. She had lumps on the left side of her head. The lumps were covered by her hair. She blotted her lip with a tissue until it stopped bleeding.

"Do you want a drink?"

"He took all my money, I can't pay you."

The barkeep set an un-cracked bottle of Jim Beam in front of her with a glass and a bucket of ice. They asked her who could come help her. She said the only person that could help her now was a man named Peter who worked at The Man Trap. "I have to be there at noon tomorrow. I just got a job as a dancer," said Gene.

The women promised to call Peter in the morning and if he wouldn't come and get her they would give her a job.

"What do you people do?" she asked as she looked around at the strange group who had saved her life.

"We're Carnies. We work in side shows all over the country. We come back to Gyp'town in the fall and winter here. We always have need of a pretty woman. You can be a dancer with one of our shows," they said.

"Maybe I will do that," said Gene. "But I have to warn Peter about that man. He nearly killed me tonight."

"Do what you want. But we'll take you in with us if you have nowhere to go."

"That's right," said the Crab Boy.

"You won't call the police about this?" begged Gene. "He will kill me for sure if you call the police."

"We never call the police," said the Crab Boy. "The police think we're freaks. The police won't help us."

***

In the morning Gene woke up to the sound of a train barreling through town. It took her a minute to realize where she was. She was in a room in the back of the Showtime Bar. She was on a cot and covered with a quilt. She got up and went to the bathroom. She inspected her face. The only damage she could see was her split lip and she thought she could cover that with lipstick. In the barroom there was a bottle of Jim Beam on a table. She looked like she had only had a few drinks. Her head was pretty clear. She remembered the bar patrons were going to call Peter.

"Let's see if he picks me up?" She pushed one hand down in her right front pocket and felt cash. That couldn't be right, Clem took all my money, she thought. She pulled out the bills in her pocket. There were five twenty dollar bills. The carnies.

These are good people, Gene thought.

Gene went back on the cot and started to cry, and she fell back asleep.

Chapter 30

After returning to the police station and depositing the evidence found during the search of Clem's old house, Faircloth and Randell went to the Toy Town Landfill.

They were going to search the public refuse dump for a piece of carpet, 9 foot by 12 foot, brown in color. They brought a sample of the wall to wall carpet that remained in Clem's house to the refuse center. The people at the dump would use the sample of carpet to attempt a match with the carpet in the dump.

Randell and Faircloth talked to the site supervisor at the dump. They asked how many 9' by 12' rugs or carpets are sent to the site for disposal each month. ("That's a common size, probably 30 to 40 pieces that size.") Are many of the pieces stained? ("Probably most are stained, ripped or worn through.") Do you have a special way of treating or handling the rugs? ("No, most of them are foul and we try to spray them with disinfectant and deodorant if we can't burn them in the boiler right away. But we want to burn them as soon as we can.") What kind of back load of carpet do you have at this time? ("We probably have 100 pieces waiting to be burned.")

"Don't burn them. We need to look at those pieces right now," said Randell.

The supervisor loaned the officers a truck and gave them a map and sent them on their way. The dump was one of the few refuse systems in the country that incorporated a furnace to burn the garbage to produce electricity. So all the refuse was culled for garbage that would burn and that garbage was the fuel for the boiler. The boiler produced the steam that turned the generator that produced electricity. State of the Art.

Faircloth drove and Randell navigated as they negotiated around huge piles of garbage. Ultimately, they found a pyramid of carpet and a crane that had a hook. The hook was attached to a single piece of carpet and the carpet was lifted and placed in a dump truck and taken to the main building where it was mixed with other fibers such as paper and wood pulp and all these items were shredded and mixed, and then they went into the furnace.

As they watched the operation they could see that it would be almost impossible to sort the pieces according to size. The best they could do would be to watch as the crane picked up each piece and if it appeared to match the piece they wanted they would have it set aside. The supervisor was right. The pile of material smelled god-awful. It would gag you if the wind was just right.

Randell looked at Faircloth but he didn't have to ask, Faircloth just said, "It has to be done. I will stay here and see what we can find. We don't need both of us up here at the land fill."

Randell thanked him. He drove to the office of the landfill and asked the supervisor if they would take the truck back to his partner.

"How can you stand that smell?" asked Randell.

"Vanilla. We put vanilla extract in a handkerchief and wear the handkerchief over our face and noses. It works real well." Vanilla nose gay.

"Would you give my partner some vanilla extract and a bandana?"

The supervisor said he would. He also offered to give Faircloth a truck with a radio to relay any message Faircloth had back to Randell at the police station.

***

Detective Randell put his feet up on his desk. He was going through Faircloth's notes from his trip to the headquarters of The

Oar House's parent company in Jacksonville, Florida. Faircloth was thorough. He had even brought back brochures that he picked up in the reception room of the corporate office. One folder identified the club locations and the names and photographs of the managers at each club.

Randell looked at the names. The print was small but there on the last page was a photo of the manager of The Oar House. Smiling back at Randell was a picture of Clemenso M. Bondi, who was shorn bald and clean-shaven.

On the next to last page was the photograph of Derek Kline, the manager of The Man Trap in Tampa.

Derek Kline, thought Detective Randell. Someone with the initials "D. K.", who has a connection to Lori Schaeffer through their common employment. Derek Kline. It seems to be too obvious. But these folks thought they were immune – they would never be caught, or so they thought.

Randell ordered a copy of the DMV file on Derek Kline. The information included a physical description. He was 5' 6" tall, and weighed 150lbs.

The photo in the DMV file showed a man who could be described as swarthy and foreign; like a gypsy.

This gets better and better, thought Randell.

***

Randell was re-reading Faircloth's notes, making sure he had not missed any of the facts contained in the file. One of the clerks came to his desk and told him to pick up the phone. "The supervisor of the Toy Town dump is on the line."

"Listen, your man out at the carpet pile just called in and said you need to get out here right away. He says you should bring the Medical Examiner."

Randell got up and left the building and turned on the emergency lights on his vehicle and began to book it down the road. This was the first time in many years that he had driven with his lights flashing. While he drove he was patched through to the ME's office by radio and he spoke to a pathologist. He explained that he needed a doctor at the Toy Town dump STAT.

The ME said she would come herself, "if you feel it was that important".

"Yes I do," said Randell.

"I will be there in five minutes. I can come into the dump from the back way. Where is the body?"

"In the carpet pile" said Randell.

"God. It stinks in there," said the ME. "It's like a dead, wet dog."

"It sure does stink," agreed Randell. He didn't think MEs were bothered by smell, as they can take the smell of a ripe corpse. But then he realized she was commenting on the smell of the old carpets. It was a different smell than a corpse. She could actually smell the nasty carpets. She wasn't used to that smell. She would probably wretch. Randell hoped she did wretch. The ME always made fun of the officers who lost their lunch when they had to view an autopsy.

***

The ME was at the scene when Randell arrived. Faircloth was leaning over against the Toy Town truck that had been lent to the police. The dump truck driver and the crane operator were huddled about a 100 feet away from the oriental carpet that was still hanging in the air on the hook from the crane. On the ground there was an object about 5' 6" long. As Randell walked toward the object he could see it was a corpse of a woman. Randell went back to the car and called for a technician to photograph the body and other officers to secure the scene.

He went over to Faircloth. The ME joined them. They were all giving the body a wide berth.

"So what happened?" said Randell and the ME almost simultaneously.

Faircloth took a deep breath through the vanilla scented bandana and then he said, "I had been helping the men hook up the carpets so the crane could hoist them into the dump truck. This here carpet, actually it's an oriental rug if you look at it closely. This rug was all rolled up like it was being taken to be cleaned. I thought it must have gotten in the pile with the other discards by mistake. Anyway, I attached the hook on the cable from the crane to the rug and the rug was being hoisted and I was underneath and I figured I better move back. The rug was unfurling and then it got stuck. The crane operator can make the cable on the crane slip down by stepping on the clutch and the rug would drop and then he would pop the clutch and the rug would snap and unfurl. That's what he did and the bounce made the rug continue to unroll and this body fell out and landed at my feet. I wasn't prepared for that and it totally grossed me out. I was looking for a brown carpet not an oriental rug with a body."

They all looked at each other: "So. Did you do anything after that?"

"I told everyone to turn off the engines to their vehicles and get back from the body and wait for the cavalry. And so, here you are. I'm expecting you and the doctor will take over from here" said Faircloth, who was pale, clammy and sweaty.

There were other vehicles that came to the scene. Randell had the two officers in the first car to arrive put up crime scene tape— yellow tape.

The technician was told to photograph the scene and measure the location of the vehicles using the body as the focal point. After that the ME began a field exam. She could see that the body was a female, dead for a couple of weeks; probably she had sustained a nonfatal gunshot wound to the left forearm. It appeared she suffocated.

"Can you tell me if there are any wounds to the torso and face?" Randell called to the doctor from his position next to Faircloth.

"There are scars to the face. 'X' marks to the forehead and both cheeks. There also appears to be 'X' marks on the chest. There are initials on the breasts. Looks like a 'D' and a 'K'," said the ME.

"Were the wounds healed at the time of death?"

"It appears so. They appear to be fresh scars," the ME repeated.

Randell went back to his car. He had a thermos of black coffee. He brought it out to Faircloth. Faircloth took a mouthful, gargled and spit.

Randell went back to his car. He called the station and had his call patched through to the State Attorney's office. John Hale was in court, said his secretary. Randell relayed the message that it looked like they had found Lori Schaeffer's body. The secretary said she would give Hale the message as soon as he was back to his office.

The ME had called for an ambulance from her office and two assistants. The assistants had carefully rolled the body on its side. There was a wide, one and one half inch puncture wound to the back at the dorsal spine. The wound was a slit type wound. There was also a shoe print impressed in the corpse's back. The photo tech took pictures for the ME. Measurements of the boot print showed it belonged to a size 14 shoe. The shoe's width was a triple D. It had been re-heeled with a "Cat's Paw" replacement heel. The aides from the ME's office rolled the body back onto a stretcher, then onto a gurney.

The ME told the assistants to stop and wait. She looked at the face of the corpse and noted that water had trickled out of its mouth. The ME captured a sample of the water in a tube and corked it. She told her assistants to load the body and take it to the office and schedule the autopsy for her calendar. ASAP.

The ME went over to Randell and Faircloth and spoke in confidence: "She has a knife wound to the back, probably severing her spine, but I still think she may have drowned. Regardless, the wound or the drowning didn't happen in the dump. Do you know how the body got here?"

"No." Randell went to the radio and called the supervisor at the dump and asked him if there was a way to tell where the Oriental rug came from. The supervisor said he would ask around and call back. The rug would have been a special pick-up called in by a resident or it was found in the woods or a ditch. There were special crews that handled that kind of pick-up. He would talk to those crews.

Randell apologized to the supervisor because he had to continue to search to see if the 9 foot by 12 foot piece of brown carpet was in the pile. The Oriental rug did not match the swatch of carpet the police brought from Clem's house.

"No more bodies are going to fall out of the carpets, are they?" asked the dump supervisor.

"We hope not," said Randell.

***

Randell and Faircloth left the dump when the piece of 9x12 brown carpet was found. It had been a long day. Both the rug and the carpet were delivered to the evidence department, but there was a revolt. The technicians refused to put the two pieces of floor covering in the evidence room.

As a result of the insurrection by the technicians, Randell rented a storage locker and had it moved to the station and it was placed along the property line as far back from the building as possible. Randell asked the supervisor at the dump where they could purchase vanilla extract in bulk and once it was delivered, the janitors at the police station were required to spray the outside of the locker daily to ward off the stench. Randell kept the key to the storage locker. Really, though, no key was necessary. The smell of the locker repelled the criminal element and the curious.

Chapter 31

Peter, the assistant manager at The Man Trap, arrived at the Showtime Bar at 10 am. He had received a call from the janitor informing him that Gene was at the Gyp'Town bar. Peter asked the janitor if he had seen a red-haired woman. The janitor took Peter to a back room and there on a cot covered with a quilt was a woman sleeping soundly.

Peter hated to wake Gene but he had to be at work at 11 a.m. Peter shook Gene's shoulder softly and her eye lids opened in slow motion and the lenses in her eyes focused and she was looking at Peter, and she smiled.

"I wondered if you would come for me," she said.

Then as Gene removed the quilt Peter could see she was hurt. She moved slowly and carefully. She had a cut lip. Her mouth was bruised where Clem had slapped her. There were also bruises that had been colored red that then faded to black at both ears and the rear area of her cheeks.

"You won't be doing any dancing tonight," said Peter.

"I have to go in. I can't lose this job."

"What happened to you?"

Gene explained that her boyfriend had gotten drunk and beat her up. Then she blurted out, "He says that he is going to kill Derek."

"I don't understand. Why would he kill Derek?"

"He says Derek killed a girl he loved named Lori."

"What is your boyfriend's name?"

"Clemenso Me Bondi."

"I know him. He is called 'Clem'. He ran the club in St. Petersburg. He is a big, mean guy."

Peter helped Gene fold up the quilt and helped her get in the restroom to clean up. She had bruises on her back and both arms. She did not know exactly how she was injured in those areas of her body but she explained she had opened the door to Clem's car while it was moving and she had rolled on the asphalt pavement in the road. She pulled down her slacks and she was a mass of bruises on her hips and buttocks.

"Poor Gene," said Peter. "Can you walk to my car? We'll go see Derek and see what he thinks."

"I don't think I should go. You tell Derek that Clem is going to kill him in the bar. Clem made me audition for the job at the Man Trap to get information about the layout of the club."

"Is that why you asked for the floor plan of the bar and the location of all the exits?" asked Peter.

"Yes."

Peter agreed that if Gene went back to the club and told Derek her story that he would likely to be upset with her. He might even kill her.

"Derek isn't going to give you a reward for stealing the floor plan for Clem so he knows the best way to attack him," said Peter. "You're right, you better not go back to the club."

Peter looked at her and spoke in a straight masculine voice. "You need to get away and don't come back."

"I will stay here. These people will help me. They are like you and me," said Gene. "We are all freaks. The good freaks."

Peter left. Gene went back to the cot. The janitor told her he would wake her at noon when the bar opened. She would have to leave then.

She asked where she could find the bar patrons that were in the bar when the fight occurred. The janitor said that they all live with the other Carnies along Nundy Road and he would take her there. He said that in the evening he passed the road on his way home.

Gene thanked him and she fell back to sleep.

***

It was 11 a.m. Peter went in the rear door entrance of The Man Trap that led directly to Derek's office. He opened the emergency door and he was standing behind Derek who was sitting at his desk. Dereck began to curse, "Haven't I told you not to come in that way. You will give me a heart attack."

"I needed to talk to you and I didn't want anyone to see me come in the office through the front door."

"Don't come in the emergency door again. Understand?"

"Yes, but boss you need to know that Clem is out to kill you," said Peter.

"What now?"

"When I went to pick up Gene she said she wasn't coming in to work. She had been beat up badly by Clem. Clem is her boyfriend. She said Clem had sent her in for the tryout. The reason was for her to get the layout of the bar so he could get in and kill you," said Peter.

"Did she say why he wanted me dead?"

"She says you killed Lori, Clem's girlfriend."

Derek didn't answer. Derek knew Clem thought it was Derek's fault that Lori was dead. In a convoluted way, Clem blamed Derek for Lori's death. There was no way Gene would know Clem thought that Derek killed Lori if she hadn't talked to Clem. And if she talked to Clem, Clem was in town and it was true Clem intended to kill him.

Derek opened his desk drawer and pulled out his gun and put it in the rear of his waistband.

"Thanks Peter, you go on and open up like nothing's wrong. If anyone asks about Gene, just say she was a no show."

"Okay boss," said Peter. "But you need to know she wanted to come in. I told her she is too bruised up and hurt to dance."

"Do you think she will come back?" asked Derek. He was hoping she would.

"She wants to, Boss. I think she will be back."

"She was too good to be true."

***

Derek called headquarters in Jacksonville and asked to speak to operations. When he started to tell his tale of woe he was interrupted and told to call another number from a payphone. Derek left the bar, walked across the street to the gas station next door and used their phone to make the call to the new phone number. Paranoia or wiretap?

Derek explained the situation. He was told he would have to handle the matter himself. Derek reminded the man that the last time he handled it they ended up with chaos in St. Petersburg. Lori was cut, then she and Clem left town. Now Clem wanted to kill him.

"You are paid a good wage to resolve issues at work," said Operations.

"This man is going to kill me." Derek pleaded for help.

"I understand what you are saying. If you think you need more security, hire some more men. But you figure it out. We are not going to tell you what to do or pay the cost of the solution. You determine what best resolves the dispute."

Operations hung up.

***

Derek got Peter into his office and told him to hire four or five men for the night for extra security. Derek wanted the men to be able to handle a gun. Peter said he would make some calls.

Derek told Peter one of the men was to stand guard outside the exit from his office and one man was to stand outside the office door inside the club. No one was to be allowed in his office.

"I'm not going to run away, but I'm not stupid. I'm staying in the office and the guards can take me home and watch me there tonight."

Chapter 32

Clem was driving north on US 301, looking for a place to hide after being pummeled the night before at the Showtime Bar. He drove through North Tampa; it was rural with agricultural businesses; dairy farms, chicken farms, horse farms and small truck farms, growing vegetables and citrus. He passed through Zephyrhills and, small as it was, and as far as it was from Tampa (20 miles), even that town seemed too close to Gyp'town.

When he got to Lacoochee, with its single, small motel set way back off the road, he knew he was home. He asked the motel manager if he was still in Hillsborough County.

"No. You're in the heart of Dixie," said the manager. "I'm proud to say you are standing in Summer County."

"Is there a hunting store around? Firearms. Rifles. Ammo."

"Sure is, just down the road."

"Can I do some target practice in the woods in back of your motel if I'm a guest?"

"Absolutely, just aim away from the building," the manager laughed.

Clem checked in. Threw his suitcase in the room. It looked like a bedroom in a hunting lodge. The walls were covered in pecky cypress. The wood was probably harvested from trees on the Withlacoochee River and milled in the old Cummer Sawmill in Lacoochee. "Tank Cypress" is what the wood was called.

Clem drove up the road as he was directed and came upon a business that had a sign: "Huntin' N Fishin".

Must be the place, thought Clem.

He got out of his car and took his pistol with him. He held it by his side with his fingers and his thumb. He asked the manager if there was a gunsmith who could look at it. "It doesn't seem to shoot true," said Clem. "It' shoots all over the place, not where I aim it."

"Uh huh," the manager replied as he took the weapon and looked at it; checked that it was unloaded; spun the cylinder, and looked down the barrel. "Looks alright to me."

The owner called over a worker who was in an apron.

"That's a .44 Magnum Colt 'Anaconda'. I never have seen one of those up close and personal." The worker was excited seeing the weapon.

The owner gave the man in the apron the gun.

"Go fire a shot in the barrel and see what it does," said the owner.

The owner motioned for Clem to give him a bullet from the box he had in his hand. The worker took the gun to the back of the shop, loaded the one cartridge and fired the gun into a 55 gallon barrel full of water. The shot roared through the building and all three men smiled like little boys.

"Looks good to me," said the worker. "It's got a hell of a recoil. I think you just need to get the feel of the gun when it's fired. You need practice. Fire that baby. You may also need to use both hands."

Clem bought five boxes of .44 Cal Magnum cartridges and some targets. The man asked if he was going to start a war with all that ammo. Clem said he wanted to "be prepared". Then he walked out the door; got in his crème over brown Bel-Air, and he drove back through the town heading back to the motel.

He passed Lacoochee High School. The classes had just been let out and the kids blocked the road as they crossed the street. There was a sugar shack, malt shop across from the school and there were mostly girls out on the street. "Easy pickings," thought Clem.

He parked. The boys took a close look at his car. Clem had spent a lot of time cleaning and hand waxing it. The Anaconda and the shells were on the front seat. One of the boys reached in and picked up the hand gun and the group of boys passed the silver-plated weapon around.

There were two girls who were in the crowd with the boys. They were bold. They looked like they were more interested in Clem than the pistol or the car. Clem noticed. He took his gun from the group and retrieved all his ammunition. The kids had broken open a box of ammunition and were taking cartridges as souvenirs.

The group crowded around Clem, who was a foot taller than the biggest boy. Clem raised his arm and hand in the air with the revolver and fired one shot. The gun exploded in a very controlled way, controlled like the way a Harley pan head engine sounds as it lopes when it is in neutral and you are just sitting there, waiting for the light to change.

The town was silenced by the shot. No one said anything. They were waiting for the next shot. This had to be the start of a war. Then, all together the crowd began to laugh as they collectively decided that Clem was harmless. All the kids piled into the malt shop. Clem put the gun into the glove box in the dashboard of his car along with the boxes of shells and he followed the crowd and he went over to the cash register. A sign said "take out". He ordered a burger and fries and a chocolate milk shake. He waited by the register and talked to the cashier until the food was delivered. A couple of the girls inside were looking at him and talking, comparing notes.

The food was delivered and Clem paid. He went outside and got in his car and began to munch the meal. The two girls came out and leaned into the open window on the passenger side of the car and asked if Clem would give them a ride in his car.

"Sure," said Clem. "You girls from around here?"

"That's what we were going to ask you," they said and giggled. "Where you from?"

Clem did not reply. He reached over and pushed the door open.

There was nothing special Clem did to get the two girls into the car. They should have understood the potential danger, Clem thought. Clem drove to the motel. The girls were familiar with the building; they were not strangers to the place.

Clem got the gun from the glove box and ammo and some targets and tacks and he and the girls went into the woods behind the motel. Clem pushed the tacks into the targets then stuck them to the trees at various heights and distances.

He took the gun and aimed like the gunsmith showed him. He fired and waited to recover from the recoil and then fired again. If he caught any part of the paper target with the slug, the target was destroyed. The girls wanted to try. Clem said "no" until they were begging.

"Okay. Okay," said Clem. "But I've got to hold the gun with you or it will break your arm."

The girls agreed and one at a time they snuggled in, and like a big bear, Clem corralled each girl separately with his arms and helped each of them hold the weapon and squeeze the trigger. They shook with the recoil as the bullet pushed out of the muzzle of the gun.

"God," the girls said, and shivered.

After the girls each shot the weapon, Clem took the gun and began to fire one shot at a time using his right hand; each time holding his right wrist with his left hand and firing until he had to re-load. He emptied one full box of shells and eliminated all the targets. In the end he was firing at tree limbs. He could take down a limb six inches in diameter if he hit the meat of the limb with the slug. One shot did terrible damage.

After he fired a box of shells, the girls wanted Clem to take them in the motel room.

Clem let them beg a bit. It made him feel good to have a woman want him. Clem probably would have taken the girls up on their offer any other time. But the Fat Lady at the Showtime Bar in Gypsumton had about pulled Clem's testicles out of his crotch. When he had even an inkling of arousal he felt pain in his intestines. He thought he maybe had a hernia. There was no way he could satisfy these two girls. Maybe he would come back some day, but it wouldn't be today.

"No. No. No," said Clem. "I need to take you back to the malt shop. It's getting late." They got in the car reluctantly and he drove back to the school and he let the girls out. They thanked him for a "really good time".

Clem went back to the motel. He was in his room and it was getting dark. It was October, still Eastern Standard Time. He turned on the light over the desk and sat down and looked at the floor plan for The Man Trap that Gene had left him. He quickly saw that Derek was vulnerable if he was in his office. There were doors that led directly into his office from the outside. If Derek was in his office, Clem could break down the door and finish him off. Clem became riled up just at the thought. Revenge.

Clem threw his clothes into his suitcase and got in the car and drove south toward Tampa. He would mail the motel owner the key.

Part VIII

Being good or being bad
are habits that become easier over time
with practice.

Chapter 33

Gene next awoke at 1:15 p.m. She was lying on the cot curled under the quilt with her red hair dangling down to the floor. The janitor at the Showtime Bar was shaking her shoulder and telling her it was time to go.

"Here, put this on. The weather has changed. It's much colder." The janitor gave her a jacket that had a liner He also gave her a pile of other clothes. "Take what you need."

Gene went in the bathroom and washed up. The bruises on her face and what she could see of those on her back, hips and thighs were darker. But she felt more limber. The extra sleep had done her some good. She threw away the T-shirt and pants she had been given at The Man Trap. She had no underwear. Her bra and hot pants were part of her costume and they were back in her locker with the rest of her pirate costume.

In the armload of clothes Gene found a clean T-shirt and a blouse with a collar and a sweatshirt and a wind breaker. There were also blue jeans. The jeans fit her a little loose but there was a belt so the pants wouldn't fall down. There were wool socks and boots. The boots fit perfect.

"How do I look?" She modeled the clothes.

"Well, except for the bruises on your face, you look great," said the barkeep.

"Agreed." Said the janitor.

"The boss let you sleep in," said the janitor. "There were no customers this morning when we opened. It's going to be a windy day and cold. It may hit the 40s tonight."

"We have been coming down here to winter for 30 years or so and it has never been this cold in October," said the bartender.

"I understand you want to see the sights in Gyp'town?" asked the janitor.

"I do. I want to learn all about it," said Gene.

"Most of the sights are on Nundy. The road has a special zoning to accommodate the Carny trade. The County government understood that show business folks needed a place to go where they could rehearse their acts and fix their rides in the winter. It's all the better for show people if you can go somewhere where it is warm in the winter. It's too cold up north to work outside. Sarasota has the circus and Gyp'town has the Carnies and the side shows."

Gene became excited at the thought of the sights to see on Nundy Road. Her mother had taken her to the circus and she saw the side shows and listened to the barkers hawk their acts when she was a kid. She went to movies a lot, too. That's how Gene learned to walk like a woman. And it was how she learned to wear make-up, and dress. She learned that she could communicate by changing the way she was dressed or wore her clothes and painted her face.

"You take a walk down Nundy Road. No one will bother you. After you're through, if you want to help here at the bar, you have a job as long as you want," said the bartender. "Think about it."

The janitor walked with her out the front door. They crossed the tracks and went south two blocks and turned west on Nundy Road.

"I'm going to leave you here. The road's about three miles long and then it ends at a sharp left turn. Have you got your money?" asked the janitor.

Gene reached into her pocket and pulled out the five twenty dollar bills. "Yes, I am still rich."

"I'll see you then, good luck."

Gene wandered down Nundy. She walked in a lackadaisical style, wiping her hair from her face as it blew in her mouth and eyes. The air was brisk, in the 50's. It caused her to tear up a bit. She came to a house with a fenced yard. A man was practicing with two white Arabian horses. They were going through their routine. The horses ran in a circle inside a ring and there were dogs that jumped on the horses' backs. The dogs were very agile and athletic. They could somersault to the front and to the back. Through all their tricks the dogs' mouths were open and their tongues flopped around. As she continued walking, men in another yard were repairing a ride called 'The Octopus'. They were operating a welder and one man was hammering away with a sledge, removing a dent from the apparatus that locked a passenger in place during the operation of the ride.

Further along, she saw elephants and camels grazing on hay, munching vigorously. They were untethered, standing next to their trainer. The house with the elephants and camels also had two white tigers. They were in cages set on the porch of the house. The animals were prowling back and forth. They looked healthy, with rippling muscles that flexed with each movement. They seemed content but couldn't help looking ominous and they made Gene nervous.

Gene was approached by a man she thought she recognized. He was very tall and slender. He asked her to wait and he went in the house and came out with a very fat woman.

"Hi, Dearie. I want you to have this." She handed her a long, red-knitted wool scarf.

"Oh, it's beautiful. Thank you." Gene remembered the two from the rumble in the bar the night before.

"It will keep you warm," said the woman. "Are you feeling better today?"

"Yes, I am much better," she said as she adopted an affectation in her stride, and she strutted and waved the end of the red scarf.

"I feel better and even pretty." She shook her red hair. She was acting like a tease.

"You take care," said the woman who waddled with great effort up the stairs to her porch and then sat in a super-size rocking chair and cackled and laughed. "You look good," she hollered as Gene sashayed up the street in a miasma of activity, with people greeting her as she passed and answering her questions. The midget and the dwarf; "We are just little people," they explained.

"I can see that." She looked carefully at their fingers. "You're beautiful."

"Have you seen the trapeze artist?' asked the little people.

"Not yet," she said, but soon she did. He was working without a net. He had two other aerialists with him. They were in training, said an on-looker.

"Could I do that some day?" asked Gene.

"Sure," said the crowd of munchkins that were surrounding her and parading down Nundy Road by her side, seeing all the sights. It was like she was still sleeping on the cot in the bar, dreaming. She was floating above the road, being carried with the cold breeze.

***

Gene got to the end of the road, the road took a sharp left like the janitor said it would, and the name of the road to the left was an ordinary name, like Central Avenue or North Street. (Unmemorable.) There were no more little people following her and there were no more people in costumes, beautiful women and men in tights risking their lives flying through the air, or bending the will of great beasts with a whip. They all disappeared when she left Nundy Road. Were they all just a dream? Perhaps?

Gene took the left turn and she came to another road. Then she took another left and she was heading back toward US 301. Farther along, she crossed the railroad tracks and she went back into the Showtime. She looked at the inside of the bar and it looked like home. Louisiana, maybe.

She went in the door. She took off her coat and turned and knew there would be a coat rack. There was one there just as she thought there would be. She hung up her jacket and scarf.

"Do you want me to wipe down the tables first?" Gene asked the man behind the bar.

"That would be good," said the bartender. "Afterward, take a rest. Tonight is a busy night at the bar."

***

As she was instructed, Gene fell asleep on the cot. She had the dream she sometimes had when she was exhausted and felt her life was in turmoil. She was always comforted by the dream because afterward, when she awoke, everything in her life seemed to get better.

The dream involved her mother. She was a resident of New Orleans. Her mother owned a wooden house and lived there alone. It was property that had been in the family for over a hundred years. Her mother died and Gene had inherited the house. Gene learned of her death by way of a letter from an attorney who had taken care of her family's affairs for years. The letter took forever to find her. Gene had been on the road, working a bit, then moving on. Sometimes she was with a friend, male or female, just companionship, nothing serious.

When the US Postal Service caught up with her she was in Cedar Rapids. The weather was starting to turn cold and she and her friends were intending to head south. It took Gene a while to make the trip home, but she made it safely and found the attorney.

Gene was her mother's sole heir. The lawyer explained that while Gene was gone the Probate Court had allowed the sale of the family home. It was sold for very little because it was infested with Asian termites and the city condemned it and tore it down. The city purchased the lot at a foreclosure sale. The net proceeds from the sale of the house after paying to have the house razed was $500.

Her mother also had a death policy. Gene remembered the insurance man who came to the front door each week to collect the $1.50 premium on the policy. Gene's mother joked that when she left the earth there would be money for a proper funeral and burial. New Orleans was below sea level and the burial plots were above ground. Gene's family had a plot with a marble crypt. There was enough space for her mother. But what her mother meant by a "proper burial" was a parade.

After the attorney was paid and the court took its fees, and the cost of demolition of the house, no longer a home, was paid, there was $329.50. Gene asked the lawyer to arrange the funeral and gave him $300. He said that was enough. Gene went to a second hand store and she bought a wedding dress for the funeral.

Barefoot, she mingled with the "So Sad Band".

Then, Gene danced with great fervor as the band and the gent in the tux holding the umbrella danced to beat away the devil and sadness. They danced and played down Bourbon Street. Others knew her mother and joined in, as did drunks and tourists. The parade ended at the cemetery with a wail of rejoicing and noise that rose to the heavens. Gene knew her mother heard the glorious noise. Gene went in the cemetery and went to the family crypt. Over the door the name CAMERON was carved in the stone. Gene had a key to the iron door. She opened it and went in. There was a fresh marble slab that had been placed in the wall where her Mother had been laid. Gene felt the stone and it was warm. Gene lay on the ground in the warmth of her Mother's glow and she slept a sleep that brought her close to death. Her breath was shallow and her heart slowed to a silent flutter. As she was almost there, gone from this Earth, in the tunnel with bright white light, she was snatched from death by a shudder she felt on her shoulder.

"Wake up Gene, wake up."

Chapter 34

As John Hale walked out of the oversized doors of Courtroom A, he was handed a note by the bailiff. This is never a good sign, he thought and he folded the paper in two and slipped it into his pocket without reading it.

Hale went to a side room next to the courtrooms. The room had a desk and a chair and a phone. The room was a convenience for attorneys only. The note had to be from Mary. She had been with him for over 25 years. She had lasted longer than all three of his wives.

"What's up Mary?"

"Detective George Randell needs to see you. He says he found Lori Schaeffer."

"Great!"

"I think she's dead, Mr. Hale."

"So where is Randell?" said Hale. "I'm still in downtown St. Pete."

"He's coming back from Toy Town Landfill. I would imagine he will be at the station shortly."

"Hook us up and call me back."

John Hale sat with his yellow legal pad. For Hale the pad was an 8.5x14 inch doodle pad. A psychiatrist would have had a field day. His writing was miniscule. The letters were so small you could hardly discern what was written on the page. Hale always felt he could deny the content of the scribbling because it was undecipherable. But Mary could read his writing. She often was required to type the notes, minus the large looping lines, which were abstractions of swans. There were swans in all manner of flight and activity and repose. Probably the swans represented repression. But really, who the hell cared? thought Hale.

When Mary typed the notes she also purposely failed to include Mr. Hale's observations of his competitors in the court room. He commented on opposing attorneys, witnesses and court personnel. He saved his most biting comments for the judiciary. Awful, horrible things flowed from his pen in obscenity, cattiness and drivel. Someone must have beaten him as a child and he must have been denied sexual gratification with regularity by his wives. But really, who the hell cared?

The phone rang. "The policemen will meet you at your private office in the courthouse in 10 minutes," said Mary.

Hale threw his pad and pen in his briefcase and stalked off to his private office located on the third floor. He was the only person with a key to the room and he limited the people who were allowed to visit him there. Mary was the gatekeeper. Hale enjoyed the perks of his position as State Attorney. Besides the glee he sometimes felt turning the screws on an accused or on an attorney, he had a nice new car (the color of the car was a burgundy hue and he was the only official in the judicial system who had that color car). At work, when he reviewed a file, he wrote on the paperwork with a pen with purple-colored ink. No one else in the office was allowed a pen with purple ink. If the writing was in purple ink it was the ideation of John Hale, and everyone had to know it and respect it.

As Hale was struggling with the key in the door to his private office, Randell and Faircloth met him at the door. The three of them tried to make the key work. The key fit the lock but it wouldn't turn the cylinder and release the bolt.

"Maybe it's a different key," said Faircloth.

Hale tried another key and the bolt disengaged and the three men entered the room and sat down around Hale's desk.

"So you found Lori Schaeffer?"

"Yes," said Randell. "We found her body in the Toy Town dump. She was rolled up in an oriental rug. The supervisor at Toy Town was able to determine the rug was found in that small cypress swamp next to the interstate."

"That's the second body they found there," said Hale.

"Yeah, sanitation checks the spot monthly since the first body was discovered," said Faircloth.

"That was embarrassing," said Hale, remembering the case. "The first corpse was the body of a woman who laid out there for almost 20 years before they found it. The guy that killed that woman killed two more people before the body in the swamp was found."

"Sanitation didn't realize there was a body in the second rug in the swamp. The carpet was rolled up when they found it and they left it rolled up and took it to the dump and threw it in a pile of carpets a couple of weeks ago," said Randell.

"What was the date they found the rug with the body of Lori Schaeffer?" asked Hale.

"According to the supervisor it was found on the 20th."

"When on the 20th was the body found?" asked Hale, not revealing his thought process.

"The supervisor said the rug was found in the morning on the 20th," said Faircloth.

Faircloth and Randell did not understand the significance of the date and time the body was found. When Hale first heard from Mary that Lori's body had been found he immediately assumed she had been killed by Alesse and Magyar to silence Lori as a witness. Lori Schaeffer was the only person who could identify the two as the men who assaulted her. If the body was found in the swamp on the 20th in the morning, Magyar had the perfect alibi for the murder of Lori Schaeffer because he was in jail. He had been there for three weeks.

Now John Hale had to consider if Alesse had murdered Lori by himself. Maybe he and Magyar plotted to have Alesse commit the crime by himself. But then when did the plot occur? Did Alesse visit Magyar in jail? No, there was no visit. Then it had to be that Magyar's attorney took messages back and forth to the two men. As he considered these possibilities, Hale realized how ridiculous they were. In a very short time Hale realized Magyar and Alesse were not guilty, in fact they were innocent.

Randell noticed that Hale was not listening to the explanation they were giving of their theory of the assault and the murder. The two cops thought the probable suspect was Derek Kline. They didn't know the motive for the assault but felt it had something to do with work at the topless joints. They figured the motive for Derek Kline to kill Lori was to shut her up so she couldn't identify him as her assailant and testify against him.

"Mr. Hale, are you okay?" asked Randell.

"I'm a little dizzy, I think I have the flu," said Hale. "Do we have to do this now?"

"No, we wanted you to be updated, and you wanted me to tell you as soon as we found Lori Schaeffer. That's the only reason for this meeting," said Randell. "We still have more investigation to complete. We need to go to Tampa and try to interview Derek Kline," said Randell.

Hale nodded. Who is Kline? he thought. Hale had not heard a word the officers said. His mind was clouded with rage. He was going to have to let Alesse and Magyar go. He didn't think he could stand it.

***

The officers left and went back to the station. They had the Chief of Police in St. Petersburg contacting the Chief in Tampa to tell him that Faircloth and Randell were going to conduct an investigation of a murder that had occurred in St. Pete. The men would be interviewing witnesses in Tampa. It was a matter of courtesy to call the other jurisdiction, but also a matter of safety for the men. The men didn't want to be stopped by the police in Tampa and charged with impersonating a police officer. Then Faircloth and Randell went out to dinner. No telling when they would have time to eat once they were across Tampa Bay.

***

It was 2 p.m.

Hale called Mary. He told her to first check and see if Judge Waters was the on call duty judge in the afternoon. He told her to tell the judge's secretary that the judge may need all the court personnel available in court to take a plea to a charge.

Mary called back. "He says he's always available to take a plea to get rid of a case," said Mary.

"Good, now call attorneys James DeMarco and Tom Night and tell them to be in my private office with their clients, Magyar and Alesse at 4:00 p.m. Call Judge Waters back and tell him we may not be before him until 5:30 p.m."

It was presently 2:30 p.m.

***

"This is Mary. The Judge can stay until 6:00 if you need him that late. He says he's available straight through from now to 6:00. Just come to his chambers when you are ready. He says you need to have the court file with you."

"Order it from the Clerk, will you?" asked Hale.

"I did," said Mary.

"What about the attorneys and their clients?"

"They will be there at your office at 3:15 p.m.," said Mary.

***

It was 3:15 p.m.

There were five men huddled around Hale's desk.

"I brought you here to discuss settlement of this case," said Hale. "Since Richard Cook died I have spent a lot of my time trying to personally investigate this case."

"Have you located Lori Schaeffer?" asked Tom.

"To be honest, I have not," Hale lied. "But we do have some leads that we are still following up on."

"What about Clemenso Bondi? Have you located him?" asked James DeMarco.

"No, we haven't," said Hale. "Again we have leads."

"Will you have them available for the trial?"

"That is the $64,000 question," said Hale. "I'm not sure where they are and that's why I asked you here to talk about a plea deal."

"If the witnesses aren't available to testify, the case against our clients is over," said James DeMarco. He was feeling pretty good now. He anticipated when the meeting was called that Hale was going to tell them he had found the witnesses and Hale was going to try to cram a settlement with a long sentence in jail down their clients' throats. Instead, the defense was in the catbird seat.

"Why are we here, exactly?" asked Tom.

"We are here to decide if you're clients are going to have a life in the future without a long jail sentence," said Hale. "The aggravated battery charge carries a sentence of 15 years. The facts in this case are heinous. I expect the court would impose a maximum sentence of 15 years with probation afterward, upon conviction. That's assuming these boys will survive jail. The inmates are pretty hard on prisoners who cut up women." Hale smiled at Tommy.

"John, I need you to drop the theatrics' and tell us the offer," said Tom.

"Five years," said Hale.

Tom began to pack his bag. "I thought you were going to be serious. Alphonse will lose his career if he pleads to any sentence that involves jail or an adjudication of guilt."

"Mr. Magyar's thinking more like a non-jail sentence, nolo contendere to a simple assault charge with one day's probation and a withhold of adjudication," said James.

"That might be alright," Tom agreed. Tom knew that The Florida Bar Association would not prevent Alesse from being admitted to practice law if he was charged with a misdemeanor (simple assault was a misdemeanor.) and he was not convicted (if there is a withhold of adjudication there is no conviction). Further, Tom knew both clients would be eligible to have the record of the arrest expunged so there would be no record of an arrest.

"You all stay inside and talk," said Hale. "I have to get the Court file. I have a plea hearing scheduled before Judge Waters if you want to accept the plea deal."

"Do you agree with our proposal?" asked Tom.

"Yes," said Hale. He had no other choice.

James and Tom and Alphonse and Tommy spoke after Hale left the room. Tom explained what all the talk meant and the consequences of the deal being offered by the State. They were giving up a trial. But if they went to trial and were convicted their lives were ruined. They understood. Alphonse was aware the plea would not affect his ability to become a lawyer. He had already felt the sting of discrimination as the result of his arrest. His wife would just have to understand why he accepted the plea deal. If she couldn't, she could divorce him, he thought.

The four men agreed the result was fair under the circumstances. By pleading Nolo Contendere they were not pleading guilty, they were only agreeing the State had enough evidence to prove a prima fascia case to a misdemeanor, simple assault.

***

It was 5:15 p.m.

Court personnel were assembled in Courtroom A, Judge Waters presiding. The clerk read the case number. Tommy and Alphonse were placed under oath. The judge asked the State Attorney to state the offer made to the defendants. Hale did. The judge then questioned the defendants to determine whether they understood the rights they were giving up in return for the plea bargain.

After being satisfied the defendants knew what they were doing and the rights they were giving up, the court said he would approve the deal. But first he looked at the State Attorney. "John, are you sure this is what you want to do? I know the facts in this case."

"I'm doing the best I can do," said Hale.

The judge nodded his head and said he accepted the plea and sentenced Tommy and Alphonse as per the agreement. The judge got up and left the bench.

The Bailiff said, "All rise."

Part IX

Revenge and vengeance
fail to satisfy.

Chapter 35

Randell and Faircloth had been forced to wait for their chief to talk to the Chief of the Tampa Police Department to advise the Tampa Chief that two detectives from St. Petersburg were going to interview Derek Kline at The Man Trap regarding the aggravated battery and the murder of Lori Schaeffer.

Both detectives were glad for the delay, because they were unable to determine what Derek Kline's motive might have been for him to commit those crimes. It was easy to assign a motive to Clemenso Bondi. The relationship between the pair (they were lovers) provided ample motive for violence.

The detectives had yet to interview Sarah Rogers. She now resided in Clem and Lori's house since her promotion to supervisor of The Oar House. If they couldn't interview Derek this night, they could finish up the investigation in St. Pete by talking to Sarah.

Randell and Faircloth drove together to The Oar House in Randell's unmarked vehicle. They pulled into the parking lot and spoke to the attendant. He called inside on his two-way radio and was told to bring the detectives into Sarah's office by way of her private entrance so that the police were not seen by the patrons walking through the club.

Sarah was not a cordial person. She could be quite curt as Randell had found from his dealings with her when the search warrant was served. Randell felt that if they could obtain any information it would regard the carpet and the rug they found at the Toy Town Landfill.

Sarah kept the men standing.

"We have a few questions," said Randell. "I asked you about the carpet in Clem's house when we served the search warrant. We found a piece of carpet at the dump."

"I had nothing to do with the carpet," said Sarah. "There was no carpet in the living room when I moved in."

"You were Lori's best friend. You lived in her apartment in The Gateway after she moved in with Clem."

"Yes, but what's the point?"

"As Lori's best friend, didn't you visit her after she moved into Clem's house?"

"Yes."

"Wasn't there carpet there when you visited?"

"I can't remember."

"Was there any floor covering?"

"There might have been a carpet," said Sarah, reconsidering.

"Was there an oriental rug?" asked Faircloth.

"I believe there was an oriental rug when I visited."

"Did you ever see a carpet or a rug in the living room after you moved in?"

"No."

"You reported the attack when Lori was assaulted?"

"Correct."

"Where did you find Lori, at Clem's house or in the apartment at The Gateway?"

"She was at her apartment in The Gateway."

"That's the apartment you took over and sub-leased?"

"Correct."

"Where did you find Lori?"

In the living room. On the terrazzo floor."

"Was there blood on the floor?"

"Yes, I believe so."

"How did Lori get to the hospital?"

"I took her."

"How did you know she was in the apartment and needed help?"

"I can't remember."

"Did she call you?"

"I don't know."

"Did someone else call you?"

"Maybe."

"You aren't making much sense," said Faircloth. "How could you not remember how you came to find Lori injured and bleeding in the living room at her apartment in The Gateway?"

"I don't know."

"Was there blood on the floor?"

"I told you there was."

"We have pictures of the living room floor." Randell took the pictures from a folder in his file and laid them on the desk top. The photos of the living room floor did not show blood on the floor. "Where is the blood?"

"I must have cleaned the blood up after I took Lori to the hospital."

"Are you saying the police technicians didn't take pictures that night?"

"I don't know."

"These photographs were taken of Lori's apartment while you and Lori were at the hospital," said Faircloth. "There is no blood on the floor in these pictures. It would seem like the floor had to have been cleaned before you took Lori to the hospital."

Sarah began to look like she was staring into headlights. She became very quiet. She looked down. The detectives knew it was best to be quiet. Sarah was trapped. She had to have time to fully realize that fact. She would either break off the interview or she would tell all she knew. They would have to let her tell the story in her own way, like a fact machine with no emotion.

Sarah finally spoke the truth. "I got a call from Richard Cook the night Lori was cut. He told me Lori was at Clem's house with Clem and Richard. There was blood on the wall to wall carpet in the living room in Clem's house. I was told to take her to the ER and tell the doctor that I had found her at her apartment in The Gateway. If the doctor or if the police asked me any questions I was just supposed to say I got a call from Lori and I went to her apartment and found her there. I was not to say I found her at Clem's house. Clem was not to be involved.

"I later learned from Richard that Lori was cut by Derek Kline on orders from the corporate office in Jacksonville. It was punishment because Clem and Lori broke the rules regarding employees living together. After the police got involved, Richard was put in charge of the case. Richard tried to keep a lid on the case but he couldn't control the police. They were just doing their job ... trying to solve the crime. Lori was a little crazy to begin with, but the attack and the cutting and disfigurement took her over the top. Even though Richard and Clem tried to undermine the investigation, she identified two people as the men who attacked her, when they were innocent. Then the defense lawyers began to pressure Clem and Lori because it was obvious their clients were not guilty.

"Richard and Clem became afraid they would be caught because they couldn't control Lori, then Clem and Lori took off and hid so the case would be dismissed.

"So when Clem left, the company gave me a promotion to Clem's job."

Sarah stopped speaking. Sarah had admitted she gave a false police report. She had avoided a perjury charge because she had never been put under oath when she told her lie about finding Lori at her apartment.

After speaking to Sarah, the detectives had the motive for the aggravated assault and probable cause to arrest Derek Kline.

"Do you know where Lori is at the present time?" asked Randell.

"I saw Clem about a week ago and he said he took her to North Carolina and she was with her family."

Randell asked her directly. "Is Lori dead?"

"I don't believe so. I think she and Clem left town and she is in Carolina with her mother."

"We are going to have to speak to the State Attorney about this and we will be back to you," said Randell.

***

When Faircloth and Randell left the club exiting the private door, they drove to the police station and Randell typed the notes of the interview with Sarah Rogers. Faircloth read the notes to see if he was in agreement and the detectives both signed the report.

It had been raining all night and now it was pouring. They went in Randell's office and called Mary, the secretary at John Hale's office and she agreed to locate the State Attorney. She told them she would have him call them.

Hale called and complained about the time of the call. It was after midnight.

"We need your advice," they both said into the phone.

"Will just one of you speak or I won't be able to hear anything with you fellas talking into the speaker phone."

Randell began to explain about the interview with Sarah. He told Hale that she had admitted that she had lied when she reported the assault and that the lie was told at the request of

Detective Richard Cook. That Sarah also reported Lori's assailant was Derek Kline. That Sarah was unaware Lori was a murder victim. That Tommy Magyar and Alphonse Alesse were innocent of the aggravated assault.

"Well," said Hale. "You will see what I did in the paper tomorrow. I made a plea deal with Magyar and Alesse earlier today. The case is closed."

"That's terrible," said Faircloth. "It is wrong."

"I let them plead to simple assault. They will have no record of the conviction," said Hale.

"What are we supposed to do with Derek Kline? He's the real criminal. If you take a plea from Magyar and Alesse it says Kline was not Lori's assailant. You aren't telling us to let Kline go, are you?" Randell was on his feet yelling into the phone.

"Whether I prosecute him or not is my prerogative," said Hale, and he hung up the phone.

Randell and Faircloth just looked at each other. In frustration, Randell threw the pile of papers off his desk.

Faircloth picked them up. "What are we going to do?"

Randell straightened out the papers. On top was a note signed by the chief stating that the Tampa Police Chief gave permission for the detectives to conduct their investigation of the aggravated battery and murder of Lori Schaeffer.

Randell showed the note from the chief to Faircloth. "We are going to Tampa as soon as The Man Trap opens tomorrow and we are going to interview Derek Kline. We still have an open case for Lori's murder," said Randell. "If we establish probable cause to make the arrest of Kline, Hale will be in a crack if he doesn't prosecute him."

The heavy rain continued to fall.

Chapter 36

As Clem pulled out of the driveway of the Hunter's Motel and looked to the north, he could see a storm was coming. He hoped he could stay ahead of it as he drove south.

In the fall, if you had a storm that developed late in the year that came out of the Caribbean Sea, it could develop into a hurricane that hit Florida from the southwest. If the storm came from the north it was a Nor'easter. In either event, you had a storm that would last a day or two and produce heavy, blinding rain.

Clem drove on US 98/301. The traffic was slow, so he made poor time, and the storm, which was moving at 40 to 50 miles per hour, caught him as he came into Dade City. Clem did not intend to stop until he arrived at The Man Trap, but the storm made a change in his plans. He needed food and stopped in the outskirts of the town at a Bar-B-Q restaurant. He ordered a full slab of ribs with beans and slaw.

He used the facilities while he waited for his order. He didn't want to stand in the crowd of men who had been sent by their wives to pick up dinner. Clem did not know if there had been a news bulletin that he was a wanted man. If there was no BOLO (be on the lookout) someone could still recognize him. He would not know the person. He had a poor memory? He had been hit in the head too many times, or he speared too many players with his head first tackles.

Clem heard the cashier call out that his order was ready and he paid and left and he got in his car.

He turned his Chevy to the right (southward) as he pulled out of the parking lot just as the rain started to fall again. He put a pork rib in his mouth. The meat was so tender that he could suck it off the bone. The sauce was not too spicy, it was just right. He was distracted by the rib and drifted into the oncoming lane and a car had to swerve out of his way.

Naturally it was a Dade City patrol car.

Clem watched the police car in his rear view mirror. The car pulled into the parking lot of the Bar-B-Q. Was the cop going to ignore his reckless driving? The cop could be using the lot to turn around. The brush and trees grew right up to the right of way of the road and it was hard to find a place to turn around.

The law turned into the lot but the cop didn't turn around and come back out. Lucky for Clem, the cop's wife must have placed an order for take-out, thought Clem. Clem was still nervous. The cop had a radio. He could have called in to have a partner up the road pull him over. I had better be safe than sorry, thought Clem. I need to get off the main road. So Clem made the first left turn on an access road for a large orange juice processing plant (Lykes Pasco). He drove past the plant. He pulled out another rib and sucked the meat off the bone as he listened to the radio and drove slowly.

The rain stopped and then became a drizzle. Then large, silver dollar size drops with hail pelted the car and then came the deluge. He put the ribs away and concentrated on the narrow back road. He was passing fields and farm houses, barns and out buildings that housed machines to care for orange trees. Clem had to wipe the inside of the windshield to see where he was going. He drove at a crawl. The road had 90 degree left and right turns. He must have traveled five miles, he thought. The road changed from one with an asphalt cap to a lime rock road. Then he crossed a wooden bridge. There was a sign ahead that said: "Office".

There was a right hand turn. He took that road but it was a mistake. He wound around in circles in a grove of tall pine timber and finally came to a dead end at the Withlacoochee River. Clem was unaware, but he was on the west side of the Green Swamp, a 322,000 acre woodland. The swamp was a dome of water. The rain was heavy each year over the swamp. The swamp soaked up the rainwater and then expelled it into streams that turned into four rivers: the Hillsborough, that flowed south; the Peace River, that went east and then south; the Ocklawaha, that flowed north and west, and the Withlacoochee, that headed east then south then west, then north and finally it went west again into the Gulf of Mexico.

Clem dead ended at a portion of the Withlacoochee River. There was a shack on the river. He decided to ride out the storm there. He grabbed his food and his suitcase. He ran through the rain. Still soaked. The bright side; the back door to the shack was open. It had a tin roof and the heavy rain beat the roof silly. There was a sink in the one room shack. He washed. The water smelled like sulfur and had a strange taste, chalky like.

There were cots along the back wall of the shack with a bed roll on each cot. There was a small front porch where you could see the river. There was a walkway to the right. The boardwalk was fifty feet long and led to a small building ... the facilities. The outhouse emptied the human waste into the river. As he had used water at the sink to wash his face Clem hoped the facilities emptied its human waste downstream.

Clem sat on a rocking chair on the porch. He finished his meal and put the box on the floor. He went inside. It was getting cool. There was a stove in the shack but no wood. Clem lay on a cot and fell asleep. For the first time in years he slept for about a seven hour stretch without waking. The rain continued and the sound helped him sleep.

***

Clem stirred. He saw a truck's headlight beam shining into the windows of the shack. Clem fixed the bed roll on the cot. He packed his bag and remembered the food box on the porch. He threw it out the front door off the porch, sat in the rocker and waited.

Clem hoped the man in the truck would come in so he could explain himself. If he didn't come in and left, it meant the police would be called and that would be bad.

Clem heard the back door creak open. He got up and faced into the shack from the door of the porch. The person who was now inside aimed a strong flashlight beam on Clem.

"I was trying to get out of the storm and I got lost. I saw the shack and thought I would wait it out," said Clem.

The person who had come in the back door of the shack had a shotgun. "A person can get lost here in this forest. I'll give you that," said a woman's voice. She was dressed in a full length yellow rain coat.

"If you could show me the way out I will be on my way," said Clem.

"Close the door behind me and follow my truck. I'll get you to the bridge. If you stay on the road after the bridge it will get you back to the highway."

"Thank you," said Clem. The rain was steady. Clem drove his car behind the truck until he got to the bridge. The woman waved him on. He drove to US Highway 98/301 and continued south into Tampa.

***

It was 10:00 a.m. as Clem drove past The Man Trap. The club was closed.

"I need to start over. I've lost a day," thought Clem. He drove to the Howard Frankland Bridge and drove across Tampa Bay. He went to Williams Park in downtown St. Petersburg and found some shelter under the band shell. He waited for the rain to stop. He stood with a group of bums that were waiting for a free lunch. St. Vincent De Paul arrived in a beat up Ford station wagon. The do-gooders set up a table and carried a large metal soup tureen filled with tomato soup and sandwiches to the table. The meal was meager, but hot. It was cold outside, still 40 degrees F. The coldest day in October. A new record.

***

It was 1 p.m. in the afternoon. The rain only came in spurts now. But still no sunshine. The afternoon paper, The Evening

Independent, would be free now since there had been 24 continuous hours without sunshine in St. Petersburg (the Sunshine City). The give-away promotion was started by the editor of the newspaper 25 years ago. Clem stood in line at a news rack and got his free paper and went back to the bench under the roof of the band shell and read the paper.

Part two of the thin paper had the gossip column and courts section, followed by the Classifieds. There in the court section was a small story about the sentencing of a pair of men for a simple assault. Clem recognized the facts, this was Lori's case. There was a quotation from the State Attorney in which John Hale stated that after the investigation the case had turned out to be very weak and this was a good disposition of the charges under the circumstances. There was a statement made by the defense attorneys. They said their clients did not admit they were guilty and only entered their pleas because the deal offered by the State Attorney was so lenient. More bull hockey, thought Clem. But he was happy. If the case was resolved the police wouldn't be looking for him, or so he thought. It should be easier for him to get to Derek, or so Clem thought.

Clem needed to kill some time and get off the streets. He thought a minute and then he laughed out loud. He walked down the street and got in his car and drove west from downtown. In ten minutes he drove past the Quick Mart and made a left and drove to the front of his old house. Sarah lived here now but she would be at work. He turned off the ignition switch and took his suitcase and went to the front door. He had three keys left from back when he managed the club and lived in the old house. He tried each of the keys in the front door. The last key opened the lock. He went inside. He sat in his big Stratolounger in the living room and pushed back and laid there a minute. He felt something hard by his left thigh. It was a .22 caliber pistol. He put the gun on the table next to the recliner and fell asleep.

Chapter 37

Clem awoke from his long nap in his recliner. But he did not feel rested and he was stiff. He saw the .22 caliber firearm on the table by his chair. He picked it up and put the gun in his pocket and checked the time. It was 3 p.m. The topless clubs opened at 2 p.m. and Derek Kline should be finishing his management duties and settling in for a long night. They would close at 2 a.m.

The rain had stopped but it was still overcast and gray. It looked like there would only be a break in the storm and it would start again soon. Clem walked out front. There was a lady standing at the bay window of her house. She was looking out and staring at him. He shot her an obscene gesture using the middle finger on his right hand and climbed in his car and scratched off ... squealing his tires ... heading for Tampa.

Clem drove across the Howard Frankland Bridge. It was being rebuilt, and soon there would be twin spans, but no one thought it would help the congestion crossing Tampa Bay. The locals called the bridge "The Frankenstein." It was overused and dangerous. There were three bridges across the bay where there needed to be six.

Clem was trying to think of the best place to lay in wait for Derek. Clem had the layout Gene had obtained from Peter the day she successfully tried out to be a dancer at the club. It showed the private entrance from Derek's office to the outside that would allow a person to exit at the back of the building. That private exit opened onto a small area used for overflow parking. From the parking lot one had the view of a fence and the rear of numerous commercial businesses. Strip joints were restricted to parts of the

City that had no schools or churches. So the clubs tended to be in industrial and commercial areas that wouldn't be concerned with the activity in the building. Most likely the clubs drew many of their patrons from those industrial and commercial businesses.

Once Clem arrived in the neighborhood in the Dale Mabry area near Tampa Stadium, he drove in front of the buildings that abutted the rear of The Man Trap's property. Times were tough and a number of businesses were closed. He found a large abandoned building and he drove to the rear. From there he could see the rear of the club and the overflow parking lot and the private exit door that connected to the secret back door from Derek's office.

Next to the back door, he saw Derek's Kawasaki motorcycle.

Clem drove to a sandwich shop and bought a Cuban and plantain chips (like potato chips but made with a type of banana) and a six-pack of long neck Buds, (the "King of Beers"). He drove back to the rear of the abandoned building and began to pull around to the back. Ahead, at the door at Derek's private exit sat a security guard in a blue/gray colored uniform. He was an old man. He had a black cap with a shiny plastic brim and red epaulettes on each shoulder. He had an old style, two inch wide gun belt with bullets and holster and a .38 caliber Police "Positive" Special handgun. Clem figured he was a retired cop. The cop saw Clem and his car. The guard got up from his seat and he crouched in the "at ready" position. Clem waved to calm him down and continued to drive along the fence that separated the club from the businesses. The guard sat back down on his gray metal folding chair as Clem drove away.

There were other businesses that were vacant behind the club, and Clem chose another one with better cover. At the rear of a large, empty warehouse there was a small grove of Australian pines that grew along the fence. Clem parked among the trees. The guard couldn't see him as Clem sat leaning up against a tree trunk and watching the rear of the building. The guard was watching nothing in particular. It was hard to understand how the guard could stay awake, especially since they gave him a chair. He could prop his head against the wall and in the cool breeze in the late fall afternoon in the low sun, any normal male mammal would fall asleep. But not the cop, he dutifully stayed wide awake.

***

Peter was having a rough day in paradise. The ice machine broke during the night and they had trouble finding a local repairman. There was a question if the patrons would stay and watch the naked women if there was no ice cold beer. Probably not, they decided.

Derek was in a sour mood. He had two security guards who babysat him the night before and he got little sleep. He had to pay the guards out of his own pocket because they were there to protect him and not the business. Worse, the guards didn't make him feel safe. They were old retired Tampa police officers. Derek guessed they were in their early 70s.

The last problem was that Sarah had phoned to tell him that the police had visited her at the club late at night asking her questions about Clem and Richard and Lori and him. Derek didn't like that at all. Time had slipped by since he assaulted Lori and he had almost forgotten about the crime. He had pushed those memories back behind other more immediate problems, like the fact that Clem said he was going to kill him.

"Lord, give me peace," Derek repeated like a mantra as he walked in circles inside his office.

"Lord, help me," repeated Derek. Derek asked for the Lord's aid many times in the day. The Lord never helped him or answered his prayers. Actually, he asked for the Lord's help to confirm there was no Lord. And if there was no Lord there was no hell. If he believed in hell, he would not be so essentially bad to the bone. If he believed in the Lord, he would not feel as he did, that people who do good are just fools.

"The ice machine repair man just entered the club," said Peter as he walked in Derek's office.

"Finally, some good news," Derek said to Peter.

"Yeah, Boss. Good news," said Peter. "We have cold beer."

"Sarah says I may get a visit from the law. I am going to stay in my office and work on the accounting books. The auditors will be in tomorrow. I haven't been able to reconcile the accounts. If the cops come, tell them I'm not here."

"Okay," said Peter.

"I also think I'm going to fire the extra security guards."

"I don't think you should do that," said Peter. "They are the only security men we got that have guns."

"I've got a gun," said Derek. Peter was not reassured.

***

At 3:45 p.m. it began to rain again. The clouds were dark as smoke from a tire on fire and the wind swirled. Clem got in his car and the security guard at the private exit at the club went inside the tunnel and propped open the door so he had shelter. The storm was now carrying some gale force winds.

Meanwhile, in the front of The Man Trap, Faircloth and Randell pulled up to the valet parking space in their unmarked police car. The parking space had an overhang and was out of the weather. Randell was driving and he took the parking stub from the attendant. He watched where his car was parked and then he and Faircloth went inside the club.

The doorman opened the front door and the detectives were hit with a blast of disco, smoke and the smell of "Eau de Tavern". The odor of stale beer and vomit. Faircloth looked around. The ticket taker asked for their membership cards. They showed their badges.

The attendant left and went in a side door and came out with Peter.

"What do you officers want?"

"We're here to see Derek Kline."

"I'll check to see if he's here," said Peter. "Meanwhile, have a seat."

Peter directed the men to a front row seat and winked at the dancer, as if to say, "These are cops. Don't do anything that will get you or me arrested." Peter went inside the back of the bar and rapped on Derek's door.

"Who is it?"

"Me," said Peter.

Derek unlocked the door. "What? I'm working on the books."

"The cops are here and want to speak to you."

"Stall them as long as you can."

Peter went into the club and told the detectives that Derek was working and he would be out as soon as he could. "What can I get you to drink?"

The men requested orange juice from a can they could unseal themselves. They said they could wait a short while but they expected Derek to be out soon. Peter said he understood.

Derek put the books in the safe. He removed a stack of $100 bills and grabbed his motorcycle helmet and walked casually through the private exit. The guard was standing there. Derek told the guard that he left something at home and he would be back soon. Derek told the guard to go inside and tell Peter he left the premises but "don't tell anyone else". The guard said okay and Derek left.

***

Clem had been watching the open door at the rear of The Man Trap. He could no longer see the guard. Clem moved toward the fence, even though it was raining. This might be his chance to cross the fence and enter the building without anyone being aware. As Clem was climbing the fence he saw Derek come out of the door. Clem turned away from the fence and dropped to the ground. Derek got on the motorcycle; kick started the motor, put it in gear and roared away.

Clem hurried into his car leaving the sandwich and beer on the ground. He backed away from the grove of Australian pines and drove to the access road in front of the row of commercial buildings. He could turn left or right. Depending on the direction he turned, he would either be behind Derek's motorcycle or Derek would escape because Clem didn't know where Derek was headed. Clem chose to turn left, drove to the end of the street and stopped at the stop sign. He looked left. He couldn't see anything but rain. Snake eyes, he thought. Derek got away.

Clem turned his car around and went in the opposite direction until he got to the stop sign on the opposite end of the access road. He decided to turn right. He went about 200 yards and decided that turning right was wrong and he made a U-turn and headed back in the other direction.

Clem thought the only logical place Derek would go was to his house.

Clem didn't know Tampa well, but he remembered that Derek's house was near The Man Trap. Sarah had told him that Derek's house was on Arrow Street. Clem began to crisscross back and forth in the neighborhoods within ten blocks of the club. He thought he had little likelihood of success, but he was determined to end Derek's life.

***

Meanwhile, inside the Man Trap, Det. Faircloth arose from his front row seat. He found Peter trying to sneak into a back door. He stopped him and said it appeared Peter and Derek were not being cooperative. Peter said he would check on Derek personally. He walked through the door into the back room. Minutes later he came out and said he was told Derek had gone home to pick up some paperwork. Faircloth asked for the address. Peter gave him the correct address, (1324 Arrow Street). But Peter lied and said he had never been to the house and couldn't give accurate directions. He did offer that the orange juice the detectives were given was free of charge.

Faircloth collected Randell and they left the club. The valet delivered their unmarked car.

"Where is 1324 Arrow Street from the club?" asked Faircloth. Though the officers had been to Derek's house before when they followed Sarah, they were lost now.

"You mean the boss' place?" asked the valet.

"Yes."

"It's a little tricky. Let me draw you a map." The valet got paper and pencil and drew and then explained how to get to the house. He even pointed out the directions and landmarks. "You can tell if he's at home if his motorcycle is parked in front. He has a Kawasaki."

"Thanks," said the men. They were familiar with the Kawasaki. They left the club, following the valet's directions.

***

Clem continued his search for Arrow Street. He looked down and noticed the fuel gage registered a quarter tank below empty. I must be on fumes, he thought. Just ahead he saw a Sun Oil gas station. He pulled in. Even in the rain, the attendant opened the hood and checked the fluids. The Chevy needed a quart of oil and a little water.

"Do you want an oil change? You need one quart already."

"Not today. Just top off the oil and fill up the gas tank."

The attendant came to the window of the Chevy. Total charge including fuel was $16.

Clem gave him a twenty. When the man came back with the change, Clem asked the attendant if he knew where Arrow Street was located.

"I sure do. It's a little tricky to find though. The road is real narrow and you'll get a ticket if you park on the sidewalk. It's a dead end street and it has a cul-de-sac with a bunch of trees and bushes at one end. If you don't have a map you will drive around all day trying to find it."

The attendant drew a map and gave Clem hand directions pointing the way.

"Thank you," said Clem. "If I finish up soon with the house-call, I'll come back and get the oil change."

Clem had lied. Clem went out of his way to lie. It was his habit to do the wrong thing. It's hard to be good if you constantly commit bad acts. Goodness is habit-forming. It's easy to be good if you stay in practice. Clem did not stay in practice to do anything – except to do things that were bad.

Chapter 38

Randell had a premonition. After the valet at The Man Trap retrieved their unmarked car and gave directions to Derek's house, Randell pulled over in the parking lot. Randell never wore his service revolver, or any other weapon. He reached under the seat of his car and patted the carpet until he found his .45 caliber Colt. It was secured in its holster with the strap engaged. He had ammunition in the glove box. He handed the gun to Faircloth, who checked to see if a round was in the chamber. There was, but he found the clip was empty. He loaded the clip. There was an extra clip in the glove compartment. Faircloth gave Randell the gun. Faircloth reached over and put the extra clip and a handful of loose rounds in Randell's inside coat pocket.

Faircloth had a .38 caliber Police "Positive" Special that had been issued to him on graduation from the police academy. He had been required to pay for the gun … the cost was deducted from his salary a few dollars every other pay period. The City Fathers figured that if he had to pay for the gun there was incentive for him not to lose it. The revolver was loaded. He had the gun in a holster on a belt and he had extra bullets in small leather cases on the belt.

"I hope I don't have to use this gun," said Randell. "It will be the first time I have fired it in a couple of years. I never have fired the gun in the line of duty at a suspect."

"Me either," said Faircloth, "but I have only been on the force two and a half years."

Randell listened as Faircloth read the valet's directions from the note. Arrow Street was a dead end street with a cul-de-sac at the end that allowed a vehicle to turn around. The street was like a rabbit hole. A driver had to circle a warren of streets until you found the entrance to the street. Because of the trees and bushes at the end of the street it was hard to distinguish the existence of the cul-de-sac, but Randell noted there was a sign that said: "Arrow Street".

The weather was still blustery, and because of the cloud cover it was dark as night, but the rain had stopped. The men had their windows rolled down. It was cold. As their car turned onto Arrow Street they could hear gunshots. They drove further and saw a '56 Chevy that had crashed into the front door of a house. The front wall of the house had collapsed and the roof was sagging because it lacked the support of the front wall. A piece of ornamental iron was loose but still swinging from the force of the collision of the car with the house.

There was a Kawasaki motorcycle that was over on its side but didn't appear damaged. The Chevy had suffered major damage to the front and passenger side. The driver's door was open. The officers could see the muzzle flash of Clem's .44 caliber Magnum revolver that was being fired inside the house. They could hear the sound of two weapons. Both were high caliber weapons, they guessed. They guessed right. One was a revolver and the other was a semi-automatic.

Randell doubted the Chevy could be extricated from the front of the house on its own power, but to be safe, he pulled up behind the older car to block it. The St. Petersburg policemen opened their doors and stayed low behind the doors once they got out of the car. They had no other cover available to them besides the cars in front of the house. They peeked around the side of the doors of their car and looked through the car's window port. From the sound of the shots, which were random, it appeared there were two shooters and they were at opposite sides of the house, probably shooting from doorways of rooms on either side of the inside of the house. Best guess ... the shooters were 40 feet apart.

Faircloth grabbed the radio and contacted the station in St. Petersburg and reported their location. Dispatch in St. Petersburg called his report of "shots fired" to Tampa Police. Faircloth felt sure a neighbor had made a report but it was just 5:00 in the afternoon and there might be no one at home yet.

Within a minute or two of rolling up behind the Chevy, the policemen hiding behind the doors of their unmarked police car began to take fire from the house. The detectives looked at each other as if to say: "What did we do to cause that?" In any event, the men began to feel uncomfortable. Faircloth signaled that he would move closer to the house to try to see what was going on inside the house. As he moved forward, crawling on his stomach toward the Chevy, he heard a third weapon that seemed like it was a small caliber pistol, like a .22.

Faircloth pushed himself against the trunk of the Chevy and he was able to see into the hole the car made in the front wall of the house. There was a huge living room inside the front wall. It was sunken about three feet below floor level. The shooters were battling across the sunken living room. Faircloth yelled "Police" when the shooters were reloading. It was then that the ping of the .22 caliber weapon was fired at his position from his left. Faircloth figured there were only two shooters with three guns. The person on the left had a .22 and a .44 caliber cannon and the person on the right had a .38 semi-automatic.

Faircloth went back to report what he saw.

"Let's stay out of it, let them kill each other," said Randell. "I just got confirmation. Tampa Police are on their way."

The shooter on the left squeezed off four quick rounds from his weapons. There was no reply from the right.

There was a lull. Randell was uncomfortable squatting down with all his weight on his knees. He was too old for this, he thought. He sat down on the ground. At that time, a large athletic male came running out of the house firing at the officers with both guns. Faircloth dove to the right and heard a terrible scream from Randell who was on his left. The big athletic man was attempting to steal the unmarked car and he had been able to enter the driver side of the vehicle and pull the shifter into reverse. The car moved back and Faircloth got to his knees and fired two shots into the open passenger door. He missed the man. Randell never fired a shot. The driver was able to hit the accelerator and the car shot backwards. The passenger door hit Faircloth's arm and he lost his gun. When the car got in the street the driver slammed on the brakes and the car doors flew forward and then as the unmarked police car accelerated the doors sprang backward and slammed shut.

Randell was still screaming in pain and he looked at Faircloth and said, "Could you give me some help?"

Faircloth's forearm felt like it was broken, but he got up and went to his partner. Randell was missing his left foot and the stump was pumping blood into a puddle on the ground. The femoral artery within the thigh feeds blood to the tibial artery and the perennial artery feeds blood to the dorsal artery of the foot. The .44 caliber bullet hit the two bones (tibia and fibula) in the lower leg above the ankle and broke the bones and tore the arteries and Randell's left foot was imperfectly, but totally amputated from the rest of his leg.

Faircloth looked for something to twist around Randell's leg to stop the blood flow from the stump. He noticed the cuff on Randell's pants.

Faircloth had carried a pocket knife since he was a kid. He opened the knife and poked a hole through the trousers just above the cuff. He closed the knife and inserted the closed knife in the hole in the material and began to twist the cuff with the knife. The cuff closed around the stump and acted as a tourniquet. The bleeding decreased almost totally as he twisted the cuff, making it tight on the stump of Randell's leg.

Tampa Police arrived. There were two cars. They were quick and professional and helped Randell, who was still screaming a deep roar at the pain from the ugly wound. Faircloth was holding the left leg, up above Randell's heart, staring at the wound. The police had a field tourniquet, which was efficient. They got

Faircloth off to the side. One of the officers looked for the foot and shoe. He found it near the gutter on the concrete driveway. He stood by the appendage waiting for the ambulance.

The ambulance arrived at the scene in short order. The attendant removed the field tourniquet and covered and wrapped Randell's stump. The bleeding stopped. They loaded Randell into the ambulance. An officer showed the attendant the foot, shoe and sock on the ground. The attendant retrieved the object and the attendant packed the foot and shoe and sock in ice in a Styrofoam chest and the ambulance drove quickly to Tampa General Hospital's emergency room.

Faircloth stayed at the scene. He explained to the Tampa Police that the person that shot his partner had stolen their unmarked police car. The police said they saw the car speed out of Arrow Street as they turned in. Faircloth described the car and the police radioed the information to headquarters.

Faircloth warned the police as they started to inspect the house that there was a second shooter still inside. The officers drew their weapons and entered the house from the front. They found Derek's body in a front bedroom. He had superficial wounds to his right arm and flank. The wound that killed him was to the neck. A bullet struck the wood from the door jamb, which splintered, and a sliver of the wood had sliced an artery in Derek's neck. He had plopped back on the bed after being hit. He bled to death. He lay there with his eyes and mouth wide open. From his expression it appeared Derek was surprised that he could be killed in a gun fight.

***

When St. Petersburg's Police Chief arrived at the scene, he found that Faircloth had been treated at the scene. His arm was not broken, but bruised. It was in a sling.

The Chief had been advised of the gunfight by radio as he drove to Tampa. He was already fully aware of the case. First, it had been unusual having a victim being cut on her face and chest;

then she had failed to cooperate with the police; then the complaints of mistaken identities, the witnesses fleeing, then the death of Richard Cook, the chief detective assigned to the case and now this ... a shootout in Tampa involving his officers, and to add to the indignity, one of his cars was stolen.

When Tampa Police finished with Faircloth, the officer and the chief went to the hospital. Randell was in surgery. A team of doctors was trying to re-attach his foot. Heroic surgery. The men were sent to a waiting room. There was a middle-aged Negro woman and two young Negro men in the room huddled together.

The chief had never met Randell's family in the near 20 years the detective had been on the force. He knew his office had notified his next of kin. He was embarrassed that he didn't know them, but assumed they had to be Randell's family. He went over and said hello. They were gracious, accepting his best wishes for Randell's recovery. The chief said he or Faircloth would remain at the hospital until there was news, good or bad.

Randell's wife took Faircloth's hand. "You're George's partner. He likes you a lot." She smiled at him.

"Thank you, ma'am," said Faircloth.

The men went over to the corner. The chief wanted an update of the case. Faircloth said he and Randell had been very upset with the fact that Tommy Magyar and Alphonse Alesse had pleaded to Lori's assault. The State Attorney knew that he couldn't prove the case against the men and that they were innocent.

Faircloth warned the chief that he and Randell intended to make that right.

"I understand." The chief wondered if it wasn't about time for him to retire. "Who was the man who shot Randell?"

"I had never seen him before. I think he was the fellow they call Clem," said Faircloth. "The DMV says the '56 Chevy was owned by a man named Clemenso M. Bondi. He ran The Oar House strip club in St. Petersburg."

The chief looked at Faircloth. "From everything you and Randell have discovered, who is it that knows the most about the assault and murder of Lori Schaeffer, the murder of Anthony Stewart, the probable murder of Det. Richard Cook, and the death of Derek Kline?"

"Sarah Rogers, the manager of The Oar House," said Faircloth. "She's the person we need to talk to under oath now."

The chief said he would talk to State Attorney Hale and have him set her for a statement under oath if she wouldn't talk to them voluntarily. Do you think you can get her to talk to you?" asked the chief.

"Yes, I can." said Faircloth. "I don't think Hale is going to help us much. We, the police, need to take the initiative. Hale is going to try to hush this up and cover his butt."

By midnight it became clear to Randell's surgeons that they were not going to be able to re-attach his foot. There was too much damage to the nerves, arteries and veins at the site of the traumatic amputation. The surgeons felt they had a more than 50% chance of saving Randell's life if the foot was removed and the stump was dressed. But the possibility of infection increased the chance of death to more than 50% if the foot was re-attached. So the doctors abandoned the consideration of saving Randell's foot and concentrated on saving the detective's life.

Chapter 39

Clem had thought that Derek, being a short, fat, out of shape dude, would be easy pickings. Clem caught Derek as he entered the front door of his home on Arrow Street. But Derek saw the '56 Chevy pulling in the driveway and he was able to grab his weapon and fire three rounds hitting the windshield of Clem's car as Derek got inside the house.

Clem accelerated and his car hit the front door and wall of the house. The roof of the house partially collapsed. Clem got out of the car and into the house and there was a gunfight in the house, with the living room being the no-man's land of the battle. Derek's new couch sustained numerous wounds.

Then the unmarked police car pulled in behind Clem's Chevy and the men in the house began taking fire from the outside on their flank. They had to return fire to the front against the men in the police car.

Derek was jumping out from behind the wall of a bedroom and then shooting and then popping back behind the wall for cover. Clem had a number of close calls. Then Clem waited for Derek to fire and when Derek jumped back behind the wall, Clem fired four rounds at the wall. The wall was made of gypsum board. Derek's only protection was a thin half-inch skin of dry wall attached to furring strips on each side of the wall. Clem fired the four shots at the wall in a cluster in the area he believed Derek was standing. The strategy paid off. One of the bullets hit a furring strip. The wood splintered and a sliver hit Derek in the neck and burst his carotid artery and knocked him on the bed, where he bled to death.

The two officers continued to fire random shots into the house. Then Faircloth started to move in to flank Clem's position and Clem decided he needed to leave. There were no shots being fired by Derek, so he believed he had inflicted the damage he intended. Time to go. Clem barreled out of the front of the house like he was a defensive tackle attacking his opponent, hitting low. But as Clem got out of the house his foot hit a remnant of the wall of the house. Clem tripped. His right hand holding the gun hit the ground and the force of the impact caused the gun to discharge accidentally. That bullet was the projectile that hit Randell's left lower extremity, separating his foot from his leg.

Clem pushed himself up. He swung his body in the front driver door of the unmarked car. The engine was running and he put the car in reverse. He accelerated.

At that time, Faircloth fired his service weapon into the police car. Two shots. Neither shot hit Clem but they caused him to react with renewed purpose. He accelerated even more. The car leaped back, then forward, as Clem put the car in forward gear once he reached the street. The front doors slammed shut as the vehicle sped forward down the street. He blew through the stop sign as two Tampa Police cars rounded the corner, pulling into Arrow Street.

All the drivers were amazed there was no collision. All of the drivers congratulated themselves for avoiding a collision.

The police continued to 1324 Arrow Street. The roof was sagging and the wall was collapsed. They had work to do. It looked like a bomb had gone off.

***

After the skirmish, Clem drove to Dale Mabry and then headed south for no particular reason. He was starving. He went in an all-night restaurant and ate waffles. The waitress flirted. He gave her a big tip, a fiver on a three dollar tab. He was thinking maybe she should go with him but he didn't know how to explain that he was driving an unmarked police car. Clem drove west on US Highway

92. He got the car washed. He used the restroom to clean up. He would have to get some clothes. His suitcase was in the '56 Chevy. He was going to miss that car. He tipped the car wash attendant two bucks.

"Oh, thank you sir," said the attendant. Clem nodded. He never tipped anyone but he had an uncontrollable compulsion to do something good for someone today after killing Derek in the gunfight.

Clem drove east. He was heading to Daytona Beach, but the car started to misfire. Bad gas, he thought. He pulled over at a filling station at the intersection of US 92 and US 301. Clem told the mechanic the car was acting up and he had to call the police station in St. Petersburg and they would tell him what to do with the car. The mechanic said there was no problem parking the car there for a while. The mechanic felt the man made no sense. The man said he would go next door to call. Why not use the police radio in the car to call, he thought. But the mechanic was busy. The next day the police car was still there. The mechanic had no idea when the policeman from St. Petersburg left. He was too damn busy, he thought. It was Tampa.

In the confusion, Clem had simply walked away from the gas station. He looked for a vehicle. He was a little confused. He walked down the side street. He saw a truck driver get out of a small delivery van, a red Ford. The lettering on the truck was yellow and said: "Tom's Potato Chips". He walked over to the truck. The keys were in the ignition. The delivery man had left the keys in the truck in case someone needed to move the vehicle while he was inside selling product and taking the store's order for potato chips. Clem got in the van and drove away. Clem drove south on US 301. He stopped in a Quick Mart parking lot. He went in the back of the potato chip van. He found a cash box with a few dollar bills and a lot of change. He took some bar-b-que chips, opened the bag, jumbo size and munched a bunch. "Tom's Chips" was the brand. Clem's favorite.

***

Clem drove south. It was familiar. Riverview. He remembered the fish camp. He had the key to the fishing cabin, he thought. He pulled up to the side of the cabin he had rented with Gene. He dug around in his pants and pulled out a ring of keys. He tried a couple of keys in the door but no luck. He went to the side of the cabin and pushed up an unlocked window. He climbed in and became dizzy and fell on the bed and slept. Out for the count. This was unusual, he rarely took a nap. But this was the second day in a row he was dizzy and then napped.

***

Back in St. Petersburg, Faircloth went back to The Oar House. Sarah had a bouncer direct him to her office and she spoke to him promptly. She was dressed in a navy blue business suit with blue high heels and stockings.

"Where's your partner?" she asked.

"He was shot by Clem." Just the facts.

"Jeez," said Sarah. "Will he live?"

"I think so," said Faircloth. "Will you voluntarily speak to the Police Chief of St. Petersburg and tell the chief the truth. Will you tell all you know about Cook, Lori and Clem and Derek?"

"Yes I will. I can't keep up with these people. They are crazy. I will be the next one found dead in the bushes."

"Will you sit down with an artist. Help him draw a picture of Clem the way he looked when you saw him last?"

"He had a driver's license. Won't they have a photo?"

"The DMV shows him with no facial hair and he's bald."

"I'll help. Can I go with you now? I need protection."

"Do you know if Clem's fingerprints are on record anywhere?"

"We all have to be fingerprinted before the Florida Restaurant Commission will let us manage one of these strip clubs. Clem would have his prints recorded with them."

Sarah and Faircloth left the club through the private exit. Faircloth had a loner vehicle from the police department. He drove back to the station with Sarah.

***

It was dark when Clem heard the knock on the front door of the cabin. The owner was at the door. Clem explained that he would need the room again for a couple of days. The owner recognized him. Clem told him he tried the front door key but it didn't work. So he came in through the window.

"Changed the lock after the fire," said the owner.

"What fire?" asked Clem.

"Someone burned up your girlfriend's clothes and belongings," the owner said. "You must have had quite a fight." The owner was grinning. "There was no damage to the cabin so I did not report the fire. No harm. No foul."

"You know how it is?" said Clem. "Did she come back by? I haven't seen her in a couple of days."

"Haven't seen her either," said the owner.

"How much do I owe you?"

"It'll be $15 per night."

"Here's $30," said Clem as he counted out bills and quarters. "Can I park the van where it is now?"

"No problem," said the owner. "You working for Tom's Potato Chips now?"

"Yes, I just got hired."

***

Faircloth settled Sarah down in Randell's office. She took off her high heels, put her feet up under her in an upholstered chair, tucked her head in her open palm and fell asleep. He went to Forensics and asked that the department contact the restaurant commission and get Derek and Clem's fingerprints and compare them to the unknown prints found on the wall plug from Det. Richard Cook's ventilation machine at the hospital and from the bathroom in Cook's house.

Faircloth then went to look for a desk in a squad room and he worked on his report.

The chief came by and told Faircloth he had an appointment with John Hale the next day. "Anything he needs to know?"

"Sarah is here in Randell's office. She says she will volunteer and be truthful and tell the State Attorney anything he wants to know about Clem, Lori, Richard and Derek and the operation of the strip clubs."

"Okay, will she help us with a police artist?"

"Yes, but first," asked Faircloth. "Do you promise that if Hale refuses to take Sarah's statement that you will do it? We need an official record of these events."

"Yes," said the chief. "I will take her statement."

Before the chief left, Forensics advised they were able to examine and compare Clem Bondi's prints from the Restaurant Commission with the prints in Det. Richard Cook's bathroom, and on the plug for the ventilator Cook was attached to at the hospital. They matched the prints as belonging to those of Clemenso M. Bondi.

Chapter 40

The blood red potato chip van stuck out like a sore thumb. Even though Clem had parked on the far side of the cabin someone driving up or down US 301 would have an excellent view of the van, both coming and going.

Clem thought he had done the best he could concealing the van and he wasn't going to worry about it anymore. Clem was mentally exhausted. Clem thought, If the police see the red van and come to arrest me I will just deal with it then.

Clem checked his stash of weapons. He had the .44 caliber Magnum and a pocket full of loose shells. The rest of the shells in the unopened boxes were in his suitcase in the '56 Chevy that he abandoned at Derek's house. He still had his heavy knife and the .22 caliber handgun that he stole from Sarah. He had only fired four shots from the pistol, but he had no additional bullets for the gun.

But this should be enough artillery to bring down a little girl, thought Clem.

Clem was now concentrating his efforts on killing Gene. He was angry as a result of the events of the proceeding day. He was reminded of her and the whipping she and her friends gave him at the Showtime Bar. He decided that he would counterattack this evening and kill her for the embarrassment she caused him.

Meanwhile, the carny folk at Gyp'town had forgotten Clem. They had won the fight, fair and square, and they were confident they could do it again if Clem returned. So they didn't dwell on him as a continuing danger. The people of Gyp'town had gone on with their lives and pretty much forgotten Clem in the last two days.

Gene was not sure they were done with the man. She knew he harbored deep grudges and he was single minded in his approach to life. If someone hurt him, he would hurt them back. He had learned that lesson in football. You could not let an injury go unanswered. That was why he developed his spearing technique. He would run and launch his body at a target and lower his head at the last second and smash into the opponent with his helmet and all the weight of his body. Normally, if he performed the spear successfully, the recipient of the spear was disabled for the game and sometimes for months.

Clem knew that the Carnies would forget the fight because they had won. If they had lost, there would have been a lesson remembered, a scar that would tell them they had to be on guard.

Clem figured Gene would still be at the Showtime and the best time to attack Gene would be at night when the Showtime bar had a crowd. He would also be able to strike out at the others in the bar who had humbled him two days ago.

***

After all that thinking, getting the group of ideas and emotions to a kernel, an essence of a thought, Clem deserved a drink. He knew not to take the van out on the street until it was dark and the vehicle would be less obvious. So he walked to the liquor store about a mile north of his cabin.

After purchasing his bottle and after opening it, and taking a few slugs of the whiskey as he walked down the street, he was stopped by the police. Two officers were on patrol doing what their sergeant told them to do, cleaning up the drunks along US 301 and the railroad tracks. To the east of the tracks there was a tangle of acres of wild bushes and trees and a number of large hobo camps. The officers thought Clem was one of the hobos, but he didn't have that smell of bum that was a sign of the underclass, the homeless, with no running water or sewer system.

The police asked for his residence address and Clem explained he was living in a cabin in the fish camp. He showed them his key. He was definitely not drunk and he let the police frisk him for a weapon. He was unarmed. He was polite. He wasn't a hobo. They let him go. No probable cause for anything unless the cops lied and made up a crime. He wasn't drunk in public or drinking within 50 feet of a liquor store or bar. So there was no crime and they did the right thing and let Clem go. But Clem didn't seem right to the officers. They had a feeling. They got in their car and drove to the fish camp and arrived ahead of him. They spoke to the owner of the camp. He verified that Clem was staying there. The police looked at the red van. They checked the registration. There were no wants for the vehicle. Inexplicably, the van had not been reported stolen at that time.

The police left before Clem got back to the cabin. When Clem walked up to his cabin the owner told him the police had been by asking questions.

"No worry, I have never been arrested for anything. I'm clean as the driven snow."

Clem took his key and opened the cabin door. Inside, he took a glass and filled it with whiskey. Earlier, he had found a bank bag full of loose change in the van. The change had been collected by the salesman from vending machines. There were coin rollers in the bag. To pass the time he began to roll the coins, quarters first, then dimes and nickels. It took him another glass of whiskey to finish the task. He counted the haul, $285.70. Then he went to sleep, passed out in the upholstered chair in the cabin.

***

At the Showtime in Gyp'town it had only taken Gene the last couple of days to fall into the routine of the job as waitress at the bar. The barkeeper, Phil Smith, was very kind. She had not yet found a place to live. She was still sleeping on the cot in the backroom of the saloon. She slept soundly and her open wounds had healed, no pain, and the bruises on her thighs and buttocks were yellow and healing. Her circulatory system had cleaned the hematoma from her behind. Her face was completely healed. A person's face is flush with blood from the heart pumping life into the brain and the blood quickly heals injury to the face.

In the odd atmosphere of Gyp'town, and with the citizens who lived on Nundy Street, Gene fit in as the beautiful gypsy woman. It became her life role in short order. She was no longer the floozy.

One could imagine that Gene would live in a horse-drawn covered wagon. That she cooked her meals on a campfire, incorporating the roots and small animals she could gather into a stew, simmered for hours in an iron kettle. Rather, and in truth, she cooked hamburger on a gas grill at the rear of the bar and slathered the bun with mustard, catsup and mayonnaise before she ate it.

But Gene dressed to look like a gypsy. She wore a peasant dress gathered at the waist with a knotted belt. She wore slippers, not shoes. Her hair fell in piles of red from her head. Her face was strong, with high cheek bones. A man would look at her and he could not help himself, he would be filled with desire and longing. It was surprising that she had fallen so low as to consider her lot in life was to be the punching bag for a person like Clem Bondi. She had had no confidence in herself and when she looked in the mirror when she was with Clem she saw herself as ugly, not the beauty she now saw in the room length mirror behind the bar at the Showtime, where she served drinks with a smile and a gentle, demure laugh.

Probably the thing that changed Gene's demeanor even more than the fact that she felt safe in Gyp'town, was that she had not had a drink since Clem had run off. She saw herself differently when she was not in a confused haze. Gene made up her mind that she did not want to go there again. No more alcohol.

The bartender was the same as Gene, except he was a drunk who had not had a drink for 23 years and 78 days. He kept the coffee pot perking for him and Gene. He was someone Gene could learn a lot from and she was willing to learn.

***

Clem woke up in the chair in the cabin. The rolls of coins were on the table. He had fallen asleep in the chair as was his habit. He felt particularly stiff and sore. He had only elevated one of his feet on an old beat up hassock. His other leg and knee hurt. He took a long drink of whiskey. He found his watch. It was 1 a.m. He gathered the coins and his weapons and went out to the van. This van has to be hot by now, he thought. But maybe since it was late and dark the police wouldn't notice, and he decided to take a chance and drive the van.

Clem relieved himself on the ground next to his vehicle. It was cold outside and steam rose from his warm stream of pee. He unlocked the door, put the guns, knife and change on the bench seat, turned the key in the Ford Econoline van and pulled out onto US 301 and drove south. There were no streetlights until he got to the Gypsumton town limits. Clem pulled in the parking lot of the Showtime. He armed himself with the .22 caliber pistol. He strolled casually to the front door. He pushed open the door to the bar. The barman was looking down, wiping the bar. Phil was closing shop.

"We're closed," said Phil. There was no one in the room but the barman.

"I just want a short one," said Clem.

The barman recognized the voice. He put his hands on the bar, lifted his head and looked into Clem's eyes, smiled and said "I don't guess it will hurt anything if it's a short one." Phil's gaze was steady and he was hoping against hope.

Clem came to the bar and sat at a stool. "Where's Gene?" All of the rage Clem felt for the patrons who beat him up was in his eyes and his anger was directed at the barkeep.

The barman lied. "She left two days ago. She's a rambling rose."

Phil knew he was a dead man when he saw Clem's eyes. Phil had no ability to stop Clem from killing him, but he did not panic. He was calm. Clem lifted his right hand with the .22. He fired the weapon two times. The barman was dead before he hit the floor. One bullet hit his aorta. Clem had a feeling of satisfaction killing Phil. It relieved his rage at the people of Gyp'town, but not the rage for Gene.

Gene heard the gunshot. She knew her friend Phil, the barman, was dead. There were no screams or groans. She did not hear anything except the heavy footfalls of a big man heading toward the back room. Gene ran out the back door, pushed it closed and latched it on the outside. She ran to the front, crossed the road and crossed the railroad tracks.

Clem ran into the back door thinking it was open. He could not stop. He crashed into the door and broke it off at its hinges. He was out in the back but could not see Gene. He ran to the front of the bar and got in his Tom's Potato Chip van. There was a long train that came through town from Miami at 1:30 a.m. He saw Gene cross the tracks just as the train flew by doing 60 mph. This was the last chance the engineer had to make up a little time before Tampa. The engineer saw the woman run across the tracks and he sounded a long warning horn blast.

Clem started the van and pulled up to the light at US 301 and Nundy, waiting for the train to pass. It was carrying over two hundred cars filled with automobiles that had landed in the Port of Miami. They had come from Japan through the Panama Canal.

It was forever, Clem thought, as he watched the cars pass by. Finally Clem watched the caboose pass and he looked up and down the access road. He could not see her. He drove over the tracks and got on the access road next to the tracks. He headed north. He had not seen Gene head south. He drove four or five miles with no sight of her. He decided to turn around when he was back in Riverview on the south side of the Alaphia River. She can't have swam across the river, he thought.

He drove back along the access road heading south. Ahead he saw a car stopped. The dome light of the interior of the car allowed him to see a woman with red hair get in the vehicle. Clem accelerated. He caught the car as it pulled over the tracks at a crossing and headed south on US 301. The two cars sped past the power plant and the phosphate processing facility with its mountain of phosphate from the mines in Polk County. Finally, desperate to stop the vehicle, Clem rammed the rear of the car and it spun out of control. The driver was able to stop along the right of way in the weeds. Gene jumped out of the car even before it stopped. She ran west toward Tampa Bay. She heard two shots, loud ones.

To get to the water she had to pass through a wooded area and a swamp. This part of Tampa Bay was an estuary known as Cockroach Bay. She had no idea if Clem could swim but she felt that heading for the water was the right thing to do. She could hear him crashing through the underbrush close at her heels. She began to dodge back and forth, cutting like a running back. Serpentine.

She felt she could feel Clem's breath on her neck.

Why didn't he shoot her, she thought?

Then she could no longer hear the sound of heavy feet and she jogged left at a mangrove tree. In a couple of seconds she heard a crash. Clem had impacted the tree trunk with his head. He laid there below the tree, tangled in the tree roots.

Gene turned around and could see Clem on the ground. She came back to within ten feet of the man. He was not moving. Gene found a dry place to sit down and she watched Clem. He was on his chest. The air roots of the mangrove tree propped his head out of the water.

As Gene stared at Clem, his eyes popped open but there was no movement in his upper or lower extremities except for his eyes which darted about angrily.

She continued to watch for any other sign of movement besides his eyes. Nothing happened, he did not move even his little finger.

But he was mean and sly as she very well knew, so she did not get near him. Finally he spoke.

"Help me, Gene. I can't move."

Gene did not believe him. She walked further back to the edge of the mangroves and sat down again and watched him from a distance. He stayed still from his neck down. Gene waited. It seemed like an hour. She could hear him saying "Help me" over and over. His pleas began to bother her and so she back-tracked out of the swamp and the woods to US 301 until she could not hear him.

As she walked back she saw Clem's silver plated gun on the ground. He must have dropped it, she thought. She left the gun where it lay. Once she was back to US 301, she saw the car she had been in, it was catawampus on the side of the road. The old man had been shot in the side. The wound was through and through. He was alive and being treated by paramedics. The red Ford van was on the side of the road. The lights were smashed and the bumper was pushed in. The wind shield was broken from the impact of a body. Clem must have hit the windshield. He was not wearing his seat belt. Yet another transgression.

The police were there, investigating, measuring the scene. They were told by the driver of the car that a man and a woman had run from the scene into the woods toward the bay. Officers from the three other police cars were off the road and the police were searching for the woman and the man who chased her into the woods. You could see their flashlight beams cutting through the night. The sky was turning gray from black. It would be dawn soon and there was a ground fog rising from the swamp, so it was hard to see anything lying on the ground.

The two officers who were measuring the accident scene were familiar with the van. They had seen it at the fish camp in Riverview. The officers were upset that they hadn't rousted Clem for anything and got him off the streets.

Gene walked out of the woods and over to the police. They questioned her. She told them she was the woman in the car that was rammed by the red Ford van. She asked them if they had been to the Showtime Bar and she asked, "Is the bartender still alive?"

The police did not know about the shooting at the bar. These patrolmen were closest in time and distance to the Showtime and they got in their car with Gene in the back seat and they headed north with all deliberate speed with their sirens blaring. As they drove, Gene explained what happened in the bar. That she was in the back room; she heard two shots and ran out the back. She explained that Clem had tried to kill her two nights ago and the Carnies had saved her.

When they entered the bar there was no sound after they called out "Police". The officers found Phil's body behind the bar and called for a homicide detective.

While they waited outside the murder scene, the sun came up. Gene asked the police if they were familiar with the tides in Tampa Bay.

"What is the tide now?" she asked. "Is it high or low?"

One officer explained that Tampa Bay was a long body of water and the tide changed depending on where you were located on the bay. "It's low tide right now here in Cockroach Bay and will be high tide here at noontime," said the officer, who spent his off hours fishing.

Gene considered what the policeman said about the tides and then said, "Once the homicide detective gets here, I need to show you something else down by the water in Cockroach Bay. We need to get there before noon," she emphasized.

The End

Epilogue

Events within a year afterward

Epilogue

When the story broke in the newspaper about The Man Trap, The Oar House, and the attendant death and destruction, State Attorney John Hale became the subject of much controversy. What had been a "no news" story buried as filler among the obituaries, had become front page news and the subject of editorial comment in newspapers throughout the country.

A criminal case involving the murders of six people was sensational. But in addition, John Hale had solicited pleas from Tommy Magyar and Alphonse Alesse when he knew they were innocent.

The legal question was whether Hale had an obligation to disclose information to the defense that proved their clients were innocent. The issue had been heard by the US Supreme Court in the past in the case of Maryland vs. Brady. Although the facts in that case were different, the ruling instructed prosecutors that they had an obligation to provide exculpatory evidence that could exonerate a defendant to the defendant's attorney. Hale's failure to provide evidence that proved the accused was innocent went a step farther and was considered so egregious that there was a question of whether John Hale would lose his license to practice law, and whether the Governor of the State of Florida would remove him from office.

Hale avoided official action by blaming Detective Richard Cook for setting up Tommy and Alphonse. Hale also dismissed the cases against the men on his own motion. Hale also was a good Republican. Hale continued to be elected as State Attorney. No one wanted his job and no one ran against him.

Immediately after the plea deal, Tommy and Theresa left St. Petersburg and caught up with the work crew that had been traveling since his arrest and was now into the Southeast US. They never returned to the State of Florida.

Alphonse and his wife, Francis, divorced later in the year. It was her decision. Alphonse finished law school at Stetson University and came back and worked for Darlene and Tom.

James DeMarco also worked with the firm and he took over the cases involving insurance defense that had been handled by Roger "Roger, Roger" Adams before his death.

Jim Faircloth was hired to replace Anthony Stewart as the firm's investigator. DeMarco and Faircloth continued to handle pro bono criminal defense work.

John "Big John" Curry died of an overdose of painkillers.

Regina "Gene" Cameron stayed with the Gyp'Town Carnies and played the part of the gypsy woman when they were on the road. She worked in the Showtime Bar during the winter. She remained sober at least to this point in time.

Clemenso "Clem" Me Bondi remained paralyzed from the neck down and did not utter a word after he was pulled out of the mud on the shore of Cockroach Bay. Because of the injuries he suffered to his brain and spine, he did not stand trial for the deaths of Lori Schaeffer, Anthony Stewart, Richard Cook, Derek Kline, George Randell and Phil Smith, the barkeep. Bondi was found incapacitated to proceed to trial but remained at Florida State Hospital in Chattahoochee, where he received treatment in an attempt to rehabilitate him so he could stand trial, be found guilty of murder and executed. Because he was paralyzed he suffered from bed sores, he would probably die of sepsis from the decubitus ulcers. His care in the State hospital was poor. The nurses failed to turn him regularly, resulting in his skin breaking down from pressure sores. Although Clem did not communicate that he felt pain, he knew his flesh was rotting because of the smell.

Sarah Rogers moved in with her Aunt in Tampa. She could not get work and most recently, she applied to enter law school.

George Randell died as a result of the injury from the gunshot wound to his leg. He never recovered from the surgery. A good number of officers, including Jim Faircloth, attended the funeral; however, no one from The Gas Plant Community besides Randell's family were there.

The Police Chief of St. Petersburg volunteered when he gave his retirement speech that George Randell had never been treated fairly during his almost twenty years of service as a patrolman and detective. The chief admitted the unfair treatment was a consequence of his race and prejudicial attitudes on the force. The chief apologized to the Randell family. The newspaper failed to report the chief's musings regarding the fact the police department was racist. It was old news said the editor.

At least some of the inequity suffered by George Randell provided a foothold to other black officers who followed his career on the force.

Preview to Indian Hollow Road

Chapter 1

"Predator"

The police in Summer County had been on alert for a predator who, over seven years, had kidnapped and killed five young girls. The young girls were off walking to middle school or last seen on a school bus and then they disappeared.

The police were targeting a white male, 25 to 50 years of age, because that's who the FBI criminal psychologists believed committed the crimes. They were also looking for a red, rusty truck because that vaguely described vehicle had surfaced as a vehicle seen at or near the scene of the kidnappings.

There had never been a witness who came forward who saw a kidnapping or who knew the perpetrator of the crime. So there was no description of the criminal other than the educated guess of the FBI profilers. There was no hard evidence as to the identity of a suspect.

The Summer County Police were on guard this day because there was another girl missing on the way to school. She only had to walk two blocks to the bus stop from her home, but she never arrived.

***

It is foggy near to and inland of the west coast of Florida in the spring. A ground fog hangs over the surface of the land and burns off at about mid-morning.

The children at the bus stop on Indian Hollow Road, all middle schoolers, reported that the fog was thick the morning that Becky

Sue Painter went missing. The classmates reported the fact that Becky was not at the bus stop to the bus driver. The driver was late and said she would tell the principal when she finished her route. Becky was probably sick, thought the driver. Summer County was rural and it was a Black Jack Oak forest and the oak pollen was thick with the new growth of leaves each spring. The school kids were susceptible to allergy attacks from the oak pollen and the day Becky went missing the driver noted at least five students absent due to sickness, although those student's parents had provided a note for the absence.

The principal's secretary called the Summer Sheriff's office with the report that Becky Sue Painter was not at school and the school had not received word from her grandmother that she was ill. The grandmother had no phone.

Since the children in Summer County had begun to go missing, the Sheriff had assigned a deputy to investigate reports of missing children. Parents, guardians and schools were encouraged to report their children missing to the Sheriff's office as soon as the fact was discovered.

The FBI said one or two detectives should be assigned to this duty and they would be required to remain current on any report of a missing child in the region. There were now five girls that were lost to the predator. Three bodies had been found. All three were buried in shallow graves and had been dug up by animals, probably coyotes, and then the remains were discovered by humans. All three children were found in rural fields. Most of the fields were just off the interstate (I-75) and the fields were progressively farther away from Summer County and closer to Gainesville, to the north of the place where the children were kidnapped.

Two other children, young girls, (in addition to the bodies of the three children found) were missing and the only explanation for their disappearance was that they were kidnapped and had been murdered.

Over the years the gap of time between when the child was last seen and then reported missing had shrunken considerably. Becky was reported to the detective by the principal's secretary to be suspiciously absent from school within two hours of when her grandmother sent her out the door of the trailer where they lived.

This was the first missing child report of the day. Detective Joseph Rainey was on duty and he immediately went to Becky's home. She lived in a double wide trailer at the end of a short, dead end, limited access road that was just off Indian Hollow Road in the country outside (east and north) of the city limits of New Retirement City.

Det. Rainey interviewed the Grandmother, Alma Lee and discovered the following:

Becky was not angry or upset when she left out the door. She loved school. She had done her homework. There was no reason she wouldn't want to go to school that day. She never skipped school. If she was sick she stayed at home in bed. She was not sick that day and she did not suffer an allergic reaction from the oak pollen.

She had friends on the bus. No one bullied her. She got along with everyone.

She was an average student and she got average grades.

Her parents were gone. They never saw her.

Alma Lee said, "Her father, my son, is still in prison. Her mother is out west in Sturgis, at least that's the last I know. She never visits or calls."

The State awarded the grandmother custody. Becky's mother and father failed to care for the child. The mother had other children who she birthed and spread over the country who were living in foster care. "Five children, I think," said Ms. Lee.

"My son never had anything to do with Becky. He never writes her, or calls. He was a drug dealer. He doesn't care about anything but drugs."

The grandmother had not seen anything suspicious that morning. There was no vehicle or stranger hanging about. Maybe she saw an old red truck up the street yesterday or maybe last week, but she was not sure. "There are a lot of red trucks around," she commented.

Det. Rainey broke off the interview and went to his car and called the sheriff.

"This could be another abduction. There is a report of a missing female child and the sighting of a red truck the day before," said the detective.

The sheriff called the riding club and the bloodhound handlers from the State Prison.

Rainey continued the interview. Becky did not drink or use drugs ...

***

The bloodhounds were on the scene in 25 minutes. Alma Lee retrieved a pair of dirty shorts belonging to Becky to give the hounds a scent. They picked up the trail easily and followed it up the dirt access road to a large wax myrtle bush. There was a field of tall grass behind (east) of the wax myrtle.

There was a trail into the grass. "Do not disturb the trail," ordered the detective.

"We'll loop around and see if the trail comes out of the grass up on Indian Hollow Road," said the dog handler.

Det. Rainey followed the trail but did not disturb the path. He stayed out to the side of the path and came to an area where the grass was beaten down as though someone had been rolling in the grass. It was trampled, maybe the scene of a struggle. Rainey saw a white rag in the area.

"We found a trail out of the grass," yelled the dog handler. "There are tire tracks at that spot."

"Get those dogs out of that area. Go down the road and see if you can pick up the scent anywhere else." Rainey walked back to the wax myrtle bush and then up the access road to Indian Hollow Road and he found the trail out of the tall grass. It looked like the trail had only been made by a single individual who was coming out of the grass to the spot where the tire tracks were located.

"How much did Becky weigh?" Rainey asked Alma Lee when he got back to his car.

"She was pretty good size ... maybe 95 pounds. She is five feet tall," said the grandmother.

The dog handler returned. "The dogs couldn't find anything more. We went a 100 yards up and down the road. Did you see the blood near the tracks?" asked the handler.

"Damn, no I did not." Rainey had not walked in the right of way. He avoided the tire tracks and the footprints where the trail emerged from the tall grass.

Rainey got on the radio. The sheriff picked up immediately.

"I need forensics ... Blood ... Footprints ... Tire tracks. Mostly, I need a cherry picker so we don't contaminate this scene.

The sheriff called the electric power company and commandeered one of their trucks with a cherry picker (a long mechanical arm with a bucket to hold a man) and the men to operate it. The electric company wanted to know who was going to pay.

"You get that equipment out to Indian Hollow Road now, or someone is going to be arrested." The sheriff was very dramatic and not well liked by the civilians who dealt with him.

The sheriff got back on the radio to Rainey. "What are we looking for?"

"An old red truck on or near Indian Hollow Road near or on Interstate 75. You need to contact the Highway Patrol as well as all the local authorities. The truck has at least a two hour head start. I need the riding club to search along the other access roads off of Indian Hollow Road to see if they can find anything. The girl may have been thrown in the woods alongside the road if the perpetrator got spooked."

"Okay ... Done ... I will be there in 15 minutes," and he asked "What was the child wearing?"

"The grandmother reported she had a pink cotton dress with a red sweater, buttoned up to the neck. She had on cowboy boots. She always wore them. She has a pink backpack with horses printed on the pack."

The power company truck arrived. The employees beeped its horn from its position on the gravel road. The truck had been just a couple of miles away when they were ordered to go to the scene.

Detective Rainey ran up the access road from the double wide to Indian Hollow Road, where the bucket truck with the cherry picker was located. Once the arm of the cherry picker was extended, the machine would reach 75 feet in the air. With stabilizer pads in place the machine would extend horizontally out over the long grass so Rainey could see what was in the field from the basket at the end of the arm extended above the grass.

As the men stabilized the machine, Rainey got in the basket and waited to take it up in the air. One of the men from the power company jumped in to operate the basket.

"I'm looking for the path through that grass."

The operator swung the basket over the grass and then maneuvered upward so they got a good view. There were drag marks from the access road near the large wax myrtle bush to the trampled down area in the center of the grass and there was a single foot path out of the grass to Indian Hollow Road.

The operator pointed to the location of two objects – a backpack and a red sweater – that looked like they were thrown into the grass away from the area where the grass had been trampled like someone had rolled around in a tussle.

Forensics arrived.

"I need you to get photos," yelled Rainey to the technician over the noise of the utility vehicle. Traffic was backing up on the road. The deputy called in for traffic control.

Rainey had the operator maneuver over to the gravel road and he drew a map showing the drag trail and the trampled area and the footpath out of the grass and the general location of the backpack and sweater and the white rag.

Rainey gave the map to Forensics and said, "Make sure you also get photos of these items with a Polaroid in case we have a screw up with the 35 mm camera."

Rainey's mind conjured what happened. The criminal parked on the side of Indian Hollow Road. He walked into the tall grass to the bush by the access road from the double wide and hid by the wax myrtle. As Becky walked by the wax myrtle, the criminal grabbed her and dragged her into the grass. There was a struggle and Becky was rendered unconscious. He took off her sweater and the backpack and threw them into the grass. He picked her up and carried her to the red truck in his arms and put her in the truck somewhere, either the front seat or in the back. He drove off, probably east to the interstate.

Rainey took the crime scene technicians to the south side right of way of Indian Hollow Road, where the handler stood. The dogs were in their cage on the handler's truck. The handler pointed out the location of the foot path track coming out of the grass, and the location of the blood, and the vehicle tracks where a vehicle drove off the road onto the right of way and parked off the road.

The two technicians took photos of the tracks and foot prints and blood on the grass. The blood technician said it was a lot of blood, probably from a facial wound. The tech took samples of the blood. The print technician said that he saw only one track in and one track out. The footprint was made by the same shoe, probably a man's shoe, a boot maybe, from the shape of the imprint of the heel in the soil.

"It is probably a cowboy boot and the man was heavy." said the tech. "The boot really sunk in the dirt. There was a distinct, fresh imprint ... Good evidence."

Rainey yelled at the operator to try to follow the track out of the grass to the gravel road. "Look for child size cowboy boots."

If she was unconscious and she was carried out, the boots could have slipped off her feet, Rainey thought.

"There, in the path," said the photographer. "The boots are just inside the area where the grass is trampled."

"Get Polaroids of the boots where they lay," said Rainey.

***

The sheriff arrived and he was at the double wide consoling Alma Lee. With this criminal on the loose, any mother or grandmother was concerned if they had a middle school aged girl living in Summer County. Some parents had left the area. They simply moved away from Summer County. They worried their child would be kidnapped. They had no faith the sheriff would find the perpetrator and protect their child. The odds of the return of a child who went missing were remote. Five girls were lost and none returned alive over the last seven years.

The sheriff had won the election on the promise he would find the perpetrator of these awful crimes. It's time for me to put up or shut up, thought the sheriff. Two of the five children had been lost on his watch. Now the number taken was six. The sheriff thought about where he might find a job in the private sector if he didn't make an arrest for this crime.

"Do you suspect anyone who might have done this, Ms. Lee?" asked the sheriff.

"No."

"Have you noticed anyone in the neighborhood who might have had an unhealthy interest in Becky?"

"Unhealthy?" Alma Lee stared blankly at the sheriff. She was in her 60's, dull and worn out. The word "unhealthy" was foreign to her when used in this context.

"A pervert, ma'am."

"Oh no, no one like that. We stay to ourselves. We don't go to parties or socialize. Becky has friends but they are all girls and I don't think she knows about the birds and the bees yet. I haven't told her. I hoped they would teach her in school. She knows she has private parts and no one but the doctor is to touch her there."

"What does she enjoy?"

"She wants a horse. She thinks she's a cowgirl. Let me show you." Alma Lee took the sheriff into Beck's bedroom. There were horses everywhere. There were posters on the wall and stuffed horses on the bed and a rocking horse with a real horse hair tail.

"I see," said the sheriff. He began to tear up. His youngest daughter loved horses. Jesus, he thought. "Where is that son of a bitch?" he mumbled.

"What?" said Alma Lee.

"Do you have anyone to be with you? Friends ... Church ... Family ..."

"No, just Becky."

"Come with me." The sheriff went to the car and called in to headquarters and made arrangements for a female deputy to stay with Ms. Lee until they knew what was what. It was too horrible to even say what they would find, if they could find anything of Becky. More likely than not, Becky would become another ghost.

***

The sheriff stayed by Alma's side until the female deputy arrived. "Do you like coffee?" he asked.

"I do."

"This is Martha, a special deputy. She will help you. Show her where the coffee is and she will help you make it" said the sheriff as he walked up the access road to the power truck.

The technicians were still working. The sheriff pulled Rainey aside. He asked for an update.

Rainey told the sheriff what they had found and what he conjectured from the facts on the ground.

"Where do you think Becky is right now?"

"She is in the red truck or she has been dumped on the side of the road between here and the Gainesville exit on I-75. My guess is she is somewhere in Paynes Prairie."

"Is that what your gut says or do you have hard evidence?"

"We found the last body near Wilder. I figured the next likely spot to bury a body with easy access from Interstate 75 is the large preserve at Paynes Prairie."

"Then trust your gut. Go to Paynes Prairie," said the sheriff. "This is all technician crap here where she was snatched. We need to find the girl. She'll be dead soon if she's not dead already."

"Can you get me the chopper?"

"Hell, yes, it's on the way," said the sheriff. "They will meet you up the road near the interstate."

Rainey got in his car and drove to the interstate three miles to the east with another deputy. Rainey got out of the car and the deputy stopped traffic and laid out some flares in the road to mark an area for a landing pad for the helicopter.

The chopper landed and Rainey boarded. The pilot took off and headed north. Thirty minutes later they were at the Micanopy exit just before Paynes Prairie.

Rainey directed the pilot to follow the fence line along the interstate. When they found nothing, not even tracks where a vehicle had driven on the right of way into the grass, Rainey directed the pilot out over the prairie. The prairie was nothing more than a swamp with about 21,000 acres of sedge brush and wax myrtle and understory tree growth – bay, tupelo and wild apricot trees.

They found no red truck but they were utterly amazed. In a rutted road they saw the body of a female child dressed in a red print cotton dress. She was shoeless and moving.

They called in the location, requesting an ambulance and investigators.

The crime scene had matriculated from Indian Hollow Road to a spot in Paynes Prairie 40 miles north.

The chopper landed. Rainey told the pilot to stay with the aircraft and fly about 100 feet above the ground so the cavalry could find them. Then Rainey jumped from the chopper.

Rainey ran down the rutted dirt road to Becky. She was alive and sobbing.

Rainey held Becky in his arms. He looked up to see if he saw anything that was large and red, but he saw nothing, just a bunch of green vegetation. Rainey knew the criminal was close. They had to be patient and they would catch him.

Rainey was just happy they saved the child.

To purchase the next book in the
Thomas Night Crime Novel series,
please visit Amazon.com.

www.ingramcontent.com/pod-product-compliance
Lightning Source LLC
Chambersburg PA
CBHW030155200626
46812CB00017B/2083